THIS FRESH HELL

Edited by Katya de Becerra and Narrelle M. Harris

Clan Destine
PRESS

First published by Clan Destine Press in 2023

Clan Destine Press
PO Box 121, Bittern
Victoria, 3918 Australia

National Library of Australia Cataloguing-In-Publication data:

EDITORS: Narrelle M. Harris & Katya de Becerra

THIS FRESH HELL

ISBN: 978-1-922904-33-1 (hardback)
ISBN: 978-1-922904-34-8 (paperback)
ISBN: 978-1-922904-35-5 (eBook)

Cover Art by Claire L. Smith
Cover Design by © Willsin Rowe
Design & Typesetting by Clan Destine Press

Clan Destine
P R E S S

www.clandestinepress.net

Katya dedicates this anthology to all the brave souls who ventured into the depths of haunted houses and came back.

Narrelle dedicates this anthology to all the misunderstood monsters.

CONTENTS

EDITORS' NOTE

Foreign words are usually italicised, unless they are not considered foreign in the context of the story, such as in stories featuring bilingual characters or set in locations, where languages other than English are spoken. We have also gone with authors' preferences, where those were expressed.

General content advisory: this is a horror collection, with stories ranging from supernatural, dark and spooky to light and humorous.

Unless the story is set in North America, where US spelling is appropriate, Australian spelling is used throughout.

FOREWORD

If you're a horror fan, like we are, chances are you have a favourite horror trope. Katya, for instance, loves a horror house story, while Narrelle loves a good monster. But after decades of stories being told about new families moving in to haunted houses, can there ever be an unexpected ending? Can an alternate point of view give old ideas a new lease on life? Can monsters be understood? Can shifting shadow reveal new depths of darkness?

These questions are at the heart of this anthology.

We have reached out to the authors we admire, emerging and established, and challenged them to pick a horror trope and write a story that subverts or reimagines it.

We are so pleased with the result!

Our authors have tackled old and dusty horror tropes by mixing genres, interrogating problematic assumptions and challenging western hegemony on what makes compelling horror. *This Fresh Hell* is bursting at the seams with incredible and diverse storytelling. It will take you to the sizzling Australian outback and the deep suburbs of Sydney, to the haunted beaches of West Java and historical Scotland, where mythic beasts roam in the deadly fog. You will come face to face with the devil, in his many forms, and ride the haunted lift down to the suffocating bowels of a haunted ship.

So cross your fingers, plan your escapes, wear your amulets (but nothing green) and take your chances as you step inside… these fresh hells.

Enjoy,
Katya and Narrelle

THE DARK MAN, BY REFERRAL

CHUCK McKENZIE

THE SMALL CARDBOARD SIGN PINNED TO THE TRAY READ *"'ORRIBLE 'AIRY Spiders — $1 Each"* in spooky lettering. James kept his eyes on it; partly because he found the obvious misspellings thrilling in a way he couldn't have put into words, and partly (mostly) because it meant he could sort of keep an eye on the Dark Man without looking at his face, and James didn't want to get a good look at that face, because he felt that if he did he would lose his mind.

James thought about all the times Trent had yelled that the Dark Man would come for him for being a little shit, which to James — up until a few moments ago — had been a far less frightening thought than the prospect of what Trent might do to him. Now, though, he was gripped by a fear so all-consuming that he couldn't even summon the ability to run the dozen or so steps that would take him from the deepening dusk to the (relative) safety of home. Instead, because it was all he could seem to do, he focused upon the sign and upon not looking at the Dark Man's face.

The brief glimpse James had caught of that face, as he'd turned from waving goodnight to Tim and impossibly found the legendary monster of Stanhope standing before him in the street, had given him a sense of *wrongness* that went beyond fear; it was the same feeling he'd often felt when watching Dad's favourite old horror movies on Saturday nights, but now inducing nausea instead of thrills, without Dad there to cuddle him.

'Master James Kent?' the Dark Man asked.

James blinked, automatically looked up from the sign (*'Look at me when I'm talking to you, ya little shit!'*) and cringed in expectation of awfulness, before realising he could hardly even see the Dark Man's face, hidden in shadow thrown by the black, wide-brimmed hat the Dark Man wore. And the Dark Man's clothes…well, he looked like he was wearing one of those robes that nuns wore, and the thought almost made James giggle. Then his thoughts turned back to his immediate situation, and the urge to giggle died. Even standing a few metres away, the Dark Man towered in a way that adults only did when they were up close and about to hurt you.

James opened his mouth but found himself unable to utter a word.

'I do apologise if I've alarmed you, Master James. That certainly wasn't my intention.' The Dark Man's voice was deep and rich, and made James think of Christopher Lee in the *Dracula* movies.

'How…do you know my name?' James managed.

'I know your name, Master James, because I have in fact been *referred* to you.' The Dark Man paused. 'Do you know what *referred* means?'

James shook his head. He thought maybe it meant something medical, as he'd heard his doctor use the word before.

'It means that someone who has found my services useful has specifically suggested I approach you, because they feel that you, also, might value my services. In other words, they *referred* me to you.'

James stared into the shadows covering the Dark Man's face, feeling it looked too *still* in there when the Dark Man spoke. 'Who…*referred* me?' he asked, rolling the word around his mouth.

'Ah, now, that would be Master Timothy Brown, at number forty-two.'

James automatically turned his head to look down the street, half-expecting to see Tim standing there. All he saw was the sun beginning to slip below the horizon, and with that came the thought of being caught in complete darkness alone with the Dark Man.

James hurriedly turned back, to find the Dark Man had silently closed the gap between them. He was now definitely within grabbing distance, arms outstretched. James stumbled back a pace. But the Dark Man stood motionless, black-gloved hands holding out the tray to James.

It was one of those wooden trays that James sometimes saw old men in suits holding when he went to the railway station with Mum. Instead of poppies and pins, though, this tray was filled with…well, James guessed they were the 'Orrible 'Airy Spiders mentioned on the sign; a mass of whitish-grey egg-shaped objects, each with multiple long, furry legs extending in all directions, and dozens of tiny red eyes clustered around a weird, puckered orifice. No fangs or spinnerets, so not very much like spiders at all, thought James. They glistened like rotten peaches and jiggled slightly, even though the Dark Man was standing perfectly still.

'Why do they look all sticky?'

'Because they *are* sticky. One throws them against a wall, and the stickiness allows them to walk down that wall.'

James had seen sticky toys that worked the same way before, though he'd never owned one. And suddenly, despite the grossness of the things – or maybe even because of it – he really wanted one.

'Would you like one?' the Dark Man asked, as though reading James' thoughts.

James instinctively reached out towards the tray, then hesitated. 'I don't have any money,' he admitted. 'And I'm not supposed to take stuff from strangers.'

The hat dipped in acknowledgement. 'A sensible policy. Master Timothy calls me Mister Black, as does Mistress Heather Noake on the corner, whom I believe you also know, and several other Masters and Mistresses hereabouts.'

'Okay.'

'You see, Master James, the wonderful thing about referrals is that the person referring me to another already knows and trusts me, just as they know and trust you, so you needn't worry about me despite me being a stranger.'

James began to nod, then suddenly remembered a scene from one of Dad's movies where a clown in a drain introduces himself to a little boy and tells the boy that the two of them are no longer strangers, and then… But the clown in that movie hadn't been *referred*. And how would the Dark Man – Mister Black – know everyone's names if they didn't already know *him*? And anyway, Mister Black could already have grabbed James a dozen times over if he'd wanted to, so…

'Okay,' James said again. 'Yeah. That makes sense, I guess.'

'As to the cost,' and here, Mister Black pushed the tray a little closer to James, 'there is none.'

'It says a dollar on the sign.'

'That sign,' Mister Black said, 'is for adults, who would not understand that some do not require money for their services.'

James nodded, not really understanding. He reached out and gingerly pulled one of the Spiders from the top of the tray. It quivered in his hand, sticking lightly to his skin, cool and feeling like a half-set jelly. The red eyes stared blindly up at him. 'Thank you,' he said, remembering his manners.

'You are very welcome,' Mister Black intoned, withdrawing the tray. 'I hope you will enjoy it. Oh. And, ah,' he added, as James began to turn away. 'Should you find at any point that you no longer require the Spider, all you need do is simply bring it out to the street, and I shall collect it.'

'Okay,' said James, thinking how unlikely it was that he'd want to return a toy. 'But how will you know to be here if I do?'

'I'll know,' said Mister Black. And he watched as James turned and raced the darkness home.

James lay face-up and wrong-way-around on his bed, flinging the Spider at the wall as though it were a tennis ball. At first, he tried throwing as hard as he could, but found that the mattress prevented him from pulling his arm back sufficiently to aim properly. The Spider ended up splatting just above the bed-head then dropping a centimetre or two before hitting the wooden frame, whereupon it would simply peel off the wall and drop behind the pillows, forcing James to sit up and rummage for it.

After a few such attempts he changed tactics and tried lobbing the Spider like a shot-put, placing it in his palm then pulling his arm back flat against the mattress next to his head before "releasing", like one of those giant Roman catapults. The Spider flew in a graceful arc, hit the top of the wall, and stuck there for a moment, shuddering. James allowed himself a small, muted cheer. The Spider began a slow roll down the wall, rubbery legs shooting out to slap against the plaster then detaching as they were drawn in under the egg-shaped body, only to spray out again in a shower of grasping limbs as the body completed each roll. It took about ten seconds for the Spider to hit the bed-head this time, whereupon it bounced off the top and dropped onto the pillow below, then rolled down and came to rest against the soles of James' feet.

Cool.

James retrieved the Spider, before resuming his catapulting position. On the second try, the Spider rolled past his foot and ended up just short of James' outstretched hand. That was odd. The bed was perfectly flat, and he wouldn't have thought the sticky toy could roll half the length of the mattress. He craned his neck and regarded the Spider warily. The Spider seemed to stare back at him, red eyes glistening.

James hesitated, then stretched out his hand, retrieved the Spider, and tried another throw. This time, the Spider rolled all the way into James' outstretched hand, jiggling against his palm. James held the Spider up to his face, not sure what it was he was looking for.

On the next throw, the Spider hit the wall and dropped straight down behind the pillows again.

James scrambled to retrieve the toy, noting that the Spider was now coated with a thin layer of dust that presumably counteracted the stickiness. James rubbed at the dust, then licked his finger and tried again, with no success. Annoyed, he rolled off his bed and left his room.

Mum was in the kitchen, cutting vegetables. The muffled sound of the telly told James that Trent was in the living room.

'Mum?'

'What's up, buddy?' Mum favoured him with a bright smile.

'How do you clean sticky toys?'

'Sticky toys?' Mum spotted the Spider in James' hand. 'Ah, wall-walkers. Umm…warm soapy water, I think.'

'Won't that wash the sticky stuff off it?'

'I don't think so. In fact, I think it sort of revitalises it?'

'How?'

'Not sure. Heard it somewhere. Want me to Google it?'

'Google what?' asked Trent from the kitchen doorway, and James' heart shrank.

'Cleaning one of those wall-walkers,' Mum said, too brightly. 'One of those things you throw against the wall, and it sort of crawls down.'

'Yeah, I know what a wall-walker is. I'm not fuggin' stupid.'

Mum's smile vanished, and her eyes briefly met James'. *Don't poke the bear.* Trent's tone had been lightly mocking, but that could easily escalate.

'Ay, Jimmy. Show us.'

James slowly turned, keeping his upturned palm close to his body.

Trent sniffed, ran the back of his hand across his nose, and slouched into the kitchen. Came in close (*too close*) to James, towering over him, looking down at the Spider with a sneering half-smile on his face. 'Where'd ya get it?'

'A…friend gave it to me.'

Trent snorted. Looked up to smirk at Mum. Then back at James, darkness clouding his features. The loosened tie hanging beneath five-o-clock jowls made Trent look a bit like a mean Homer Simpson.. 'Steal it, didya?'

'No!' There was a time when Mum would have immediately jumped in to defend James, but James knew Mum had learned the hard way to not do that. The faint scar across his cheek prickled in anticipation.

'Who gave it to ya, then?'

'Tim.' James met Trent's gaze and held it.

Trent stared, then gave Mum a querying look.

'James' friend from up the road.'

Trent looked back at James. 'And Timmy'll back that up, will he?'

James was suddenly confident that Tim would do exactly that. It occurred to him that neither he nor any of the other kids would want to tell an adult about Mister Black. It was a shared secret, like a sort of club, and the notion gave him a thrill. 'Yep,' he said.

Trent eyed him coldly, then sniffed again. 'Better not be lying, or there'll be *consequences*. The Dark Man doesn't like kids who lie.'

James only just managed to hold back an hysterical giggle.

'Dinner?' Trent asked, not breaking eye contact with James.

'Ten minutes. Just gotta boil–'

'Fine.' Trent slouched back out of the kitchen. A few seconds later, the volume of the telly increased.

Mum exhaled quietly and James turned to find she'd already gone back to preparing dinner. *Why do you let him stay here, Mum?* But there was no point asking the same old question. Once, Mum would have said it was because she was lonely. But James knew that was no longer the reason.

Sometimes he wished Trent was just…gone. He couldn't quite bring himself to wish anything worse, after Dad's accident.

'Mum?'

'Mm?'

'Do you think the Dark Man is real?'

Mum's gaze flickering momentarily to the kitchen doorway. She took a couple of steps closer to James and, lowering her voice, said: 'Do *you* think the Dark Man's real?'

James considered how best to answer, then simply shrugged. It seemed the safest response.

'Okay then. Well, no, he's not real. At least, not the Dark Man Trent talks about.' Seeing James' blank look, she sighed. 'Monsters aren't real, buddy. What happened was…there was a sickness that made a lot of locals really ill, and some of them died, and I think people just made up this story about a Dark Man to sort of…help them cope with it. Sometimes it's easier to blame a person, or even a made-up monster, than it is to blame a random disease.'

'Why?'

'Dunno. It's just something people do. And this all happened decades ago, long enough for the Dark Man to pass into local legend.'

James digested that. 'So…Dad grew up in Stanhope. Was he here when all this happened?'

'Yeah, he was. Trent, too.'

James frowned. 'Dad loved horror stuff, but he never told me anything about the Dark Man, or the sickness, or anything like that.'

'Sometimes real life is scarier than horror. The disease affected people that Dad knew, and I think maybe he just didn't want to remember. He never told me much about it either, even after I moved here to be with him. And he probably didn't want to talk about the Dark Man either, because the legend's now so closely linked to the true story. Does that make sense?'

'I guess. Did Trent know people who got sick? Or died?'

'Probably, yeah.'

'So why does *he* always talk about the Dark Man?'

'Trent…just wants you to behave.' The pain of the lie was obvious on Mum's face. 'If someone told you the Dark Man would get you if you didn't wash your hands after you went to the toilet, you'd wash your hands, wouldn't you? And then you hopefully wouldn't have any disease on your hands. So really, those sorts of legends are meant to keep you safe.'

James gave Mum a *look*.

'Okay, so sometimes people just make up stuff to get kids to behave. Remember when you used to believe in Santa, and you'd behave so Santa would bring you toys?'

'I was eight. I'm twelve now.'

Mum smiled sadly. 'Yeah. Just about ready to move out and get a job.'

James snorted.

'Okay, enough talk about scary stuff,' Mum said. 'Go wash up, buddy.' She nodded towards the Spider. 'And give that thing a wash too, if you like.'

James nodded and turned towards the kitchen door.

'James?'

James turned back.

'Don't use any of what we've discussed as an excuse to—'

'I won't!' James said, emphatically.

'And maybe just don't mention this talk at all, okay?'

James nodded.

'Good boy.'

Mum and James were already eating dinner – one of the few discourtesies Trent would allow (except for those occasions when he didn't) – when the swearing began out in the hall. They froze, forks half-raised to their mouths.

'The fugg is this??' Trent thundered, striding into the kitchen. James cringed as Trent thrust out his fist, rubbery grey legs dangling between his fingers.

Mum swallowed her food, looking ill. 'That's just James' toy—'

'*I know what it is!*' Trent rounded on her, and she shrank into herself. 'Ya think I'm fuggin' *retarded*??' He swung back to glare at James, looking like a dog about to attack. 'What's it doing in the fuggin' bathroom?' A beat. '*Eh??*

'I had to wash it,' James croaked. He wished Mum would say something, defend him, even if it meant that Trent's rage focused upon her instead. His cheek prickled.

'THEN YOU WASH IT OUTSIDE!!'

Mum made a small noise. Trent swung back to her, leaning over her, pushing his face into hers. 'WHAT??'

Mum licked her lips. 'I just...Trent, where's the harm?'

An expression of rabid incredulity crossed Trent's face. 'Leavin' his shit all over the fuggin' place? It's not his fuggin' HOUSE!!'

James suddenly found himself filled with utter rage. *It's not yours either! It's mine and Mum's and Dad's, and one day I'll be big enough to throw you out if Mum won't do it!*

Something of what he was thinking must have shown on his face. Trent looked at him, and his expression went blank. Then he smiled.

Oh shit, thought James.

Trent straightened up and casually strolled over to James, then squatted down on his haunches so their faces were level. 'Whaddaya thinking, Jimmy?' he asked quietly. 'Maybe you wanna have a go, eh?'

I'd like to punch you so hard you cry.

'Yeah? Wanna take a swing?'

The silence stretched forever.

'Yeah, that's what I thought.' Trent started to straighten, then abruptly thrust his face back towards James with a grunt. A fake-out attack. James had known it was coming, but still couldn't keep from flinching, and was immediately filled with self-loathing.

Trent gave a short, ugly bark of laughter. 'Fugg with me, and there'll be fuggin' *consequences*.' He spun on his heel and flung the Spider hard through the kitchen doorway. A soft thud sounded from the hallway beyond. Trent grabbed his plate, gave James and Mum a hard stare, then loped back to the lounge room to eat in front of the telly.

After a long silence, Mum reached over and touched James' hand. 'Hang in there, buddy,' she murmured. 'Things'll get better.'

James pulled his hand away and went back to eating his dinner, carefully regarding the plate in front of him. Only once did he look up, to find Mum staring miserably at him. The shame in her eyes made him feel so bad that he went back to staring at his plate again.

After talking about all the usual stuff – school, mutual friends, girls, and so on – James asked Tim the question he really wanted an answer to:

'Why did you refer Mister Black to me?'

Tim dropped his gaze to the road. 'Remember when you came to school with stitches across your cheek?' He glanced up at James. 'And you told us all you'd run full speed into a door frame?'

James flushed, hoping Tim couldn't see it in the gloom.

'Yeah. Well. Last school holidays I got some really bad bruising, here.' He clamped his right hand tightly around his left wrist for a moment. 'Healed up before school started again. There were other times, though.' He gave James a hard look. 'Heather referred Mister Black to me. And I haven't had any more bruising since.'

James couldn't get a fix on what Tim was saying, and couldn't think of the right questions to ask. The look Tim was giving him was beginning to make him squirm.

'Don't worry,' Tim said, eventually. 'It'll all make sense.'

'*What* will?' James asked, frustrated. 'I don't understand!'

'You will. I promise. And then things'll be better.'

'My mum always says that,' James blurted sourly.

'Mine too. And now things *are* better. You'll see.'

James shook his head in exasperation, then noticed how dark it had become. 'I better get going. Trent's in a shitty mood today. I'm surprised he's not out here yelling for me to come in.'

'Yeah, my dad used to do that,' Tim said. He smiled, and the interplay of shadow and light from the nearest lamp-post seemed to stretch the smile into a maniacal Joker's grin. 'But he's sick at the moment. *Really* sick. So.' Tim shrugged. 'Later.' He turned and ambled away into the darkness.

'Has your dad got Covid?' James called after him. Tim didn't reply.

Trent was already snoring in front of the telly when James got back inside. James spent a few minutes unsuccessfully searching the hallway for the Spider, before sadly concluding that Trent had disposed of it. James said goodnight to Mum, who was sitting at her work laptop in the kitchen, then went to bed and glared at the ceiling until he fell asleep.

'Late shift today?' Mum asked hesitantly.

Trent slumped into his seat with a groan. 'Not going. Already rung in.'

'How come?'

'Feel like shit.'

James risked a quick glance up from his cornflakes. Trent had dark smudges under his eyes, a contrast to his pallid, sweaty face.

Mum gave Trent a worried look. 'Yeah. You don't look great. Maybe a bit of breakfast?'

Trent grunted. 'No breakfast. Gonna sleep it off.'

'Okay. But maybe go to bed, yeah? You might have cricked your neck last night on the couch.'

'Nah, I'll stick with the couch.' Trent gave Mum a bleary look, daring her to push the point. She didn't.

So, Trent had spent the night in the lounge room. It suddenly occurred to James that his Spider might be in there also. Maybe it had bounced off the hallway wall. And if so, Trent obviously hadn't found it or they'd be hearing all about it right now.

James eyed the kitchen doorway, weighing his chances of checking out the lounge room before Mum had to drive him to school on her way to work.

'Should you go and get a Covid test?' Mum asked. 'A few people in the street have been getting sick. They had to take Glen Brown to hospital, though Jane says it's not Covid. God, that's all we need, another outbreak, probably a lockdown—'

'Fuggsake, it's just 'flu!' Trent snapped, though with less force than James would have expected.

'Okay then. Well, stay warm and drink plenty of water. James? All set? Need to be in the car in five, buddy.'

'But—' *But you're not supposed to go to work or school if you've been around someone with Covid. You have to get a test, and then wait at home until—*

Mum's eyes flicked to the back of Trent's head, then back to James.

Home all day with Trent.

'Just…need to get my pencil case,' James mumbled, through a final mouthful of cereal.

Mum glanced at James' schoolbag, sitting on the floor beside his chair. 'Okay. Go on, then.'

James got up, moved carefully past Trent, and went down the hallway towards his room. Then he quietly doubled back and slipped into the lounge room. He scanned the floor, then dropped to his hands and knees and peered underneath the couch. Nothing. Then, despite knowing it was an utterly ridiculous place to look, James leaned over the back of the couch, and pulled aside the cushions.

And there it was. Looking up at him, quivering.

James snatched up the Spider and examined it quickly. All in one piece. No legs torn off. Indeed, the Spider looked *healthier* than when James had seen it last, the colour having changed from sickly grey-white to a pinkish-grey. Maybe that was just something it did. James was sure he'd heard of toys that did that.

The grating of chair legs on linoleum jolted him back to the moment. Instinctively he stuffed the Spider back behind the cushions, then scuttled out into the hallway. A half-second later, Trent loomed in the kitchen doorway. 'Whaddya doing? Where's your pencil case?'

'I think it's in my bag after all.' No reaction. 'I thought I hadn't packed it, but I think I just need to have a better look.'

Trent eyed him, then grunted and shuffled past James and vanished into the lounge room. James went into the kitchen, where Mum was jingling the car keys.

'I heard that. In your bag after all, you reckon?' She smiled and unzipped his school bag, revealing the pencil case sitting on top of his books and lunch box. 'Well, whaddya know?' Mum leaned towards James and stage-whispered: 'You must've had a Man's Look the first time, eh?' The tone was jovial, but the look in her eye told James her "bullshit detector" was pinging.

He lowered his gaze. 'Yeah.'

'Well, that's okay. Got everything now? Let's go.' She didn't call out to Trent as they left.

The house was silent when they got home that afternoon. After looking in on Trent, asleep in the lounge room, Mum rifled through the fridge for the makings of dinner, while James hesitated at the hallway door. In the darkness beyond, he could hear the familiar rasp of Trent's snoring. Mum stopped moving behind him, and James could feel her eyes on the back of his head. 'Go on, then,' she urged. 'Homework?'

'A little bit.'

'Okay, homework first, then you can go outside for a bit while it's still light. Quietly, though.'

As soon as he got to his room, James fished his school laptop out of his bag, opened it up on his desk and began Googling. There were a few mentions of the Dark Man as a local legend; a black-clad monster who preyed upon naughty children. There were maybe a dozen links to articles about the "Stanhope Outbreak" of 1989, all of which mentioned a "wasting disease" that affected ninety-three people, twenty-seven of whom had died. All adults. No kids. One article mentioned that Stanhope actually had a long history of unexplained outbreaks going back almost 150 years and occurring at intervals of a few decades, the 1989 outbreak being the most recent. At the end of that article, the journalist suggested that the legend of the Dark Man had started with the founding of the town in 1857, as it seemed a "rather old fashioned" tale.

Um…Slenderman? The Blair Witch? Then James saw the article was from 1993, long before either of those things.

And that was it. Nothing more. Although maybe the site blocker on the laptop was filtering out anything more gory or creepy.

Then James remembered the Spider.

James crept down the hallway and paused at the open door to the lounge room, peering into the gloom beyond. The blinds were down, thin rays of daylight filtering in at the bottom in a way that made the darkness inside seem like it was made of brown dust. James strained his eyes as shapes in the darkness began to resolve themselves, and he took a step in the direction of the couch.

A floorboard creaked under his foot, and he froze.

The snoring stopped. Something rolled sluggishly in the dark. A groan. Some muttered gibberish. Then a sudden cessation of movement and sound.

James took a step back.

'Wha're you doing?' Trent's voice was slow and slurred.

James licked his lips and said: 'We're home.'

A beat. 'You're home.' It wasn't a question. It didn't even sound like Trent's usual trick of repeating something you'd said to make you feel stupid for saying it. It was more like Trent was trying to get his head around the words, repeating them simply to get a feel for the meaning. Like his head wasn't in the right space.

A strange feeling overcame James; a sudden thrill he'd never before experienced outside of the school playground. The sensing of weakness in another. An immediate desire to push and see what happened, regardless of *consequences*. He hesitated. Then–

'That's what I said. We're home,' he said, not quite adopting the level of contempt that Trent would have under the same circumstances.

Silence.

'What?' The word came crisp and clear, without slurring.

Oh shit.

'WHAT?' Trent bellowed, and James suffered a moment of utter regret, frozen to the spot, before Trent reared up out of the darkness like a malevolent jack-in-the-box, jumping up from the couch. 'YOU WATCH YOUR FUGGIN'–!'

And then he stopped and folded in upon himself without actually collapsing, tilting forwards, arms flopping by his sides, mouth dropping open. He looked, thought James, like the flapping inflated figure at the place where Mum got the car serviced, but with the air gushing out of it, and that was somehow even more alarming than the threat of Trent's violence.

Something bulbous and gelid fell from Trent's neck, hit the floor with a soft thud, and rolled under the couch.

'MUM!' James yelled, and instantly Mum was there. *She must've been standing outside the lounge room since Trent started yelling*, thought James, *but she only came in when I yelled too. Was she waiting until he started hitting me?*

Trent staggered, clutched at the side of the couch, and half-sat, half-fell on to the armrest, gasping like a beached fish. His face was so pale that the dim light from the hallway seemed to make it glow.

Mum pushed past James to Trent's side. 'What's wrong?' Trent goggled at her, shakily raising a hand to press his fingers into the soft flesh of his neck. Mum pushed his fingers aside. James leaned forward, expecting to see bruising, blood, bite-marks. Nothing but sweat and stubble. Mum peered into Trent's face. 'Trent? Trent! Can you breathe?' No response. Mum gave a huff of panic and irritation. 'Come on, come out to the kitchen…' She bent and heaved one of Trent's arms up over her shoulder, wrangling him into a standing position, then shuffled both of them out of the lounge room.

James hesitated, then knelt down on the carpet and stuck his hand under the couch. His fingers closed around the Spider almost immediately, and he withdrew his arm to examine it. The thing quivered (or throbbed?) against his palm — surely *bigger* than the last time he'd seen it. And it felt warm. Hot, even. Even in the gloom, James could see the Spider's pink tinge had deepened almost to crimson.

James had the impression of a creature that had just enjoyed a hearty meal.

'James!'

James bounced to his feet, thrust the Spider into his pocket, and ran to the kitchen.

Mum had Trent sitting at the table. 'Did you see what happened?' she asked. 'He keeps touching his neck, but there's no injury, and I think he's breathing okay, but — Trent? Shall I call an ambulance?' Trent shook his head emphatically, and made as if to get up, groaning weakly.

Mum placed a hand against his chest. 'No, stop, you need to—'

Trent glared at her. Mum blanched as Trent slowly grasped her offending hand, his fingers scrabbling for purchase, seeking out the familiar weak spots, the holds where fingers could be crushed together.

Eventually, without any obvious effort, Mum pulled her hand free, placed it upon Trent's own, and pushed it down against the table. Then held it there. Trent grunted, the muscles in his arm flexing ineffectually.

An expression crept over Mum's face that James had never seen there before.

'Hey, buddy,' she said to James, 'how about you go to your room for a bit? I'm going to give the hospital a call, okay?'

James went to his room, lay on his bed and held the Spider, listening to Mum talk on the phone, her voice high and urgent at first, slowly lowering in pitch as the call continued. Then a second, far more restrained call. Then the sounds of Mum helping Trent to the bedroom. Eventually Mum appeared in the doorway to James' room.

'We can't get Trent into hospital just yet. The local ones are all full of Covid patients.'

'Okay,' said James, and then, because he felt like maybe it was the question Mum would expect him to ask: 'Does Trent have Covid?'

'The ambos said it didn't sound like it, but whatever he's got still seems pretty bad. I'll duck out soon and pick up some tests for all of us. In the meantime, maybe just stay in your room. Tim's mum says there's a few people in the street with something similar, so…y'know.'

'Kids?'

'Parents. But you'd hate to be the first kid with it, eh?'

'Sure.'

'Just let me know if you need anything before I pop out.'

'Can I go out and talk to Tim?' James nodded towards the darkening window. 'He's usually out there around now.'

'Well…I mean, not if there's a chance Trent has Covid.' Mum lowered her eyes. 'You and I shouldn't even have gone to school and work today, really, except–'

'What if I just talk to him from the driveway?'

Mum mulled it over. 'Okay, sure. But keep your distance, okay?'

'It was attached to his *neck*.'

Tim nodded. 'How's it looking?'

'What do you mean?'

'Like, is it looking…well fed?'

'Yeah,' James said, slowly. 'It is.'

'Cool. And how's Trent looking?'

'Not great.'

'And…how do you feel about that?'

James considered. 'Fine.'

'Can I give you some advice? When he's sleeping, try to make sure the Spider's always in the room with him. It'll move things along quicker.'

'I will. Thanks,' James said.

'You're welcome,' Tim replied.

After he got back inside, James lay on his bed until Mum went out to get the Covid tests. Then he took the Spider, opened the door to Mum's room, stood listening to Trent's gurgling snores for a moment, then gently tossed the Spider into the darkness underarm and closed the door again. Then he went to the lounge room and watched all the cartoons that Trent never let him watch anymore.

The tests came back negative for all three of them. Regardless, Trent couldn't even talk the next day. Mum called her work and Trent's and the school to say they'd all be off for the next day or so, then left James at home for several hours while she dragged Trent to the doctor.

James went into Mum's room and found the Spider, swollen, red and pulsing, beneath Trent's sweat-stained pillow. He took it to the bathroom and cleaned the accumulated muck off it, then brought the Spider to the lounge room. He sat it on the couch beside him, making sure its eyes were facing the right way, and they watched telly together.

The daytime kids' shows were a bit too childish now for James, but he found them comforting. At some point he began talking to the Spider. Asking questions. *What are you? Are you alive, or part of Mister Black, or something else entirely? How are you making Trent sick?*

The Spider remained silent, so eventually James switched to just talking about Stuff. About Dad, and how life had been before, and how much James missed him every day, and how Mum still cried sometimes when Trent wasn't home and she thought James wasn't watching; about Trent, and the things he did, and what James wished would happen to Trent. And he cried a bit, and then a lot, and afterwards felt better than he'd felt in a very long time. And when he heard Mum's car pull into the driveway, he returned the Spider to Mum's room — stowing it back beneath Trent's pillow — and lay on his bed and pretended to read a book.

After much huffing and puffing as she put Trent to bed again, Mum came to James' doorway. 'Hey, buddy. All good?'

James gave her the thumbs up.

Mum smiled tiredly. 'Sorry we took so long. The GP sent us straight on to hospital to get a diagnosis, but they couldn't tell us what Trent's got either, and they still don't have room to admit him for treatment. Just keep on keeping your distance from him, okay?'

'No problem. When do I go back to school?'

'Not for another few days. Whatever this thing is that Trent's got, it's nasty, and we don't want to go spreading it.'

'Can we do something if we don't get sick?'

Mum gave James a funny look. 'Like what?'

'Maybe the zoo? It's been ages. If Trent's still sick, he doesn't need to come with us.' He turned back to his book and pretended not to see the way Mum stared at him, until she finally left.

That night, Mum slept on the couch so as to distance herself from Trent. James considered sneaking into Mum's room to check on the

Spider but figured that Trent wasn't likely to tidy the bedclothes, so the Spider would probably stay safely hidden. Cosied up to Trent.

James drifted off to sleep with a small smile on his lips.

The next day Trent couldn't even get out of bed. Mum and James sat quietly in the lounge room for a while, reading. Eventually, Mum sighed, then gave James a look; the sort of look she'd not given him since Trent had come into their lives. The sort of look that hinted at impending fun.

'How about I plug in the PlayStation?'

'What?'

Mum grinned impishly. 'No? Worried I'll whip your butt?'

And Mum had pulled the PS4 out of the cupboard, the box grimy with dust and fluff, and the two of them had set it up and played *Spider-Man* for the rest of the day. It was only when his belly rumbled that James realised it was way past dinnertime. At that thought, he stiffened.

'What's wrong?' Mum asked. And then her eyes widened. She stared out of the window, taking in the darkness beyond, then scrambled to her feet and rushed from the room.

James waited, his guts tightening. Waited for the outrage over dinner being late.

A few moments later, Mum came back into the lounge room. 'Trent's not hungry,' she said, then paused. 'I didn't get anything ready for dinner, so…maybe takeaway? We could get McDonald's.'

And they did.

The day after that, they all stayed home again.

It was a good day.

Trent stayed in bed, silent and unmoving.

James and Mum played Monster Hunter all day, with pizza for lunch, eaten on the couch. Dinner was home-made hamburgers with oven-baked chips.

Afterwards, James went outside and talked to Tim from a socially responsible distance. They talked about all the cool movies being put on hold because of the pandemic. They talked about school and girls. They talked about sports and the latest electronic games. They talked about cars. And comics. And then, finally:

'My dad's being admitted to a care facility,' Tim said. 'He can't do anything for himself anymore. Can't get out of bed. Can't feed himself. Can't even wipe his own arse. Doctor says it's some sort of wasting disease. Might be a long-term thing.'

'Huh,' James said. 'And…how do you feel about that?'

Tim's teeth glowed in the lamplight. 'Fine.'

'I Googled the Dark Man.'

'Yeah. I think we all do.'

'There's hardly anything there.'

Tim was silent for a moment, then said: 'I think the outbreaks have been small enough that they don't really rate much attention outside of Stanhope. This one won't flag any attention at all, I reckon – not with Covid going on everywhere. And there wouldn't be many adults still in Stanhope who know what's *really* going on – adults who were kids back in 1989, I mean. The ones who got referred. I reckon most of them moved away. Maybe they forgot. Or wrote him off as an imaginary friend they had as a kid.'

'Yeah. And if there *are* any who knew, and stayed, and remembered…I think they'd try really hard to not grow up to be like the adults who got sick.'

'Yeah.'

They stood for a while, looking at the sunset.

'Feels like we should…pinkie-swear, or something,' James said eventually. 'Y'know. Secrets. Vow to never become arseholes. That sort of thing.'

'Dude!' Tim said, sternly. 'I'm not touching you. There's still a Covid pandemic on!'

They laughed at that for far longer than seemed reasonable.

'Trent.'

Trent squirmed and blinked against the sudden glare of the bedroom light. He wheezed softly, then locked eyes with James, standing at the bedside. The confusion on his face slowly morphed to anger. He wheezed again, and the muscles in his neck tightened like knotted rope as he attempted to sit up. He stopped and lay trembling, glaring weakly at James.

'You're going to have to be nice to us now, Trent,' James said. 'To me and Mum. I don't think you'll ever be well enough again to hurt us, but if you don't act nice…well. I think that's why some of the adults died back in 1989. Maybe some of the people who got sick were so awful that they ended up with pillows over their faces.'

Trent's eyes widened, his gaze flickering to the door behind James.

James leaned in over Trent. 'Mum just went to the toilet. We've got a couple of minutes to chat. Anyway, even if you do get well enough to talk properly again, if you tell Mum she wouldn't believe you. And if you try to hurt her or make her feel bad, there'll be…consequences.'

The look in Trent's eyes changed.

James smiled.

The toilet flushed. 'Ah.' James pulled back the bedsheets, then slid a hand down into Trent's armpit and pulled out something red and swollen and throbbing. 'If it helps to make you behave, Trent–' James held the Spider up for Trent to see, '–just think of me as your personal Dark Man.'

He switched off the lights and closed the door as he left the bedroom, leaving Trent alone in the dark.

James put a few steps between the bedroom and himself as Mum came out of the bathroom. She gave him a smile. 'You look like a man on a mission. Looking forward to getting back to school tomorrow?'

James shrugged. 'I just need to take something out for Tim.'

'Haven't you already spoken to Tim?'

'It's that toy I borrowed from him.' James held up the Spider, prodding it with his finger to make it look as though *he* was causing it to quiver. 'Ten minutes? He's waiting outside.'

'Five minutes.' Mum hovered for a moment, then unexpectedly enveloped James in a bear hug. 'You're a good kid, James,' she said. 'Things'll get better. You'll see.'

'I know,' James said, as he hugged Mum back.

Mister Black was already waiting in the street, tray clasped between gloved hands. He extended the tray and James carefully deposited his Spider on top of the others. The rubbery mass briefly shuddered as one. Mister Black made a soft gurgling noise and twitched in ways that a human being couldn't possibly have managed. A stray ray of light from the setting sun momentarily lanced the darkness beneath Mister Black's hat, and James saw a flash of flesh-coloured latex with gaping black holes where eyes and a mouth should have been.

'The Spider…'

Mister Black slowly straightened up, face once again in darkness. 'Yes?'

'It didn't just make Trent sick, did it? As he got sicker, the Spider got…healthier. It took something from him.'

'Well observed, Master James. Go on.'

James considered. 'Something it can only find in a certain sort of person. Something *you* need. The Spider collects it, and then you…' He gestured vaguely.

'Exactly so, Master James. And I thank you for assisting in the process.' Mister Black hesitated. 'I do hope these facts do not undermine the benefits of my service in your eyes?'

'Oh, no, not at all!'

There was a long pause.

'And…do you have a…*referral* for me?' Mister Black asked, at length.

'I was thinking about that.' He pointed further up the street. 'Steven Moore, at number sixty-eight. He's not in my class, but we've talked. And sometimes I've been in the changing room getting into my PE kit at the same time he's getting out of his, and I've seen purple marks across his back that he tries to hide. The first time I thought they were birthmarks, but they were in different places the next time.' He paused. 'Is that an okay *referral*?'

The brim of Mister Black's hat dipped again. 'An *excellent* referral. Thank you, Master James.'

'You're welcome.'

'And with our contract completed, I must bid you farewell.' Mister Black bowed slightly. then began to glide smoothly away.

James' mind swirled with questions, but the one that blurted from his lips was: 'You're not really a monster, are you?'

Mister Black stopped abruptly, and James felt a sudden qualm, more afraid he'd been rude than anything else.

Mister Black turned back to James. 'I suppose,' he said, 'that rather depends upon your *definition* of a monster. Don't you think?'

A beat. Then James nodded thoughtfully. 'Yeah. I think you're right.'

'Well then.'

'Thank you!' James blurted.

'You are most welcome, Master James.' Another small bow, and

Mister Black moved away. James watched him vanish into the lengthening shadows as the sun slipped below the horizon. Then he stood for a while longer, looking up at the stars, just enjoying the warm evening air and the sounds of other children playing in the street after dark.

AFTER I FOUND HER

CLAIRE LOW

DOWN ONE OF THOSE STREETS IN MY NEIGHBOURHOOD, THE ONE WITH THE bird baths and hatchbacks and party balloons lost in trees, a black plastic garbage bag catches my eye and for a moment, I can't breathe. I see a hand: tiny, pink and fleshy – the soft hand of lotion commercials – poking out as though waving. A chill creeps over me. Someone killed their baby.

My husband, Noah, always blasé about everything – before I have a chance to cry out, he has pulled that…that thing out of the bag. Body bag, says my brain. 'Hey, a doll,' he says, unmoved.

'Just a doll?' My whole body unclenches. 'Jeeeeesuuuusss, I was so scared. I thought that was a real baby.'

'This? Nah.' With the practiced hands of a dedicated scavenger, he's already flipping the doll this way and that, searching its clothes for tags, assessing its condition. The doll makes a soft clicking sound. Its eyes are designed to snap open and shut as its weight is shifted. So, I suppose, the little girl who lays it down to nap in a cot will be satisfied as its blue peepers close and it lies there, a perfect still angel in gentle repose.

'Darling? Leave it. We don't want that one.'

'Yes, we do,' he says.

There's a scraping feeling inside me, as though someone is running a crochet hook somewhere within the walls of my gut. 'No, please – does it not seem like a bad omen?' I gesture at my stomach but Noah doesn't see as he's tapping search terms into his phone, like he always does. Always looking up the resale value of things.

'It's a MyLovely,' he says. 'People get like 200 bucks for these. Because they're so lifelike. See?' He hands the doll to me.

It's surprisingly heavy and in even worse shape than I thought. The clothes are worn and ripped. A miniature wig has been glued to its head, askew. One set of eyelashes fell off and have been inexpertly glued back on, with some of the glue cutting a cloudy path through one eye.

But the other eye is pretty and bright, catching the sun like the cheap sparkle of a plastic tiara. The skin – silicone, maybe – is soft and almost warm, it nearly responds to the touch of a finger. This used to be someone's dream baby girl. Despite everything, holding the doll, her weight so suggestive of a real baby, I feel the stirrings of something within me and give myself a shake.

'I could fix her,' I say, my mind already racing ahead with how I could do this: wash the suit, stitch up the rips or redress her. Find out what's under the wig. Clean the marks off her face, scrape the gunk off her eye.

''Course you could,' replies Noah, gently plucking her from my hands and dropping her, less gently, into a reusable supermarket bag. She joins the other small things we have dug up from council clean-up today: *The Best of Hall and Oates* on CD and a chipped enamel mug. We walk on and there's a rattling from within the bag, a clicking. Maybe it's the sound of that tiny hand that had so spooked me jostling against the mug.

'I thought it'd finally happened – we'd found a body.'

'C'mon, Jess, no.' He spins me around and takes my chin in his hand. I flinch slightly, remembering where that hand has been. Green eyes meet my brown ones. 'Not going to happen around here. We live near where the prime minister lives.' He lets go and our steps fall into rhythm again. 'Would you maybe consider less of that true crime podcast?'

'Hey, do I tell you to listen to less of the cricket? *You're Wrong About* isn't even a true crime podcast, if you'd only give it a try.'

He's begun to dig through a box of toys.

'The Prom Mom episode, that's what I was reminded of.'

No answer. It's not like he stuffs his fingers in his ears and goes, 'lalala, I am not listening', but it almost is. Selective hearing. I raise my voice slightly.

'…and she threw away her baby, and her sorority sisters found it in the rubbish, I think they all ended up with PTSD, who wouldn't…'

He's inspecting a Teletubby – crusty and caked over. It's tossed back.

'And the trial was about whether she'd discarded a stillborn or murdered her child…'

He prods a grimy Hello Kitty, pulls a face and keeps sifting.

When I heard of the Prom Mom, my mind could only go to the logistics. Hands, freshly manicured at the mall, reaching between legs to deliver her own infant, the truth of the matter being so unpalatable to her that she'd been deeply in denial until this exact moment. Pulling with strength? Gentleness? And then the blood and also the umbilical cord and what must have been the baby's first cry – and its last. Did she put her hand over its impossible eyes before throwing it in the garbage? And then wash her hands with the inadequate pink soap from one of those stainless steel dispensers common to the kinds of venues where they have the prom? And wipe herself between her legs with the rough paper towels? What happened to the placenta?

I thought of the the thrown-away baby all blue, naked and covered in slime, and I had more questions

Like birth went so smoothly that she hadn't cried or screamed her make-up off? There wasn't any blood or gore on her gown? She walked and danced just fine, in patent leather mall heels, no need for stitches or giant pads or scratchy mesh underwear? People couldn't tell until they saw the state of the bathroom?

Noah does not notice I've drifted off as he is sorting through a large pile of clothing that looks like it's languished for 15 years before being hauled to the curb, just flung there, not in boxes or in bags but in a giant nest.

'Besides, we have found really nasty stuff, I know you remember. Like the sack of…'

'…dirty underwear?' he grunts as he pulls a T-shirt inside out, searching for designer labels.

We laugh, though it brings back memories of a whole body shudder. 'I wanted to light my arm on fire. Just get me a whole new arm.'

'And what about the—'

'Wig?' I say. 'I screamed so loud that day.' Left out well past Halloween, it was languishing inside a black bin liner with acres of artificial spiderwebs and a tacky plastic lei. 'I screamed because it was wet.' There was something about reaching into a bag and feeling what could have been a disembodied head. Also, the polyester fibres of the fake hair, though they still had the cheap chemical smell of the dollar store, felt a lot like cleaning my own long strands out of the bathroom drain. 'It aged me 10 years.'

'Making you what, 31?'

'Ahh you.' I snuggle under his arm, the one that isn't holding the bag. 'There isn't much else out here.' I gesture at dismal piles of three-legged flatpack furniture, rusted filing cabinets vomiting dull memories and ragged old mops. We head for home with our modest haul.

And the bag goes *click click*.

I understand why some people stare as we dig through garbage left out for council clean-up — we do it with the relish of a rat with a dripping cinnamon bun. It's the sense of endless possibility. People throw out literal cash. If you are patient and fearless, treasure can be found: jewel-bright miniature paintings. Ornate chairs upholstered in dusty rose velvet. A Commodore computer, found among books about Jane Fonda and Richard Nixon. The last one fetched us $600 in cash so promptly I thought I was dreaming; I had taken it to be a strange-looking keyboard.

The money we make goes into a jar. Over the years it has been labelled "Bali holiday" and "Road trip". Right now it says "IVF". Remembering a pair of jeans we sold, I tip $25 in and those three letters stare at me in a silent rebuke. *You weren't good enough. Your body couldn't do what it was supposed to do. You weren't woman enough.*

I feel like crying and it must be the hormones they've had to pump into me. Bitterly, I think, most women can do this for free. It's OK though. We aren't paying for the treatments solely in petty cash: sales of an antique table here and a secondhand book there. It's just that what we want most, the centre of our life, goes on the jar label.

IVF. It has taken so long, been so difficult, painful and expensive.

My body is prodded, inspected and injected in hopes a lucky cell will set out on a voyage on its seas. Sometimes, I feel my body is not my own. I'm a sort of vessel.

Noah comes into the kitchen, washes the chipped mug we found, and stashes the CD with our music collection. 'Whatcha doing?'

His voice is always gentle but these days because he understands how much I am like an overburdened suitcase, the tensile strength of a zipper struggling to hold me together, his voice is so gentle it could soothe a kitten to sleep.

'Twenty-five dollars for the jar,' I say. 'For the jeans.'

Just last week we found storage containers of discarded men's clothes: all folded, clean, polite clothes. Enough to dress a man in all weathers, seasons, and occasions. Either his woman had also kicked him to the curb or he was walking around naked. That had been my joke at the time. Right now, even though I see my husband and I love him, I can barely smile.

He reads my expression. Folds me into his chest. There's that bright sunshine smell. 'Shh, shh, it will happen. I promise.'

'You don't know that.'

'Well, you don't know that it won't.'

He pushes the sides of my mouth up into the semblance of a smile and when he lets go, I let the silence hang in the room.

Releasing me for a moment, he pulls the doll out of the bag. 'Here, take your mind off things.' I know he doesn't intend to be cruel but it feels cruel. Take my mind off things? With this? He hands me the soft old toothbrush I use for restoration, a rag, rubbing alcohol, make-up wipes, my travel sewing kit. And he leaves the room. I hear canned laughter from the lounge room; he's turned on the TV.

I tilt the doll this way and that, and her one good eye clicks open and shut. The glue-caked other eye remains wide open, staring. 'It will be all right,' I say to her – unless I'm saying it to myself.

First, the makeup wipes. They fail to bring about much improvement to the dark marks on her face and hands. They could be ink, they could be dye. Nail polish, maybe? Rubbing alcohol next and a cotton ball. She feels slightly sticky and swiping the rubbing alcohol all over her removes this feeling, at least a little bit. 'What happened to you?' Having started muttering to her, I don't seem to be able to stop. Progress is minimal and when I've had enough of trying to fix her – it – this thing – I lower her into a large-sized packing box, lined with tissue paper. She looks awkward, displaced.

Though she's lying down, neither eye, not the working one nor the stuck one, closes. So she stares up at me, up at the ceiling, up at nothing. I feel an urge to try to close her eyes or cover her face but give myself another shake. Just a toy. Just an object. I can make $200. Go with it.

That night, after a heavy dinner, the kind that gets served to me when I'm being consoled – steak, potatoes and cheese gratin, sparkling water in my wine glass and red wine in his, and a large scoop of ice cream – I fall asleep well after Noah does. As REM sleep comes for me, I see her, the doll. One blue eye searching around, roving in its socket restlessly; the other eye staring at nothing. The little hands curl open and closed. Then, her chest begins to tear, just a little at first, until it bursts open and a huge rat surges out. Dark, slick fur and a naked pink tail and those little fleshy paws. It shrieks and runs towards me. I wake up gasping, coated in sweat, an oily feeling of revulsion rising in me like bile.

I need water. My clock says 2:18am. I push my feet into slippers and pick up an empty glass, then wander over to the kitchen. The fridge hums and the soles of my slippers make a shhh, shhh sound against the rental carpet. I turn on the tap, drink, then fix my eyes on the clock on the microwave. Its display is blank, a plain black face. I dislike coming out of bed at night. Never want to see any of the cockroaches that rustle around out of their hiding places.

As I finish one glass of water and refill, the sound is faint: *click click*. Must be the fridge or maybe the house settling. Or – shudder – some vermin scuttling. Something like that. As I return to bed and hold myself stiffly there, I can't help thinking of the one gluey eye that can't close and is staring into the dark right now, bright blue.

In the morning, Noah's not around – he's gone to the gym, leaving behind a large coffee he made with our machine and cereal, fruit. 'I am alone,' I think to myself. 'Except…am I?'

Two hundred dollars. I'm doing this for $200.

With supplies in hand – rubbing alcohol, sewing kit, make-up wipes – I go to pick up the doll. We keep everything in the second bedroom, everything: teetering piles of secondhand books, 1960s kitchenware, enough clothes to outfit an army of TikTok girls and their mothers…

She's not in the box.

She's not in the box?! Did Noah move her?

I spot her in the room, sitting upright. That feeling, that cold, scraping feeling, it's back. She faces the wall. Blank stare, both eyes open. Sitting in a way that, were she a real child, you would have said looked dejected. 'What...?'

I mutter, 'You were supposed to get some rest.' I'm talking to myself. Not a good sign.

I put down my repair supplies. Picking her up for a moment, I do what Noah did earlier and flip up the inner tag of her clothes from inside the collar. 'Emily? Your name is Emily?'

Her head moves. It spins on the axis of her neck, turning to face me for one second before clattering to the floor. I scream and drop her body. Remembering the beheaded Barbies of my childhood, I look at the neck and what's left behind with morbid interest. A sort of ball socket is there, the same pinkish colour as her skin. It's covered with mould, thick and black. Meanwhile, her head, tipped onto its side, rests near my feet. Her lips, designed to be parted slightly for pretend bottle-feeds form a faint "oh" of surprise.

Mould. We can't sell her. I'd rather set her on fire.

The shock has me crying. Shoulders shaking. Still teary and on edge, with my stomach clenched like a fist, I hear Noah's key in the front door.

He appears in the room, a large, comforting presence and two big arms. 'Baby?' He takes in the headless doll on the floor and the popped off head near my feet. 'What happened?'

'I don't know! Her head fell off! But before that...she wasn't where I left her yesterday! I left her in a packing box. Did you move her there?' I point. 'To the wall?'

His eyes are large and his brow furrows. 'No. I didn't touch it. Not since I first picked it up.'

Gently, very gently, he picks the doll up from the floor. Picks up alcohol spray and a microfibre cloth and wipes the mould off the neck and the ball socket. It disappears. Picks up the head that gives the impression of staring wildly around in shock at its predicament and forces it back on. 'See, all fine.'

Though it is much better with her head back on, the scraping feeling is back, the scratching. The rising tension inside my stomach, all taut like violin strings. 'We can't sell her. We should get rid of her.'

'Sure we will. The mould was easy to remove. You'll fix all the other things right up.'

'She...she..she...' I gulp. I don't want to admit this.

'...Yes?'

'She disturbs me.' I don't want to meet Noah's eyes. I am worried about what I will see there.

I glance up for a moment. His brow is still furrowed.

'You think I'm crazy!'

'I don't, baby, I don't, OK.' He holds me by the shoulders and I raise my eyes up to him. 'But you've got to see – this isn't different from fixing a bicycle or glueing a vase back together. Both of which you have done. It's just plastic and fabric.'

'Plastic and fabric?'

'That's right, nothing more.'

'But how did she move to the wall?'

'Jess, it didn't move. You must've put it there and forgotten about it.'

'I would know! I'm not a flake. I'm not making this up.'

'Didn't say you were. His eyes are large and fixed on me, the pupils are dark tunnels and I feel myself falling in. 'But you've been under a lot of pressure lately.'

You could say that: overfilled gutters, overdue bill notice, hormone shots, doctor's appointments, pee on a stick and pee on another, tampons, new tooth-grinding mouthguard, breathing exercises.

I can feel my mouth pulling into a downturned line. 'If you want her fixed so badly, why don't you do it?'

'Jess, you know I can't, you're the crafty one, not me.'

He's right. He's always been more of a brute strength guy than a fine tools guy.

'It will be OK. We'll take care of you.'

There's still this feeling on my skin, a prickling sensation. 'Who's "we"?'

'Me and Mum, of course.' He means his mother. He says in a cajoling voice, 'Chicken pot pie.' He knows I love that pie. Here we go.

It's fine. Honestly. It's fine. But just fine. Compared with other women's stories of cruelty, of passive aggression, I know I have nothing to complain about. It's just not where I want to be. Why does he think this would comfort me? More than fishsticks on hot buttered toast in front of the TV?

His mother Berenice smells like the kind of bar soap that has a black and gilt sticker in the middle and is always lightly dusted in talcum powder. Warm, comforting food in her hand, acidic tongue in her mouth. Her hair is always pulled back so tightly that to look at her makes my own scalp hurt. Wry, dry, in all honesty someone I could have been friends with but for her vested interest in my uterus.

I get a powdery peck on the cheek. At dinner, over her overfilled glass of wine, and a similar one for her Noah, and iced water with a wedge of lemon in mine, she fixes me with this look. It's not a glare, but not not-a-glare. 'So? No news yet?'

I glance over at Noah and take a big sip of water to avoid answering. 'No,' he says.

She has served us, of all things, cream-sauced quail. In my case, unseasoned, just in case, I guess, an excess of flavour makes it harder for the right cells to bed down in me.

'Oh? Well. How very disappointing. By the time I was your age, my two boys were already three and five years old. I cannot imagine how challenging it must be.'

I put a large mouthful of quail in my mouth and choke slightly. Noah pats me on the back. He doesn't say anything to the woman in front of us, stiffly coiffed and with eyebrows tattooed on.

'Tell me, Jessica, how are you spending your days? Maybe we can change something about that, make it easier for you. We must try.'

How am I spending my days? My mind searches frantically, spinning the way someone's life flashes before their eyes while they drown. I see myself sorting mail, mending pants, laundry, laundry and laundry, packet cake mix, multi-vitamin tablets, hunting for Noah's lost socks. The doll pops into my mind and I gesture with my hand, as though to push that thought away from me.

Seeing my dazed expression, Noah jumps in. 'A doll. She's restoring a valuable doll.'

'A doll?' Berenice says, like she has never heard of such a thing. 'For the baby?'

I shake my head.

'Well, then, why on earth would you devote your energy to something of that nature?'

I take another bite of quail and let Noah field that one. Berenice hates that we pick up used things and sort through garbage for fun. While Noah explains, I can feel myself wavering in and out. It's hot in her apartment. As I turn my gaze to her, to the fine furrow between her eyebrows, her home feels airless and tiny. Her eyes, they're the bluest, most piercing eyes I've ever seen. No one else in the family has them. Noah's are green.

I blink and see, for two seconds, the doll's eyes in her face. Bright blue, like hers, but glassy, one coated in glue. They look right at me, they look into me. I gasp and drop my fork; it clatters onto her Italian chequerboard tiles.

'Silly goose,' she says coldly. As my vision swims back into place, her eyes are ordinary once more, regarding me with pity and a few grains of contempt. 'If you want to be a mother, is it not time to focus on something else, something better? Don't you think?'

On the drive home, I say to Noah through gritted teeth, 'That wasn't chicken pot pie.'

'No,' he admits. 'It wasn't.'

Sleep is elusive these days. Tonight, I feel bone-tiredness but no wave of relief as my brain powers down. One reason might be dinner. The quail had a creamy sauce. Then, after the cream, a dessert with fresh lemon in it. Feeling my insides bloating and curdling, I feel balloon-tight, the way I imagine pregnancy might feel. My mouthguard in, my anti-frown patches glued on, my white noise machine whirring. All of these things to help me drift away. I am not drifting.

A clock stares with its red numeral display: 1:08.

The white noise is meant to cover sound, to hide it in a whirl of other sounds blended together. Still, I hear the whispers of the night. A dog barking in the distance. Trucks rumbling. A motorcycle revving. Crickets rubbing their legs to their bodies like they're playing the violin.

Then: *click click.*

I shudder and pull the sheets and blankets right up to my chin, the way I have since I was first shifted out of a cot and into what was then hailed as a big-girl bed. Noah is snoring beside me. No signs of turmoil, gastrointestinal or otherwise.

I hear it again: *click click*. Please let it be literally anything. A cockroach scuttling. A rat tap-dancing. Please, anything but the recently re-headed doll's eyes opening in the dark. Those eyes that had appeared in Berenice's face. Why had they? Had I been that hot? That sick? Am I sick?

Then something worse: a grizzling. A faint cry. Then a louder one.

It's baby cries, unmistakably, coming from within the second bedroom. 'No,' I whisper, pinching myself. 'This isn't real.'

Noah has not heard anything. He sleeps sweetly, gently, with a faint smile about his lips.

The cries eventually stop and I shiver in the dark, though it isn't cold. I shiver for hours. I am still trembling when sleep finally comes.

The next morning, over toast and thick lashings of butter and Vegemite with coffee, the good kind, freshly brewed, I look at Noah. 'Did you... did you...' I gulp like I had when I first confessed the doll frightened me. 'Did you hear anything? Last night?'

He's all fresh and handsome, soft and showered, he looks like a dream and I am a walking nightmare: dark circles under bloodshot eyes. 'No, sweetie. What did you hear?'

'Crying. I heard baby cries. In the night. In our house.'

He's smiling, shaking his head. 'Come here,' he says, folding me into his arms. Warm, comfortable like a sofa. 'It's just anxiety. Or maybe you were dreaming? I didn't hear anything.'

'I couldn't sleep,' I say fretfully. 'It wasn't my anxiety. I was awake. The cries were real.'

'So much stress on you lately,' he murmurs, kissing the top of my head. 'So much.'

I swipe a hand over the sore spot in my thigh. No one ever talks about how many needles there will be. The pricking, the prodding, always administering the sharp tip into my own fleshy body. Blood tests. Then, days of feeling weepy and sore-breasted, just as likely to weep at a Thai life insurance commercial as the latest Disney/Pixar offering. In short, a wreck. And it's this state that Noah thinks is responsible, for, well, everything.

He says, 'We can get rid of it. If you want to. I think maybe it's no good for you.'

I flinch at the word "it". 'You mean "her". Emily's a "her".'

'OK, sweetie, sure. I think we should maybe get rid of her. This was a bad idea. I never wanted to get you into this state.'

"Into this state" makes me sound like I'm sitting there polishing both barrels of a shotgun, muttering under my breath. But there *is* a state: whitish cast to my skin, blue shadows under the eyes, a haunted look. New grey hairs mingling with the brown. Nails bitten to the quick. "This state" began months ago, maybe years, but Emily has added an extra layer of anguish.

I slam my fist on the table. 'No.'

'...No?'

'It's not even about the money anymore. It's something else.' I pull my hands through my hair, tugging out several strands, and fling them onto the carpet, the beige suburban carpet with its beige suburban stains. 'We found her for a reason. You and me. She...needs...to be rescued.'

He's looking at me the way he does when I read too much into my horoscope or ask if he thinks we need a pink Himalayan salt lamp.

'Look, it's hard to explain. But she didn't deserve to be thrown away. She didn't deserve what happened to her.'

'It...is not...a person...' he says, enunciating each word.

My lips are dry, cracked, bleeding. I lick them, knowing this will make them drier. 'I know. But, I've been thinking. About the Prom Mom's baby – the real one, the one that got thrown away? What happened to her? After the autopsy, the trial, everything? Did they, did they...' I gulp and tears come quickly. 'Did they throw her away?'

'I don't know.' His eyes are large again, big green pools and a little teary too. 'Sweetie, I don't want you to think about dolls, or dead babies, or any of this stuff. It's not good for you.'

I slam my fist down again, biting the inside of my cheeks to keep from screaming. 'How do you know? How do you know anything about anything?'

The nightly cries reach me. They get to me. The way humans – women, mothers, people, who give birth in particular – are hardwired to respond to baby cries. They found the part of me that needs to give care, fix things, solve problems. The same part of me destined to dry tears, run towards overflowing bathtubs, chipped teeth, a hundred tiny disasters, maybe more.

I spend the whole day with her. Her eyes, piercingly blue, they keep click-clicking as I move her around. I want to close those eyes. The screwball side of me wonders what it would be like to cover them with something, anything. Eye mask, goggles, sunglasses. Anything but their endless glassy stare. Real babies often have this stare too. I try to ignore it, ignore everything. I don't...I don't want to make it dark for her. Dark like the inside of that garbage bag. Black plastic, deep stench. Tiny hand escaping as though waving for help, for freedom.

I strip the clothes off her and wash them by hand. Pegged outside to dry, they're desperately small. The clothes have a newly acquired sunshine smell and I add tiny stitches to the rips, thread new pink ribbon through the collar. Gently push the stuffing back into that cloth torso and stitch up the holes with compassionate stitches. The torso is soft throughout. No voice box. No sound-maker. I know it's not possible for her to be crying, to be doing anything, and I also know she is.

The world disappears as I put all my energy into her. Every last bit of me. I don't eat or sip water. Noah tries to offer me things like coffee and sandwiches, but eventually he walks away.

I bathe her soft pink skin, so eerily lifelike, soft to the touch, very nearly warm. I use rubbing alcohol, then bleach on the marks scrawled on her. Powerful strength pimple cream and sunlight start to bring about results. Finally, some baby shampoo, solvent and a careful hand to prise the strange wig off her. Underneath, a sparsely populated scalp – soft and tender as if to suggest a still-forming skull. The spot where new parents kiss a baby, all love-drunk and high on that smell.

She's so much better. I re-dress her. Everything is better, except that gluey eye.

It's late. Darkness has come and Noah returns. He waves at me until I turn my eyes to him. 'Hey. Did you have a good day?' He's talking the way you would to a frightened deer.

'I think so.'

'I went to CC,' he says – this is what we call council clean-up. 'And I found this.' He holds out a baby monitor. I stare back at him, unsure if he means to be cruel or if the cruelty is by accident.

He adds, 'It works and everything.'

Still holding Emily, I say. 'We don't. Have a baby. Sweetheart.' It comes out all stilted and wrong, like I have forgotten how to be a person.

'I want to prove that the doll is just a doll, OK?'

'Noah. This is a terrible idea.'

'You won't have to be scared of her at night if you see her doing nothing. Nothing! I guess she wasn't so bad after all; you've spent the whole day with her.'

'Noah. No.'

'OK,' he says, deflated. 'It'll be here if you change your mind.'

'Excuse me,' I say briskly, carrying Emily with me as I go.

As I take her to the bathroom sink to fetch warm water to rinse the marks I have scrubbed with chemicals, I catch a glimpse in the mirror of myself holding her. The effect is startling – so much like the baby I want, and in every way, not the baby I want. Too lifelike and not lifelike enough. The more I restore her, the more dead she seems.

Was the Prom Mom's child a stillbirth or was she murdered? The question comes into my head as I go past the mirror, until Emily's bright blue eyes, eyes that seem to lock onto my own, to follow my gaze, jolt me back to reality.

Getting out of bed in the night has felt worse lately. It feels absurd to be afraid of the dark at my age, but here we are. I go with my empty water glass to the living room, towards the kitchen. Noah left one of the lamps on after an evening of reading. The light illuminates a screen on the coffee table.

He set up the baby monitor? Even though I didn't want him to? I move to place it face down. On the screen, she's there. It's Emily. The scraping feeling is back, worse than ever, coming from within me. She's moving. Looking better and more complete, with her fresh clothes and cleaned stains and her blush pink skin – it's always nearly warm, just a tiny bit. And she's pulling herself along. Not crawling, more like dragging herself by the hands as though paralysed from the waist down. Like a mermaid moving on the shore.

I feel paralysed, prickling all over.

Like a person who becomes aware she is being watched, her head turns abruptly, turns my way. One bright blue eye and one glue-caked eye look at me through the screen, straight at me, right into my soul. I clap both hands over my mouth. Would it be easiest to evacuate myself and Noah, throw a lit match at the house as we go, never look back?

Her mouth forms more of an "oh" shape and one of those dragging hands, in a small fist, comes up to her face. Swipes at the gunked over eye. Another movement of her mouth, something like a stifled cry.

'You can't sleep with your eye like that,' I whisper. 'And I can't sleep either.'

I run into the bedroom. 'Noah, Noah, Noah, Noah!'

'Mmm hmmm?'

'She's moving, she's crawling, look, you can see.'

I drag a sleep-mussed Noah over to the baby monitor.

The screen is black. Cold. Like it's never been switched on, like it never worked at all.

'What, babe?'

'She was...she was...'

The blank screen looks back at me. Nothing.

Noah takes my hand. 'Back to bed?' He switches off the lamp as he leads me away. The darkness swallows us up and I keep holding onto that warm hand like it's the only real thing left on earth.

In the dark, I hear it, it's faint but I hear it. *Click click.*

I whisper urgently, 'Do you hear that?'

Noah's voice is sweet as ever. 'No. There's nothing. I promise you, nothing at all. Come back to bed.'

Click click. Then a muffled cry.

'That!' I say, excited that I might be able to show him what I'm experiencing is real. 'The clicking sound, it's her eyes. Then that other sound, it's like a cry.'

'It's time to come back to bed,' he says, slowly. Like a man with a dozen cartons of eggs stacked on top of each other, the whole situation more precarious by the second.

He leads me back to our bed and, as though I am five years old, tucks me in, squaring the blanket under my feet. 'Good night.'

'You don't believe me.'

'There's nothing to believe. There's just...nothing. Nothing to worry about. There isn't one single thing.'

Noah finds his words more convincing than I do. He's drifted off again in five minutes or less, snoring. And the click-clicks and the muffled cries – and louder cries, those too – they last for hours in the night.

Not one sound wakes him. His rhythmic breathing and the cries, the awful cries, they go into a place deep inside me, a place where they will keep echoing forever.

In the morning, he makes me a cup of tea. It's weak herbal tea. He is judging me, through tea.

'You OK, babe?' His whole forehead is creased up. He studies my sleepless face. I know – from the way my eyes itch and droop, how dry they are, the raggedness of my nails, my chapped lips – he can see every last drop of misery in me; I wear it all for the world to see.

'Fine.'

'You sure about that?'

'Yep.'

I sip the tea. Basically hot water. He's softened me up with two honey jumbles on the side. Once I bite one, words – and crumbs – start spilling out of my mouth.

'You really don't hear anything?'

'I don't. I'm not lying. I never have.' Noah takes one of my feet, picks it up, plops it into his lap like a tired puppy and begins to rub the sole. 'I'm very sorry about all this. I should never have insisted we take the doll. The money's not important. You are.'

His hand is warm. I see in my mind's eye a flash of Emily's little fist poking out of the garbage bag, sun-warmed and sticky. He continues, 'So I have good news. I found a buyer.'

'You what?'

'A buyer. They will only do $150 but I figured it would be better to have it gone and you sleeping through the night again. I never meant for this to stress you out so much.'

I gape at him. 'Why? How could you do that?'

'I thought this is what we wanted. She looks perfect now, and it would be better for you for her to go.'

'It's not that, it's not.' I'm so frustrated I'm about to cry. 'I wasn't finished working on her. Emily still needs my help.'

Noah just stares. 'I looked up whether all the hormone stuff we've got you on could make you hallucinate.'

I feel like roaring at him, tearing the table in half. 'She won't rest. She'll never rest until I finish fixing her.'

'It...is...a...doll.' He takes my face in his hands and I swat them away in irritation. 'Jess, look at me. It's not alive. Never was. Whatever you're going through, it's in your mind.'

'I am not crazy,' I hiss. I run a hand through my hair so viciously that a good clump of it falls out. 'Let me finish repairing her.'

'Jess, you need help.'

'No. Just leave me. Leave me with Emily. I can fix her. Fix everything. Then she'll be able to rest.'

I storm into the room with all the craft supplies, the cleaning products, the unsold items we have spirited away from roadsides where they were abandoned.

Emily is there. Face up, where I left her. One eye open, one eye closed. I just want her to close both eyes. Noah is right: other than that, Emily is perfect.

I start scraping at the glue with cotton swabs and chemical solutions. Powerful strength de-gunkers. The sort of stuff they use to remove all those price stickers on shelves when they move stock around. Nothing works. I am going to ruin it, ruin her eye, ruin everything. It stays under the stubborn glue, that piercing blue, doomed to peer forever through a layer of hardened adhesive. It must be like staring up through the ice of a beautiful Nordic lake. Everything a little fractured, a little distorted.

'How did this happen to you?'

It's stuck. I'm stuck. I can't finish the job. She'll always be like this, and those cries are destined to find me every night. I begin to cry big, heavy sobs. There is a lot of sadness in me: for the doll that disturbs my sleep, for the Prom Mom and her discarded baby, for the life she wanted and the life of the infant. For the lives of the girls who found the miniature corpse wrapped in plastic. For Noah, who hears nothing and therefore feels as removed from me and my reality as someone drifting away on an ice floe.

The buyer. Can I just give the doll away? In this state? No. She'll terrify them with her cries, so eerie they will throw her away again. Burn her, maybe. Send her to the bottom of a frozen lake. I can't bear the thought of her: no rest eternally, staring in the dark with one forever-opened eye.

It takes hours. It takes strong chemicals. It takes a tiny screwdriver to chip away at the glue and a tiny brush, a sable haired paintbrush, but little by little, the glue starts to come off.

Then it's gone. No glue. I hold Emily up to the light coming through the window. Two blue eyes, as bright and clear as each other. I sweep away any fine crumbs of glue with the soft paintbrush and, finally, polish the surface of the eyeball with a lens cleaning cloth. The eyelashes that someone had stuck so inaccurately I glue back where they belong. I use tweezers and patience, holding my breath. No glue smears on her eye this time.

I shift her weight and *click*, both her eyes snap shut. The placid beauty of her face is quite something. 'You really are pretty,' I whisper. The serenity of her face sends a wave of peace through me. My body relaxes.

I carry her out towards Noah. 'I'm heading out. Cancel the sale.'

'But babe, $150.'

'We were wrong to try and sell her. I just needed to fix her. Everything will be OK now.'

'Wait, where are you taking her?'

'I'm going to lay her to rest.'

He swallows hard and nods. We share a computer; I have seen his search history: fertility issues and depression. Fertility issues and psychosis. And he lets me go.

There's a shady little area on the edge of town near the cemetery. Perhaps I can bury her there, nearly among the human dead. Drop a handkerchief over her face so her blush-pink cheeks will not be soiled by the handfuls of earth I will toss in.

On a mostly empty bus, I hold her on my lap. In every way like the baby I want. In no way like the baby I want.

A small voice at my elbow startles me. 'Is that a dolly?' It's a little girl, aged seven or so.

'You'll have to excuse her,' says a flustered woman I take to be her mother. 'She's at a curious age. But I have to admit, I was curious too. I thought that was a real baby.'

'No,' I say simply.

'Oh,' the woman says. 'Oh, how strange.' She catches herself, shakes herself as if to dislodge her accidental rudeness and dabs at her brimming eyes. 'I'm sorry, I didn't mean that rudely. I…I've had a hard time lately.'

Her daughter waggles the doll's foot, fascinated. The child looks up and concurs in the blunt way of children. 'Mummy is sad a lot.'

Her mother nods and stifles a sniffing sound. 'We should leave the lady alone.'

But the girl, entranced by the doll, is still holding onto its miniature foot.

'It's OK,' I say. 'Really.' I pull a tissue out of a packet in my handbag and offer it to the mother. She begins to cry deeply – rivers of misery flow out of her as she holds herself together with as much dignity as she can.

'Sorry,' she whispers. 'Sorry. But...' she lowers her voice. 'I miscarried last week. I didn't know it could happen after I had a healthy one.' She nods at her daughter, who is prodding the doll in its soft cloth middle. 'And the doll, the doll reminded me of, I suppose, what I had lost and I...'

She trails off and cries some more. I pass her the entire 10-pack of tissues.

It's then I realise – I can't bury Emily. I can't have her lying in darkness, underground. I set her upright and her eyes snap open properly, satisfyingly after all I've been through, removing the glue. The little girl makes a pleased squeak.

An idea comes to me. 'Here,' I say to the mother. 'You can have the doll. For your daughter, I mean.'

'Oh,' she says, surprised. 'Oh...I don't know. It might be like seeing a ghost.'

'It will be fine,' I insist. And I'm sure it will be. Since I repaired her, that scraping feeling, that dark scratching inside me, has gone away. I don't think she'll cry anymore. 'I was just going to take her to the op shop as a donation.' I put the doll in the child's arms.

'Really?' the woman says, still tentative. Her daughter, oblivious to our discussion, is singing a song to Emily. Perhaps seeing how difficult it would be to prise her child away from the doll, she relents. 'Ummm, thank you.'

She scrounges in her wallet for a moment, digging out what turns out to be a voucher for a very nice salon. 'Here, you need this more than I do.'

She means I look like death, and I do. But I understand the intent. 'Thanks. It's been a real time for me as well.'

49

'Women like us,' she says. 'We need to care for ourselves as much as we care for others.'

I take the voucher and stick it in my purse. I watch as the woman and her child go away, with the doll firmly clasped in the little girl's embrace. Its eyes stay closed though she's holding it upright. It looks, for all the world, at peace.

'Bye,' I whisper.

When I get home, Noah is cooking dinner: pasta and cheese sauce. He is mollifying me. It works, too. I come and put my arms around him, rest my head against his heart.

'The doll's gone, huh?'

'Yes, gone.'

When his eyes meet mine, I hope he can see that lightness has come back into my body.

'It was my fault. I should never have made you take something you never wanted.'

I shake my head. 'It was both of us.'

That night, I scrub myself clean under an extra hot shower and fall gratefully into bed, certain I will sleep a solid eight hours, maybe 10.

In bed, both of us fed on stupefying amounts of cheesy pasta, a wave of sleep takes Noah immediately and I am not far behind.

Then I hear it. Faint at first, then loud, then ear-splitting. It's cries, baby cries. They're unmistakable. Full-throated.

'No,' I whisper. My mind conjures up a terrible image. The doll, dragging itself forward as it had on the baby monitor, has found its way back to me. The cries are so real this time. The scraping feeling returns. 'It's not possible.' I pinch myself viciously, hoping to wake up. Nothing. I stare at Noah, his beautiful face in peaceful profile as he sleeps, handsome in the way of a Roman coin, undisturbed. I say, under my breath: 'It's in my mind, it's in my mind, it's in my mind, it's not real...'

The cries fade out to silence and the silence hangs, punctured occasionally by distant cars and the rumble of trucks. Streetlights filter through the slats of our blinds. I chew the insides of my cheeks and listen to my stomach acid sloshing inside me.

In the morning, my face in the mirror is creased and crumpled, with heavy blue circles under my eyes. Noah, fresh as though on holiday, says, 'Ahh, babe, another bad night?'

'The cries came back! They did! Even without the doll!' I look at him, terrified. 'Why? Why don't you hear anything?'

'Because,' he says gently, 'because there's nothing to hear, my love.'

I think the answer is probably closer to this: he can't hear anything when he sleeps. On honeymoon in Bordeaux, he failed to hear a siren ordering us to evacuate the hotel in the night. I had to slap him awake.

'I am not insane!'

'I never said you were, not once. Come here.' He tries to fold me against his body but, shaking, I push past him and storm out.

We don't have the kind of apartment complex in which you talk to the neighbours so I'm not surprised to not recognise a woman standing there, strapping an infant into a gorgeous beast of a baby carrier, the kind that costs as much as a car repayment. She is as big as the sun and radiates serene energy, the happiness of a woman who has fulfilled one of her wishes. The child in her carrier kicks its miniature legs; one baby sock wrinkles down slightly.

I mutter at the baby, 'Oh, it's real.'

'What?' says its mother, turning a genial face to mine.

'I said, "Must be so surreal" – you know, new motherhood and all.'

'Oh yes,' she says, hoisting the child to her chest, love-drunk and all. 'You never quite imagine exactly what it will be like and all of a sudden, she's here and you realise, it could not have been any other way.'

'You're new to the building?'

'Oh no, just visiting. I came to stay with my sister for a few days. You know her? Marcelle, 8B.'

The baby's eyes are bright blue. I shiver. The mother catches my expression.

'Don't worry. I'm sure whatever it is you're going through, it will be a lot better soon.'

Just then, the baby turns bright red and flails its fists. It begins to squall, to cry its small lungs out. I have never heard it in the daytime before.

'I'd better let you go.'

The baby's cries come back at all hours of the day and night. Not once does Noah react. He continues in that calm way of his – folding shirts, turning pages, typing.

'You really don't hear that?'

He's wide-eyed. 'Hear what?'

I sigh heavily. Just whose idea was it to have a baby? With this guy, I see visions of a future in which I must do every night-time feeding. Where the person who must always respond to our child, if we ever get one, is me. Babies – whether real or silicone – are inaudible to him.

The cries next door start to strangle me, to choke off what little ability I have to sleep. He will never hear anything. So he'll never haul himself up from bed, and sterilise a bottle, and offer it, unless I ask him to. Years will go by.

In the bathroom, crabby and sore, I pee onto a stick. Two lines. It finally happened. The dark scraping feeling, the scratching inside, it's back.

The baby next door screams and screams. I yell over the sound, 'Noah! The test is positive!'

He yells back, 'What?'

'I'm pregnant,' I roar over the baby's screams.

'Huh?'

'Noah, I am pregnant!' I'm yelling enough to tear my throat, yelling over those baby screams, yelling as though adrift in a raft on the ocean.

Nobody hears me.

NULLARBOR

RAYMOND GATES

KAREN WOKE TO THE FEELING THAT SHE HAD FALLEN ASLEEP INSIDE AN oven.

It was hot and bright. She could tell it was bright even with her eyes closed. Everything was red behind her eyelids. She raised her arm to shield her eyes, wincing as her neck and shoulders protested the stiffness that had settled into them. She opened her eyes to slits and her vision changed from red to a brilliant, uniform blue. Heat radiated off the windshield, making her feel like an ant under a magnifying glass.

Karen sat up behind the wheel of her old Toyota Corolla. Her throat wasn't just dry but evacuated of moisture. She smacked her lips together and ran her tongue over them. Her tongue felt rough and raspy, her lips cracked. She turned and found a half empty bottle of water beside her. She grabbed it, quickly unscrewed the lid and upended it into her mouth. The water was warm but at least it was wet. She managed to swish some around the inside of her mouth before swallowing it, resisted gagging, and then took another gulp and did the same. She considered pouring the remainder over her face, however, some primal instinct reminded her this was the only water she had. Instead, she splashed a little into her palm and wiped her eyes and as much of her face as she could. As her vision and mind began to clear, Karen realised she was in the shit.

She'd left Kalgoorlie the previous day, leaving behind a worthless bar job and an even more worthless boyfriend. The trip wasn't planned; she had woken up that day and realised she couldn't recognise the face that stared back from the bathroom mirror. It wasn't just the cut lip or the bruise coming out on her cheek. It was the resignation in her eyes, and realising she was on the cusp of accepting that this was her life. In the next moment, she'd dressed, thrown some clothes and a few trinkets in a bag, grabbed her keys, her purse and her phone, and headed out the door. She would go back to Adelaide and try to reconnect with the woman she'd been before coming to this godforsaken place five years ago.

She drove until the needle hovered above E and managed to coerce the car to a truck stop by the Balladonia Hotel. She'd considered a hot meal and a cold beer, but she wanted to put as much distance between her and Craig as she could. She'd switched off her phone to stop the incessant texts and calls. However, she couldn't escape the idea that somehow he knew where she was and was catching up to her.

She had settled for the fuel, some junk food, and the largest bottle of water she could find, and got back on the road.

She'd made it to Eucla well after the sun had disappeared, and stopped at a roadhouse reported to be the last chance for food and fuel before entering the Nullarbor. It was devoid of customers except for a few truckers either getting ready to leave or bunk down for the night.

That she was across the border eased her fears, but not enough to pass the night at the motel. She took the time to refill the tank and to eat some real food – if you could call the dried-out burger and wedges the hot bar offered real – and a hot cup of coffee. She also took the chance to check her phone while spending some quality time with the bathroom facilities.

She skipped past the notifications from Craig, her boss (ex-boss now, she supposed) and a few unknown numbers. She replied to the texts from concerned friends confirming she was alive and would be in touch again soon.

As she finished the last reply, her phone lit up with Craig's face. She swiped to end the call and switched the phone off again. *Bastard*. She needed to get moving again.

She waved to the giant kangaroo standing sentry just beyond the roadhouse entrance as she swung onto the Eyre highway. Though hers was the only vehicle on the road, she didn't stop checking her rear-view mirror for tell-tale lights for a while.

The open plain and multitude of stars was beautiful, somehow peaceful, at first. Yet as the kilometres passed and the scenery didn't seem to change, it became agoraphobic. The unending passage of white lines down the centre of the road was hypnotic and threatened to lull her to sleep. The radio only picked up one station on the AM band and while drawling country music wasn't her taste, with nothing to see but as much road as her headlights would reach, it was at least some company. Occasional relief came in the form of the news on the hour.

'South Australian police have confirmed a fourth report of missing persons in the Nullarbor region,' the reporter droned. 'Sandra Parks and her husband Michael were last seen at a truckstop in Ceduna three days ago and were believed to be heading west along the Eyre highway. Family members in Perth reported the couple missing when they failed to arrive for a planned visit. This latest report follows a series of disappearances in the region, including a family of four from Melbourne, a Western Australian police officer, and a student from— …'

A loud BANG came from the front of the car.

The noise made her jump and she immediately thought she had hit an animal. The car leaned to the driver's side and at first made a flapping, then a grinding sound against the bitumen. Fortunately, it was still steerable, and when she'd slowed down enough, she eased it off the road onto the shoulder.

She got out to inspect the damage using the light from her phone. A strip of rubber clung to the rim; the rest of the tyre was no doubt in pieces along the road behind her.

Karen had never learned any sort of car maintenance beyond making sure there was petrol in the tank, which was why she had premium membership to a roadside assistance service. She checked her phone.

No reception. She held her arm high, waved it around, even moved around the car as if the signal were there but being elusive. Not so much as a single bar appeared.

Fuck. The idea of teaching herself to change a tyre in the middle of the night, in the middle of nowhere, was almost as unappealing as being stuck here. In her mind she heard her mother say, 'beggars can't be choosers'. She'd always hated when her mother was right.

Karen popped the boot of the car and pulled up the floor mat to reveal an empty space where the spare tyre should have been.

For a moment all she could do was stare, as if the tyre were just obscured by shadow and if she looked long enough it would reappear. When it didn't, she slumped to the ground, crossed her arms over her drawn up knees and lay her head against them.

What the hell am I going to do now?

She checked her phone again to see if bars had magically appeared. They hadn't. She dialled the emergency number anyway. Nothing.

The back of her car lit up, silhouetting her against it. She rose to her feet. In the near total darkness, the lights approaching her were like twin suns, forcing her to first shield her eyes, then look away. The ground became brighter, the dust an ashen grey, like a photographic negative. A loud, chugging rumble drew closer, accompanied by a high-pitched hiss of escaping air.

Karen attempted another look. She was bathed in light, almost pure white, surrounded by little dots of orange or yellow.

A male voice emanated from the light.

'Oi! You all right?'

The voice was too blokey to be God or aliens, yet still Karen stepped around to the side of her car. She heard the thump of boots on the ground, then gravelly footsteps approaching. A large, lumbering figure partially blotted out the light.

'You okay, love?' There was warmth in the voice. Genuine concern. 'You break down or somethin'?'

Karen stopped backing away; however, she still wished she had something more substantial in her hand than her phone.

'Got a flat,' she said, and inwardly cringed at the shake in her voice.

'Oh, that all?' the man said. The footsteps had stopped, and Karen's eyes were adjusting enough to make out some features.

He stood about six feet tall, broad shouldered and even more broad across the belly. He looked to be in shorts and a singlet with a peaked cap on his head. She still couldn't make out his face, but a long beard danced in the light whenever he spoke.

'I'll change her for you if you like. Won't take me long.' He moved towards the back of her car.

'I haven't got a spare,' she said.

'Haven't got a spare?' The man snorted. 'What the bloody hell are you doin' out here then? This isn't the place to be without a spare.'

'It wasn't exactly part of the plan,' Karen said, a little more strength in her voice.

The man chuckled. 'Yeah, I reckon it wasn't.' He took a couple of steps towards her. 'Well, we better get ya outta here, eh?'

'I just need some help,' she started. 'Can't you call somebody? On your CB or whatever?'

'I could,' he said."But it's not gonna be much use. No RAA out here, love. No local towies till the sun's up at least, and even then, it'll take a while to get anyone out here.'

He took another step towards her. 'Look. Your best bet'd be to come with me. I can get you to Yatala.' He spread his hands open from his sides. 'You don't wanna be stuck out here by yourself. At least you'd be a lot more comfortable while you wait for help.'

He made sense, yet Karen retreated towards the front of her car. In her experience, no one was that helpful that quickly without having an ulterior motive. The words from the last news report on the radio drifted through her mind.

'Can't you just call a cop?' she asked.

'I could,' he said, 'but you'd be lucky if there's one within coo-ee of here. In fact, you're bloody lucky I come along. You can go days out here without seeing another soul.'

He made to step forward yet again, then stopped. 'Listen,' he said 'I don't blame ya for being cagey around some strange fella who pops up outta nowhere. Frankly, in my book it makes you smart. But ya can't stay here, and I can't hang around here all night either.' He thumbed back over his shoulder. 'I got a load I've gotta have in Melbourne tomorrow or it's my arse.'

His words registered and fought her fear and despair. The lights behind him must be a large semi-trailer. She looked past him and saw the large grill of the truck emblazoned with a Kenworth logo. She relaxed a little, but kept her distance.

'Look, I'm Macca,' he said. 'Big Mac, they call me" He tapped his belly with both hands; it made a drum-like sound. 'Not just 'cause I don't mind a burger.' The hint of a toothy smile appeared in the darkness. 'I've got a wife and a couple of youngen's at home countin' on me to keep my job, and a boss who's got thirty other blokes waitin' for a driver to screw up so they can take his run. One way or another I've gotta get back on the road.' He extended a hand towards her. 'Don't make me the arsehole that left a lady stranded in the middle of the desert.'

Karen didn't know what to do. She knew she couldn't stay out here, especially not when the next vehicle might be Craig's. She'd met her fair share of truckies at the bar back in Kalgoorlie, and Big Mac would fit right in with them. He seemed genuine enough, yet the fine hairs on the back of her neck stayed at attention.

What choice did she have?

A loud WHOOP-WHOOP pierced the air from behind Big Mac and his truck. Moments later, a third figure appeared by the side of the road, illuminated by the truck's lights. From the blue shirt, trousers, and cap he was clearly a police officer. He held a torch up by the side of his face and swept its beam from Big Mac to Karen.

'What's going on?' the officer asked.

'G'day mate,' Big Mac replied and approached the newcomer. The officer raised his free hand by way of telling him to stop, which he did. 'You're just in time. This young lady lost a tyre and hasn't got a spare. I was gonna give her a lift but now you're here you'll be able to sort her out, eh?'

The officer kept the light focused on Karen. 'That the case, miss?' he asked.

'Yes,' Karen said, and gestured toward her car. The beam played over to the car, revealed the tyreless rim, then returned to her face. 'This guy just pulled over to help me.'

The officer lowered the torch slightly, taking the glare out of Karen's eyes. 'Not the sort of place you want to get a flat without a spare,' he said. Karen resisted a sarcastic reply.

'You both got some ID?' he asked.

Karen's licence was in her purse in the car. Big Mac's was in his truck. The officer told each to retrieve them. 'You want my logbook too?' Big Mac asked. The officer shook his head.

Karen presented her ID first. Up close, the officer looked young, in his mid-to-late twenties, and physically fit, though the uniform was a little baggy on him. He glanced over her licence quickly. 'Where are you headed to, Miss Green?'

'Adelaide,' she said. 'Going back home"

'Says Kalgoorlie's home here,' he said, indicating her licence he still held.

'I lived in Kalgoorlie the last five years. But it's not home.'

Big Mac came strolling up. This close, and with the cop beside her, he wasn't nearly as threatening. He was middle-aged, with weather-beaten and darkened skin, a bushy moustache and beard down to the centre of his chest, and big, thick hands. His eyes were particularly noticeable; a brilliant, almost iridescent blue, as if lit with some inner light.

The cop handed Karen's licence back and inspected Big Mac's. He shone his torch on the truck and its Victorian licence plate. 'You're a long way from home,' the cop said.

'Yeah,' Big Mac replied. 'I do a round trip to Perth a couple of times a month. Only worth it if ya can get a backload, so sometimes you've got to hang around for a bit.' He nodded towards Karen. 'Like I said to her, just lucky I was on the road tonight.'

The officer murmured a reply, returned Big Mac's licence, and turned back to Karen.

'Well, Ms Green, I can get you back to the station at Eucla and we can get you some assistance in the morning. In the meantime,' he turned back to Big Mac. 'I imagine you need to be getting on your way.'

'Too right,' Big Mac nodded and then gave Karen a curt, almost embarrassed smile. 'Nice to meet ya. Hope it's not like this next time.' His smile became warmer then and the blue in his eyes grew even brighter. Then he walked back to his truck.

The officer gestured towards Karen's car. 'Why don't you grab anything essential you need and we'll get you out of here?'

'What about my car?'

'Just lock it up. It'll be safe till we get someone out here, but you can't be too careful.'

Karen grabbed her purse and bag. By the time she locked the car, Big Mac's truck was rolling past them with its double trailers. His air horn sounded two blasts by way of farewell.

Everything was darker once he'd gone. The lights from the officer's car, a four-wheel drive cruiser, were nowhere near as bright, or as numerous, as the truck's.

Karen followed the officer to his vehicle. He opened the rear passenger door for her. 'You can sit back here, please,' he said. She pushed her bag along the seat, then slid in beside it. The officer closed the door and then moved to the driver's side. A thick wire screen separated the front and rear compartments, and Karen realised a very different kind of passenger would normally sit here.

The officer drove back the way she had come. Karen looked out the back window, thinking that she might see the fading lights of Big Mac's truck, but they had already been swallowed up by the night. Looking ahead, she wondered if she would see oncoming lights, indicating Craig's pursuit. She decided not to mention this to the officer, dreading the inquiry that would come with it. She could explain later if she had to.

They drove in silence, save for the occasional squark emitted over the police radio. No other vehicles appeared on the road either in front or behind them, and despite herself, Karen found her eyes continuously wanting to close.

After some time, the officer slowed and turned onto another road.

Calling it a road was being generous; it was little more than a dusty, bumpy trail, which the four-wheel drive handled well. The change in pitch and smoothness of the journey roused Karen from her near slumber.

'Where are we?' she asked.

'Almost there,' the officer replied without taking his eyes from the road.

Karen looked out her window. What formless features she could discern were no different than those on the rest of the journey. As they jostled along, something in the back of her mind nagged at her like a hangnail.

'I thought the highway was famous for being the longest stretch of straight road in the country,' she said.

'It is,' the officer replied.

'So, why did we turn off?'

The smile of a predator was reflected in the rear-view mirror.

'I had a feeling you'd be a smart bitch,' he said.

Karen pulled at her door handle. It wouldn't release. She leaned across to try the other door. Her hand touched something tacky on the seat. A dark stain, not quite dry, had spread over the seat and now partially coated her hand.

She ignored it and pulled the other handle. That door wouldn't open either.

She turned and kicked out at the window next to her. Her shoe thudded against it, but it did not crack. She tried again, and again, crying out with each attempt. The non-cop driving chuckled.

'Kick all you want,' he said. 'These pig cars are reinforced just for that reason.'

'Let me out!'

His smile grew and he laughed more. He kept one hand on the steering wheel, the other lifting to show her what he was holding. At first, she couldn't tell what it was, but as he turned it this way and that, it became clear. A knife, one side curved and wicked sharp, the other jagged. What Craig would have called a Rambo knife.

'We're going to have so much fun.' His voice dropped almost to a whisper. 'Oh, so much fun'

Karen screamed and beat her hands against the wire barricade between them. When he ignored her, she threaded her fingers through and tugged at it. That got him to glance back, and his expression turned from delight to rage. He lashed out with the knife; it tinged as it struck the wire. The clumsy attempt was enough for her to pull her hands away.

'Let me go!' she screamed again. Hot tears burned her cheeks.

In an instant, the car's cabin lit up as if someone had struck a flare, only white instead of red. A deafening roar, like some prehistoric animal, blotted out all other sound: *WHOARRRRRRRRRR!*

Karen glanced out the rear window. Shrouded in light was a symbol: a red circle with two letters, one above the other.

K. W.

With a thump, the four-wheel drive lurched forward, sending Karen crashing against the panel behind the driver's seat. The car fishtailed e before the driver got it back under control. Karen scrambled back into her seat just as the next impact came. It jolted her forward again and she struck the wire cage with her forehead. They swerved, but not as severely. Then the car accelerated.

Again, that terrible sound blasted, enveloping them. For an insane moment, Karen thought of the dinosaurs roaring in *Jurassic Park*. This was much louder.

Then there was a metallic crunch and everything shifted sideways.

Karen felt as if she was on a round-a-bout that had been spun too fast. She was pressed back against the seat, then into the corner where the seat met the door. Then everything upended and she was on the roof, then back on the seat, then on the roof again. There was a moment of weightlessness, and a horrible screeching like nails on a blackboard.

And then nothing.

The next thing she knew, something was tugging at her leg. She raised her head as much as she could. Someone, or something, was trying to drag her out of the car.

Karen screamed and kicked out with the little strength she could muster.

'Easy!' a familiar voice said. 'Easy, love! I'm tryin' to help ya!'

Karen tried to kick once more but her leg would barely respond. There was pain, but it was dull. Resigned to her fate, she let herself be pulled free.

The cool air roused her enough to see the shape looming over her. A face, and within it twin pools of brilliant blue.

'I gotcha, love.'

Karen wanted to say her name wasn't "love", but as she went to speak, everything went black.

Karen opened her eyes. She was surrounded by a circle of faces, none of whom she recognised. She tried to scrabble away from them but her whole body shrieked in protest.

'Whoa, hold on honey,' a woman, who probably wasn't as old as her leathery wrinkled face, suggested. 'You're okay. No one here's gonna hurt you.'

The other faces, a mix of old and young, male and female, withdrew somewhat. Karen could see their concern.

'It's all right.' The woman touched Karen's face. She was gentle despite her skin being rough and calloused. 'You're all right. Well, you're a bit bruised and battered but you're all right.'

Karen stared into the woman's face. Focusing on the one rather than the many helped quell the spiralling fear building up inside her.

'Where am I?' she asked.

'You're at the Yatala roadhouse,' the woman replied. 'We found you on the doorstep a little while ago when we came to open up.'

Karen struggled to make sense of what the woman was saying. She realised she was lying on a blanket on the floor. She tried sitting up. The room spun and the woman had to catch her before she fell.

'Take it easy,' the woman said. 'Jim, go get her some water, wouldya?' The woman placed an arm around her shoulder and slowly helped Karen into a sitting position. Everything throbbed and ached, but everything still seemed to move, as well.

A man returned with a glass of water. Karen sipped at it, then gulped the rest down.

'Well, that looks like it hit the spot,' the woman said and smiled. She took the glass from Karen and handed it back to the man. 'Get her another will ya, love?'

Karen's senses were sharpening up. 'How did I get here?'

'We were hoping you could tell us,' the woman replied. 'You look like you've been through the wringer, love. What happened to ya?'

Karen slowly shook her head. 'I don't know.' She searched through the fog of her memory. 'There was this guy. He was a cop. But he wasn't a cop. And then the car was rolling and–…'

Karen's eyes widened and she gripped the woman's arm. 'The truckie! Is he here?'

'Truckie?' The woman looked up at the other faces.

One of the men shook his head. 'Don't look at me,' he said. 'I never seen her before.'

'No,' Karen said. 'His name was Mac. Or Macca. Or something like that.'

The woman grinned. 'Darlin', do you know how many truckies called Macca blow through here on any given day?'

'No,' Karen said, exasperated. The man who'd gone to fetch more water – Jim, she guessed – had returned and offered her the glass.

She took it and held on to it. 'He was different. He had–' An image came to her mind. 'He had the most amazing blue eyes.'

'Oh shit,' Jim said. 'She's talking about Big Mac.'

Some of those present backed further away. Others turned and left. The woman's face creased with concern.

'Yes!' Karen said. 'Big Mac! That's him!'

'Big Mac brought you here, eh?' the woman said. She shook her head and looked at Jim. 'It's been a while.'

'I thought we'd seen the last of 'im,' said Jim. 'Must be at least two? Three years?'

'Must be,' the woman agreed.

'Wait. You know him?' Karen said. 'Where is he?'

The woman sighed. 'Oh, he's long gone now,' she said. 'But every now and then he pays us a visit. Usually with some stray he's found out on the Nullarbor. Never even occurred to me you might be one.'

'I don't understand. One what?'

'One of the ones he saves.' The woman looked directly into Karen's eyes. 'Every once in a while, someone runs into trouble out on the Nullarbor. Sometimes their car breaks down. Or they run out of petrol. Or some are just mad buggers who think they can wander off and explore the desert. The lucky ones get found by Big Mac, and he picks them up and brings them here or Eucla. Makes sure people are safe, see?' The woman smiled. 'He was always a good fella. Bit of a larrikin, but always a good fella.'

'But he saved me,' Karen said. Her eyes widened. 'He probably knows everything that happened! Do you know him? Do you know how I can reach him?'

The woman's smile faded, and she became stern. 'You can't reach him.'

'But you know the guy. He must stop in here. Wouldn't someone know how to reach him?'

The woman shook her head. 'You don't understand. You can't reach him.' She drew a long breath and exhaled slowly. 'Big Mac's truck got cleaned up by a train at a crossing just outside of Ceduna.

'Big Mac's been dead nearly twenty years.'

A LITTLE OVERBOARD

SARAH ROBINSON-HATCH

Join us!

This Valentine's Day, come aboard the historical *Polly Woodside** for a night of unforgettable spooky fun.

Sit back and relax while our professional photographer (and talented matchmaker) helps you find your soulmate.

PLUS bottomless themed cocktails!

Singles only.

* believed to be haunted

The thing Polly hated most – more than the gaudy pink hearts strung up over the moored ship's deck, more than the sea of bodies gyrating out of time to the beat – was small talk.

'Sssso whaddaya do for a living?' the girl with curly brown hair slurred, her glossy lips pulling into a slow smile, city lights reflected in her glasses.

Polly attempted to look like she wasn't about to hurl herself off the historical ship and into the murky, sewer-scented Yarra River. Her fingers skated over the material of her scratchy white dress until they landed on her hips. 'Well, I suppose I–'

'I'm in marketing,' interrupted the blonde next to Polly, cheeks pink in the warm night air.

The stretched grin slipped from Polly's mouth, shattering on the sticky floorboards under her. The ship smelled of alcohol and too much body spray.

'That's sooo cool.' The brunette tilted her head towards the blonde, raising the almost finished, bright pink *Love on the Titanic* cocktail to her lips. She shifted in her heels slightly, almost bumping Polly's shoulder. 'I'm a graphic designer.'

'Oh really?' The blonde placed a soft hand on the brunette's arm.

'Hey.' A voice carried over the buzz of the drunken crowd, but Polly dismissed it. Surely, it wasn't addressing her.

Polly stepped in closer, pretending for a moment that she was a part of this. That she could *ever* be a part of this – a flirty conversation over a drink. If only she could just skip the small talk, this would be bearable. Nice, even.

Though there was only one person she really wanted to talk to after years of isolation and she wasn't here.

And she never will be, Polly thought. The realisation wasn't new, but it still stung like alcohol on an open wound. Sharp. Biting. Impossible to ignore.

Polly tried to shove that familiar lonely feeling aside, then she cleared her throat and asked the two women, 'How often do you think about your own mortality?'

Her question hung in the air, ignored.

'*Hey.*' There was that voice again, louder this time. It cut through the music and the small talk like a bow through calm waters.

Polly looked over her shoulder, breath hitching in her throat.

A woman who didn't appear much older than her (all things considered), long black hair pulled into a ponytail, was looking right at her.

Her. Polly, the one no one ever noticed, more ghost than girl.

Unsure, Polly glanced behind her quickly, and, when she saw no one there, she raised a finger to her chest and cocked her head.

'Yeah you, silly!' The woman beamed at her. A fancy camera was looped around her neck, the sleeves of her black dress pushed up her forearms. 'Can't you find anyone to talk to? On Valentine's Day?'

Polly shrugged. 'I am not sure I am their type.'

The woman gave her a look – smiling, squinting slightly – like she didn't quite believe her. 'How could you not be anyone's type? You're a catch.' She extended a hand. 'I'm Nora. Event photographer and matchmaker extraordinaire. Find your soulmate, et cetera, et cetera.'

'P-Polly,' Polly said, the name feeling foreign in her mouth. It'd been so long since–

Nora smirked. 'You sure about that?'

'Excuse me?' Polly's brows knitted together.

Nora laughed. 'No I just meant– You didn't sound sure. But I'm kidding. It's a joke.' Pink rose onto her cheeks, spreading across them like light across the sky at dawn. 'Pretty big coincidence, you sharing a name with this ship. The *Polly Woodside.*'

'Who is to say the ship does not share a name with me?' Polly said, offering a coy smile. The corner of her mouth tugged up, a dimple pushing into a single cheek, caressed by strands of white-blonde hair that had come loose from her braid.

Nora laughed again, rolling her eyes. 'You're right. How dare I assume.' Her gaze lingered on Polly a beat longer, long enough to jolt Polly's brain into action – *This was happening. This was really happening* – and then Nora cleared her throat. Her eyes slid across the dancing figures, nothing more than shadowy silhouettes against the bright city lights. Back to business. 'I'm sure we can find a partner for you.'

And the moment shattered.

Polly felt the lightness evaporate like fizz escaping from a can of soft drink, gone in an instant. Her fingers curled in the material of her dress as she followed Nora's gaze across the ship's deck. Dancing bodies, pulsating lights, beat thumping through the floorboards. Snippets of carefree chatter, small talk… She could never be a part of that, even if she wanted to be.

'Come on,' Nora said. She reached out, placing a warm hand on Polly's shoulder.

Polly flinched under her touch. She pulled away before she could stop herself, the feeling of human connection so foreign on her skin.

'Sorry,' she blurted, clocking Nora's widened eyes. 'I…' *I did not think you could do that.*

Nora raised her palms in apology, letting the camera hanging from her shoulder bump into her hip. 'No, my bad.' She looked at Polly again. 'You know, if you're not up to meeting anyone, that's fine. There's no pressure.'

'No, it's not that…' Polly said, shaking her head. 'It's just that I've already met someone.'

Nora took a tiny step in, shifting her weight to the other foot. This close to her, Polly could see freckles smattered over her nose and across her cheeks, like someone had flicked a wet paintbrush at her. 'Oh yeah?' Nora smiled.

Polly wanted to tell her. Wanted to explain how she felt, how no one had ever seen her like this woman had, and how she was pretty sure this might be her only shot. But then the beat dropped and a gaggle of girls screeched, and she didn't really want to be yelling all that through the sound of some singer crooning about watermelon and sugar highs.

'Follow me,' Polly said instead, dipping her head in the direction of the small cabin above the ship.

Polly led Nora through the sea of people until the colourful lights melted away and the music faded. They slipped through the open door into the cabin and descended the steep stairs to the room below.

Only one set of footsteps echoed.

'Why did you bring me down here?' Nora asked when they reached the bottom. The room was shadowy and forgotten, unlike the deck above. All the light that permeated the room seeped from a string of pink hearts on one wall, reflected in the framed photographs hung opposite. A few old mannequins sporting costume shop pirate outfits that had been passed off as "historically accurate" during the guided tours of the ship stood in one corner, covered in dust and cobwebs.

Polly knew every inch of her ship. She knew which floorboards creaked, knew where the cold drafts snuck through the slats in the wood, knew the exact spot where she took her final breath, cold and alone, her blood running in rivulets across the deck and dripping into the rooms below.

Right here.

Sometimes she swore she could still smell the metallic tang in the stale, dusty air.

'I want to show you something,' she said to the woman before her.

Nora watched her with a small smile and wide, curious eyes. She readjusted her camera strap. 'Better be quick. I'm meant to be working.'

'Your job is matchmaking as well, right?' Polly floated towards the framed photos on the hundred year-old wall.

'Yeah,' Nora said slowly.

'Then you're the only one that can help me. But first…' Polly stopped in front of a picture of the ship set against a stormy background, rocks jutting from the water. It was just an artist's interpretation, but the way it made her feel was so… *real*. It was almost like she was on that ship back in the day, *this ship*, and hating every second of it – except on those rare occasions when she saw *her*.

Polly could imagine her there, perched on the rocks, singing as sailors flung themselves into the depths.

Nora leaned in, close enough that Polly could see Nora's reflection in the glass, a blush on her cheeks, wide eyes watching her. Polly's eyes slid down to Nora's lips then back up again, and when she breathed, Polly could almost feel the rise of her chest against the fabric of her dress. Feel the warmth of Nora's breath on her bare neck.

But she tuned all that out.

Instead, Polly let the memories of her long-ago beloved wash over her – the horror, the beauty, the *awe* – until a tingle passed through her. It spread from her chest through her spine, right down to her fingertips. Her pale skin rippled and shifted as her true form took hold.

'This is me,' she whispered, looking down at the exposed bones of her fingertips. Her skin dripped from the cartilage of her forearms, hanging in loose, age-eaten strands. Something was slick at her neck. She didn't have to look at the glass – didn't want to – to know her throat was wet with centuries-old blood. Her blood.

Nora stumbled back from Polly, mouth hanging open in a silent scream. The camera slid from her shoulder. The sound of the lens shattering on the floorboards cut through her ragged breathing. Her lips moved, and finally, a quiet 'No no no *no*,' slipped through them.

'Did you not wonder why no one else noticed me at the party?' Polly said, her voice hushed like waves in the distance. 'Did you not wonder why I was so surprised you approached and were able to talk to me?'

Nora's wide eyes filled with tears. She didn't blink – couldn't blink – but still tears ran down her cheeks like rivers of blood. 'W-W-Who are you?'

'I told you. I am Polly.' She stepped closer to Nora, but when the woman tried to retreat, the only place she could go was into the wall behind her. Nora was trapped, at Polly's mercy. 'I am this ship and this ship is me. We've been one and the same for so long I can barely remember a time before.'

'You can't be,' Nora whispered, ashen and shaking. 'How is this possible?'

Polly stopped her movement, but Nora didn't. Her shoulders were pressed into the hard wood of the wall, the corner of the frame digging into her back as she tried to create more distance between them.

'You are right. I am not Polly,' said the ghost who was not a girl, but who was not Polly either. 'That is the name I gave myself.' *Because I cannot remember my own.* She met Nora's eyes and caught a glimpse of her own reflection in the glass behind her.

Black, bottomless pits for eyes. Straggly hair. Cheekbones that cut through her flesh. Teeth exposed through her rotting lips, a putrid grey.

'Please,' Nora sniffled. 'Don't hurt me.'

'Hurt you?' Polly tried to give her a smile, but the skin stretched uncomfortably across her bones. 'No. I need you to help me.'

'W-What?' Nora stuttered, eyebrows tugging together. Tears streaked her pale cheeks, eyes rimmed with red. 'How can I possibly help you?'

'It seems you are the only one who can see me. It was meant to be.' Polly ran her boney fingers over the rags of her dress. No longer was it the clean, shining silk she'd conjured for the party. This dress was rugged with age, covered in blood and dirt and grime. 'You can help me find my soulmate. You said so yourself.'

'I'm not sure—'

'*Please*,' Polly said. The desperation in her voice surprised her. 'You are the first person I have spoken to in decades. *Centuries.* I don't know how this is possible, or why, but there's something special about you. You can see me when no one else can, and so I cannot let you leave without taking me to her.'

Nora had stopped crying, the streaks already drying on her cheeks. She'd stopped shaking too. All that remained was a nervous twitch to her fingers that dug into the skin of her goose-bumped arms.

'Who is she?' Nora asked.

'She is…' God, how would Polly even begin to explain when she didn't even know the name of her beloved? All Polly knew was how her love made her feel. 'She is remarkable. There is no one like her. Every day since I have been moored here, I dream of her. Of one day being properly introduced at last…' Her voice trailed off, eyes looking out the porthole on the wall.

Nora softened slightly, looking at Polly. She wasn't a monster, or a demon. She was just someone who wanted to be loved. Isn't that all anyone ever wanted?

For a moment, Polly imagined she could see the girl she'd spoken of — the love of her life, perched on one of the rocks as the *Polly Woodside* passed. The men on board always drifted towards her song, helplessly enraptured. The memories of her life all those years ago were blurry, faded like a Polaroid left in the sun, but the image of her crush was crystal clear.

Polly's cavernous black pits itched. Was she… crying?

Nora's fearful eyes took on a different shape, eyebrows sloping up in the middle. Her lips extended into a thin line, the rigidness of her posture slipping. 'Why haven't you gone to her then? If you love her this much, what's stopped you?'

'I cannot move the ship on my own.' Polly reached out to graze the walls with her boney fingers. The wood was cold. Or maybe it was herself that was cold, the heat never being able to permeate her body, nothing ever touching her. Until – impossibly – Nora. 'My love waited for me each trip, always in the same spot in Bass Strait. She has been there for centuries. I just hope…'

'What?' Nora's voice was soft. Caring. She took a step forward.

Polly could have sworn Nora flinched when she met her gaze, but she didn't look away.

71

'I hope she is still there. That she has not found a lover in my absence.'

Nora offered a small smile. 'So let's go find this girl you're crushing on.'

'"Crushing on"?'

'Falling for.' Nora explained. 'Y'know, interested in. Romantically or...'

'You know... I have never spoken to her.' The confession burned through Polly, making her gaze drop to the sticky floor. It hurt to admit that in all those years of passing her as they sailed the Strait, she never once dared speak to the woman who she was so enamoured by.

'Well,' Nora said. When Polly met Nora's eyes once more, she saw the glint of hope in them. 'We'll have to fix that. And your lack of slang education. You need a sleducation.'

'Sle–'

Nora waved a hand. 'Never mind.' Then her eyes slid back down, trailing over Polly's raggedy dress. The skin dripping from her arms. The blackened ends of her bones. 'But if we're doing this, we need to do it properly.'

Polly frowned, tilting her head so the few remaining strands poking out of her discoloured skull tickled her exposed collarbones. 'What do you mean?'

No one realised that the *Polly Woodside* was never meant to leave the Yarra. The partygoers were either too drunk, flinging their bodies in time with the music on the deck, or busy making out with their one true love they met an hour earlier, or both. Either way, no one said anything or tried to stop them – or rather, Nora – as she told the crew there had been a change of plans and the event organisers were expecting the *Polly* to set sail into the harbour.

Polly stood at the darkened stern of the ship, hair moving like writhing tendrils. The two girls were out of sight of the singles back here, the city lights a distant haze. Waves thudded against the ship like a heartbeat.

'So I can say something like, *you're my ride or die*,' Polly said. 'Or *I promise to never ghost you*. But isn't that confusing? I mean...' She gestured at herself. 'Look at me. Is all this not a little... overboard? Is that the word you used before?'

Nora shook her head and gestured for Polly to continue. 'You're doing great.'

Polly cleared her throat and launched back into her recitation. She was getting the hang of this. Wooing the love of her life with modern slang was going to be easy. 'I think we should DTR, because I am DTF.'

Nora cringed. 'Maybe leave that part out for now.'

'Would it help if I explained the acronyms to her?'

'I think we should move on,' Nora said quickly. Her arms were covered in goosebumps, the wind knotting her hair. 'You've nailed that. Hundo P. Congrats.'

Polly gave her a satisfied grin. Then she brought both her arms up slowly, bending one arm over her forehead and stretching out the other to the side, just like Nora had shown her.

'What are you—'

'Dab?' Polly said, still in position, looking at Nora from beneath a forearm.

'Absolutely not.'

Polly lowered both arms, unable to keep the grin from her face.

'However,' Nora continued, pointing a knowing finger at the ghost. 'We should practise the questions you're going to ask her as well.'

'What type of questions?' Polly's anxiety rose within her. She'd memorised the slang. She knew all the hand signals. But now she had to wrap her head around questions too?

'I dunno, like, asking her about her favourite music.' Nora shrugged. 'What she likes doing on the weekend. That kind of stuff.'

Repulsion crept up Polly's spine. 'No way. I despise small talk.'

'Why do you hate it so much?'

'Do you know how many sailors I've had to listen to over the years?' Polly shuddered at the memories.

'Okay, yeah, fair enough.' Nora waved a hand. 'Skip the small talk then. I'm sure she won't mind. Just think about all the amazing times you two are going to have together instead.'

Polly inhaled, smelling the salt and the seaweed and the humidity in the air. This was going to go fine. Better than fine, in fact. She was finally going to meet the love of her life.

Polly could almost picture it – approaching her love on the rocks, jumping into the water and swimming up beside her. Feeling her cool, scaly skin beneath her boney fingers. Watching her ribs rise and fall as she devoured human flesh, turning the water crimson.

She had already waited over a century for this, but somehow the last twenty minutes had been more unbearable than all the years of loneliness and hopelessness put together. Her true love was so close, and yet still felt too far away to bear.

'What now?' Polly's fingers twisted in the shabby material of her white dress.

Nora's nose crinkled. 'You don't happen to have any other clothes, do you?'

Polly looked down at what she was wearing. She'd gotten used to the stains, the smell, the way it hung from her skeletal frame. She crossed her arms over her chest. 'I think we might be in a spot of bother.'

'We'll figure something out,' Nora said quickly. 'There's gotta be some bar aprons we could fashion into a skirt or...' She gasped. 'The mannequins!'

Polly didn't wait for Nora. She slipped through the floorboards, body melting into the ether and rearranging in the room below. She didn't want to waste a single second when she could be preparing to meet the love of her life.

Nora joined Polly a moment later, approaching her in the corner of the darkened room.

Polly ran her fingertips over the scratchy fabric of a pirate shirt. It was hardly the glittery dresses or slick suits worn by the people above them as they met their supposed soulmates. 'Are you sure she will like me in this?'

'I mean,' Nora said slowly, eyes flicking over the costume. 'I'm not saying you have to *change* for anyone, but we're dressing to impress, right?'

'Right,' Polly said. Nora knew what she was doing. And plus, anything was better than the dress she was currently sporting, covered in blood and grime and god knows what else from a hundred years at sea. A slow smile crawled across her face. 'Let me see if I can...'

The ghost trailed off and she reached out, the ends of her boney fingers glowing a pale blue, tingling like they always did when she passed through something, be it a wall or a body. She stepped *into* the mannequin and disappeared through the fabric.

Everything was dark for a moment. No light could reach her, the sounds around her became muffled. She could feel the plastic pressing into her, not like a weight but like stepping out into the cold after being warmed by a fire.

'*Polly?*' came Nora's uncertain voice.

Polly pushed against the pressure, light snaking through the cracks that formed around her. She shoved her way back into the world, feeling the plastic of the mannequin snap off and drop to the floor like a snake shedding its skin. The costume dropped onto her in its place, covering her old dress with the sleeves of the pirate shirt.

Nora leapt back, her wide eyes unblinking as Polly stood where the mannequin had been. Shards of plastic were scattered around her feet, a single unmoving eye staring up at her from the floorboards. It was almost accusatory.

'Do I look better?' Polly asked, one hand moving to feel her new get-up. Then she cocked her head at Nora, awaiting her verdict. 'What do you think?'

Nora's mouth opened and closed, eyes blinking. 'I-I think you should never do that again.'

A slight mischievous smile tugged at Polly's lips. 'Do what?'

Nora rolled her eyes. 'Okay,' she said, assessing the sailor's shirt hanging off Polly's bony shoulders and the too-long trousers. 'Not exactly the brilliant idea I thought it was.'

Polly stretched her arms. 'It is tolerable.'

'That's the problem,' Nora said. She folded her arms, circling Polly to inspect the outfit from all angles. 'We're going for the *wow* factor. The thirst trap.'

'Would *that*,' she said, motioning to what Nora had on, 'be considered a thirst trap?'

'They're just my work clothes.' Nora shrugged, fingers grazing the hem of her dress. 'Nothing special.'

Polly looked at the sleek black fabric Nora donned, tight at her waist and slightly flared at her hips. It was simple, elegant… *perfect*.

'Do you think, perhaps…' Polly trailed off. A small, sheepish smile. 'She might like your outfit better?'

Nora glared at her. 'You're *not* doing your weird ghost thing with me.'

An hour later, standing on the deck in Nora's clothes, Polly stared out across the ocean with longing in her heart and all the slang Nora taught her running in a loop inside her dead, leaking brain. She tapped the bones of her fingers against the railing, hearing the satisfying *clink* on metal.

'Stop it,' Nora said, looking down at the ghost's hands.

'I am not doing anything.'

'You're making *me* anxious. Just chill, okay?' Nora offered a small smile. The wind caught the loose fabric of her dusty pirate shirt sleeves, making them flap in the wind. 'She's gonna love you. And if she doesn't, then at least you've learned some slang and have a cool new outfit. Right?'

Polly didn't want to consider that possibility – that maybe the girl she'd been lusting over for decades, *centuries*, might not like her in the same way. 'Yeah,' she said, her voice hollow.

Just as the word left her mouth, the clouds parted and the moonlight fell on the wave crests. They shone in the dark, stretching into the blackness that dripped from the sky into the water, the horizon indistinguishable. And there, in the distance, was *her*.

The siren.

Bones jutted from where her ribs should be, sticking through her gorgeous green-tinged skin. Gills lashed against the sides of her face, hair a beautiful, wiry mess.

She was the most stunning creature Polly had ever laid eyes on.

'Is that her?' Nora asked, squinting into the darkness.

'Yes,' Polly breathed. 'The love of my life.'

The siren looked just as she did all those years ago, singing to the sailors on Polly's ship as they passed, luring them out into the moonlight and watching with glee as they tumbled into the water below. Her feasts dyed the sea red. She was beautiful. Powerful. *Unstoppable*.

'She's a–'

'Siren,' Polly filled in, right as Nora uttered the word *'monster'* with such contempt it made Polly shiver.

'Excuse me?' Polly whipped around to face Nora properly, hands balling into fists. 'You don't know anything. She's a *hero*. She saved me from countless men when I lived aboard this ship.'

'You mean she murdered them.'

'They deserved it. You have no idea what they did to me. If it were not for her...' Polly broke off. Tears welled in the inky black pits where her eyes used to be. 'I love her. And I'm going to spend the rest of my life with her. No matter what.'

Nora inched back. 'I really don't like this, Polly.'

'Then leave. I got what I needed from you.'

'I thought we were–'

'We were what?'

'Friends!' Nora exploded. The second the word escaped her, she clapped a hand over her mouth.

Nora's expression changed from horrified, to sad, to angry. Her eyebrows tugged together and she crossed her arms over her chest. She was shivering. 'I think you should be the one to leave. You don't need the ship anymore. You have her.'

'Fine.' Something clenched in Polly's cavernous, rotting chest. Was it... regret? She shoved the feeling aside and stepped to the ship's railing, looking over the edge.

The siren looked up at her with her six dreamy eyes, webbed fingers clinging onto the rocky surface she was perched on. She opened her mouth, exposing all her razor-sharp teeth. Polly thought she was smiling at her, but her mouth made the shape of words unheard over the deafening music. No one would fall prey to her tonight.

She was all Polly's. Like she'd always dreamt about.

Polly felt something clench painfully in the pit of her rotten stomach. Her hands balled into fists, bone scraping against bone. She took in a deep breath she didn't need and tried to expel her nerves. She'd learnt modern slang, she was wearing a fierce outfit... She could do this. She didn't need Nora anymore.

She looked over her shoulder at the girl standing behind her in the pirate costume, sucked in a deep breath, then hurled herself off the ship's railing.

Polly didn't feel the impact of the water. Couldn't feel the freezing waves batter into her. But that didn't matter. All that mattered was the siren. As Polly climbed the rocks, she gave the siren her best smile.

'Hellllooo,' the siren cooed, a single forked tongue lashing out of her mouth. Dark, crusted blood was smeared from one of her cheeks right down to her gilled neck. She had recently dined.

'Hi,' Polly said. Fear suddenly clenched at her throat, making it hard to push the words out. All she had to do was remember what Nora said. She moved closer to the siren. 'Um… How is it… hanging?'

The siren cocked her head at Polly. 'What a curious being you are.'

Nervous laughter bubbled up inside Polly. 'I meant, how are you? Do you… remember me?'

'Of course I do.'

Relief washed through Polly, warm and sweet. 'Well, good. I have been thinking about you for centuries. You are the love of my life, and I want to spend every second with you. I never want to be apart again.'

'Sooo,' the siren said, tilting her head. 'What's your favourite colour?'

'Huh?'

'If we are to spend the rest of eternity together, I want to know everything about you.' The siren offered Polly a too-stretched smile. 'Your favourite food. Your hobbies. What you dream of when you sleep.'

Polly swallowed. 'Do you mind if we skip the small talk?'

The siren grabbed hold of Polly's boney arm, pointed nails digging into what was left of her flesh. *'Tell me.'*

The ghost glanced over her shoulder, clocking the *Polly Woodside* farther away than she remembered. Were they… leaving her? Abandoning her here? Suddenly her palms felt all sweaty, which shouldn't have been possible. The breaths she didn't need to take came fast and hard.

The *Polly Woodside* cut through the waves, the black enveloping it until it was once more one with the darkness. A cloud passed in front of the moon and the dreamy glow on the waves was gone.

All Polly could hear was the crashing of the sea. The siren's wheezing breaths. The hammering of her own decaying heart.

It wasn't too late if she left now. She could cut through the water like she did before and catch up to the ship.

'Well,' Polly told the siren. 'This has been lovely. But I should go–'

'I don't think so.' The siren's other arm snaked around Polly's torso, squeezing tightly. Polly's brittle ribs bent under the monster's force. 'You said we would spend eternity together.'

Polly struggled to break free, but she couldn't. She pushed at the siren's webbed hands, trying to get some purchase on the rock, but her feet kept slipping on the slimy surface.

'Tell me,' the siren repeated, her voice sinking right into Polly's ear. 'How has your day been?'

Polly screamed.

DEEP IN THE MIST

ELLE BEAUMONT

THE FIRST TIME ISLA WITNESSED A SACRIFICE SHE WAS EIGHT YEARS OLD. A girl of sixteen had walked down the trodden path of the seaside village, with no music, no flowers strewn through twine decorating her path. Just an oppressive weight that threatened to pull Isla down into the fertile soil. For this was a funeral, not a celebration.

Today, the process began again. Today, a sacrifice would be chosen and prepared for their eventual death.

The large village of Tir a' Cheo gathered on the ground above the cliffside, forming a circle. Each family remained huddled together, gripping onto their younger children. Isla couldn't blame them. She was a young woman now and free from the ritual of sacrifice, but her sister Aileen wasn't.

A burly man stepped into the middle of the circle. Red braids dangled down his shoulders and two more from his beard. Chieftain Ross.

'It is with a heavy heart, that we must choose the next life for the mist."

Isla grabbed her sister's hand and squeezed it. Aileen was destined for so much more than the bloody village of Tir a Cheo', there was no way it would be her. But then hadn't every family thought the same about their children, too?

Each family came together in the spring, and again in the fall, casting their decision on which child they'd give up. Their lives depended on strands of sea grass. Whosoever chose the shortest one would be sacrificed. The fate of a boy or girl depended on such a trivial act amid a monumental decision. It wasn't lost on Isla how this process took place during the most important farming times of the year.

Some families tried to justify the choice, for the child in question was too lazy, too simple-minded, or some other half-witted notion. But largely, it was done with a purpose – who had children to spare? Who had given up a child not that long ago? It was sickening, but it was their way of life and it cast a somber mood heavier than the mist over the village.

It was no wonder so many villagers of Isla's age ran far away from this place before they could have children of their own. Aileen turned her head and looked at Isla, offering a tense smile.

Behind Isla stood a comforting presence. She didn't have to turn her head to know Bram, her heart's love, was there.

The villagers were silent and their eyes were trained on the chieftain. He stroked his chin, bit his bottom lip, and shifted on his feet. The chieftain hated this as much as everyone else. He bent down to pick up a bundle of sea grass from a basket and held it out. 'Families, step forward.'

Each mother or father stepped forward, selected a strand, and eyed it worriedly. Isla frowned as her father shakily drew the last one.

'Fates, who have you chosen?' Chieftain Ross raised his voice, looking to the sky.

At once, those who held the grass came together in a circle, comparing the length. It was Isla's father who sobbed in realization. Instantly, she wanted to vomit.

'Fate has decided. Aileen of the Ervin family, I am sorry, my child.'

Isla's body grew cold. She hadn't heard correctly, had she? But as her mother cried out, fell to her knees, and clutched the ground, she knew. Everyone's eyes were on them, full of sadness, pity, and heartbreak.

Aileen turned to her, burying her face into her shoulder. All Isla could do was hold her sister tight, and bite down hard on her tongue to keep from crying and succumbing to the mounting despair.

This was the way of life in the village of Tir a' Cheo, where the young lives always hung in the balance of life and death.

The mist didn't care whether it was a boy or a girl, but it did prefer a young life. Those between the ages of twelve and seventeen. Why? No one knew. Perhaps it was that they were still innocent – if the mist didn't receive a child, it'd spit the sacrifice back out, and the crops would wither for the season. So many would perish from starvation.

Bram's hand rubbed against Isla's back, bringing her to the present. She squeezed Aileen so tightly she thought she'd crack a rib. 'I will find a way, *mo chridhe*, there is another way. There must be.'

No matter what it cost her, Isla would find a way to ensure her sister was safe.

Isla's hair ruffled in the wind, sending auburn curls into her eyes. She pulled her knees into her chest, wishing she could will herself into the lavender fabric of her kirtle. The roaring of the waves crashing onto the shore was enough to deafen her, yet somehow the gulls crying above managed to be heard.

In a fortnight, the next offering would be gifted to the mist. Her little sister, Aileen.

Why couldn't it have been her instead? Isla, in her mind, had misused her twenty-one years. She hadn't lived as freely as Aileen, hadn't been so kind to her parents, and always tested their patience. So, why Aileen? Why had fate chosen someone so pure? Was that the reasoning? A pristine life to counterbalance the wickedness lingering in the mist?

Isla brought her fists to her eyes and forced back the sob lodged in her throat.

A calm presence settled beside her on the knoll and when she dropped her hands, she beheld Bram McTavish. His unruly dark hair hung over his light green eyes and if that hadn't been enough to set Isla's heart aflutter, then the dusting of hair on his cheeks and his full, cherry lips certainly was.

'A rainstorm is coming,' he said, knocking his knee into hers. 'It bodes well for us if the month is rained out.'

What he said was true. The rain, for whatever reason, kept the mist at bay. But it didn't bode well for the village if their crops were drowned in the early months.

Isla tilted her face toward the fading sun's warmth. Nightfall would be upon them soon. 'And then what?' she whispered and turned to face Bram. His eyes softened as he closed the distance between them, resting his forehead against hers.

'Mo leannan,' he breathed against Isla's lips, then tenderly captured them.

Bram tasted of the sea, of honey and promises. Isla had loved him ever since she lobbed a stone at his head for teasing her cousin for his bright orange hair and freckles.

Isla pressed her hand against his chest, forcing him backward until he laid on the grass. She crawled on top of him, smiling as he fought to lean forward. It didn't take much for him to upend her. Isla fell to the side, laughing even as Bram's lips trailed kisses along her neck. If only light-hearted moments like this lasted.

His hand squeezed her hip, and the familiar flutter of desire flapped its wings within her chest. 'Stay with me here,' Isla whispered.

Raindrops plopped against her temple, cooler than the warm spring air, but she wanted this moment with Bram, needed it.

'I have no desire to leave.' Bram lifted his hand, brushed curls away from her eyes and stared down at her. 'I will stay with you for as long as you'd like.' His nose dragged along the hollow of her throat, teasing, promising.

And selfishly, Isla wanted him to take away her pain, the building sorrow, all of it. She couldn't get the day out of her head, her sister being chosen, her mother sobbing on the ground. She needed an escape - in the rain, on the grassy knoll, with feverish, desperate kisses.

The fragrance of supper wafted from Isla's stone home built into the side of the hill. It was larger than most, considering her father had several head of steer and sheep. A luxury most didn't possess.

Isla did her best to sneak into the hut, but Aileen spotted her. She lifted a finger to her lips, silencing her little sister before spiriting away into their shared bedroom. It was of modest means, two simple beds and a chamber pot, but it was enough for them.

Quickly, she peeled off her soaking kirtle and grabbed another chemise. Her skin was still sensitive from lovemaking. Isla pulled the chemise down over her head, then drew a burgundy kirtle over her head as well.

'Why don't you marry?' Aileen asked softly from the doorway. 'He loves you.'

Isla knew that, and she loved him with everything too. Bram had asked her to marry him once when Isla was eighteen, but she'd feared them being ripped apart, one of them becoming another victim of the mist. He'd never asked again, and she was frightened she'd missed her chance.

'Nothing in life is so simple.' Isla pulled Aileen in for an embrace. 'I love him too. I think he knows that.' She stroked her sister's back, then gave her long, chestnut braid a gentle tug.

Maybe one day Bram would ask her again. But to even consider a life of happiness when her sister was facing certain death... Isla couldn't allow herself even a sliver of joy.

'You deserve your own life, Isla, you deserve one another.' Within Aileen's warm brown eyes, Isla saw so much wisdom, so much life left to live.

None of this was fair.

'Girls!' their mother called. 'We'll be suppin' without your father. He's taking advantage of the rain and burning the kelp.' Kelp extracted from the sea was what they used for their gardens, it was why their soil was so rich and healthy.

As if the mist had heard, howls filled the air, scraping at Isla's ears and nerves. Then a bellowing echoed across the hillside, down to her marrow.

Her mother stilled, gripping onto the skirt of her kirtle. 'Gods save us all.'

Isla's eyes darted around their home, then focused on the wooden door. Instead of howling, groans filled the air, hardly muted by the downpour of rain. They were safe for now, with the rain falling. The mist never came for them during the rain. Still, fear filled her to the brim. She reached for Aileen and held her close to her breast, as if the mist would snake its way into their home and steal her away.

'It'll stay at bay. Fret not, now let's eat.' Her mother milled around their home, placing steaming bowls of lamb stew down.

Reluctantly, Isla released her sister and moved to her chair. But it wasn't just she who stared down at her food, unwilling to touch it. Isla could feel the weight of the situation pressing on her chest, wrapping itself like a noose around her neck.

In only a fortnight Aileen would be gone.

In the morning, the rain still pelted the land. A familiar melody pinging off her father's tools didn't inspire Isla to roll out of her bed. As if the village's mood hadn't been solemn enough, Aileen being chosen had plunged Isla into a dour mood.

'Isla!' her mother called. 'Bram is here to call on you.' She huffed. 'Don't leave him standing in the rain!'

Isla sat up and looked around for Aileen, but she wasn't in her bed. She'd likely gone to the stable to tend to the cows. Aileen had been off ever since the gathering. She'd even gone so far as to say she wanted no pity, for no one to hover over her. Isla respected her sister's wishes, but god's wounds, she wanted to hold onto Aileen while she still had her.

'Isla!' her mother bellowed. 'Don't leave him outside!'

This time, Isla bolted from her bed, combed her fingers through her hair and whipped on her kirtle. She darted into the kitchen, looking again for Aileen, but she wasn't there. A knot formed in her stomach, even more so as she noted her mother's red-rimmed eyes.

Bram entered a moment later. He was tall enough so that he had to bend forward so his head didn't hit the ceiling.

Rivulets of rain trickled down his hair, onto the dirt floor. His full lips tilted into a grin that could inspire the oldest of hearts to race. 'I brought my mother's latest dyes for you.' He lifted the covered woven basket,, almost seeming bashful in the presence of Isla's mother. 'I thought you'd like to go riding.' Bram handed the basket to Isla, laughter dancing in his eyes before he glanced at her mother.

Her mother's lips pressed into a thin line. 'I don't think—'

She dropped the dyes to the floor. 'Yes, I would.' Isla darted out of her home. Soft whisperings of rain trickled down her face, dampening her hair immediately, but she didn't care. She wanted this for herself, even if it was selfish to set aside her worries for her sister's fate.

Bram followed behind her, his heavy footfall sloshing in the muck. Outside, he hoisted Isla onto his mare's back, then himself.

Isla gasped as his heated lips ran a trail of kisses down her neck, promising her so much more.

'Why are you not with your father?' She knew that Robert McTavish would be burning the kelp in the pits with the rest of the men. 'Shirking your duties.' Isla clucked her tongue, but as Bram reached around for the reins, his hand squeezed her thigh.

'I had other plans.' He nipped her neck. 'Like spending time with you, in the rain...'

The chestnut mare galloped through the once green hillside. In the rain, the earth churned up, creating a mud pit. It was the wet season and happened every year.

Isla glanced down the hillside, toward the crashing waves of the sea. Heavy smoke filled the air as the men of the Tir a' Cheo burned piles of kelp, creating the ash that kept their soil rich. The sea provided the village with an endless supply of it. If not for the cursed mist, the land would be a fertile paradise. Isla coughed as the wind brought thick, dark clouds closer to them. Movement caught her attention near the shore. Perhaps it was her imagination, but a dark, looming figure hurled *something*. Mist shifted along the rocks, shrouding whatever *it* was.

An ear-splitting wail carried over the tumultuous sea and the whipping windows. Bram stiffened behind her, and Isla knew she hadn't been imagining it. 'Do you see that?' she rasped, clutching onto the mare's mane.

'Bloody hell, what is that?' Bram leaned forward, his arm curling around her even tighter.

Another animalistic scream rolled around the hillside, setting Isla's nerves aflame.

Her teeth chattered as she clutched onto Bram's arm. 'We should go. We should warn the others.'

'It's raining,' Bram said.

Isla knew the mist wouldn't come for them while it was raining, but the rain couldn't last forever, and the mist was only going to get more and more agitated.

'The rain will stop at some point. It always does.' And her little sister would be forced to die. Isla wiped a tear from her cheek. 'Why is this the way? Why must we sacrifice so many?'

'I don't know.' Bram was quiet for a time before continuing. 'They say it's to keep us safe. To keep the peace with the mist.'

'Do you believe that?' Isla whispered, her voice nearly lost with the wind.

Bram shook his head. 'I don't know anymore. How safe are we if we have to continue giving up our own? For what reason?'

To appease the mist, to stop the pestilence…

But why?

Not knowing the root of it always bothered Isla. Ever since she'd first seen that girl led into the mist, heard her screams… there had to be a substantial reason. Bram couldn't understand what it was like to lose a sibling, but at least he was empathetic. If it meant making Isla happy, he'd do anything she asked. Yet, that wasn't what she wanted. Isla could've asked Bram to help her escape the village with Aileen, and leave the tainted land behind. But this village was her home, the only one she'd ever known. She wouldn't leave her parents behind. She had to stay and change the village within.

Isla needed to stop the mist. But how? She was not a fabled hero of old, with magic and spells to cast. She was no use with a weapon. Isla wasn't a revolutionary, for many had talked about stopping the mist before, and yet, they'd never come up with a way to do it. How could they stop *mist* from forming, after all? If Aileen hadn't been chosen, Isla wondered if she'd even consider trying to stop the sacrifice from happening.

The odds were stacked against her, but she truly wanted the deaths to end once and for all. But her motivation was for Aileen to be saved. For there to be peace. Something had to be done.

Isla jerked back, cementing herself against Bram as a flock of sheep ran toward them. They bleated in passing, assuring her that they were indeed sheep, and not some beastie bent on slaughtering them. Still, her heart pounded wildly.

Another shrill shriek jarred Isla's nerves further as a rock landed on top of the hill, not far from them. Bram tugged back on his mare's reins, and she dutifully edged backward. How could the rock reach where they were? The creature must've been sheer muscle.

And then she saw it, emerging from the waves.

Try as Isla may, she couldn't fully make out the figure, but it was larger than the tallest man in the village. Something must have spooked it, for it lurched back into the sea, and at the same moment the sky fully opened and drenched Isla instantly.

Rivulets poured down onto her back as the rain cascaded down Bram's hair and body. 'We should head back. It's getting bad.'

'No.' Isla pulled her eyes from the fading figure, then looked over her shoulder. 'We came out here for a reason.' And if anyone could chase the chill from her bones, it was Bram and his full, delicious lips branding her body. She didn't want to think of the monster in the sea, or the mist, or her sister's impending death. She wanted to forget it all.

'As you wish,' he murmured, spurring his mare on toward the woodline. Bram dismounted and helped Isla down, his hands lingering on the curve of her hips. Heat simmered in his green eyes, igniting her blood. There was a sense of hesitation coming from him, however, and Isla couldn't blame him after they'd witnessed the creature hurling rocks at Tir a' Cheo.

He was as scared as she was. Yet, all she wanted was to blot out the fear, erase it from her mind.

Bram's fingers brushed against Isla's cheeks, then slid into her sopping wet curls as he walked her backward, into the bite of a tree's bark. 'Come back to me,' he murmured, then pressed a warm kiss against her lips. There was his taste of sea air and honey. A taste Isla could never get enough of. When he dropped his hands, it was to gather hers in his and he pinned them against the tree. His fingers squeezed her hands gently, rooting her to the moment, to him.

And Isla let him take her away, to a place of bliss.

In the evening, the rain stopped, and with it, the melody of droplets pelting her father's tools. Golden rays peeked through the cracks of the hut, brighter than the hearth and tallow candles.

Isla ventured to the door, opening it to let the warm sun bathe her. Despite the heavenly appearance of the hillside, tension as tight as a bow string filled her home.

'We are still safe,' Isla said, glancing down at her sister who joined her. 'There are far too many puddles. We still have time.' Who was she reassuring? Herself, or her sister?

Aileen nodded.

Isla wasn't certain which was worse. Losing her sister to the beast of the sea, or potentially losing an entire year's worth of crops. The latter, of course, meant possibly starving over the harsh, long winter, but the former... She loosed a shaky breath and wrapped her arm around Aileen's shoulder. A life without her sister seemed a worse fate.

The sun hadn't peeked through the clouds in a week. Relief flooded through Isla, like the rains in the fields, drowning the young seedlings.

She sat on a stool situated beside one of her favorite cows, Tessie, and milked her. Isla gave in to the ritual of Tessie lowing softly and the spray of milk in the bucket.

'Isla!' Aileen's voice cut through the rhythmic sound. 'Isla, I've just been to see Adair Stewart, and he says the weather will be turning for the better.' Her words were rushed, breathless, and her usually pale cheeks were red.

Isla's fingers stilled on the cow's teats. Adair fancied himself a weather diviner, and while he was accurate quite often, he wasn't *always* right. 'He cannot know that for certain,' she replied curtly, returning to milking.

'You know he does! He is seldom wrong.'

Aileen shifted behind her, then her feet proceeded to fall heavily on the dirt. Isla didn't have to turn around to know she was pacing – she knew her sister like the back of her hand. 'We've run out of time, Isla.'

Run out of time.

'No,' Isla choked on the word. 'I'll find another way.' She stood and grabbed a hold of her sister's arm. 'I will find another way,' she said more firmly, then tugged Aileen against her. This was how complacency bred, wasn't it? Isla could wish herself away from the coast, but when it came down to it, moving away was a terrifying thought. And the reality that her sister was still of an age to be selected for a sacrifice kept her rooted in Tir a' Cheo.

That night, Aileen huddled close to her, and Isla buried her nose into her sister's hair, committing her soft jasmine fragrance to memory. For as long as she could remember, none had tried to deny the mist a sacrifice. The thought alone was foolish, since it could bring pestilence upon the land, ensuring they'd all die... but still, there had to be a way.

Unable to sleep, Isla peeled herself from Aileen's snoring figure and crept into the common room. To her surprise, her mother sat at the table with a lit candle and a cup of tea. Her shoulders were hunched forward and her eyes puffy and red. She'd been crying.

'Oh, Isla, I didn't mean to wake you.' She shook her head and sipped the tea.

Isla laughed mirthlessly. 'I won't be sleeping any time soon.'

Her mother's tired eyes flicked over to her. 'I know.'

Questions itched at the roof of her mouth. She had to know more about the ritual, and why the villagers were so complacent. 'Why do we do it? Why does Tir a' Cheo have to pay with a young life?'

Time passed, enough that Isla thought her mother would ignore her altogether, but then, she sighed. 'You know it is to keep peace and our land prosperous.' She paused, tapping her finger against her cup. 'This thing that plagues us, the *Nuckelavee*,' she whispered the name, glancing to the side before continuing, 'It's a creature of the sea. No one remembers why or where it came from, but when my grandmother was a child, the village started the sacrifices then. Or rather, were forced to.' Her mother grew quiet and fussed with her skirt. 'Crops and livestock were dead, the only thing left to harvest was kelp and then fish. Until even that had run its course. So many died that winter from starvation and illness.'

The heavy braid on her shoulder slipped forward as she set the cup down. 'One evening, the beast came into the village and took a young boy, and the crops returned to health. And the livestock that were ailing were miraculously well again.'

'What?' Isla had never heard this story before. Until now, it was only *the mist* and what it demanded from them twice a year. 'What exactly is the Nuckelavee?'

Her mother narrowed her eyes. 'Shh, child. Don't say the name too loud, or it'll hear you. We don't speak its name—we don't talk about it.' She rubbed her temples. 'A demon, a creature... No one knows for sure. But what we do know is that if we sacrifice one of our own, relative peace settles on the land. No pestilence, no mass starving.'

Of course, there had been stories passed around the villagers, meant to scare children into behaving, with the harsh reality that one day maybe they'd be a sacrifice. That a creature beyond the mist would come in the middle of the night and take them. But the notion there truly was a demon or some kind of *beast* horrified Isla. 'Has anyone tried to stop the n...creature, or at least communicate with it?

'To what end?'

'To live, Mama, to live.'

'And what do you think we are doing, my girl? We are already doing all we can. Some villagers leave and never turn back, but this has been our home for hundreds of years.'

Isla's heart sank to the pit of her stomach. *A home of death, where children pay the price for pride.* 'I don't understand. The villagers would rather stay in a cursed land than seek freedom from it?'

Her mother stared at her, long and hard, with an expression that bore every speck of exhaustion, worry, and dread. 'I once had a sister, you know. You are her spitting image.'

Isla's heart leaped wildly. This was another story she'd never heard before. Even her grandmother, when she was alive, had never mentioned this.

'She was chosen by the village and I thought myself clever enough to find a way to stop it. We were going to run away, flee the village once and for all.' Her mother pressed her lips together as fresh tears spilled onto her cheeks. 'She'd told her lover what we were going to do, and he must have told someone else. For on the eve of our leaving, the villagers swarmed our home, pulled Catrin from her bed, and tied her to a post. They made an example out of her.'

Horror ignited every nerve in Isla's body. She gasped and covered her mouth. 'Why have you never told me?'

'Because it doesn't matter. None of it does, Isla. We can try all we like, but we are as tied to this village as it is to us. So, whatever you are planning, I suggest you forget it. This is the way it is and shall be. We've all accepted it, it's time that you did as well.'

Adair had been right. *May the gods curse him to lose his long blond hair.* The rain had stopped and warmth touched the land, drying up the puddles. A knot formed in Isla's stomach, because she knew it meant their time was up. The Nuckelavee could now cross the land and demand its sacrifice.

A somber mood fell over the village. Hamish wouldn't sing, the Wallace girls wouldn't dance, and Isla's mother wouldn't speak, not as she embroidered the neckline of Aileen's white sacrificial gown and not as she crafted a crown of heather for her.

It was just as well, for Isla didn't know what to say, or how to ease her parents' breaking hearts when her own had shattered into oblivion.

Still, hope filled Isla that perhaps it wouldn't be *today*. She hovered around Aileen outside, refusing Bram's requests for a ride, ignoring the helpless look in his eyes.

'*Mo chridhe,* you know what I said when you were born, and I held you for the first time?' Isla said to her sister, forcing a lightness into her voice that she didn't feel, and smiled, despite wanting to sob.

'What?' Aileen asked.

'I'd always protect you. I vowed it like I was a knight sworn into your service.' Isla laughed, immediately regretting it, for tears pricked her eyes. 'And maybe I am, for you're the fairest maiden on the isle.' She reached down and plucked a white flower from the tall grass and stuck it in Aileen's hair.

'Isla?' Aileen's soft smile faded and her brow furrowed. 'Will you do me a favor?'

'Anything.'

She turned her eyes to Isla's, unshed tears glimmering in them. 'Marry Bram, run away from Tir a' Cheo, and have his children like you've wanted to for years now. Live a life I won't be able to. Please.'

Each word was an arrow to Isla's heart. It was a simple ask, but one that held weight. Isla wrapped her arms around Aileen's small frame. 'Gods, why choose you out of everyone else?' she whispered.

Aileen's body shook as she wept into Isla's shoulder.

When both had cried until they couldn't anymore, they sat together on the grassy knoll overlooking the sea. Gulls laughed above, heckling the land dwellers as if mocking their dismay.

A horn blew in the distance. Isla knew the bellowing well, had heard it since she could remember. Dread filled her.

'No,' she blurted, grabbing Aileen's hand. 'It cannot have you. I won't let it.' Isla's eyes flicked toward the woodline. Beyond it, a pathway led to the shoreline. Only the fishermen dared to use it.

'Aileen, it's time.' It was their father who spoke. No doubt their mother couldn't bring herself to fetch them. He turned his bloodshot eyes to Isla, silently pleading with her to release her sister.

She did, for his sake, then followed them back to the hut.

Aileen was whisked away to their room to dress for the ritual. All the while, numbness crept into Isla.

When her sister emerged, she was clothed in white, her chestnut hair loose and the heather crown nestled on top of her head. If it weren't for the tears welling in her mother's eyes, or the sob twisting her father's features, one may think Aileen was dressed for a wedding, but this was not a ceremony of marriage unless death was to be her groom.

The horn bellowed again, this time a warning to hurry.

One by one, they followed Aileen out of the hut.

The numbness kept Isla from crying or speaking. But as the entire village marched toward the mist which snaked out of the woods and licked at the grass, a burst of life erupted within Isla. The beast wouldn't take her sister.

While the rest of the villagers lined the way, creating an aisle for Aileen to walk down, Isla pulled away from her family.

Bram's hand caught hers and tugged. 'Don't, Isla–' The rest of his words were cut short as she yanked her hand away. She shot him a pained glance, then turned toward the approaching mist.

A guttural rumble, almost like a purr, came from beyond the curtain of fog. *No, no, no. Not Aileen.* Clicking, like bone hitting bone, echoed off the trees. Without another thought, Isla bolted forward and shoved Aileen out of the way.

Isla smiled in relief, but it was short-lived as a grotesque hand reached out and dragged her into the mist.

Somewhere, someone was screaming and as Isla sucked in a breath, she realized it was her. *Oh gods, please, if you're listening, help me.* She couldn't bring herself to make another sound as she peered down at the appendage holding her.

Red muscle, covered in white tendons held onto her so tightly she could scarcely breathe. Beneath the surface of it, blue blood flowed like a river.

Click, click, click.

That noise again…

The Nuckelavee.

Isla dared to look up at the creature and regretted it instantly. No story did this being justice, for it had no flesh and, as far as she could see, no bone, save for its human-like teeth. Its arms were far too long and, had she not been held by one of its hands, its knuckles would have grazed the ground. But that wasn't the most alarming part, no. Isla swallowed a scream when she saw that the creature had the torso and head of a man rising from the back of a horse-like body. The human skull had a pair of yellow eyes, but the creature's equine head possessed only one giant eye.

Isla vomited.

The Nuckelavee loosened its grip as if repulsed and it was all the room Isla needed to wriggle out of its grip.

She hit the ground with a thud and scurried away, but she didn't get very far. Something collided with the back of her shoulder, shoving her forward.

Pain shot through her.

The heavy sound of horses' hooves falling approached. Isla chanced looking over her aching shoulder. The Nuckelavee was looming over her. One hand outstretched, it was pinning her in place. As it withdrew, blood dripped from its claws. Her blood.

It regarded her in silence, as if unsure of what to do with her.

Didn't it just kill all the ones before me? Instantly? She recalled the sound of bones snapping, the shrill screams…

She spat at the ground. 'If you're going to kill me, just get it over with already.'

The Nuckelavee shook its head and reached down, grabbing Isla once again. This time, she didn't have the energy to fight, and if it meant her sister would live, so be it.

The beast carried her through the woods, down the path and toward the shore, but rather than dragging her to the depths, it ventured into a deep cave.

So deep that the rocky formation ceased glimmering in the faint light.

The Nuckelavee tossed her onto the sandy floor. She patted the air in front of her and found the rigid stone of the cave. She then searched the ground and her hand met what she supposed was bone. Isla swallowed another scream.

The beast means to savor my death.

The creature hissed, shoving Isla roughly.

'What? What do you want from us?' she shrieked. 'I can't bloody see you and I certainly can't understand you!'

A heavy sigh was her reply, then a moment later, several hundred small green gems lit up like embers. Brighter than all of the candles lit in her home.

Isla's relief lasted seconds, because as she glanced down at the sand, she realized she was surrounded by piles of bones. Human remains.

She screeched and scooted backward, tearing her skirt in the process.

The Nuckelavee didn't advance on her, but it watched in rapt fascination.

With both parts of the creature staring at her, Isla would've welcomed the pitch black of the cave.

As the time passed, there was no way to determine when it was day or night. Isla forced herself to sleep, although it was difficult with the watchful creature in the corner of the cave.

She'd discovered the creature slept too. Its breathing would grow heavy and slow.

Her mouth was parched from a lack of water and her stomach ached from hunger. Three...four days in the cave? Mayhaps, this was how she'd die. Slow and drawn out. If she could fall asleep and peacefully pass away–

A wail resonated off the cave walls, forcing Isla to cover her ears. She stumbled to her feet and edged closer to where the Nuckelavee's cries originated.

Isla's hands remained against the cave wall, using it to guide her toward the entrance. She nearly fell to her knees from the exertion.

The beast lobbed a rock as large as her head at the cliff where the village resided. *But why? The Nuckelavee already has what it wanted.* Smoke billowed upward. Isla knew what it meant. They were burning kelp for the crops.

The beast charged toward the cliffside, hammering its fists into the earth until blue blood poured down its arms. It reminded her of the day she and Bram rode to the hilltop, watching the creature toss rocks from afar.

Her boot caught on a rock and the demon homed in on her. Two yellow eyes on the human-like face, and the one on the equine. It galloped over to her, baring its teeth in a snarl, but Isla had no energy to run. She collapsed to her knees, then onto her face, and knew no more.

When she came to, the beast was trying to right her. Isla's head lolled back, forcing her to look at the hellish creature. 'Water…food…' she rasped.

It glanced around, then motioned toward the sea with a garish hand. She supposed it meant sea water.

'If I drink the sea water then I'll surely die.' And mayhap it was for the best at this point. She didn't want to suffer.

She caught herself as the beast retreated out of the cave. It returned moments later with an oyster. Isla looked askance from the shellfish to the creature. Crushing the shell with ease, it offered the innards to her.

There were times she'd eaten oysters with Bram, but they'd never tasted as good as this one did now. Salty and sweet. Still, she knew her thirst would only increase the more brine she consumed.

'They are good, but I need fresh water too.'

Her captor gnashed its teeth together.

For a moment, they stared at one another in silence, then the single yellow eye rolled to the side as the equine wheezed. The human-like portion lifted its hands and grasped onto Isla's shoulders.

A scream bubbled up, but she lacked the energy to voice it, and it came out more of a sob. *Just kill me already.* But it didn't. Instead, images that didn't belong to her flickered into her mind. The dark gray sky opening, raining down, and it burned like embers on her skin. She stepped into a puddle and was certain flames were licking at her feet. Smoke billowed into the air, black and heavy, smelling of death. Heat erupted within her chest, threatening to yank her down to the sand. It wasn't just pain; it was agonizing pinpricks all over her flesh. Fury that wasn't her own threatened to black her vision out.

Kelp burning. Villagers overfishing, waste being tossed into the sea. Each new image brought a new wave of anger and understanding.

The kelp burning. Isla's eyes widened. Every instance she'd heard the Nuckelavee wail, it was during the burning.

'It hurts you, doesn't it?'

The creature growled and nodded. As it withdrew a hand, one of its claws scraped along her chin. More images coasted through her mind, of all the lives the Nuckelavee took for punishment. Punishment for destroying the sea, for tainting it, for taking too much from it.

Lidless eyes narrowed on Isla. She understood, but why show her any of this? She thought of the girl she'd seen sacrificed and all those before and after her. The crunching snap of bones as the victims walked through the mist…

'What do you want from *me?* Why keep me alive and no one else?'

A wet sigh escaped the Nuckelavee, then its human torso bent as it prodded her chest, where her heart was. 'Change,' it croaked. The word was nearly lost on her, sounding more like a growl. When she said nothing, it bent to scoop up a bone, which looked human. The Nuckelavee grit its teeth together, then crushed the bone until it was no more than dust scattered on the breeze.

Isla jolted backward. Change? What did it mean by that? She wanted to ask for an explanation, but it was evident even simple words were difficult for the beast. 'Change,' she at last echoed. Could the creature mean it wanted her to change her village's entire way of living? How would she convince them to cease burning the kelp? Tossing their refuse into the sea? 'If you're going to kill me then just do it. I cannot change the minds of an entire village.'

'Heart,' the beast groaned and it sounded much like rocks tumbling against one another, grating on every one of Isla's singed nerves.

Too exhausted to even speak anymore, she lowered her head. The oyster sat heavily in her stomach, and Isla wished she hadn't taken the offering. Water, that's what she needed so desperately.

She yelped as she was picked up. The Nuckelavee's hands squeezed her as it trotted out of the cave. Light seared her eyes as it washed over her face, kissed her skin with a heat she hadn't experienced in what felt like eons.

The beast halted at the path to the woods, set her down, and proceeded to dig furiously at the ground. It hissed, lurching backward as it stopped, shook its hands as if they'd been burned, then motioned to her.

When she didn't move, the Nuckelavee pushed Isla forward with enough force that her knees buckled. She braced herself with her hands, and as she looked down to the hole, she realized there was water. *Fresh water.*

She cupped her hands and greedily dipped them in, then raised the pool of water to her chapped lips. Sweet, heavenly water. Isla drank until her stomach sloshed.

'Thank you,' she murmured.

The demon only nodded in response.

Isla squinted. Beyond the Nuckelavee, on the cliffside, she could make out a figure. She wondered if they saw her; saw the beast too.

Bram, is that you?

Aileen?

It didn't matter. She was the prisoner of the Nuckelavee and he'd no doubt kill her soon.

Isla lost all sense of time once she was in the depths of the cave again. The only company she had was the Nuckelavee and its winking lights. Most days she wasn't allowed out of the cave unless it was to drink water, since it couldn't fetch it for her.

Why keep me alive? Why insist I can change anything?

The Nuckelavee shrieked at the entrance, pulling Isla from her morose musings. She rolled onto her side and forced herself to her feet

It couldn't have been a kelp burning day, for that was...she flexed her fingers by her side, unsure of what day it even was. Frowning, Isla stepped closer to the entrance. The beast frantically paced back and forth. Its knuckles dragged against the sand, creating ruts for the seawater to run through.

She followed its line of sight, then spotted Bram standing at the bottom of the path. His eyes widened the moment he caught sight of her, and he bolted forward, only halting when the Nuckelavee bellowed and pounded its torn knuckles against its chest.

'Isla! My gods, you're alive.' Bram frantically glanced from the beast to her. 'I had hoped...*Mo leannan.*' His voice shook with the threat of tears.

She was dreaming, she must've been, lost to the darkness of the cave. But as Bram pressed forward, the Nuckelavee allowed it.

Bram's fingers brushed tangled curls from her face and his lips peppered kisses along her brow, cheeks, and lips. 'You are real,' he whispered as if he was unsure still.

'Am I?' she choked and threw her arms around his neck, squeezing him.

'How? How can this be?' He searched her gaze.

Isla didn't know. Out of all the sacrifices to survive, why her? But then again, how many had been willing to sacrifice themselves in place of another?

She tilted her head back to look up at the Nuckelavee. The beast could easily pull Bram apart as if he were no more than a blade of grass. But this very beast also had kept her alive. She knew from the memories it'd shared with her that it truly wanted a change.

'The Nuckelavee is the sea's guardian. It will come in the mist to take a life because we are sullying the ocean.' Isla bit her bottom lip and her brow furrowed as she shifted her gaze from Bram to the demon again. 'I never asked, but if we cannot burn kelp, how do we improve our soil?' There was only so much cow pats and sheep droppings could do.

Bram gaped at the horse's eye, then not so subtly shoved Isla behind him.

The Nuckelavee mimicked planting seeds, then scooped up a handful of seaweed and covered them. It leaned forward, looming over Bram and Isla. One of its claws poked Bram in the chest before he pointed toward the pathway.

Isla wondered for a moment if it wanted just Bram to leave, but then its claw jabbed her too.

'Go,' it said in a voice like waves crashing on the shore. 'Change.'

Bram didn't need another prompt. He took her hand and pulled her along, only pausing to look back once to ensure it wasn't a trap.

Isla ran as fast as her legs would take her. Up the pathway, into the woods, and out again into the village.

The village!

No one waited for Isla as she returned with Bram. She frowned.

'None knew I ventured to find you,' Bram said, as if he could read her mind.

Although a new lightness lifted her spirits, there was still a weight in her chest. A silent promise she'd made, to try and change the ways of the village.

Bram walked her to the front door of her family's hut and squeezed her hands so tightly she thought he'd break her bones. 'I love you, Isla.'

His words warmed her soul. 'Enough to venture into the den of a demon.' She leaned up to capture his lips in a quick kiss. 'I love you... enough to marry you.'

Bram's eyes widened, but whatever he was about to say in reply was cut short as the door opened and Aileen ran out, flinging herself at Isla.

'You're back and you're alive.' Aileen sobbed loud enough to alert the neighbors and her parents.

Isla, though weary to the bone, told her entire family and Bram of her time with the Nuckelavee and the promise she'd made in the dark.

The village hosted a feast in honor of Isla's return, celebrating how she'd braved the Nuckelavee. Rumors circulated of Isla defeating the beast, but she assured them it was alive and well.

'It's time for a change,' she said, telling them how things must be from now on, how to save the villagers' sons and daughters. 'For it is all our fault for poisoning the sea and enraging the Nuckelavee.'

Murmurs rose in the crowd and they cast accusing glances at one another. Some outright denied they were the cause, others lowered their gaze in shame.

'For every extra fish taken, every mollusc, we inspired hatred in the beast. And every time we burn the kelp, reducing it to ash we use to fertilize our soil, it's yet another thing we take from the sea. But what do we give back? Refuse. Sickness.' Isla pressed a hand to her heart, which pounded wildly. If she hoped to change the way the village was, the Nuckelavee was right… she needed heart.

'We will change!' The village answered in unison.

And, for a time, they did. They ceased tossing their rubbish into the sea and stopped burning the kelp. The need for fishing wasn't as great as before, for the crops flourished in the summer and the livestock was healthy.

On the day of Isla's wedding, everyone in the village swooped in on her family's home. Pots and pans clanged loudly, overpowering the twittering birds, and the fiddlers. It seemed as if it had been forever since there had been such joy in Tir a' Cheo.

Ewan, Bram's best friend, laid a wet kiss against her cheek, then offered his arm to her. His auburn hair hung in braids by his shoulders. 'Oh, lass, everyone has been waiting for this day for far too long. Let's give them a bit of a show.' His dark brown eyes sparkled with mischief.

With a tug, Ewan led her out of the house. Bram, dressed in his ceremonial kilt, stood beside Aileen, but his eyes were focused entirely on Isla.

The wedding walk started, Isla took up the cream skirt, and the riotous party wound its way to the cliffside.

And there, she married her lifelong friend, who, gods willing, would become her lifelong partner.

But all good things and happiness must come to an end, and Tir a' Cheo was the land of death, after all.

Two months after her wedding, Isla sat carding wool outside her home. *Our home. Me and Bram.*

Aileen had ducked out of her chores and instead perched on a stool next to Isla.

'When am I to be an aunt?' Aileen groused.

Isla clucked her tongue. She wanted children, wanted more than anything to give Bram a home filled with laughter and stomping feet. 'When the gods will it.'

The familiar scent of smoke suddenly tickled her throat. It wasn't from a chimney, for it didn't smell like wood. No, it was the smell of kelp burning. Her eyes widened and she dropped her tools and ran for the burning pits.

'Stop!' she cried. Isla's gaze flicked to the cloudless sky. No rain was on the way; it wouldn't protect them. 'Put it out, now, you fools!'

A blood-curdling cry cut through the crackle-pop of the kelp, then the bellow that sank so deep into Isla's bones it made her want to vomit. The Nuckelavee.

'It comes for revenge. You didn't listen,' she choked on her sob. 'Put it out and you may live yet.' Isla turned away from them and ran across the hillside, toward the tree-line which she could barely make out through a mist so thick it may as well have been a curtain. Bram and his father were running towards the fires, past the trees and the mist.

A hand emerged from the wall of fog, something glinting in it. A long object that–

Bram darted away from the blow, but his father wasn't as fortunate. The long spear-like weapon impaled him. Blood spilled from his mouth, down his chin, and onto his linen shirt.

'My gods, no,' Isla shouted hoarsely and ran to help Bram pull his flailing father away.

Instead of running, or hiding, the villagers gathered their arms and banded together, readying to take on the Nuckelavee. The very idea sickened Isla, for they'd never win, surely. And mayhaps a small part of her didn't want them to, either.

Another hand darted out from the mist, grabbing onto another villager, and while he successfully slashed open the Nuckelavee's limb, he was crushed in the beast's grip moments later.

When Bram's father was dragged to safety, Isla started forward, but an arm around her waist halted her.

'No. I won't stand by and watch you go again.' Tears spilled down Bram's cheeks and Isla leaned in for a lingering kiss. He knew as well as she did that this could be their last.

Without a word, she pulled away and ran to the mist. 'Stop! Nuckelavee, hear me. And Tir a' Cheo! Hear me! Peace. I have told you what must be done, and you didn't listen, so your debt is death. The Nuckelavee is alive and well, as you see. I cannot control it, but it was willing to give us a chance and you didn't honor it.'

Murmurs filled the space, then the gnashing of the Nuckelavee's teeth.

Hot breath washed over Isla's neck as the equine portion of the beast breathed on her. Claws grazed the top of Isla's head and she wondered if now was when she'd die. She'd failed, after all.

"We believe now. We will change,' Chieftain Ross rushed forward. His face was drawn and pale.

'It is too late,' Isla hissed. The claws raked down her head, beneath her chin, and to her cheek.

Bram swore but didn't approach, in fear of what the Nuckelavee would do.

Isla's heart thrummed loud enough in her ears that she could count every beat, like a skin drum. The beast's knuckles ran along her chest and visions of a life without death flashed in her mind, then another with a field of dead crops, livestock and bodies littering the ground.

A final reminder.

'I promise to do what I can. To protect your sea,' Isla told the creature. 'For there to be no more deaths in our village. Peace between us and you.'

The Nuckelavee purred, then retreated behind the mist. Slowly, as it walked away, the mist receded.

Isla's shoulders sagged. She would do what she could to remind the people of Tir a' Cheo of the deal they had made. And should they ever forget this bargain, the Nuckelavee would come for them all.

But that was the trouble with humans, wasn't it? Change never lasted.

After the Nuckelavee returned to the sea, Isla confronted Chieftain Ross, determined to *truly* change the villagers for good, for the better.

'Chieftain,' Isla said, joining him above the cliffs.

He looked down at her. Gratitude shone in his gaze, but he didn't smile. 'Isla, we owe you so much. How can we repay you?'

In that moment, she knew how, and a way to ensure her family and the rest of the villagers would remain safe. 'You won't like my request, but it is the only way.' Isla exhaled, teeth clenching. 'Leave Tir a' Cheo. Take the villagers and head inland. You won't be tempted to burn kelp, or sully the water. Leave and never return.'

Perhaps an argument brewed at the tip of his tongue, for his lips pressed together in a thin line and his eyes narrowed. But in the end, Chieftain Ross sighed. 'It is time we truly change, isn't it?'

'Someone needs to break this wretched cycle.' She motioned to the sea, watching as the waves crashed against the rocks.

'What of you, Isla? You cannot stay behind.'

She had to. If anyone ever came upon Tir a' Cheo, they'd need to know.

'I must protect the sea or the Nuckelavee will not be so kind next time.'

In the end, the creature of the sea took nearly everything from Isla. What she gave herself up for was packed in the back of a cart.

Aileen sobbed, clinging to Isla. 'You promised me you'd run away with Bram. You promised!'

'And I promised to keep you safe and find another way for you to live. I did that for you.' She kissed her sister's tear stained cheek. 'This is my gift to you. A new life, a better one.'

With that, Isla embraced her parents and somehow kept herself from dissolving into tears. Hope blossomed in her chest for her family—the villagers. If they could have a brighter beginning away from here, staying in Tir a' Cheo would be worth it.

'I love you so much, Isla,' her mother said, squeezing her to the point her ribs ached.

Isla swallowed roughly. 'And I you. Be well and happy.'

Her parents climbed into the cart and as the chieftain whistled, the villagers pulled away.

'What now?' Bram's voice called from behind.

Isla turned to face him, then gazed out at the sea. 'Now, we uphold our end of the bargain.'

CONTRACT LORE

JASON FRANKS

MARNIE HAD MET ENOUGH CELEBRITIES WHILE WORKING FOR C. HEYINGTON-Smythe II to know that legal practice wasn't all courtrooms and designer clothes, but the shabby office at the back of a suburban strip mall looked set to offer a particularly downmarket experience.

She pulled on the handbrake and looked at her boss, sitting in the passenger seat. 'What are we even doing here, C? This is the loser end of dudsville.'

Who hired an entertainment lawyer to negotiate funding for a software startup? Marnie couldn't think of one good reason Smythe had agreed to the enterprise, beyond whatever creepy thrill he derived from making her drive him halfway to San Fran.

Smythe yawned. 'The client is paying handsomely for our inconvenience.' He popped the door and eased his bulk out of the car.

Another year and she'd be finished with law school. If she played nice, the firm would make her an associate as soon as she had the degree. Then she'd have her own office, and some other shmuck would take over as Smythe's paralegal.

Smythe had set off at a stroll towards the client's office. Gritting her teeth, Marnie grabbed his briefcase from the back seat and rushed after him.

The client's office was just as dingy on the inside. A couple of scarred trestle tables and five mismatched chairs stood listing on the threadbare carpet. Computers squatted on every flat surface, skeletal without their cases. UML diagrams and mathematical proofs pinned to the stained grey walls flapped in the draft from the open door.

A skinny guy in a polo shirt was sitting engrossed at one of the terminals. When Smythe cleared his throat, the guy looked up as if surprised to see them.

'Oh, hello!' He came over and shook hands with the lawyer. 'Mr Smythe, I'm Arthur Pandrock. We spoke on the phone.'

Smythe released Pandrock's grip. 'This is Marnie Sudeten, my paralegal.'

Pandrock looked at her uncertainly, his hand wavering between them. She took it and shook it. His grip was stronger than she expected.

'You realise,' said Smythe, 'this engagement is not in my area of expertise.'

'I know your area of expertise, Mr Smythe,' said Pandrock. 'You've been screwing musicians out of their rights and royalties for fifty years.'

Before Smythe could respond, Pandrock continued: 'The guy we're talking to today is gonna try to do that to me. I need someone like you on my side.'

'Mr Pandrock, I don't know anything about the technology business.'

'But you know a bad contract when you see one,' replied the engineer. 'I'll handle the tech talk. You just make sure I keep what's mine.'

The door banged open. Marnie squinted at the figure silhouetted at the threshold.

The big man was in his late forties, dressed in cargo shorts, a T-shirt advertising an anime streaming service, and a pair of smudged glasses in a fashionable frame. He took a loud suck from a Slurpee and stepped into the room.

Pandrock cleared his throat. 'Mr Heyington-Smythe, Ms Sudeten, this is my associate, Craig Heffernan.'

'Call me Heifer,' said the newcomer.

'Heifer,' said Smythe.

'Heff, if you prefer. Or Huffer.'

Smythe looked Heifer up and down. 'Is this…individual…a business partner?'

Heifer blew out his lips.

'An employee?'

Heifer spluttered sarcastically.

'He's an old college buddy,' said Pandrock. 'He's helping out just for today.'

'If I was for sale, you couldn't afford me,' said Heifer.

'I immediately had you pegged as a man of means,' said Smythe.

'Heff used to own trekkerporn.com,' said Pandrock. Neither he nor Heifer seemed at all embarrassed. 'In the pre-Google days he made millions just from click-throughs.'

'Why is he here?' said Smythe.

Pandrock cut in before Heifer could retort. 'Heff's going to host the teleconference.'

'If this is going to be a teleconference,' said Smythe, 'Why couldn't we do this from my office? We have our own internet computers, you know.'

Marnie tried to contain her sigh. Smythe was incapable of navigating the internet without a legal secretary to operate the mouse for him.

'Security,' said Pandrock, suddenly nervous. 'Heff, you need a hand bringing in your gear?'

Heifer pulled his keys from his pocket and popped a flash drive in the shape of a sushi roll off the key-ring. 'Got the whole rite on here.' He flipped the flash drive into the air and caught it. 'You have a clean computer I can use?'

Pandrock fished a laptop out of a drawer and turned it on.

Heifer plugged the sushi roll into the computer. He sucked noisily from his Slurpee, and bent down to connect the laptop to an LCD monitor that was mounted on the wall. As he did so, his waistband receded to show his ass. Marnie sighed and averted her gaze.

Smythe looked at the ceiling, then his watch. 'Is this going to take long?'

Heifer shot him an over-the-ass glare.

'Not long,' said Pandrock. 'Please, have a seat.'

Smythe pulled up one of the mismatched chairs and settled his weight onto it – gently.

Pandrock addressed Heifer. 'Ready to summon?'

'Go disconnect the wireless.' Heifer took another suck from his drink. 'There's no firewall and I'd rather not risk exposing the 'net to any random hellbeast that wanders by the open portal.'

Pandrock fiddled around inside a cabinet that contained a tangle of Ethernet cables and network switches.

Marnie had taken some computing units when she was pre-law. She knew there were programs called daemons that ran silently on most computers, keeping things running behind the scenes. She'd never heard of a hellbeast before, but she guessed it was something similar. It wasn't just techies who loved fantasy stuff these days – Marnie had shelves full of books with dragons on the cover in her apartment – but middle-aged nerds like Heifer seemed to take pains to be uncool about it.

Smythe yawned.

'You really think this will work?' said Pandrock. 'You think he'll actually show up?'

'If the other party doesn't arrive, these hours are still billable,' interjected Marnie, if only to stop Smythe from speaking.

'Of course he'll manifest,' said Heifer. 'I made an appointment.'

'How'd you manage that?' asked Pandrock.

'Twitter DM.' Heifer sighed. 'Nobody cares about IRC anymore.'

'Okay, Heff,' said Pandrock, averting what sounded like the beginning of a soliloquy, 'it's your show.'

Heifer opened a primitive-looking chat client on the laptop screen and selected a name from the contacts list: JACK SCRATCH. Then he typed in the chat window:

> HEFF: Excuse me Sir. I'm here with my associate Arthur Pandrock for the Business Meeting we arranged?

A PING heralded an incoming reply. Pandrock actually jumped at the sound. Marnie supposed that she would be nervous, too, if it was her dream on the line.

> JACK SCRATCH: Be right with you, Heifer. Just let me set up my webcam.

Marnie didn't follow the world of venture capital, but Jack Scratch was a familiar name. She looked to Smythe to see if he had any idea who that was, but Smythe was resting his head on his fist with his eyes closed. In another minute he'd be snoring. Marnie elbowed him discreetly and he opened his eyes long enough to give her a reproving look.

Pandrock seemed edgy. 'Heff, shouldn't there be, like, some kind of a seal?'

A white pentagram blazoned itself across the black square in the middle of Heifer's teleconferencing app. 'There's your seal.'

'Are you sure this is cool?' said Pandrock. 'I mean, digital and all. There are gaps between pixels…'

'Analogue or digital, it's the same protocol. It's cool, trust me.'

'Have you actually tested it?'

'Sure.'

'You summoned him? With this exact software?'

'Well, not the man himself, but like, level two minions and shit. Trust me, it'll be fine.'

Marnie shifted uneasily. This was sounding more and more like a Dungeons and Dragons game these two were taking way too seriously.

Heifer pressed several keys at once. Runes scrolled across the bottom of the screen, right-to-left, and the speakers hissed sharply. Then Jack Scratch's chiselled features appeared in the middle of the pentagram.

'Hi, guys.' Jack's voice issued clearly from the little speakers on the laptop. He was handsome, for a guy with a ponytail. He had grey eyes and an easy smile.

'Great to meet you, sir,' said Heifer. He addressed the screen on the wall, not the laptop where the webcam was mounted.

'Um, hi,' said Pandrock, also to the wall screen. 'I'm Arthur Pandrock.' He gestured for Smythe to come over and the lawyer reluctantly got up from the chair. 'My attorney, C. Heyington-Smythe.'

Smythe nodded at the screen. 'Hello.'

'Who's the young lady standing in the back?' asked Jack.

'Oh,' said Smythe. 'That's my paralegal, Marnie Sudeten. She's here to assist me with the clerical work.'

By which he meant the typing. Marnie wanted to strangle him with his Yale necktie.

'Lovely to meet you all,' said the man on the screen. 'I'm the Devil.'

'This is very amusing,' rumbled Smythe, 'but I do not negotiate with mythical beings.'

'Mr Smythe, I may be eccentric, but I'm certainly not a myth.'

'I don't care how real you are,' said Smythe, in the same blustering tones with which he had intimidated dozens of sneering young musicians into signing usurious record deals. 'The Devil? You might as well sign the contract "Donald Duck". It still won't hold up.'

The Devil smiled. 'I promise you, if we successfully negotiate a contract I will sign it as a fully documented, legal human being, representing a completely legitimate business enterprise.'

'Jack Scratch,' said Marnie.

The Devil laughed. 'Or someone like him.'

Smythe stood and turned to Heifer. 'If this is a prank TV show I will not hesitate to sue, do you understand? I will sue you and your pornography business down to very your last pair of ill-fitting trousers.'

'These are tactical grade cargo shorts, dude,' replied Heifer.

Smythe wasn't sure if he was genuinely offended, but he definitely did not like the man's tone. He swept towards the door. 'Come on, Marnie. We're done here.'

Smythe faltered when he noticed that Marnie hadn't moved. He followed her gaze back to see that she was staring at the screen. Which had caught fire.

Smythe looked hard at the Devil. Then he looked down over the swell of his belly at his patent leather shoes and saw that they had caught fire as well. His two thousand dollar suit began to char as the flames rose up his legs. The pomade in his hair ignited and he could feel his skin starting to crisp and his eyeballs beginning to liquefy and…

…and then the flames vanished, and so did the pain, and he was fine, other than the damage that had been done to his quiff.

The smoke detector on the ceiling began to bleat.

'Oh shit!' Pandrock dragged a chair underneath the device and stabbed frantically at the button on its underside until the noise stopped.

'Well, then, Mr. Pandrock,' said the Devil. The flames around the undamaged screen vanished. 'I believe that you have a pitch for me?'

'Um, yes, of course,' said Pandrock, climbing unsteadily down from the chair. He took a deep breath. 'Do you want to hear the whole thing or do you, uh, already know about it?'

'I take pride in being well-informed,' said the Devil, 'But I'm not omniscient. Let's hear it.'

Heifer sat heavily on a broken swivel-chair and rolled backwards to find a better vantage from which to watch Pandrock's spiel. Smythe snapped his mouth shut and Marnie guided him back to his seat. She'd never seen the old bastard at a loss for words before. Perhaps today was a good day after all.

'All right,' said Pandrock. 'You know Big Data, right?'

'I know Big Data.'

'Well, forget about that,' said Pandrock. 'I'm going for Omega Data.'

The Devil narrowed his eyes. 'Go on.'

'Every byte that passes between every user, every device, every sensor and switch and relay,' said Pandrock. 'My technology has the capacity to harvest, store, and analyse it. All of it.'

'And how are you going to get access to this data?' said the Devil. 'If it's a social media platform I'll lay your soul to waste. On a canapé.'

'Nothing so vulgar, I assure you,' said Pandrock.

'This is the good bit,' said Heifer, rubbing his hands together.

'All right,' said the Devil. 'Tell me how you are going to acquire all the data in the world.'

'Folks will give it to me in exchange for my services.'

'Which are?'

'Micro-targeted caching,' said Pandrock. 'With all that data I can predict what users want. My systems can cache everything they're likely to need before they know it themselves. It will speed up browsing by several orders of magnitude, with no cost to end-users.'

'How will you make money from it?' said Marnie.

'Data is priceless,' said Pandrock.

'But how do you turn data into profit? Are you going to sell it?'

'No,' said Pandrock. 'You can't get away with that anymore. All data will be stored securely and safely to avoid tampering and misuse.'

Heifer sniggered. 'Like security is an actual thing,' he said. Everyone ignored him.

'Revenue comes from advertising, of course,' said the Devil. 'Now I see why you thought it would interest me. And I am interested, so please – keep talking.'

Pandrock talked. He showed slides on another laptop. He drew pictures on the whiteboard. He outlined development, manufacturing, rollout, revenue and growth. He showed plans for scaling the operation once various financial and technological milestones were reached. He talked about global markets and local personnel and corporate competitors and international policy. He spoke about every aspect of the business, and he spoke clearly and concisely, with passion and humour. Even Heifer looked impressed.

'So, what do you think?'

The Devil pursed his lips. 'I like it.'

'Uh, thanks.' Pandrock was actually blushing.

'Now, what do you want from me?'

'Money,' said Pandrock.

'Plenty of people have money,' said the Devil. 'Why come to me?'

Pandrock curled one lip. 'I'm well past forty,' he said. 'As far as venture capitalists are concerned, my best days are behind me.'

'Have you thought about Botox?'

'I don't need Botox. I need acne and a voice that hasn't broken.'

'Harsh, but true,' said Heifer.

'I'm not trying to fund buzzwords and rainbow farts,' said Pandrock. 'This is big-time, industrial-grade innovation. I want to rebuild the internet and I need a partner who won't steal my IP or yank my funding because their astrologer told them to. I want a partner who will be truly bound to the contract.'

'Which accounts for your choice of lawyer,' said the Devil.

'I figured you'd be familiar with his work,' said Pandrock.

Marnie nudged Smythe in the ribs, but he shrugged and returned his attention to the smoke detector. He looked like his brain was running a recovery cycle on his mind.

'All right,' said the Devil. 'I suppose you know the terms?'

'Oh, no,' said Pandrock. 'This is purely a money thing. I'm not selling my soul.'

'That's not how I operate.'

'But you do have money. If you fund my start-up costs, I'll give you a stake in ownership and a fair cut of the profits, which are going to be substantial.'

'What if I insist?' asked the Devil.

'You have plenty of souls already,' said Pandrock. 'You don't need mine.'

Marnie was no expert, but she was pretty sure that whenever the

Devil struck a deal, *somebody* lost their soul. Hiring Smythe to protect him had been a smart move on Pandrock's part, but could the lawyer really hold his own against the Lord of Lies? Smythe was good, there was no question, but looking at him now – sitting with his mouth open, staring at the smoke alarm – she didn't feel good about his chances.

'Tell me, Arthur Pandrock,' said the Devil, 'why do you want to build this thing?'

'Because it's what I do,' said Pandrock. 'Because I can.'

'Try again.'

'Because if I don't, somebody else will,' he said, with deeper conviction.

'No. It's because it will make you rich,' said the Devil. 'You should talk to Mammon. Greed is his purview.'

'This isn't greed. This is *ambition*.'

'I think you'll find the distinction is narrower than you expect,' said the Devil, 'But all right. This will be a monetary exchange, but I want a provision for soul-taking in the penalty clauses.'

'How's that?'

'Simple. I will give you every resource that you need to execute this project, for an agreed slice of ownership, but if you fail to deliver, I get everything – including your soul.'

'That sounds all right,' said Pandrock, 'but I'm not going to verbally agree to anything. I need a formal contract.'

'Of course,' said the Devil. 'Business is business. It's time for your lawyer to prove his worth.'

'Smythe,' said Pandrock.

Marnie elbowed him sharply. Smythe twitched, blinked. Marnie elbowed him again. '*Smythe!*'

The lawyer shook his head, inhaled, and drew himself erect. 'All right.'

Despite herself, Marnie wanted to applaud. Instead, she placed her hands on her laptop keyboard and waited.

The Devil and Smythe began to speak of contracts. They spoke in generalities first, outlining the form of the agreement; circling, trying to get a measure of one another. Pandrock and Heifer faded into the background. All Marnie could hear now was the swirl of argument and counter-argument, accompanied by the patter of the keys beneath her fingers.

Eventually, silence fell. Smythe put his hands in his pockets. 'I think it's done,' he said. Marnie withdrew her hands from the keyboard.

'I agree,' said the Devil. 'Is there anything else you would like us to discuss, Mr Pandrock?'

'If Mr Smythe is satisfied, so am I.'

'Terrific,' said Smythe. 'Marnie, may I look over the document one last time?'

She let Smythe have her seat and stretched out the crick in her neck.

Smythe scrolled through the document, nodding and humming to himself, obviously struggling with the mouse. He looked down at the keyboard and pecked out one or two additional lines to close out the contract, then smiled. 'All that's required are the signatures.'

'Great,' said the Devil. 'Just as soon as I amend your most recent addition.' A pair of manicured hands sprouted from the laptop's little screen. They were on fire. Smythe yanked his hands from the keyboard and shot back in his chair.

The Devil tapped the keys, highlighting, deleting, and replacing the offending passage with an economy of keystrokes. 'Check it out – I can type upside down. LOL.'

'I-I-I I must protest,' spluttered Smythe. 'That last clause was perfectly aligned with the terms to which we had agreed.'

'Your last clause would have prevented your client from entering into any additional contracts with me,' said the Devil. 'That is not acceptable.'

'But–'

'No,' said the Devil, firmly. 'I was a nice guy and I allowed you the contract your client wanted, but I'm not so nice that I'll forgo any opportunity to recoup my generosity at a later date.'

'I must protest.'

'It's fine,' said Pandrock. 'No one is forcing me into anything. Besides – if I need to make a new deal with the Devil, I already have a lawyer.'

Smythe sniffed and shrugged. 'You're the client.'

'Great,' said the Devil. 'Everyone's happy.' He hit some more keys and a small laser printer in the corner started to hum and fart. Pages wafted onto the out tray, one by one.

Smythe dabbed his forehead with a handkerchief. He picked up a sheaf of papers from the printer, collated a single copy of the contract, squared it and flipped through it one more time.

It was, without a doubt, the finest work of his life. The hardest fought, the most elegantly rendered, the cleverest. He had sat down to negotiate with the Devil, and he had come out ahead.

Once the documents were signed and the Devil had politely taken his leave, silence came over them.

'Does anybody smell sulphur?' said Heifer, leaning over the back of his chair.

Marnie wrinkled her nose and backed away. 'That's not sulphur.'

Heifer waggled his ass. 'You're right. It's methane.'

'You are a filthy human being,' Smythe replied. Heifer's grin broadened.

'Come on,' said Pandrock from the kitchenette. 'We should be celebrating.'

'Just don't set off any fireworks,' replied Heifer.

'How about some Cristal?' Pandrock produced an ice bucket and a magnum from behind the counter and proceeded to shake it vigorously.

'That will do nicely,' said Smythe, smiling for the first time.

Pandrock whooped and sprayed the room. Heifer was on his feet, high-fiving everyone, filling the office with his sniggering, snorting laughter. Marnie discreetly rinsed the champagne flutes in the kitchen sink.

They raised their glasses – Heifer raised his Slurpee, to which he had added his champagne – and proposed a toast. To high tech, to rock and roll, to Satan and to lawyers. Pandrock's grin was so wide it looked as though the lower half of his face had been razored open.

'So, you're satisfied, then?' said Smythe, shaking Pandrock's hand.

'Oh, man, you have no idea,' said Pandrock.

'You do realise that you've made a deal with the Devil.'

Heifer sucked noisily on the dregs of his drink. 'I'm pretty sure you were the last one to understand that,' he said. 'So why don't you keep the cautionary tales to yourself?'

'We've successfully negotiated a contract,' said Smythe. 'But that is only the first round, you understand. Business gets complicated quickly.'

'The Devil wants more, he'll have to summon himself,' said Heifer. 'Far as I'm concerned, this is over.' He shook his cup to see how much ice was left, gave it a disappointed look, and put it down on a bench top.

'Hey!' said Marnie. 'That's the signed copy!' She tried to whip the contract out from under Heifer's cup, but he snatched it away. He was surprisingly fast.

'It'll be fine,' he said, waving the soiled papers like a fan.

'Give me that!' Marnie made another grab for the contract and Heifer pulled it away again. A couple of pages fluttered free of the sheaf.

'Hey!'

'It's okay,' said Heifer indignantly. 'I got it, all right?' He bent down to collect the stray pages, treating Marnie to a second viewing of his ass. She looked away and shuddered.

'Well!' said Pandrock, waving the champagne bottle. 'Who'd like another drink?'

'Right here,' said Marnie, holding up her flute. Smythe accepted a refill with poor grace.

Still on his hands and knees, Heifer paused in the process of sorting the pages back into order. 'Huh.'

Pandrock put down the champagne. 'What is it?'

Marnie craned her neck to see what Heifer was reading. Page 15, near the bottom. The Audit clauses.

Heifer held up one hand as he reread the paragraph, his lips moving as he read. He turned the page, read a little further, then went back and read it again.

'Heff?' said Pandrock.

Heifer climbed to his feet and handed the contract back to Pandrock. 'You've agreed to give the Devil access.'

'Access to what?' said Marnie.

'Everything,' said Heifer. 'Once this goes live, he'll be in everything. Every data centre in the world. Everyone's data. Everything we touch.'

'I don't even use the internet,' said Smythe, as if it was something to be proud of.

'*You* don't,' said Heifer, 'but your bank does, and so does your proctologist. Your data is online, whether you like it or not.'

'We'll just have to make sure it doesn't get into the wrong hands, then.' Marnie wanted to scream before she'd even finished speaking.

'I'm sure the Devil can be trusted to use it for good, not ill,' said Heifer.

Pandrock shrugged. 'So what? He's a mythical entity. What's he even going to do with zettabytes of raw data?'

'Another couple years and I bet Hell will be overflowing with data scientists,' said Heifer.

'Come on,' Pandrock shook his head. 'The Devil said it himself. He's well-informed, but he's not omniscient.'

'Not yet, he isn't,' said Marnie.

A BIRTHDAY HEX

CANDACE ROBINSON

GLEAMING AGAINST THE BRIGHT SUN, A LONG STRIP OF BLACK CLOTH RESTED in Nana's palm. Charm arched a brow at it while she clasped her boyfriend's hand.

It was Charm's eighteenth birthday today, and as a surprise, her family had come to pick her up at her shared apartment with Sage.

'Come on, Sage, stop clinging to Charm and wrap the blindfold around her eyes,' her mom – Jade – singsonged, lightly smacking their hands apart.

'Don't worry,' Nana said, hugging Sage first, then handing him the dark fabric. 'We'll return Charm in time so you can have a birthday dinner with her.'

'Take your time.' Sage smiled, giving Jade a goodbye hug next. When he turned to Charm, his hazel irises were sparkling, his grin growing wider. 'Assume the position.'

Charm rolled her eyes but faced away from him as Sage's soft fingertips grazed her cheeks, his touch igniting butterflies in her stomach as they always did. She'd moved in with Sage at the end of their senior year, leaving behind their families' expensive houses to have their own space. They'd now been living together for two months in a rinky-dink apartment, working awful jobs for the time being, her at an ice cream parlour, him at a grocery store. But with Sage, it was worth every cockroach.

Darkness enveloped Charm as Sage tightened the fabric, not a single speck of light slithering in.

It was suffocating.

'Do we really need this forsaken thing?' Charm complained, tugging at the silky material of the blindfold with her hand.

'Yes, you have to wait for the *birthday* surprise,' her mom said in that singsong voice that was starting to grate on Charm.

'It's your lucky day,' Nana added. 'And there will be no purse or phone, just you.'

'Fine,' Charm grumbled. With her eyes covered, it would feel like an eternity, but she would keep those exaggerated thoughts to herself since her family was trying to do something nice for her.

'It'll beat my *fun* day at work. Have a good time, and I love you,' Sage whispered, pressing his soft lips to hers, his sandalwood scent caressing her nose.

'I love you,' Charm murmured back, wishing she could see his face.

'Come on,' Jade said. Charm could tell her mom was grinning as she took her arm and drew her away from Sage. Nana grasped Charm's other arm and together they guided her into the backseat of the car.

Jade started the car and took off a little too fast, Charm's head hitting the seat. Charm wondered where she was being taken – she'd never had a 'surprise' like this from her mom or Nana, but she was hoping it would be somewhere she hadn't been before. Maybe a park near the historical buildings in Houston or Galveston?

Time seemed to go on and on when she finally asked, 'How much longer?'

'It's only been thirty minutes, my impatient grandchild, but you must have ESP because we're here,' Nana said, laughing while removing Charm's blindfold.

The world was a blur – one big blob of mixed colours. Charm blinked until everything came into focus. A wide smile crossed Nana's cheeks as she peered around the passenger seat at her. Jade glanced back at her too, with a smile mirroring Nana's, before returning her attention to...

They weren't on a road anymore. Trees surrounded them. Jade had driven off the road and they were now buried inside a forest with no sign of pavement anywhere. A whole forest of oak trees, ones Charm had only seen in books. Her lips parted as she gazed at their wide forms, the moss dangling from gnarled branches, holes that led deep into their trunks.

Jade finally slowed to a stop in front of the largest oak tree, its crooked branches curving in all directions. Thick green vines hung from its limbs, obscuring what lay beyond. The tree looked like something out of a horror movie, one where it secretly ate babies.

What were they doing here?

'Come on,' Jade said before opening the car door at the same time Nana did.

Charm unbuckled and stepped out of the vehicle. Her lips parted as the breeze rumpled her short blue hair. She brushed her bangs from her brows, then studied the trees. Their deep green leaves rustled and their branches creaked in the wind. 'What is this?' Her heart pounded as the trees seemed to breathe in sync with her, their leaves inhaling and exhaling, their soft noises like whispers.

She's here. It's time, they appeared to say.

Charm shook her head, pushing what had to be only her imagination away. There was no way the trees could be talking.

Her long, blonde hair billowing behind her, Jade waved a hand at the giant oak. The thick green vines on the oak's right side lifted, revealing an ivory boulder, freckled with small craters, that was almost as tall as her mom.

Charm's eyes widened, her heartbeat rocketing. *What the hell?*

Jade placed a palm on her shoulder, the same hand that had made the vines *move*. 'Don't be afraid,' she said gently, her deep brown eyes – matching Charm's – holding her gaze steady. 'It's your eighteenth birthday, and you come into your magic today.'

Charm's breath hitched as she peered at the faces of her mom and Nana. *Magic?* It couldn't be true, but then she'd just seen her mom move vines without even touching them, could still hear the odd whispers of the forest. Her fingers itched to call Sage before she remembered she was told to leave her phone back at the apartment.

'What do you mean?' Charm frowned. 'Where are we?'

'We'll explain everything once we're inside.' Nana pointed to the boulder, then drew her dark braid, peppered with white streaks, over her shoulder.

Inside a rock? As if answering Charm's internal question, Nana swiped her hand to the side and a door creaked open in the centre of the boulder. The stone had been smooth, devoid of even a single crack, only moments before. For a split second, Charm wanted to run, but these weren't strangers. It was her mom, her nana, and they'd been there her whole life. They'd raised her together since Charm's dad had died before she was born. She trusted them.

Charm took a deep swallow and nodded.

Jade motioned for her to follow, and Charm padded behind her through the thick grass with Nana hovering close behind.

'It looks dark in there.' Charm squinted at the door in the boulder. 'Do you have a light?'

Jade waved her hand once more, and a weak, pale light shone from inside the boulder. Charm licked her lips and arched a brow as they ducked through the door. A pleasant, spicy-sweet aroma filled the air as Charm descended a dark stone staircase behind her mom. It was a familiar scent from her family's home. The aroma made her dizzy, filling her with lightness and expectation.

Hundreds of tiny white bulbs shone within the narrow space. Fairy lights? Beneath the warm glow, ivory brick walls led them deeper into the earth. This was...weird. Charm was desperate for her phone now, wanting to look up anything involving magic. Demons? Faeries? Witches? Angels? She'd always believed a higher power was out there, but whatever her mom and Nana's role was in this, she would soon find out.

Charm wished Sage was here, to see what she was seeing. They'd been together since the ninth grade, and he wasn't just her boyfriend but her best friend. He was sweet and funny as hell. While most high school relationships didn't last, Charm had always known he was the one. Knew it from the moment she saw him. If she hadn't experienced it for herself, she never would've believed in love at first sight, and she would've been the first to say it was bullshit. But it wasn't. Had it possibly been some kind of an intuition?

At the bottom of the stairs stood a pristine ivory archway with towering pillars on either side. Obsidian beads hung from the centre, forming a curtain. As she drew closer, through the eerie light, Charm could see the pillars weren't smooth but covered in small carvings. Naked men's bodies, twisted and stitched together into a macabre pattern, ran up and down the ivory. She frowned at the sinister art, finding it odd there were no female forms among the engravings. The men appeared to be screaming, their faces grimacing in pain. *Strange.*

A swishing sound as Jade pushed the beads aside caught Charm's attention. Jade gestured them through, and Charm inhaled sharply as she peered around the wide-open space that would make a decent-size living room. Deer and ram skulls lined the black walls, and every other inch of the area was marked in white chalk with drawings and numbers she didn't understand. Ruby-coloured chandeliers hung from the ceiling in a circle, casting their glow across the space, highlighting a massive round table beneath them. Charm counted twenty chairs surrounding it, all with black cloaks draped over their backs. On the table, in front of each chair, rested a silver goblet and a single white candle. At the centre of the table sat a small cauldron.

Charm's heart struck her rib cage, nervous at what was happening. She wasn't sure if her family was going to try to do some sort of séance, but she wouldn't join in on summoning any demons. A part of her still didn't believe this was actually happening. But the strange sweet smell of this place and the presence of her family assured her she wasn't dreaming.

'You need to tell me what's going on.' Charm folded her arms, her fingers digging into her skin. 'Are you trying to conjure the devil or something?'

Jade cocked her head and let out a high-pitched laugh. 'We don't need a man to do what we do. We answer to nature. We are each our own witch.'

Witch.

Charm sighed in relief. Nature. Nature was a good answer. Good witches then. She could deal with that.

Jade set her purse on the table and opened it to fish out a silver necklace. A purple amulet dangled at the end of the chain, the light from the chandeliers bouncing off the jewel.

'This will ignite your magic for now' – Jade held up the necklace as she moved to stand in front of Charm – 'but after tonight, when everything is finished, you won't need its help.'

'After what's finished?' Charm wrinkled her nose.

Jade ignored the question and unclasped the necklace. Charm

glanced at Nana, trying to get an answer from her, but she stayed silent too. Something was wrong. The sweet aroma of the place turned rotten.

Charm went to take a step back, yet Jade was quicker, clasping the piece of jewellery around her neck.

As soon as the amulet brushed Charm's collarbone, her heart pumped fast, too fast, while something – a wholly new sensation – coursed through her veins. A caress at first, building and building. Charm's lungs could barely keep up with the adrenaline flowing through her. It wasn't pain, but *something* else. Panicked, she clawed at her throat, trying to rip the necklace off, but it wouldn't budge. She choked as the words escaped her mouth. 'What did you *do?*'

'Relax.' Jade cradled Charm's face in her hands. 'Breathe. This amulet holds the essence of the first witch – it is ancient, its power raw. It takes a moment to get used to the magic.'

And then, as though to prove what Jade had said wasn't a lie, the rush inside Charm dulled to a soft thrum. She drank in breath after breath until each one came out steady.

Jade released Charm's face. 'You've been taking care of yourself for a long time now. By age you may be a woman, but you've been one for a while. However, tonight, you will access your birthright and become a witch. The rest of the coven is on its way and you will bring us the refreshment at 10pm sharp.'

This...this was really happening. It wasn't something Charm would wake up from. She studied her family. There were never any hints that either one had magic, could do things most people believed didn't exist. But as the energy hummed within her, raw and new, it felt right. She'd seen plenty of movies about magic. Hell, she remembered *The Craft* most clearly. Her mom had always laughed at parts that Charm had never found funny. And as she looked back over the years, maybe there *were* signs that Jade had secrets. Charm's family, these two women she loved and admired, would sometimes smell just like the inside of this boulder, but when Charm would ask them about it, they would blame it on incense. Yet Charm had never seen any incense sticks around her old house. How could they have lied to her about this?

Oblivious to Charm's anxious thoughts, Nana clapped her hands together and said, 'Now, before you return tonight, we'll drop you back at home and you'll couple with Sage, then reap his life.'

Charm's head jerked up and she stilled. *Holy hell.* Had she heard Nana correctly? No, she must not have.

'Excuse me?' she rasped, blinking hard. The amulet pulsed against her flesh. 'What did you say?'

'Sage is a good boy, but he'll need to die today.' Nana's eyes held no pity, only something that Charm interpreted as…encouragement. 'We know you have a fondness for him. We all did for ours, but you will understand once he's gone. Once true power courses through your veins.'

Nana's words rang in Charm's ears, *screaming*, the sound nearly causing her pain.

'What do you mean? What have *you done?*' Charm's hands flew to her mouth, shaking. She was hoping what her family was about to say wasn't what she was thinking. But her hope shrivelled as both women stared at her in a way that made her blood run cold. They felt like strangers to her. Worse – they felt *dangerous.*

Jade wrapped an arm around Charm's shoulders, and it was too heavy as she spoke, 'Your father, your grandfather, your great-grandfather, and so on. They've all had to die for the magic of the coven to stay strong, especially when new daughters are conceived.'

Charm ripped away from her mom and backed up into the wall, her hands trembling. 'You, you killed–'

'We had to,' Jade said, not an ounce of regret shining in her eyes. 'Our coven weakening or them dying. It's not really a choice.'

Screw the coven.

The scary images carved into the columns made sense now. Charm winced at the memory of the faces twisted in agony. Was her dad portrayed there too, included among the sacrifices? Her grandpa? Charm had never met either of them, but she'd wanted to, always wondered what her life would've been like if her dad had been there. She thought about Sage then, and about his father – one of the nicest people Charm knew. He took her to art museums and taught her to play chess.

Her mom and Nana had made life good for her, doted on her, but… was all of it a lie?

Lies behind smiles.

Nana crossed her arms and moved toward her, same as she used to when Charm was a child and not paying attention. 'You will have sex with Sage when he comes home, get his seed inside you – the amulet's magic will ensure you conceive and that it will be a daughter. Just as all the members of our coven have done over the centuries.'

Centuries?

Charm took a deep swallow, thinking again about the men engraved in the archway. So many sacrifices. All she could focus on was how her mom had killed her dad, and how her grandpa had died by Nana's hand. 'Then what?' Charm asked, wondering what they'd done after killing a man they loved.

'Then, you will gather his blood into the cauldron and mix in rosemary, mint, and three drops of your blood for the coven to drink tonight.'

Her stomach sank and nausea bubbled up her throat. 'Why does it have to be him?' Charm asked, her voice shaking. 'And why does he have to die?'

'It has to be your true love.'

'Maybe he isn't,' Charm lied. But she knew. Knew it with her whole blasted heart that he was. Knew it from the second she'd walked into that ninth-grade classroom and looked at him. Sage with his curly black hair, his vivid hazel eyes, the dimples in his cheeks, his love for awful movies, the way he ran his hands through her short hair, the way he told her he loved her.

'He is.' Nana rotated her shoulders, her expression hardening. 'Why do you think we moved here? To have you two meet and naturally fall in love.'

Charm's heart pounded. They'd *known*... That was why they hadn't argued when she'd wanted to move in with Sage. It wasn't a coincidence they'd come to Texas. This place had been specifically chosen so she could meet Sage and one day kill him. Her true love. All so that some coven she hadn't known about before today could become stronger.

'Now, this is important.' Jade straightened, her voice stern like a command. 'Will you do this and take the cauldron?'

'And what if I won't?' Charm challenged.

'Then the coven will step in,' Jade said. 'One way or another, Sage will die.'

'I understand.' Charm didn't say another word as the cauldron was placed in her hands. It didn't weigh much, but in that moment, it felt heavier than anything she'd ever held.

'Perfect.' Happy tears beaded at Jade's lashes as she smiled. 'I'm so proud of you.'

Charm struggled to breathe, but the amulet, pressed against her neck, seemed to inhale and exhale, just like the trees outside.

'Once this is done,' Nana said, 'we will leave here and make a home somewhere else. We will prepare for your daughter's arrival, and when the time comes we will locate her true love before moving once more.'

The magic pulsed underneath Charm's skin, the amulet busy at work. 'Yes.' She wanted to scream no, but she needed to get out of there, get home – away from *them* – and think of a way out of this.

Jade circled her arm around Charm's waist, her grip too tight. 'If you don't follow through,' she said, her sunny smile at odds with her words, 'there will be, shall we say, repercussions.'

'Repercussions?' Charm asked, biting her lip.

'You see, Charm,' Jade continued, her fingers playing lightly over Charm's collarbone as she lifted the pendant. 'This amulet, it can be your friend today. Or it can be your enemy.'

Nana cocked her head. 'You don't want it to be your enemy, sweetie.'

Charm nodded, but really, all she wanted was to go back to this morning, to before she'd come here. She just needed to get home.

Get home to Sage.

She wouldn't do it – wouldn't kill him. Anger boiled through her as she studied her mom and Nana, their faces serene. Charm had to force herself to look at them and smile.

Neither of them had ever had another man in their lives since murdering their true loves. Charm had been conceived *specifically* for their magic to one day grow stronger. She swallowed her disgust.

'Once you do what is asked of you, proving your loyalty to the coven, you will understand why we do this,' Jade said, as if she could sense Charm's thoughts. 'You will see that there is no other way. And once you come into your magic tonight, feel this incredible power within you, you will know that its cost is more than justified.'

Charm could barely register her mom's words.

I won't kill Sage. I won't kill Sage. I won't kill Sage. I won't kill Sage.

The amulet heated against her flesh, its warmth penetrating straight to her heart.

I will kill Sage.

Charm remained quiet as Jade started the car, the trees' breaths loud in her ears, even with the windows rolled up. She peered out the glass while Jade drove through the foliage, the sun still bright in the sky.

As the car traversed the forest, the trees' branches peeled back. Charm gasped, her eyes widening.

'The trees protect us.' Nana pointed out the window. 'No matter where we live.'

The amulet heated against Charm's chest, its warmth lingered on the entire ride back. She could feel its magic not only on her skin, but below it, massaging her muscles, swimming in her blood, and seeping into her bones until it could go no further.

Biting the inside of her cheek, she brushed her fingers against the amulet.

'The magic feels unusual at first,' Nana said, leaning around her seat. 'But once it's all done and you give into the power, you won't want to take any of it back. Sage will feel like a distant memory, after he serves his purpose. We can use our magic to get what we want – wealth, careers, fame – *anything*. It's been that way since the first witch, long ago, made a pact with a dark fae in Ireland, who gave her the amulet. It is a great honour to join our coven, and a great responsibility, too.'

Charm could see how the power might be tempting, but for the first time in her life, she hated her nana, hated her mom. She stayed silent, gripping the cauldron in her lap until they pulled into the parking lot of Charm's run-down apartment complex.

'I'll see you tonight,' Charm said, forcing a smile as she stepped out of the car. She clenched the cauldron even tighter, her nails scraping against the metal.

'I know how you're feeling right now, but after this, you'll count down the days until the moment you give this gift to your own daughter.' Jade gave her a reassuring smile.

A gift? To force her daughter to murder her true love? Was that what Charm's life would revolve around? Lying? Manipulating? Betraying? Being in denial? Was it worth the power she was promised?

'One more gift from us.' Nana opened the glove compartment and drew out a blue box with a white bow on top, then handed it out the window to Charm.

'Thank you.' Charm managed to keep her voice even as she placed the box inside the cauldron. She kept her walk steady, casual, as she headed up the metal stairs to her apartment.

Something dark jumped in front of her and hissed, baring its teeth. Charm groaned at the feral cat that hung around her building. 'Hello, Diablo.' She attempted to scoot the black cat out of the way, but it let out a low, wicked sound before darting off.

'Maybe not hiss at me next time!' she yelled at its furry back.

Once inside her apartment, she leaned against the door with a sigh of relief. Sage wasn't home yet, but he would be soon.

Charm set the cauldron with her unopened gift beneath the table in the cramped kitchen. She would get this amulet off, even if she had to cut off her own head to do it. Whatever would prevent her from killing Sage.

But no matter how hard she dug her fingers into the clasp, it wouldn't budge. The chain wasn't long enough to tear over her head either. Charm growled in frustration as she marched to one of the kitchen drawers and yanked it open. She grabbed a pair of scissors and brought their blades to the necklace, hoping to break the chain. But when she squeezed as hard as she could against the metal, it didn't give way. 'Dammit.' She hurled the scissors across the room.

Charm needed a plan – she would run. No, she couldn't do that because the coven would still kill Sage. She would tell him to run then, to a place where he couldn't be found. Clenching her jaw, she reached for her phone on the counter. The amulet heated and her fingers stilled against the phone. She wanted to scream, only no sound came out. The amulet knew everything – it could see right inside her head. She would go to Sage's work then, but just before she got to the door, her feet froze in place, her hand unable to reach the knob as she swiped through the air.

'What the hell?' Charm took a step back, gripping her hair as she went into the living room and dropped onto the futon. 'I *am* hexed...'

She studied her desk, her open laptop, the TV, the framed movie posters hanging on the walls, her and Sage's shared bookcase filled with DVDs. He always said digital wasn't the same as having the physical feel of them.

Frustrated, she pushed up from the futon and took the gift out of the cauldron, then headed into the bedroom. If she was a witch, even if she was still uninitiated, there had to be a way to break the hex. *Maybe there's an answer in this gift*, she thought while removing the lid from the box.

A gasp escaped her as her gaze fell to what rested inside – a jewelled silver dagger. Her mom and Nana had given this to her…to use on Sage. A weapon to murder him. Another invisible blade to her chest, a betrayal that kept growing.

She froze when she heard the sound of a key sliding into the lock. Sage was back early from his stocking job at the grocery store. Realising she still gripped the dagger in her hand, she shoved it into the nightstand drawer beside the bed.

As the front door opened, every memory of Sage rushed through her at once. The amulet ignited, warming her skin, becoming hotter. Every inch of her was *burning* with desire.

Charm remembered seeing Sage on her first day at the new school. Liking how his dark curly hair had hung past his shoulders. The way she had talked to him first. How his cheeks pinkened when she'd sat beside him at lunch. She'd made the first move with everything, but not with their first kiss, and not when he'd unbuttoned her jeans, which led to her wanting to touch him too. Her memories continued, moving to their first time together during eleventh grade. Every time they'd had sex, they'd always been careful, used protection.

A rustling came from the kitchen, and the thrum in her veins grew stronger. Her magic was conquering, taking root. This was the amulet's doing. It knew Sage was there – and it wanted Charm to…

She could sense the amulet's appetite, its thirst for power. It had an agency, a will of its own. It wanted and it craved.

Sage's footsteps padded toward the bedroom, toward *her*. The desire within her pulsed harder than her heart as she took a seat on the edge of the bed.

He stopped as soon as his gaze met hers, a playful smile spreading on his face, his dimples showing. 'You're back earlier than I thought. I was hoping to have a fancy meal ready for you.' His feet were bare, and he had on his dark work pants and white shirt, his hair pulled back into a low ponytail.

'That can wait.' She fought against the amulet, trying to conjure the right words. 'I need to tell you something. Come here.'

Sage furrowed his brow and stepped toward her. 'What is it? Are you all right? You're looking a little pale.' He came up to her in three long strides and lifted her chin as he sat beside her.

Charm opened her mouth to speak, to tell him everything, but the amulet wouldn't let her.

'Did the surprise not go well?' he asked, studying her face.

It didn't. Not at all. The words rested on the tip of her tongue yet wouldn't spill from her lips. 'I'll tell you about it later, but it was… unexpected,' she finally forced out. Nothing else would come.

He drew her close. 'I know they meant well. They always do.' Before today, she would've agreed.

'I love you.' She crawled into his lap, straddling his thighs. Blowing out a breath, she wrapped her arms around his neck and rested her head on his shoulder.

'I love you too.'

'Remember that one time you snuck into my room,' she whispered into the crook of his neck.

'You mean after our first date when I was too damn scared to kiss you?' He chuckled.

'Yeah.'

'What about the night you snuck into my room?' She could hear the smile in his voice.

'When I came over to make love to you for the first time but your mom walked in?'

'Yeah.'

'That was the worst.' Thankfully his mom hadn't brought up that matter ever again.

He lifted her face once more, so that her gaze locked onto his beautiful hazel eyes. 'It was perfect though. You know why?'

'Why?' she asked softly, her heart beating faster.

'Because it led us to a better first time.'

Charm thought about that night, how they'd visited an old cemetery so she could take pictures for class, then they'd walked through the woods and found an abandoned building that had once been a drive-thru theatre. They'd picnicked there before driving to the beach and setting up a tent. She'd lied to her mom, told her she was staying with a friend, and Sage had done the same. Charm was pretty sure now that her mom had known the whole time and had probably been giddy about it. Dread rolled through her.

But an idea formed.

Maybe…maybe she could distract the amulet. Maybe if she appeased it by following through with this first part, the easy part, she could gain herself more time to think of a way out of the second half. The murder.

She kissed the side of Sage's neck, making him shiver. His fingers dug into her hips as she skimmed the tip of her nose slowly up his throat, then trailed open-mouthed kisses across his jaw.

Charm knew she was being awful by not telling him the truth, but she *couldn't*. She was being a monster, a *witch*, by kissing him now. But if she didn't, the amulet would force her, and she would rather make love to him with her free will. Because this…this she could easily do.

'Dammit, this may sound stupid as hell,' he whispered, his fingers tracing soothing circles on her back. 'But each day I love you more.'

'Then I guess we're both stupid as hell,' she murmured, tears pricking at her eyes as she cupped his face and placed a soft kiss to his mouth. 'I want to be with you in a way I haven't before. Nothing between us.'

His chest heaved, and he leaned his forehead on hers. 'I want that too. If you're sure.'

Taking a deep swallow, she nodded and crashed her mouth to his. They peeled each other's clothing off, layer by layer, until there was only skin against skin. God, she was never going to get enough of him. Her lips came to his once more, same as his did hers, just as true lovers would.

Afterward, Charm wrapped her arms around him, tighter than she ever had before. Squeezing her eyes shut, she ignored the amulet's growing warmth against her collar bone. But then the heat became stronger, tugging at her, making her eyes flutter. Hot tears streamed down her cheeks, and she trembled, clenching her jaw as the pain grew sharper.

The amulet was telling her what she must do next. Open the drawer of her nightstand where her jewelled dagger rested. Remove the blade and plunge it into his heart. It would be so simple. Over in mere moments. Sage would hardly feel any pain.

Please, no. There had to be a way out of this nightmare.

There had to be.

But even as she pleaded, even as she begged, fighting with everything her heart held for Sage, Charm leaned over and her hand reached for the drawer instead.

The cauldron's lid rattled in the passenger car seat beside Charm as tears beaded her lashes. She pressed her hand against the lid to stop the sound, which reminded her of what was in the cauldron. With a deep breath, she removed her palm and turned up the radio, letting the heavy drums and guitars fill her ears while she gripped the steering wheel. Sobs threatened to choke her once again, but she was determined to focus on the road in front of her. She must think *only* of the future, of the only path left to her. She'd been left with no choice. The amulet purred against her chest, content and sated.

Charm had been driving for almost thirty minutes, and now she was looking for the spot in the forest where her family had taken her earlier. No luck yet. Not a single car's headlights had passed her down the darkened road. She wondered if the coven had placed some sort of spell on this area to keep people away.

Her phone dinged, but she didn't bother to check it. She didn't need any distractions.

Charm flicked on the high beams and squinted, knowing she was getting close.

To the right, something shifted in the darkness as she slowed. She rolled down her window, and the branches stirred, beckoning her. The limbs unfurled, creating a gateway. Heart pounding, she drove carefully over the grass, the car jostling side to side.

The sound of breathing filled her ears once more – the trees inhaling and exhaling. A humming that hadn't been there earlier drifted through the air. Charm listened closely, and it sounded like women singing.

Owls hooted and other birds screeched in the tops of the trees beneath the moon's silvery light.

Up ahead, rows of cars gleamed in Charm's headlights. She spotted her mom's white SUV, but didn't recognise any of the other vehicles.

Charm pulled to a stop, then unbuckled the cauldron and lifted it before stepping out of the car. She bit the inside of her cheek to keep from falling to pieces.

The trees' breaths came to a halt, as though they were listening, waiting for her to speak to them.

'You're right on time,' her mom called.

Charm whirled around to find Jade hovering at the boulder's open door, a lantern in her hand. Jade's blonde hair spilled down her chest over a dark hooded cloak.

Holding the cauldron tightly, Charm walked toward the light.

'You got the blood.' Jade sighed, greedily taking the cauldron from Charm's hands. 'With Sage's death, you're free now. No longer bound to someone who you may not have given a second glance to otherwise.'

That wasn't true. She'd never felt chained to Sage. Charm's chest tightened and she pushed down the emotions brewing to the surface. However, she couldn't shove them all away, and her hands clenched at her sides. The amulet purred once more, and she ignored it. 'How long did you mourn Dad?'

'After that night, I didn't. I only focused on my freedom, the magic, the future of the coven. Tomorrow, what is left of your sadness will evaporate.'

One day? That was it? How? How could Charm be expected to move on from Sage so quickly after murdering him? How could her mom have done that to Charm's dad? How could Nana? And all these other witches who she hadn't even met yet? Would any power in the world justify murder?

Charm held her tongue and followed her mom down the staircase. The fairy lights on the walls guided their way as the spicy-sweet scent enveloped her. The smell of magic, of pulsing power. A smell she had come to despise.

Humming echoed up the stairs from the room below, but Charm couldn't see anything past the beaded curtain except for slivers of light. Her eyes widened at the archway and ivory pillars, now covered in blood that spilled out from the chests of the engraved men.

Jade drew back the beads, a clinking noise echoing, revealing the table in the centre of the room that was filled except for two chairs.

The witches' heads turned in Charm's direction, eyes blazing, their smiles welcoming her to their murderous coven. Out of everyone there, Charm appeared to be the youngest. Closest to her in age was a girl with dark braids twisted around her head. The oldest witch was maybe somewhere in her nineties – age spots dotted her temples and hands, and deep wrinkles covered her face. As for the rest of them, these witches were a diverse crowd, all ages, all sizes, all skin colours. All having murdered their true love while seeming to not give a damn.

They stood from their seats, smiling with glee.

'Let me introduce Charm, our newest member,' Nana said, clasping her hands together. The witches hummed in approval, beckoning Charm closer.

Jade grinned as she set the cauldron in the centre of the table between a clear crystal ball and a modern record player. Beside a silver covered dish, tarot cards were sprawled across one side of the table as though the witches had just been using them. The death card rested in the centre, and Charm's heart quickened.

Nana motioned Charm to an empty spot beside her at the table. 'Today is a celebration, not only for my granddaughter's birthday, but for the new life she carries inside her now. Soon enough, we'll welcome the arrival of a baby girl, who one day will join us.'

Charm forced herself to smile as she placed the cloak around her shoulders and fastened it in the front.

'I'm Pamela,' a woman with bright blue eyeshadow and makeup caked on her face said. 'I've known about you since you were a wee thing. My beloved, like yours, is gone, but he served his purpose and gave me a beautiful daughter who you will meet next year.'

Served his purpose? Was there no remorse at all? From anyone?

Charm folded her arms around her stomach, where a child would already be taking shape, if what her family had said was true. Deep down, she knew it was.

Her daughter, one day, would fall in love, then…murder her beloved. The magic thumping within her grew louder as she swallowed and half-listened to the remainder of the grim stories shared around the table. Shoved off a cliff, drowned in a lake, buried alive, died from a poisonous snake bite. Jade had run over Charm's dad, claiming it was a hit and run. Nana tripped her boyfriend down the stairs, said it was an accident.

Charm's stomach churned. Most of the deaths were violent, and she didn't believe it was all the amulet's doing because the witches beamed around the table, proud of what they'd done.

'Music and then a toast,' Jade cheered, turning on the record player. *Cosmic Love* by Florence + The Machine filled the air, the singer's melodic voice caressing Charm's eardrums.

She tried not to let her horrified thoughts show across her expression as the women silently chanted their own words, words she didn't understand, to the music while lifting their candles, the flames igniting.

Jade nodded at Charm. It was time.

Stomach sinking, Charm picked up a candle – the amulet's magic coursed through her, traversing within her bloodstream to the tips of her fingers before lighting the wick. The power felt natural, easy.

Jade removed the lid from the silver dish, revealing a white-frosted cake. *Happy Birthday Charm* was written across its top.

She watched in her *Twilight Zone* state as Jade lit the birthday candles, just as she had for every birthday. But now Charm was surrounded by women she didn't know, a witch coven she was meant to join. A coven that asked for their pound of flesh, a price in blood.

When the song ended, Jade turned off the record player. 'Make a wish.'

Perspiration had gathered on Charm's palms and she rubbed them against the velvet cloak as she leaned over the cake.

Sucking in a deep breath, she blew and made the one wish she prayed would come true.

Nana removed the lid from the cauldron, took a ladle, and poured a small amount of blood into each of the goblets. The metallic scent struck Charm's nostrils when she was served her goblet last. As she stared at the liquid softly swishing in her cup, she barely held back from heaving.

'A toast to womanhood,' Nana shouted, raising her goblet high.

'To witchhood,' Jade added with a grin. 'Time for the celebration to begin. Now drink.'

The witches brought their goblets to their lips, including Charm.

A single, choking sound drifted through the air, echoing off the walls.

Charm's hands were shaking as the smiles on the witches' faces turned to grimaces. *One. Two. Three.* The witches fell to their knees, gasping for oxygen.

Charm set her goblet, still full, down on the table and inched back, the tempo of her breaths increasing.

'What did you do?' Jade gasped, clenching the sides of her head. Charm couldn't let guilt wash over her, not now. As Charm stepped to the side, Nana reached for her leg, her hand freezing midair. Nana's face grew pale, stone-like, as did the other witches' flesh.

Aside from Charm, no one moved. The room was completely still. The witches' bodies were like statues, petrified. But somehow Charm knew they could hear her. 'My daughter,' she rasped, gritting her teeth, 'will not be a part of this. Will *not* suffer from this. And she will never know about any of this. She will not have happiness taken away from her because of my selfishness, of my thirst for power.' Her gaze drifted to her mom and Nana next, their eyes unblinking and yet still able to see. 'For what you've done, you will remain like this, *powerless*, the memories of your dark deeds spinning inside your mind forever. And that is worse than death.'

The amulet around her neck lit up, heating Charm's flesh, taking, taking, *taking*. One witch's magic right after the other flowed into the jewel. Until the women were fully drained of power. The rush of what had to be dark fae magic swam through Charm's veins, coursing fast, faster. Her eyelids fluttered as she felt the power of this magic, and she *liked* it. For a moment, a part of her was tempted to leave the amulet on, see what it could do, see what *she* could do.

No! Charm wouldn't allow herself to become corrupt like the coven.

Hands shaking, she reached for the chain and let out a satisfied sigh when she unclasped it. As soon as she took the necklace off, no magic lingered inside of her. She'd sacrificed her own power to the amulet in exchange for Sage.

Her gaze fell to the women around her, their still faces filled with horror. Tears stung her eyes as she tore the cloak from her body and let it fall to her feet. Charm then ran through the beaded curtain, up the stairs. She pushed open the door of the boulder and watched it close and seal up – no one would ever find the witches.

The amulet heated against her palm but she ignored it. She shoved it into her pocket so she wouldn't have to feel its essence. Around her, the trees murmured in the night as though they understood the emotions flowing through her, and maybe they did.

She stumbled to her car, then dropped into the driver's seat. After shutting the door, she grabbed her phone and peered at the screen.

I love you. Be careful.

Disgust for what she had to do battled relief that Sage was alive. Relief won as she texted him back. *I love you. It's over. I'll be home soon.*

She hadn't thought she would be able to stop herself from murdering her true love.

Charm reached for the dagger. Brought it to Sage's throat. He froze. Peered up at her. She screamed and begged inside her head, but the amulet wasn't listening.

You want power? Isn't that what you crave, what you feed on? What if I give you the power of the coven instead? Including mine, *she pleaded, hoping that maybe the essence of the first witch was listening.*

A scream finally tore from her and she yanked her hand away from Sage's throat.

'What the hell, Charm?' Sage rasped, his eyes wide in shock. 'You could've warned me you wanted to try something a bit different.'

'Sage!' she cried, rolling away from him while he stared at the glowing amulet resting against her collarbone. 'I need blood.'

The spell had demanded Sage's blood, but if Charm had to choose between a magic that she'd never asked for or Sage, that was no choice at all. She'd pushed back tears, knowing this was not a cute and quirky witch story. It was a brutal one, and one had to be bold to survive it.

Charm took Sage's hand, slicing a diagonal line across his palm. His throat bobbed as she pinched his hand, letting the red spill from his flesh into the cauldron. She then pricked her finger and squeezed three drops of blood atop his, watching in awe as it magically filled itself to the brim with mystery blood.

'This is real,' Sage whispered, wrapping a cloth around his hand.

'I told you it was.' She frowned, adding in the rosemary and mint to the liquid. Having made her own pact with the amulet, Charm had been allowed to confess everything to Sage.

'I know, but I was hoping it wasn't.'

Charm wished it was all a nightmare too. Sage hadn't believed her at first, but he'd still been willing to let her cut his hand.

Closing her eyes, she gripped the amulet, allowing it to take her offering, her sacrifice, as was promised. The amulet warmed, growing hotter and hotter, scalding her skin. Draining her of every last drop of magic until all that she could feel was the power of the amulet itself, its thrum.

With the power of the amulet, Charm had cast a spell of her own making, to imprison one's mind, causing the potion inside the cauldron to bubble. She'd made Sage promise to stay behind, to leave town if she didn't return by midnight.

Now her hands trembled – her whole body did. The tears pricking at her eyes finally fell. This was all over. No more lies. No more manipulation. No more magic at the cost of innocent lives.

She started the engine, reclined in her seat, and let her playlist blast through the speakers. As the quick beats of *Psycho Killer* thundered, she couldn't help but laugh as she cried.

She sang and sobbed along with the lyrics while leaving the forest and the coven behind. The cars might be found, but the witches wouldn't be.

When she pulled into a parking spot at her apartment, she didn't really know how she'd gotten there. Everything had been a blur while she'd zoned out and robotically driven home.

As she pushed the key into the lock, the door flew open to Sage's worried face. 'I wish you had answered my text earlier than you did. I was so damn worried.'

'I didn't want to get distracted.' Charm stepped inside, then closed the door behind her. She cradled his face and pulled him toward her. All she needed in that moment was to kiss him, and she didn't care if it was wrong or not. She would've burned down the entire world for him if it had been necessary to save his life.

Her lips pressed to his. 'I swear, I won't cut your hand ever again. I mean, unless it's necessary.'

'You don't have to promise me anything.' He held her tight as she wept.

Charm vowed that after today, she would truly live. She would forget the horror of what she'd done, just as the witches had so easily moved past what they had done to their daughters, the terrible payments they had demanded of them, and the hearts they'd broken in the process. However, the witches wouldn't soon forget their pasts.

And her own daughter would know that true love did exist because Charm had put her and Sage first.

A soft thrum came inside her pocket where the amulet rested, purring and satisfied with Charm and its new power.

HOUSE HUNTING

NARRELLE M. HARRIS

THE GIRL IS RUNNING FROM THE HOUSE.

The house...pursues.

The girl's freckled skin is wax-white with terror; her long, red hair is tangled across her face. Her heart crashes against her ribs, a frantic creature trying to escape ahead of her body as she runs.

She stumbles through the soft, dense carpet of pine needles as she dares to look over her shoulder. She can see the smoke rising into the treetops from the house's knobbly clay chimney. She cannot see the house's charming thatched roof, its elegant gables, or the inviting trap of its vanished front gate.

She had come to the forest to collect medicinal pine resin gathering in fat globules on damaged bark and in the grains of broken branches. She should not have let herself be distracted by wildflowers – phlox and lily of the valley, sweet woodruff and Jacob's ladder, witch alder and wintergreen. She should not have entered the garden through the gap, where a gate once hung, and plucked flowers from a bed that only seemed neglected.

She meant no harm, but harm was done. Offence taken. The crackling cry of 'thief!' had commanded her startled attention. The accusation, 'witch!', rattled from the house's wooden walls.

The windows blinked and then glared.

'Rosheen,' hissed the door as the house heaved up, up, up.

The girl is running from the house that somehow knows her name; read it from her thoughts or panting breath.

The angry house is running after her.

Across the pine forest, too far for Rosheen's cries to penetrate the green, a girl – another girl – is running from a (different) house.

Her skin is smooth and brown; her brown eyes are wide and wild. Her thick, dark, braided hair, dyed with streaks of blue and pink, streams behind her as she flees, breaking free as it habitually does from the hair elastics she is always losing.

The girl staggers over splayed pine cones that have shed their seeds, and she wishes, in the second it takes to catch her breath, that she had not given in to her besetting sin, known to kill cats, and it may yet kill her.

Thirst for knowledge led her into the woods, all alone, and fate had guided her to the little wooden house. Her own impetuousness led her up the lopsided steps and through the door that sagged ajar. She lit one match from her store that usually lit incense at home, or in the temple, but it illuminated little here. She hadn't lit another.

The cold kitchen full of webs and weeds held no interest; no. She had seen the abandoned parlour and felt how the space yearned to be filled. She stepped over the threshold onto threadbare carpet and was captivated by its contents.

Curiosity guided her eyes as she examined the pictures, in which long grass and bushes seemed to wriggle when she looked away and painted clouds scudded across the patina of an aging blue sky and unseen things kept watch. It directed her hands to caress cups and candleholders, crumbling lace doilies and moth-eaten woollen tapestries. *I wonder what's inside,* it whispered to her, urging her to carefully open ancient books bound in curious leather.

Look in the mirror, Rikisha, it breathed and Rikisha obeyed the whim, as always.

A thing with teeth looked back. As Rikisha recoiled, gnarled, brittle fingers emerged from the glass and closed around her wrist.

Snoop!

Rikisha twisted, pivoted, lunged, broke that gnarled grip with dexterity that would make her basketball coach proud, and ran with speed to astonish her track coach.

Rikisha wishes, between panting breaths, that she was made some other way, with a gentle, stay-at-home, not-at-all-nosy spirit.

Who is she kidding? She knows herself, and that she will never be, or ever want to be, anyone but herself. At the same time, she really, really hopes she doesn't die today.

She looks over her shoulder. Through the trees she sees it.

The house. It's coming.

A girl is sprinting through the forest. She does not look behind.

She knows the house is gaining on her.

She's afraid, but the fear isn't as strong as the rage. That house *lied*.

Her day began all Little Red Riding Hood – a shortcut through the woods to bring flowers and lemon *polvorones* to her Abuela. After losing her path, she became Gretel without a trail of crumbs, following the promise of a friendly puff of smoke.

It ended all Goldilocks, though her hair is neither curly nor golden.

She had done no harm; only sought shelter so she could think what to do, without phone reception or any idea how her short walk had become so long and confusing. The friendly chimney smoke led her to a little house with a bright red door and white lace curtains. No-one answered her knock, and she even self-consciously called out, but the only reply was the cheery door swinging open.

The running girl is angry that the house welcomed her like that. That it *tricked* her like that. She's angry that the kitchen smelled of baking bread and the crisp red apples all heaped in a basket. She's angry that she's left Abuela's flowers on the homely wooden table, where she sat to regroup.

Not wanting to eat the pretty red apples without permission, she had put the flowers down and unwrapped the biscuits from their cloth and ribbon to mollify her hunger. The cronch, cronch, cronch of them was loud, *loud*, **loud** inside her head, so she had put her hearing aids in her pocket. It was a welcome relief, taking the pressure from behind and inside of her ears; and she said *Aaaaaaaaahhhh*, like Abuela did when she took off her walking shoes and wriggled her toes. Realising she'd eaten all the biscuits, she folded the white cloth and red ribbon and put them in her other pocket.

Thirst hit her then, but on the table was a jug of clear, fresh water; beside it, a wooden cup.

Surely a mouthful of water would not trespass too badly on absent hospitality?

In retrospect, this was her mistake. Not the water, but the naïve trust.

As she swallowed the cool, delicious water, the floorboards had begun to vibrate; the curtains to swish wildly inside the house. Muted, distant sounds beat on her eardrums, which were not built for fully deciphering them.

Words appeared, scratched into the surface of the table.

YOU DARE TO TAKE FROM ME?

The chair fell as Rosa pushed away from the words.

YOU DARE, ROSA?

Rosa ran, leaving flowers behind; leaving the hearing aids in her pocket.

She ran, afraid, then angry, with no path to follow, only the shaking of the forest floor to warn her of pursuit.

She doesn't sense the movement of what could be wild animals, also running in fear through the woods. She is too intent on fleeing to see the shadows or movement of the trees. She's too busy wondering how close the traitorous cottage is to her heels.

Rosa bursts into a tiny clearing, and halts abruptly. Through the soles of her feet, she feels the house behind her, but something just as heavy and relentless to her right; another to her left. She sees the pine trees trembling. Some unintelligible sound scuffs against her inner ear.

Wild things, she thinks, her feet and heart and rage all stopping at once.

But then she sees a girl with red hair stagger into the clearing from the right; and one second later, from the left, a girl with blue and pink hair.

And though she can't hear the houses, Rosa can see them through the trees.

On the right: a house with a thatched roof bobbing impossibly through the tall, thin pines towards them. No house should be able to navigate the gaps between the trunks, but this one shimmers and insinuates itself ever closer.

On the left: another house, narrower and taller, strobing through the trees – there/not/there/not/there.

The houses, Rosa sees, are strutting on giant chicken legs. It is almost funny except they have the feet of raptors and they scratch furrows in the ground as they inexorably close in.

Rosa turns to seek the house that is chasing her. It flickers but she knows it's close by the scent of wood smoke and burning bread.

She turns back, hoping to see escape, but suddenly finds the other two girls are right in front of her, their eyes open wide, their mouths moving too fast to read. The panic is obvious, the emphatic gestures, less so.

Rosa grabs her hearing aids and, with trembling fingers, hooks them into place. The sudden, garbled noise doesn't help.

'Stop!' she shouts. 'One at a time!'

Which is probably how they will die; though perhaps they will vanish all at once. The future is full of books devoted to their disappearance, she thinks.

'Do you know a way out?' asks the brown girl with blue and pink hair.

'No,' says Rosa.

'What can we do?' asks the red-head, her white skin flushed pink from running.

'I don't know,' Rosa confesses. She is peering at these girls, reading signs from their lips and faces and bodies as well as their sounds.

A tree trunk cracks somewhere beyond the three of them; the sound swells around them so they can't tell which house is getting closer.

'How can there be *three* of them?' demands the brown girl.

'Fairy tales,' says Rosa, because they have informed her entire day. 'Rules of three.'

'Three houses,' says the brown girl thoughtfully.

'Three bears, three pigs, three billy goats,' says the white girl.

'Three witches. Like in Macbeth,' says the brown girl.

'Maybe we get three guesses,' replies Rosa.

'Or three wishes,' says the white girl, a light in her eyes. 'Hi. I'm Rosheen.'

'Rikisha,' says the brown girl.

'Rosa,' says Rosa. 'Three girls. Three Musketeers.'

The houses are circling them. Hunting them.

'What do you have on you?' Rikisha asks.

Rosheen wears a pouch at her waist. From it, she pulls out flowers, seeds and cuttings wrapped in wax paper, and then the pocket knife she had used to collect greenery.

Rosa produces the piece of cloth and ribbon and shakes out the *polvorón* crumbs.

From her pockets, Rikisha produces a book of matches and nine hair elastics.

'What can we do with these?' Rikisha asks.

'I know.' Rosheen grins.

The houses flicker closer, but urgency births invention. A few quick words and gestures, and Rosa knows her part. She uses the knife to tear her shirt for two more cloth squares, then gives the knife back to Rosheen. Then she gathers dry pine needles and piles them on each of the three squares of cloth.

Rikisha rapidly finds three good, solid stones, as aerodynamically round as possible.

Rosheen returns with numerous, substantial lumps of sticky pine resin, which she smears over the stones before placing a large piece of resin in each square of cloth with the pine needles.

The houses are coming closer.

Rosheen places stalks and flowers and seeds in each parcel. They secure the cloths closed over the resin-smeared stones with the hair bands, three on each. Rosheen tucks small pieces of resin under the elastic, too.

The girls exchange glances. No words now, only fierce grins, a nod.

Three houses. Three girls. And they will huff and they will puff and they'll...

The thatched house finally flickers into the clearing; and then the tall house; and then the one with the red door. They loom and lean and their shutters clatter, like cruel laughter.

Rikisha lights a match and sets it to one cloth; two; three.

The densely packed needles and the resin burn.

The girls are running.

The girls are running *towards* the houses.

Rosheen seems ethereal but she is a herbalist – some kind of modern hedge witch – and robust from her exploration of the great outdoors. When she throws the stone wrapped in burning resin, it rises up in a neat arc and falls beautifully on the thatched roof. The smoke streaming off it smells of pine and of the poisonous roots of lily of the valley that she had collected in the woods.

The house screams. It runs and crashes into the pine trees. And the roof burns and burns and burns.

Rikisha is fast and bold and athletic, and she has impeccable aim with her strong left arm. Her burning stone flies through the sagging front door of the tall, wooden house full of cobwebs and crumbling, desiccated furnishings. The wallpaper catches fire first. With a great *whoomf*, the wall beneath it too, then the ceiling.

The house screams and it twists wildly, trying to shake out the fire like shaking out a matchstick, but it only sends embers into cobwebs and dust. Particles bloom into fire and then so do the rugs, the paintings, the old doilies.

The mirror. That scream is piercing.

The noise is loud and confusing. Rosa flinches from it. But she lives in worlds of both silence and sound, and she can trade one for the other. She chooses silence now, flinging aside her hearing aids and running up close to the cruel house.

She throws her burning stone through its lying windows and when the billowing curtains are eaten by flames, she's not sorry. She can see the kitchen that pretended to be sanctuary, and the stone has landed on that homely wooden table, right next to the basket of apples. The table seems too stolid to burn easily, but the basket flickers to flaming life and that fuels the fire enough.

The table burns.

The house is very possibly screaming, but Rosa is in blissful silence so she just watches that gaslighting bastard of a house lurch in a panic.

Rosa, Rosheen, Rikisha meet, back-to-back, in the centre of the clearing. The burning houses crash into the trees, and into each other, on their panicky raptor feet.

Then, flicker, flicker, flicker, the houses are gone.

Rosa feels her friends' bodies shift against her back. Rikisha moves in front of her, smiles, waves, then holds out her hand. Rosa's hearing aids are in her palm. One is broken, wires adrift, but the other seems intact, though covered in dirt. Rosa puts them in her pocket. She's not putting a dirty aid in her ear.

Rikisha seems to understand. She nods and gives Rosa the thumbs-up. Rosheen comes into view then. She listens as Rikisha explains that Rosa can't hear right now. Rosheen nods too. She makes sure Rosa can see her face before she mouths, 'Home?'

Rosa shrugs. She doesn't know where home is from here.

'I know the way,' says Rosheen's mouth.

'I think,' says Rikisha's mouth, 'Your Nan is my neighbour. We can take you.'

Her dear Abuela. She has always warned Rosa about shortcuts through the forest. Now Rosa knows why.

'Thank you,' she signs to them, making the shape of the words.

And then there are three girls, three Musketeers, three friends, walking out of the forest.

They will do great things, these roses three, and every year they will mark their origin story with a toast.

To the house hunters.

SOLACE IN A DYING HOUR

GREG HERREN

MADELEINE CHAISSON OPENED HER EYES AND KNEW THAT THE NEXT TIME she shut them would be the last.

She cocked her head to listen. Even amongst those few (some say blessed, others cursed) who could hear them, most would describe the strange sounds they made as they danced about the dark, still waters as whistling. But Madeleine was special, different, not like the others.

She heard them clearly. She knew they weren't whistling. They were *singing*.

But the sound she heard now was just the gulls over Bayou St Ferdinand shrieking as they swooped and flapped their wings looking for morsels of food.

Dirty scavengers, she thought with a scowl. She hated the gulls; had since she was a little girl growing up in this very house.

How much gull shit had she cleaned off the dock during her long lifetime? Papa would backhand her if he saw any of the dried white splotches with black pellets on the dock when he brought the boat back in from a day shrimping out in the Gulf.

'It rots the wood, you lazy *cochon,*' he'd say in his sing-song southeast Louisiana Cajun accent while she rubbed her stinging cheek. 'And who will have to rebuild the damned thing when it collapses? Don't I already work hard to keep you clothed and fed?'

Even with him years in his grave, after she began wondering if that was even true, she'd still take the bucket out and scrub the gull shit from the weathered old wood.

If I were a witch like they always said, I could have snapped my fingers and cleaned it, she thought with a snort.

Back when she could still get out of bed without help, she'd liked watching the damned birds from her window, the water's surface hidden behind the levee, always hoping one or more would fly too close to the rippled murky water of the bayou and get snatched from the air by a silent alligator drifting on the surface.

The gulls always disappeared when the singing started.

The last golden light of the day was fading. She'd dozed off during *Days of Our Lives* again. She retrieved the remote control for the enormous television her grandson Remy had mounted on the wall for her months – it seemed like years but it was just before Thanksgiving, wasn't it? – ago so she didn't have to get out of bed and use the walker to go into the living room. She'd borne her grandson's generosity with bad grace at the time, but now she was grateful for the convenience and ease. Back then, she wasn't willing to accept she'd grown feeble, and having something the size of a drive-in movie screen on her bedroom wall in place of her faded wedding pictures so she wouldn't even have to get out of bed to watch her stories seemed like nothing but pure laziness.

And no one was going to say Marie-Madeleine Jeanne delaHoussaye Chaisson had grown lazy before she died, thank you very much.

She could bear being thought a witch, but not lazy.

Wait – was that–?

She listened, but again only heard the gulls' cries. Not yet, then.

She wasn't afraid of dying, but not for any reason her parish priest Father Brad might have thought. She had seen the world she grew up in change and become nothing more than a distant memory as faded as her wedding pictures – which Remy had thoughtfully rehung alongside the big screen where some judge was making an *I-don't-think-so* face to the trashy-looking people arguing about a kidnapped dog and a pick-up truck's busted out windshield. She'd thought many times over the decades that her time was over; she'd waited for the spark that kept her heart beating to finally die away. She'd waited, listening…

The air was cold on her hand as she pressed the mute button and the judge was cut off mid-insult.

Her hearing wasn't as good as it used to be, but she knew she'd hear them singing when it was time. The sound on that big flat monster on her wall might have to be at a level that could deafen someone younger so she could hear what Marlena and Roman were up to, but the singing?

She could hear *le feu follet* over a category three hurricane.

Let everyone else think the swamp fairies were nothing more than a legend, a tale of unshriven souls haunting the wicked, an old story meant to scare children into obedience. Madeleine knew better.

Madeleine knew they were real.

She shivered and slid her hand back beneath her warm blankets and worn quilts. It was cold for Carnival. There had been a few weeks of false spring back in early February – maybe it was longer ago, she wasn't sure – but she knew today was Lundi Gras so tomorrow was Mardi Gras. Someone was in the living room – they'd never leave her completely alone now that it was just a matter of time – but there was a parade tonight over in Avignon, and no delaHoussaye or Chaisson missed a parade if they could help it, sometimes driving all the way into New Orleans for the big ones.

She watched dust motes dancing through that last fading ray of sunlight. Her house wasn't built for cold weather – no house in south Louisiana was – and the damp cold had always gone right to her bones and her joints. The heat was still running – the wall calendar from the Avignon Bank was right over the vent, and the *February* page danced in the hot air. That nice lady on the New Orleans news channel – the one with the pretty red hair whose name she could never remember – was predicting a hard freeze, even down here on the bayou. It was supposed to get down into the low twenties/high teens in New Orleans on Fat Tuesday. She thought this must surely be a sign that the end times were near. The winters kept getting colder as she got older. That Fat Tuesday the year after Katrina had been warm as summer. She could count on one hand the times it got that cold when she was younger. That red-headed lady said last night a cold rain would come first and bring the hard freeze with it.

'Maybe even snow,' she'd said in a hushed, shocked voice, her eyes widened as she looked directly into the camera lens.

Snow in south Louisiana!

It never used to snow in southeastern Louisiana. Why, snow used to be so rare down here that on those scarce occasions it did happen, it was memorable and talked about for years. But now she could think of at least three times in the last twenty years it had snowed in New Orleans. Those snows never made it down here, no, not to Redemption Parish, but this storm – that weather woman claimed that even the bayous could freeze over.

Maybe there *was* something to her great-granddaughter's endless babbling about climate change after all.

Not that Madeleine would ever tell her – *them* – that, of course. The shaved sides of their head were bad enough, all those piercings and tattoos and saying they were "nonbinary.". *We used to call them tomboys,* Madeleine had thought as her great-grandbaby – who insisted everyone call them Blaine now – explained to her patiently what "nonbinary" meant. Madeleine didn't quite understand but she–*they* seemed to be a lot happier than they had been when their mother used to push them into dresses and put bows in their hair and tried getting them to wear make-up. Blaine's mother Shelby had always dreamed of having a little girl, wanting a live doll to dress up and play with ever since she'd learned how to talk and walk and jump.

Well, man plans but God laughs, like her grandmeré used to say.

I was born during a hurricane and will die in a freeze, she thought.

They'd named her after that hurricane, too. Hurricane Madeleine. Her daddy used to call her that sometimes when he was a little too deep into his whiskey. *Here comes Hurricane Madeleine,* he'd say and pour himself another glass, laughing, the humor even reaching his coal-black eyes the way it never did when he wasn't drinking. *Make me something to eat, Hurricane Madeleine, I need something to soak up this good whiskey.*

She would, always watching his eyes. When they flattened…that was when the trouble would come.

She hadn't thought about Papa in years. He'd died when she was in her thirties – an old maid taking care of her daddy like a good daughter should – while her younger brothers and sisters got married and moved away and had children of their own. After Papa died, she knew people thought – nasty mean gossips, every last one of them bitches – Antoine Chaisson had married her for the house, the dock and the shrimp boat. He was barely twenty-two and she was almost thirty-four, old years before her time, cooking and cleaning and taking care of her old bastard of a father who took his own sweet time a-dying. Toine could have had any of the pretty girls in the parish, but he chose her.

And sometimes when he had too much whiskey, Toine did have some of those pretty girls. She didn't care, as long as he came home, and he always did, tail between his legs and sorry, with that hangdog look on his handsome face. She never said a word, even when her kids got old enough to know what was going on and say something ugly to her about their daddy.

Her oldest, Aimee, and the two younger ones had confronted her over a cast iron pot of gumbo as she cut up chicken thighs and tossed the chunks in the pot. They'd told her what she already knew, had always known, Aimee's hands on her hips and her face flushed with anger. 'What's between your daddy and me is between your daddy and me,' she'd snapped, and it had never come up again.

Toine hadn't lived much longer, come to think of it. She'd buried her husband the way she'd buried her father, not shedding a tear as friends and relatives whispered their love and condolences to her, her face a rigid mask. She'd come back to her little house along the bayou and sold the shrimp boat and raised her kids, sent them out into the world with a blessing and her love, knowing neither would shield them from pain and suffering and death.

Death would not, could not, be denied.

She listened for the singing.

Last night, after the kids and grandkids and great-grandkids came by after Mass, after they'd all kissed her brow and said nice things to her before heading home, she'd heard the singing out in the swamp beyond the far bank of the bayou, deep in the swamp. As her eyes closed in sleep, she'd smiled. They were coming, and this time they were coming for her.

She had lived a long life filled with pain but there had been love and joy and laughter, too. But now that she was dying it was hard to remember anything besides the pain. Her own maman had told her, when she was a little girl, that pain was something to endure, a trial sent by God to see if his tests would change who you were. Father Dwight told her the same when she was a little girl taking Catechism and getting ready for her confirmation. She'd taken that to heart. Pain and suffering were a test from God, so endure it and get through to the other side before forgetting it. Wasn't it better to only remember the happy things?

But now, she could barely remember those happy times. The other things – the pain, the hurt, the agony – were in the way.

She closed her eyes. She wouldn't think about that. She couldn't. That wasn't what she wanted on her mind when she died.

The corners of her mouth moved slightly up. There – she could hear it at last. It was very faint and very far away, but she knew it was them.

The spirits of the unshriven, the souls of the unconfessed.

She wondered if anyone would see the lights?

It sounded different this time. She'd heard them singing since she was a little girl, but it was always for someone else, not her. If asked to explain how the singing was different this time, how she could tell, she wouldn't have been able to put it into words. She just *knew,* and that was all that mattered, really. She'd always been special, *different,* ever since she was small, helping her mama cook and clean and take care of all the children. There was always something about her others could see, sometimes commenting on it to Maman and Papa in hushed whispers that sounded different than the usual lies adults told other adults about their children. They whispered when they talked about her difference, like they were afraid she would hear them. *And do what?* She'd always wondered, as their voices rang in her ears no matter how quietly they spoke. *What do they think I can do?*

People have always said the Delahoussayes have witch blood running through the family tree...can she see things; can she find things that are lost?...you know Remy's great-great-grandmother was hanged for it back in New Orleans before the Americans came...

And when they took the old pick-up truck into town to go to the Piggly Wiggly to get the things they couldn't catch, hunt or grow, people made the sign against the evil eye behind her back. She could see them doing it as she walked past them behind Maman's cart, wishing and wondering what they thought she was besides a little girl.

Am I a witch? She'd asked her grandmother Delahoussaye once. *Is that why everyone is afraid of me?*

Ignore those fools, the old woman had said, smelling of vanilla extract and lavender and tobacco. *They wouldn't know a witch if she cursed them right to their faces.*

She didn't remember how old she was the first time she saw the lights out in the swamp, bobbing and dancing among the ancient cypress trees, the live oaks dripping with gray beards of Spanish moss. She'd climbed up on the levee along the banks of the bayou to see them better. Their lights were beautiful, so pristine and clean and pure, and all differently colored; purples and blues and greens and pinks and reds and yellows and nearly every color in her precious box of Crayolas she'd bought with the pennies she saved at the Woolworth's in Avignon.

Singing, not whistling. And she knew this time they were singing for her.

Madeleine had lived a long and full life in her little house alongside Bayou St. Ferdinand. She'd been born in the house, the eldest of eight, all born in rapid succession, some no further apart than ten months. She'd been old for as long as she could remember, having to take care of the babies and help her mother around the house, which was far too small for ten people to be living in. But her father was a shrimper, and shrimping was hard work that paid far too little for those who caught the afternoon or evening meal for tourists or rich people in New Orleans.

She shifted under the covers. She could feel the cold air on her exposed face. She wouldn't be getting out of this bed again. Her time was coming, and she just hoped there was enough time for Father Brad to make it to give her the last rites. There were things she'd never confessed, to Father Brad or any of the many priests the Archdiocese in New Orleans had exiled out here to remote Redemption Parish. They didn't get the Church's best and brightest out here. One of them had told her, so many years ago she couldn't remember his name or his face, anything other than he always smelled like peppermints and Menthol cigarettes, that being sent to this remote out-of-the-way parish was a punishment of sorts. 'Anyone with a future in the church,' he'd said, bitterness plain on his face and in his voice, 'would never get sent to a backwater like this.'

Backwater! That one had never adjusted to life in Redemption Parish and didn't last long.

Sometimes she wondered where that priest with his hard peppermint candies and Newport cigarettes wound up when he left Our Lady of the Waters. Once she'd known, but her mind was one of those many things that didn't work the same way it used to.

It was the one before him she could never forget no matter how he tried.

Father Tony, with his wicked deep blue eyes the color of the Gulf where the water gets deep, his cleft chin and deep dimples, his big white straight teeth and curly dark hair. Tony Delvecchio, Italian by name and look, with his swarthy skin and handsome face, the way his razor stubble gave his cheeks and chin a bluish tint when you looked at him just right. Oh, he'd been a charmer, hadn't he? All the women in the parish fawned on him, showering him with attention and food and invitations, and all the while–

She cocked her head to one side. They were getting louder, coming closer.

How old was she when she'd first heard them?

A little girl, she couldn't be sure how old, really – her memory played games with her now, the way she'd played kick-the-can when she was a little girl – but it was when her Maman's last baby, her last sister, was dying. Baby Esmé had been puny, had come early after a hard pregnancy for their mother, and no one thought she'd live to see her first birthday. They hadn't let Madeleine hold her – that was how she knew something was *wrong* with Baby Esmé, the house filled with hushed whispers, and Grandmeré had come to stay with them, to cook and clean and take care of everyone.

Something was wrong with Maman, too.

Maman never got out of that bed again.

The first time she'd heard them singing outside the house was when Baby Esmé was maybe a week old – couldn't have been much older than that. No one else in the house seemed to hear the beautiful noises. She'd gone to the living room window to look out at the black still water of the bayou. She saw the lights – one yellow, one blue, one green – floating and dancing above the bayou surface, the ancient and bent swamp oaks dripping Spanish moss from their branches, the strange glowing lights staining the gray curly beards with their bright happy colors. The lights were beautiful, and she loved the way they whispered, singing dulcet tones so clear and pure they brought tears to her eyes. She reached for them, her chubby hand stopped by the wire screen, and she knew, somehow, they were waiting, but not for her.

She could almost hear them making words, words that were also filled with light and magic.

Not your time, they sang-whispered to her, *not your time, pretty girl.*

She knew everyone was worried that the baby would die. Esmé struggled for every breath she took, sometimes the inhalation so small and shallow her little chest barely moved, and her lips were tinged with blue. The doctor over at the big hospital in Avignon wanted them to bring her in, wanted to keep her overnight, run tests and poke and prod her, but Maman wanted Madame Couchon, the old woman from deep in the swamp, the one everyone whispered was a witch and made the sign against the evil eye whenever they said her name. Grandmére crossed herself and clicked her rosary beads the entire time the old witch was in with Maman working her spells and magics, but even the swamp witch and her dark powers couldn't save Esmé.

Madeleine had walked out onto the front porch as the singing got louder, looking out past the levee into the swamp.

'You hear them?' Madame Couchon, the old witch, was smoking a pipe on a corner of the porch, hidden away from the light coming through the blinds on the front window.

Madeleine wrinkled her nose. The old woman smelled sour – sweat and smoke and something else, something musky and dark Madeleine didn't like – but she took another tentative step toward her. 'You hear them, too?'

'Aye and can see them.' The old woman's reddened eyes almost glowing at her in the shadows. 'They're called *le feu follet*. Do you know what that means, little girl?'

'Foo fuh-lay?' she'd repeated slowly.

'The swamp fairies,' the old woman cackled. 'Babies and children and those souls who died before making themselves right with God – they become spirits in the swamp, dancing lights who sing and whistle and try to charm us into joining them out there in the water, so we will drown and join them.' She inclined her head towards the window. 'They come for those unshriven souls, those who don't make their peace with God or them that are too young to be confirmed in God's light. That's why I knew there was no hope for your sister. I saw them out there as I came up the walk, whistling for her.' She coughed out blue smoke, the cough wet and phlegmy. 'There's no hope for little Esmé.' Her eyes seemed to glow as Madeleine hopped down from the porch and saw them.

There were three lights that time – yellow and green and blue. They hovered and danced on the other side of the bayou, over the swamp, their singing now forming words – not in English or Cajun French, but some other language Madeleine somehow understood.

Esme, come dance with us, come join us, it's ever so much fun out here…

And Madeleine felt the urge, the need, to climb the earthen levee, swim over to the other side, and join them herself. Their song tugged at her soul, got inside her head, filled her with a longing she'd never felt before – she started to move but the old witch grabbed her arm, surprisingly strong for someone so old and bent and weary.

'No, Madeleine,' she said, her voice strong, firm, warning, 'You cannot go out there, you cannot join them without dying yourself.'

She struggled, but the claw-like hand would not shake free.

Esmé died later that night.

Maman only lasted another week.

Madeleine hadn't thought about Esmé in years, or the little funeral casket her little body was placed in before it was put into the family tomb. She could feel her father's arm heavy around their shoulders, still reeking of shrimp and sea underneath the soap and Vitalis he'd greased his thick blue-black hair into place with, the Old Navy he'd splashed on. 'You're going to have to be the lady of the house now, Maddie,' he'd whispered. 'I can't raise them babies alone.'

The lights hadn't come for Maman. Come morning she was still and cold and stiff in her bed.

Madeleine shifted under her covers, trying to find a more comfortable way to rest her body.

You remember what you did to Papa? Will you tell a priest at long last what you did?

'Confession isn't a get-out-of-jail-free card,' Father Tony – was it him? She couldn't be sure – had told her. 'And the last rites won't keep you from hell, either, Mrs Chaisson. You must confess your sins, do penance, atone, get right with God.' He fixed his eyes on her. 'You have to truly be sorry for your sins.'

You remember what you did to Father Tony?

But it wasn't Father Tony who said that; it had been Father Bill. She'd asked him when she'd first taken to her bed back – was it before Thanksgiving? Christmas? The worst part of getting old was questioning her mind all the time – *whenever* it was, she'd asked him about God and forgiveness. She'd asked when he brought her the sacrament, prayed with her that first Sunday she'd not been able to make it to Our Lady of the Waters. Father Bill was her favorite of the priests banished to Redemption Parish throughout her long life. He'd told her about his unchristian lusts for other men, how he'd prayed to God and been shown a sign that it was a calling, a test of his faith, and how once he'd given himself to God he'd found the strength to resist those urges, those whispers of the devil into his ear about the sins of the flesh and the pleasures to be found in the arms of other men. He even admitted to her that sometimes, *sometimes,* his flesh was weak and he couldn't pray the desires away, so he'd wear jeans and a tight T-shirt and visit the dens of iniquity in the French Quarter, where there were any number of sinners to choose from with which to slake his unholy passions and desires and needs. 'God always knows, and God is always ready to forgive, Mrs Chaisson,' he'd said, his greenish-blue eyes intense as they peered into hers, 'but the spirit must be willing, and the spirit must be *sorry.'*

She would have confessed to him then, spilt all the secrets burdening her soul and prostrated herself before God…but she wasn't *sorry,* was she?

God could see into her heart and would know she would do what she'd done again, without question or hesitation.

The mean-spirited old gossipy bitches of Redemption Parish thought Toine had married her for the house and Papa's shrimp boat. Toine's inability to keep his pants zipped certainly helped fuel those stories and rumors. They knew Papa was cruel and violent and smacked all of them – even Maman – around when the mood struck. But what they didn't know was that when Papa whispered that to her at the cemetery about being the woman of the house, he'd meant it in every way. Only eleven, she hadn't started bleeding yet, but that didn't matter to Papa.

Madeleine closed her eyes. She hadn't thought about this in years, so many years. So many years she'd closed her eyes and shut that door in her mind, locking the memories of Papa and what he'd done away to never be discussed again. The unclean feeling washed over her again for the first time in how many years since Papa had been put to rest in the tomb next to Maman, the way he'd made her come to his bed at night and when he'd had his fill of her, shoved her out onto the floor like so much garbage so she could creep back in the night to the bedroom she shared with her little sisters, his smell still on her and thick in her nostrils. How she hated Papa, prayed for God to kill him, prayed for the spirits in the swamp – *le feu follet* – to come take him away and save her from the years she spent there in that little house, washing his clothes and making his meals, taking his seed on the nights when he wanted her and sending her thanks to the Blessed Virgin on the nights when he didn't. She learned how much whiskey would put him to sleep and how much would make him lose his appetite for her. How many times had she climbed up onto the levee and looked into the black water of the bayou, and thought about weighting herself and jumping in?

Unclean, so unclean, she was filth in the eyes of God.

They didn't know how Toine saved her, how the handsome young man had looked past her bent body and broken spirit and saw something there he could love, found something worth loving inside of her.

They didn't know Papa wouldn't allow it. The gossips never knew that part, or any of the parts that mattered. They weren't there the night Papa threw Toine out of the house, threatening to kill him if he came near Madeleine again…

Because she was his.

They didn't know she went out to the levee that night and called them, singing to them the words she always heard them singing to her when they came to claim the souls of the unbaptized and the unshriven, or that she felt her own power rising within her as the lights began bobbing and weaving and dancing out over the swamp. Those bitches never knew what she was capable of, that *le feu follet* would come when she called for them, that she could summon them whenever she wanted—

—and they would do her bidding.

She never knew whether Toine ever suspected. There was no autopsy because no one cared that an old shrimper who lived down on the bayou died suddenly in his sleep. An autopsy wouldn't have shown anything, anyway. The spirits, the fairies, the lights had taken his soul after showing her their faces.

They were beautiful. Terrifying and ferocious, yet beautiful, despite the sharpness of their teeth and the intensity of their eyes. But their purity, the stunning magnificence of their colors, the way their wings reflected rainbows in the cold light from the moon, moved her, made her want to join them and be beautiful and free, dancing and singing out in the swamp while watching and waiting for another soul on which to feast. Madame Couchon hadn't been right, of course – the old witch knew far less than she believed she did – *le feu follet* weren't the souls of the unshriven and unbaptized; they *fed* on those souls. She watched as they fed on her father's after she'd put the rat poison in his gumbo, which she'd thrown into the bayou once he'd gone to bed.

When they had finished their feast, they'd wanted her to join them out there, and she'd held them off with a promise...that it wasn't time for her yet.

Father Tony.

She'd never confessed about Father Tony, either. She wasn't sure how great the sin was for her to continue hearing mass and taking the Eucharist with the sin of her father's death on her soul, but Father Tony was strict and stern, despite how handsome he was. He *knew* how handsome he was, the effect his dark olive face and blue-black hair and dark eyes and broad shoulders had on the women of the parish, he made much of them and flirted and teased but he was strict, he was stern and he–

He was the worst of sinners.

She had believed her grandson Peter when he told her the truth, his voice quiet and shaking with the shame of it all. Peter was only thirteen, his voice cracking and hair sprouting under his arms and on his calves, shooting up five inches almost overnight and becoming almost another person from the laughing little boy she'd loved so much. Peter wasn't a handsome boy, hadn't even been a pretty baby, if she was honest. She never understood why her daughter Amelia had married such an ugly man with the halitosis and reddish flaking patches on his arms and legs, and poor little Petey was the spitting image of his ugly father. She knew the other kids were mean to him and he didn't have many friends. He wasn't athletic and didn't like to fish and preferred to hole up with a library book than do anything vigorous. He was smart – wasn't he a doctor now, over at University Medical over in New Orleans? – but Father Tony had taken a shine to the boy, and mentored him. She thought he might even be destined for the church himself until that afternoon when he rode his bicycle over and with tears in his watery blue eyes and a halt in his voice told her what Father Tony actually meant by "taking an interest" in the boy.

That was the only other time she'd called them, her voice angry with the righteous fury of a grandmother protecting a child. There had been no rat poison that time, of course. Her voice shaking with a calm rage, she'd called some of the family men-folk over and told them – not everything, but enough – and they'd taken care of Father Tony. They'd taken one of the shrimp boats out, but not before bringing him to her and leaving him alone on the deck of the boat, a gasoline-soaked rag stuffed in his mouth, hands and feet bound. She'd climbed on board and knelt down beside him, his face bloody and battered, his now bloodshot eyes almost swollen shut, looking at her pleading for mercy. She knew he was dying, sensed it with whatever that power was inside of her that drew the singing lights to her, that same power that told her what to do with Papa.

She stood up and called them, singing in that strange language of theirs that she wasn't sure she understood, and the lights came to her again, came for Father Tony's soul and feasted upon it.

Later, Peter's father and her eldest son took the boat out, down the bayou and through the wetlands and marshes out to sea in the Gulf. The body was weighted, dropped overboard and no one ever saw Father Tony again. There was talk for a while about what happened to the handsome priest, but people often disappeared from Redemption Parish and no one ever paid too much mind to it. Peter got better, too, once the priest was gone: he lost his stammer and his skin cleared up and he went off to school and became a surgeon, the most successful of all her family, the one everyone now pointed to and used as an example.

She could still see the pain in his eyes.

It was dark now, and she could hear them coming for her. It was, at long last, her time. Would they eat her soul, she wondered, the way they'd feasted upon her father's and Father Tony's? There was time, she thought, if she could shout loud enough, maybe Father Brad could get here in time, give her the last rites, allow her to give her final confession and ask God's forgiveness, to repent of what she had done to the two men who'd hurt her the most.

She turned her head to the window. She could see their faces – the sharp teeth, the intense eyes, the beating wings casting rainbows – and was no longer afraid.

No, she wasn't sorry for what she had done, would never be sorry. She felt it happening, she felt her soul beginning to separate from her body.

Her hands were glowing now, a soft and lovely warm, pale red.

She was one of them, and now it was time for her to rejoin them.

Her soul began to sing as her body died.

PAPERWEIGHT

EUGEN BACON & CLARE E. RHODEN

J's MIND WAS FULL OF THE LIBRARIAN HE WAS OBSESSED WITH A LONG TIME.

Her name was Rukia. She sometimes came to Laneway, the café and croissanterie where he temped after hours, and on weekends. It was located near the corner of Coolangatta Terrace – between Notebook, the flower shop with velvet green décor, and Briggs, the real estate joint that announced five-bedders in ads that showed charismatic gardens and oceanic pools in resort style.

At Laneway, J stood behind a sign that said *Order Here*, and Rukia did. You'd think a girl like her would order a skinny decaf mocha, but no. It was always filtered Odyssey coffee, smashed avocado on toast, and wild organic juice that had cloves and turmeric in it.

She was some girl, that Rukia. Name like a gem and eyes to match. Emerald? Sapphire? Topaz? He never could say. His heart smashed in that avo; his stupid, wild organic heart, and the cloves and the turmeric almost stopped his breath. Felt like she had a superpower, the way her eyes lit him up.

He didn't make moves on her at the croissanterie, not with hawk-eyed Marg at his elbow, in his face, peeking up his bum. Still, he got away with things. He gave Rukia the right change and never charged an extra item for himself, as he did with other customers. How was he supposed to otherwise afford lunch?

He didn't make moves on her at the Uniting Church, either, where he sometimes tailed her from a distance. She worked at the library that folk rumoured had an ancient gemstone in it – something called a Bury Paperweight – that had intrigued J ever since he overheard Rukia and her colleague whisper about it.

The girl, Prana, she had a mouth on her. It was the first time Rukia had tagged *anything* along. Well, any*one*, but Prana could well be a thing the way she annoyed J. He wanted alone time with Rukia. He wasn't asking for a chaperone. Anyhoo… Prattly Prana – low-fat soy and manuka honey and cardamom, the hell? – left J wondering if librarians researched their drinks to have a "most arcane morning tea" contest. She couldn't keep it in, brat, brat Prana, the thing Rukia was shushing her about.

Something about a professor and the Bury Paperweight.

'What did Professor Gropy-Hands want with the Bury gem?' Prana was saying.

'Shush. Not here,' Rukia hissed, looking around.

'That thing gives me the creeps,' said the friend.

And Rukai said, 'He won't be bothering us again – and will you just shush it?' J moved closer, trying to be surreptitious about it so they wouldn't notice. It helped that the cafe was quiet. Rukia lowered her head to near Prana's ear in a whisper. 'We don't talk about that outside the Beehive, Kezzie.'

Kezzie. So that's what Prattly Prana's real name was. The way she liked odd chai, Prana suited her better.

Rukia flashed those onyx-lapis eyes at him as he handed over their drinks.

The library was not far from what J liked to call God Street – really George Street – and he liked going to prayer service, the way Pastor Methuselah made the faithful garble words and swoon. Cheapest drama you'd ever get. They spoke in tongues, muttering, and he liked to imagine each person's invisible halo. Some halos came in numbers. 8091. 7621. Others were votive lights. Sometimes he saw upside-down basins, old tires, crumbling loaves. On Rukia, he saw fragile glass in a shimmer of squares that wobbled into hexagons, then distorted waves.

The church stood on affluent land bordering tier-cake mansions with names like "The Grove" or "Palace Lake", and vintage cars parked in Fort Knox garages. Mansions with sports cars number-plated with pretty names like AMELIA, and their engines purred rather than roared.

One entered the church on a side road that hushed traffic with its sign that said: *Slow Street*, well-situated with an op shop where rich people donated off-shoulder fleurette and belle evening gowns. There was a clean carpark whose tarmac you could eat off, and Pastor Methuselah's house was on a top floor above the main prayer room.

Sometimes the church announced "community lunch and chatter" in gilded letters no-one thought to pinch, but J did – not yet pilfer, but he did think about it.

He went to some community lunches, mostly to eye Rukia from a distance as she communed with the faithful. He liked the food – they served radiance juice, elf danishes, raspberry croissants, pizza twists, escargot and lemon custard cruffins. Sure thing, he gobbled the lunch but, of course, never stayed for chatter. He'd slip out quick and try car doors in the quiet car park.

Once, he found a wallet swollen with serious dosh. Sometimes he went to the Uniting Church during Pentecost, or for baptisms – they served lunch then too – but he never let them put hands on him for prayer, spiritual resuscitation or anything like that because he didn't trust the feeling. He tried it once, and an ice-cold breeze neared with the pastor, even though it was summer and the doors were closed. J fell away quickly and skedaddled before the pastor's spirits could muck into his life.

J lived with his mother near Thomas Street – that he preferred to call Dick Street, because it also hosted his secondary school. Opposite was a primary school for Years 1 to 6, where a lollipop woman guided little ones to cross the street and jump on red seesaws and whoosh down yellow slides. If Rukia was crossing, he'd become a lollipop woman for her any day!

Sometimes J imagined Rukia was watching as he sauntered the pavement, checking out the purring cars and noting what those AMELIAs and JULIETs in their number plates left on view through the windscreen. But the lollipop woman's sweet-raisin face turned his way too often for more than a look. He couldn't move on those cars and their lonely laptops and the Prada clutchbags while Lolly Woman beamed sweetly, yet suspiciously, at him. And besides, somehow, always, Rukia was with him, those gem eyes full of powers and looking sidewise, her lips smiling… even though they weren't, really.

He imagined making his moves at the library where she worked. Over and over, he fantasised how he'd approach the unsmiling Rukia, reach across her stern desk at the reception and magnetise her into a date. He didn't think much beyond the reaching and wooing, as in how that would actually work out: where'd they go, who'd pay. He was just taken by the librarian's big-eyed stare wrapped in lashes that looked lathered in mascara, but J knew it was a natural born beauty. The fact that Rukia was unreachable, as in totally, did not hinder his infatuation – hadn't he suffered enough humiliation at the church, with the sermons, and at the library, just to gain membership, to see Rukia?

The library housed rare books. Unpublished manuscripts by famous dead people with names like van Levin, Kwacha and Woke. It had ancient maps, uncommon microfilm and single-copy hardcovers – no paperbacks – all hidden inside a honeycombed structure. The reference database said there were booklets roped in helm or burlap, not that J ever found them, but that explained why perhaps security rather than benefactor dollars might account for top steel clad in granite walls and marble-panelled windows.

Membership needed two solid referees and a statement of intent.

J's intent was clear. He wanted to murmur an oath to the librarian whose name sounded like a rare flower. He wanted to try out a wooing language that said: *I undertake not to remove from the library or to scratch or deface in any way any item belonging to this library, and to love and worship you, pash you senseless…*

Of course, he didn't write any of that in his application form. Instead, he wrote about the overwhelming attractiveness of immortalised artefacts and texts that most rightly belonged in a royal museum rather than a local library. He wrote about his life in crisis and a quest to find meaning. He wrote about vision and revolution, and his craving to be a keeper of knowledge in a marriage of ancientry and modernity by learning from the best.

He said the kind of things that might work for an exotic girl like Rukia, with her clandestine artefacts and shiny eyes.

For referees, he'd considered asking Marg, the manager at Laneway, who pretended at benevolence but pointed patrons to the specials board, above which was a sign that said *Support Local.* The croissanterie sold at the cost of a liver what J was sure were cheaply-sourced honey walnut brownies, pear and pineapple brioches and lemon meringue pies. Not that he had any proof of the ripping off, but still.

The café was unique with its photo walls, and a giant frame holding a famous soccer player's vest: Number 8. Marg rode his ass for laughable pay. No, J didn't want to engage a loser like Marg in any of his recreational activities that involved a rare library and its even rarer librarian who knew about some Bury paperweight – notwithstanding that the engagement was simply for a reference.

So he asked his English teacher Ms Tano (she told the class her name meant *five* in Swahili). She at first frowned when he approached her in the staffroom. 'I am not giving you another extension,' she said.

'Why are you so suspicious?' he said. 'It's not about my assignment.'

'Oh.' She brightened. 'You students– '

'Being a migrant is not easy, is it?' She frowned at him again. 'I'm not here to make things harder,' he said. 'I just need a favour. A reference for Beehive Library, actually.'

She brightened. 'It's good to see you summon interest in books. You can be like Abdulrazak Gurnah who won the Nobel Prize for Literature for his book *Paradise.*'

'If I write a book, it will be set in Portsea or Arthurs Seat,' said J. 'I'd write about the bluest sky and a rage of topaz waters, peaks of rocky hillocks out in the horizon.' Ms Tano smiled. 'There'd be sounds of the wash, crashing waves and low-flying gulls,' said J. 'Someone toppling off a pier and the cold hitting them first before the water swallowed them whole.' The teacher frowned. 'Nothing about paradise.'

Still, J got his reference.

Pastor Methuselah's very size affirmed the generosity of the faithful. It was hard enough getting past him through the church office door. The pastor looked at J's mambo twist braids and the blond streaks in them, his flare-hipped jumpsuit, a road-trip T-shirt and puma-soled sneakers he'd gotten cheap online, second-hand, and welcomed him with an agenda.

'Your mother – Ms Wellness, isn't it?' the pastor said. 'Doesn't sound that well.'

'How do you mean?'

'Being all that single, and raising a whole boy by herself. We could give her some guidance, but she never comes to church.'

'She works shifts at the emergency outpatient – very busy,' said J.

'Tskkk,' sighed Pastor Methuselah. 'So she's an absent mother too?'

'She works double time to save lives – the pandemic, you know? Things are tough.'

'What the world needs is to feed on eternal bread. Tell your mother how church is a blessing. Many a match is made in heaven. Look at the choir – happy couples in it.'

'Fair enough. You put the hottest chicks in town in the choir,' pointed out J.

'You can be in it too,' the pastor said.

'That would be, like, f... chill,' he lied. Nearly swore, and J reckoned Pastor Methuselah would probably have poured holy water at him and spoken in tongues. 'But today I just want a reference,' he said quickly, before any of that could happen.

'Young guns like you today get all these cravings and take whatnot for confidence.'

'I know, right? Blokes want to get jacked but they don't want to eat 'roids 'cos they'll grow tits. Doesn't bother me.'

'That's a lot of talk,' said the pastor, 'and you've come to the right place for someone to listen. I really want to help you.'

'Here's the reference form–' J started unfolding it.

The pastor stayed J's hand. 'Love gives generously. First, I am going to invite you to come and pray with me. Is there room in your heart for God to speak to you?'

'If that's what it takes.'

'Hallelujah! Let this be holy ground. We shall exalt Him, oh powerful name.' The pastor looked at J, waiting.

J looked back at him. 'Oh. Halle-lujah?'

'Amen! Take a posture before the Lord, receive Him right now as I pray for you. Place His throne upon your life!' He looked at J.

'Halle-lujah?'

'Amen!' He lay hands on J. 'Dear Father God, we beseech You–' Pastor Methuselah cried ardently.

'It could be a mother god–'

'We seek Your Presence and Your Power. We surrender to You, Father God, rest in Your TRUTH because of who You are!' He looked at J.

'Hallelujah.'

'Amen! Yes, Lord! We're on the winning side, this is our victory. Heal this lad, this sick body!' He prayed for a forever time, interjecting it with amens, some of which J mirrored, but he was glad when the pastor took both his hands, tears running down his face. 'We thank You. Amen.'

'And *amen*,' J said firmly, and removed his hands from the pastor's clutch, making it very clear that the praying was finished.

The pastor smiled through his tears. 'Liked it?'

'It was pretty chill,' lied J. But his heart stuttered with an imagining that Rukia was watching him, as he pretended to love God.

'There's a festive bonanza coming up, and we have just the part for you.'

'Sounds ace. Now the form—' J pushed it at the pastor's nose.

The pastor wrote the reference, and patted J's back. 'Don't be a stranger.'

'Sure thing. One hundred percent.'

What was he thinking? J wondered, even as he held the recommendation.

Now that J had membership, he didn't really mind the library's strange rules:

Bite your nails outside.
Don't take anything out with you.
Return all books to the counter.
Chew gum at your own peril.
Wish to know – keep the door closed to fools.

There were five rules – maybe there was something special about the number 5.

J wondered if someone had ever tried chewing gum to find out what peril happened. But he was despondent because – other than admission into the library – nothing with Rukia had gone to plan. When he'd leaned over the desk with that charmer look, Rukia did not give him a date. Her eyes said, 'Blast right off,' because her holy tongue couldn't say it.

J decided not to feel screwed, and moved to Plan B.

He'd earmarked five books from the reference database to nick: *The Aardvark Boneyard* by Idris Woke. *A Polka-dot to Uranus* by Jap Bloomberg. *The Phantom of the Nubian Desert* by Mary Mboya. *The Unfound Pyramid* by Bree Kwacha. *A Pentagram in the Rift Valley* by NHK. He'd thought *Island on a Lake of Blood* by Ripples van Levin was something special but changed his mind as he didn't really like islands or blood. What he really wanted to find was the Bury Paperweight, the ancient gemstone his Rukia and bratsy Prana were shushing about. It was somewhere in the library. That sort of artefact was grave coin on the black market.

In school Ms Tano asked, 'How's the library going?'

'No sweat,' he said. 'It's a breeze.'

In the back of his mind, the very name of the ancient gemstone paperweight wriggled like it was alive. *Find me, take me, have me*, and always a sense of Rukia's bejewelled eyes sliding at him, daring, dismissing, discounting him. *Find me. Take me. Have me.*

He wanted to hold her, but couldn't. What he wanted more right now was to find that paperweight, take it, have it in his pocket and swap it for cash.

For once he thought almost angrily of Rukia.

He wanted to prove that he was no school-boy coffee-shop nobody.

On Saturday, Pastor Methuselah swung by the croissanterie, and looked around expectantly. 'Smells of baking bread in here.'

'No shit,' said J, but the pastor kept smiling hard. 'You had a stroke or something?'

Pastor Methuselah was the last person he wanted to see. The old man had only to touch him to know, to feel that stealing-vibe thrumming through him.

No laying on of hands here, old man, J thought furiously.

'You're funny. Give me a skinny decaf mocha,' said the pastor.

J entered the order. 'You got the dole?' The pastor blinked at him. J laughed. 'What? You thought it was free or something? Because of a reference? That will be five dollars, fifty cents.'

'Now this bonanza—' the pastor tried to make conversation as J made the coffee.

'Go jerk yourself, mate.' Quickest way to rid the place of piety.

'You know what, kid? You're a hoodoo.'

'Nice. I had no father to teach me.'

The pastor grabbed his coffee and tossed down a ten-dollar note. 'See if I'll ever haul you out of trouble. Keep change!'

After he left, it was quiet at the croissanterie, J drying dishes. Just then, Marg — sitting outside under a parasol table — called him. He walked out, towel and cup in his hands to show that he was busy, and her summons a disruption.

'Pastor Methuselah looked angry. What was that about?'

'Maybe ask him. What do you want?'

'The books look a bit off, J,' she said.

'More than you?' He laughed. 'Bet you're too stunned to fire me.' He roped and threw the towel to the ground, placed the empty coffee cup deliberately and upside-down on the table right in front of her. His mother once told him that was the best way to bring out another person's stutter. 'Well, I quit.'

He wished it felt better to say that. But it worked, the way Marg stuttered.

His search was meticulous. He X-rayed the library with the growing intensity of a rejected boy. He walked from melancholy room to melancholy room, searching with the hand of a madman, the thirst of a thief.

Books thudded in a pile on the floor beside him.

Rukia approached. She looked at the books he'd yanked from the shelf. 'Are you going to read all those?'

'Maybe. Maybe not.'

'You know you can't take them out of the library.'

'Did anything about me say that I wanted to?'

'You're reading as if the world is going to end tomorrow,' she said.

'Time kills love,' he snapped.

'I forgive you,' she said. 'I forgive most everything, except ignorance.'

'Look at yourself for forgiveness.' He didn't turn until she walked away. Then he looked a long time at her straight back and the way her fingers smoothed, caressed, patted the books on the shelves as she passed them.

Finally! Right there under everyone's nose in the Gondola Room, hidden in plain sight. You wouldn't notice, until you looked closer – almost needing a magnifying glass – to distinguish the paperweight holding upright five of those single-copy hardcovers by Woke, Bloomberg, Mboya, Kwacha and NHK that J no longer cared about. It wasn't the kind of thing one immediately noticed. It was just a paperweight at first, until he touched it.

The three-dimensional pentagon against which the books on the shelf leant responded when J put hands on it as people did when the pastor lay hands on their head during prayer service. The crystalline shape glowed through his fingers, and his skin shone.

Even as he amazed at it, just then the paperweight shifted itself from perfection to five unequal sides, asymmetrical angles. He felt its rough texture like amethyst, gazed at its purplish glow through his hand. At once the marble stone hued itself into a blackish prism of granite crystals, and twinkled. J felt his feet lift off the ground and he found himself ensconced in a space between the library and the heavens, stars swirling in utmost calm in a hula hoop around his frame.

An obscene ringtone shattered the silence, a grunt and moan in climbing tempo and volume. J snapped to from spinning stars the colour of Saturn in his head. Someone said *Shhhhhh!* and he muzzled and tucked the rude device that had buzzed in his pocket. He'd put on that obscene tune to shit his mother, and now she was calling him. He barely saw her, the shifts she took at odds with human hours.

He ignored calling her back to find out what she wanted. Instead, he looked at the paperweight, now all calm and opalescent, a moonstone smooth and pearly in his shimmering hands. He put it in his pocket and started leaving. Rukia hardly looked up, just a sidewise glance of those onyx, lapis, amethyst eyes – she never spoke to him since when he snapped at her – and no alarm beeped.

J walked swiftly out of the library into dusk.

Outside was not a lit night. It was dull grey, sombre. The streets were deserted. Few passing cars had their lights on. *Waaa! Gaaa!* Five black ravens perched on a powerline, warbled and considered him with accusation in their pale eyes until their sound and silhouettes faded.

J's attention went to the paperweight that was growing heavy and heavier in his pocket. He took it out, held it for a moment, mesmerised as its colour turned a deep metamorphic blue, and then it gleamed like a tiger's eyes in a new texture and lustre of quartz.

He watched, first astonished, then in panic, as the paperweight shuffled itself out of his fingers and crawled back across his arm, down his stomach and into his pocket. J took it out again, and it lumbered back into the pocket. The third time he tried to take the paperweight, it burnt his fingers. He yowled and pulled his hand away.

He looked about him quickly. The sky dissolved as he walked, then crawled, the gemstone in his pocket now true lead-weight and chanting. *Found me. Took me. Had me. What's mine is yours*, it whispered. *Yours, yours.* He felt himself sinking and lifted a hand, reaching, reaching… But help never arrived because each of his five fingers went opaque, opalescent, solid. *Found me took me had me what's mine's yours… yours, yours.*

J dragged himself against the pulling weight, no-one there to notice his world slipping. There was the Uniting Church on God Street. Curtains parted in the upper room where Pastor Methuselah lived. J thought, as he agonisingly crawled, dragging the paperweight – or the paperweight dragging him – that he saw a face at the window. He tried waving, hopeful, but his fingers were still made of marble and it didn't matter if someone had seen him. The curtains closed.

How would he get home, wondered J glumly, and – when he did – would his mother be back from work? And how, oh how, would J explain the gemstone that was lead and burning, burning in his pocket? He pulled at his jumpsuit, tore and crawled out of its shreds.

He stood in his T-shirt and boxers, uncaring if someone might see him half-naked, when he saw the paperweight shuffling and then lumbering like a legless beast towards him from the torn clothing on the street.

Foundmetookmehadmewhatsminesyoursyoursmine…

He turned away in panic, but could do no more than belly crawl because a deep heaviness overwhelmed him. He heard the obscene ringtone, his mother calling from somewhere in his discarded pocket.

'Mum!' he cried, and reached in a flash of hope. There was a deep rumble, then a smell of sulphur. The ground started shaking, fissures forming and making an inescapable island on which he was trapped. Rocking and teetering accompanied the rumble, then *boom*!

The roadside began to crack, a long and snailing fissure moving towards him. J gave a cry and tried to crawl away, but the paperweight had already reached him and climbed on his chest, its five amorphic sides like giant fingers dragging him down on the island, as the earth opened in a bellow of illegible language.

Toundmefookmehadmewhatsnimesyoursyoursnime...

He squealed as he fell, fell, dead weight falling, hundreds of feet falling, deeper into the boom and rumble falling. Now J was trapped and bleeding in a gorge.

It seemed like forever, maybe it was just five minutes. He looked up and saw Pastor Methuselah peeking down. 'You need help, boy?'

'Amen!' cried J. 'Yes, pastor. Praise the Lord!'

'Amen. I ain't gon' say go jerk yerself. But I call it reparation. See you later.'

'No. No!' But the pastor was gone. J curled back, forlorn. He looked up. Wait – there was someone else. 'Is that you, Rukia?'

'I think you have something of mine,' she shouted down, and pointed a finger right at his heart where he lay curved in the big hole.

'Take it back!' he pleaded, his voice muffled under the weight of those five giant fingers squeezing him like his mama squeezed lime on fish. 'I'll do anything, I swear!'

Rukia laughed, a crystal tinkling he hadn't heard before, and again pointed at his heart. Sparks radiated from her finger. Her eyes took on the morphing colours of the gemstone, first a deep metamorphic blue, then gleaming like a tiger's eyes in a new texture and lustre of quartz.

He knew it! She was superpower special!

The massive fist clenching J's chest let go.

He stared, dead-eyed yet seeing, soil in his eyes, up his nostrils. The pentagonal paperweight hauled itself and lumbered like a heavyweight starfish out of water.

Foundmetookmehadmewhatsminesyoursyoursmine...

It started to climb the walls of his grave.

Find me. Take me. Have me. What's mine is yours.

It moved quicker in a scamper, slide, crawl, rippling with colour.

Then it lay smooth and calm in Rukia's hand, serene as a moonstone, still as ice.

She looked down at him, then pointed again, and J felt all the light in him rise towards the iridescent paperweight she held. He levitated in slow motion with the shine from the darkness of his tomb and flew, weightless, headfirst towards Rukia and the paperweight.

It was taking forever to reach them. A roar, and the walls below him started closing. He regretted his choices, wished he had lived different. Contributed more to his society rather than be a weight in it. He didn't know if he'd make it to the top before the crushing met him. Already it was reaching his toes. He screamed, loud, louder. But no sound came from him as the chasm gobbled his feet.

All he heard – as he wondered with a sob if it was too late to change – was Rukia's tinkling laugh and her sweet, sweetest voice.

'Rule Number Five,' she said, reminding, waiting, yet not waiting for him. '*Wish to know.*'

HARBINGER

C. VONZALE LEWIS

PINPRICKS OF UNEASE CRAWLED OVER MY SKIN AS I LOOKED UP AT THE night sky dotted with stars. The full moon's ethereal glow spilled into the Valley of the Queens, creating a pool of light on the ancient sands. In the distance, the dark pyramids rose to the heavens.

Their majestic beauty sent my mind back over a thousand years to a time when the stars were used to guide your way. A simpler time. One filled with both great wonder and terrible danger. This region held massive power. Its stories had survived thousands of years – influencing both religion and politics.

The cool wind stirred, bringing with it the marshy scent of the Nile. Its chill tickled my scalp underneath the single braid running down the center of my head.

'Shauna,' Malik prompted, rousing me from my thoughts.

A short distance ahead, a group of jeeps crowded around the stairs leading down into Queen Nefertari's tomb: the supposed resting place of The Ark of the Covenant. At least that's what I'd been led to believe. Tonight, I would learn the truth.

Sand kicked up when Malik parked behind the other vehicles at the entrance. We climbed out. A tall, middle-aged man with a ruddy complexion dressed in khaki shorts and shirt made his way toward us. He stopped in front of me. 'Mr. Hamilton instructed you to come alone,' he said, his British accent thick.

I smiled. 'Avner Price?' I recognized him from the research I'd done on the people who hired me. He inclined his head. 'I don't travel alone.'

It was a lie. I often traveled alone, but he didn't need to know that. I turned to Malik, his long hair rustling around the collar of his black t-shirt while his dark gaze remained intent on Avner. 'This is my friend and guide, Malik.' I didn't need a guide. But telling this man more about the people in my life wasn't a good idea. I preferred anonymity when it came to my personal life.

'You can remain outside,' Avner said, gaze steady on Malik.

Malik chuckled and walked around him and greeted the waiting men in Arabic.

Avner's nostrils flared as he stared at Malik's back. I shook my head and joined Malik and the workers at the tomb entrance.

Once we were all there, the workers swung open the door and stale, warm air rushed out. I descended into Nefertari's burial chamber – a quiver swimming in my gut. My skin flushed with anticipation and excitement when I ran my hand over the hieroglyphs inscribed on the door jamb leading into the "house of eternity". My fingers halted over the words:

Hereditary noblewoman; great of favors; possessor of charm, sweetness and love; mistress of Upper and Lower Egypt; the Osiris; the king's great wife, mistress of the two lands, Nefertari, beloved of Mut, revered before Osiris.

The first time I'd seen this glorious tomb, I'd soaked up its history. Too bad I couldn't spend more time with it this time.

Heavy footfalls rocked the makeshift wooden walkway between the walls. The men's urgent chatter charged the air. While I knew Arabic well, it was hard for me to follow when spoken in a rush. What I did understand were the words "curse" and "time". I slowed to allow Malik to catch up.

'They say the place is cursed,' he said in a whisper. 'Do you wish to leave?'

'Is there a problem, Dr. Landry?' Avner asked. He had taken up position behind the men in charge of the excavation.

'The men you hired seem concerned.' I said in Arabic. My statement wasn't for him. I made a point of making eye contact with the five men behind me. They turned away, refusing to meet my gaze.

The man closest to Avner whispered in his ear. Avner kept his eyes trained on me. 'I'm sure you misunderstood them,' Avner said. 'Now please. Let's keep moving.'

I hadn't misunderstood them, and he knew it. Though I suspected, if pressed, the men wouldn't admit to any concern. Money is a great motivator. And I had no doubt they had been paid well enough to swallow their obvious fear.

I looked at Malik to gauge his thoughts. 'Up to you,' he mouthed. Yeah. No sense in backing out now. All the plans had already been laid out. Besides, if I changed my mind, they would only hire someone else who would be all too willing to hand over the priceless relic. One that belonged in a museum. And I was going to make damn sure it ended up there.

I continued through the antechamber and on to the eastern annex.

The entire north wall of the annex held a depiction with an ibis-headed Thoth, god of writing, at its center. Sitting on an elaborate throne, he gazed at Queen Nefertari while she held a writer's palette, a water bowl, and a frog amulet. It was said the frog represented writing for *whm-'nh,* 'repeating life,' or more accurately, a desire for longevity.

'I, too, am a Scribe,' had been scrawled on the letter Jacob Hamilton had given me. He claimed the letter was proof of the whereabouts of The Ark of the Covenant. I still didn't understand why he'd hired me. My doctorate was in ancient civilizations and mythology. While there was some cross reference to world religions, it wasn't my focus. Sure, I had read the Bible. After all, my parents had been devout Christians. But that didn't make me an authority on Christian relics.

According to the Kebra Negast, a 700-year-old genealogy of the Solomonic dynasty, the Ark's final resting place was in the Church of Our Lady Mary of Zion in the city of Axum in Ethiopia. Brought there by Menelik, the son of the Queen of Sheba and King Solomon thousands of years ago, it was also said to be guarded by a single virgin monk.

When I mentioned this to Jacob Hamiliton, he assured me that the information he had was correct. Repeatedly.

His insistence had presented me with an irresistible set of circumstances. One, I was still trying to make a name for myself and finding The Ark of the Covenant would do just that. I wasn't too concerned with fame or fortune. My pursuits lay in learning about the past and confirming its many mysteries. And two, the money he was paying me would go a long way into helping me pay off my student debt. In the end, I took the job, putting my own plan in motion just in case his information turned out to be true.

I returned my attention to the wall. While Nefertari wasn't proclaiming to be like Thoth, her possession of the writer's palette could loosely be attributed to the line in Jacob's letter.

It would take some time for the men to break through the rock floor. So, after pointing at the most likely spot for a hidden underground structure, I stepped back and stood next to Malik.

We didn't talk, not with Avner watching our every move. One of the men stood with him while others broke into the ground with rock hammers. I wondered how they planned to cover up the damage. Not my problem, unless it ended up implicating me. We had been cautious with our correspondence. Yet, I didn't doubt they had something on me. Until I learned about their true motives, and how to counter them, I'd be on guard.

They finally broke through the floor and the large chunks of rock were quickly moved out of the way to expose a wooden trap door with a modern lock.

Seeing that lock, I realized this discovery had not been overlooked by those who had unearthed this tomb all those years ago. Nor was it proof this was truly the final resting place for the Ark.

If I had to guess, this was a hiding place for something either too dangerous or too valuable for any one person to own. All that effort. All the mechanics of what they would have had to do to construct this under the eye of everyone who had come through to either restore or view this great piece of history. They must have been reassured no one would ever find what they had hidden.

Because who would look inside an already excavated tomb?

The workers broke the lock and pulled open the trap door. A whoosh of cold stale air rushed out. I rubbed my arms and peered down into the dark void, trying to gauge the depth. Someone handed me a flashlight and I clicked it on and shone the light inside the hole. A dirt floor greeted me.

'Dr. Landry,' Avner prompted. 'Mr. Hamilton would prefer it if you entered the chamber first.'

A sigh of relief escaped me. We had wondered how I was going to capture images of what we found and slip the tracking device, currently hidden in my boot, into the Ark.

I sat on the edge of the opening but before I could jump down, I was stopped by Avner's man. 'We need your phone,' he said, eyes on the device sticking out of my pocket.

'Why?' I asked, directing my question to Avner. Might raise their alarms if I didn't protest.

'Just a precaution,' he said. 'You understand, of course.' It wasn't a question.

I handed my phone over. 'I expect it back.'

He gave me a condescending look. I turned away to hide my smirk.

Adrenaline surged through me when I pushed off the edge and soared into the icy unknown. I landed with a thump on the dirt floor. A cloud of dust swirled in the beam of light casting down from above, illuminating the small space in front of me. I clicked on my flashlight and brought the crudely constructed walls into stark relief. A litany of phrases covered the pocked surface. I let my beam rove down the wall, while I counted the varying languages represented. Nine in total. It would take time to decipher them all.

On the wall behind me, facing away from the opening, four words were carved into the wall in Greek: Το κουτί της Πανδώρας

Pandora's Box.

The Ark rested underneath the proclamation. I removed the muslin cloth, depositing more dirt and sand in the air. The frigid air pouring off the Ark buffeted me, and a cloying, putrid scent scratched at my throat.

My eyes rounded at what sat before me.

In Exodus 25:10, the Ark – referred to as a chest – is said to have been constructed using Acacia wood with gold plating inside and out, a gold band around the front, and two wide-winged angels facing each other on the lid.

Yet what lay in front of me was a rectangular block of obsidian with wooden handles and a large representation of an owl carved into the lid.

An ancient symbol of death. A single word in an unfamiliar language had been etched on the side. I moved my light over it and a chill ran down my spine as the surface rippled as if cowering from the light.

I crouched in front of it and ran my finger over the lettering, then yanked back when the cold burned my skin. I hesitated, then reached out slowly and skimmed my knuckles over the black surface. Warm. So only the lettering was cold. The entire room felt at least thirty degrees cooler than the chamber above. How was that even possible?

Commotion above pulled me out of my pondering.

'Dr. Landry?' Avner called out, urgency in his voice. 'Have you found the Ark?'

'Just a minute,' I responded.

Working quickly, I picked up the muslin cloth and pushed at the upper half of the Ark just above a faint seal around the top. After several strenuous attempts, a creak echoed, and the lid gave way. The pungent scent of dried herbs and dead things wormed their way up my nose and down my throat. I coughed, barely avoiding vomiting up the wretched stench. My hand shook as I slid my fingers into the small opening and stuck the small, flat tracking device to the wall inside the chest. Task complete, I moved the lid back in place.

Sweat broke out along my hairline – my heart rammed in my chest. I hurriedly pulled my phone – my actual phone – from my boot and took a video of the entire space as a wave of nausea overcame me.

Two men thudded down beside me. Both were wearing gloves and carrying a tarp and rope. I shifted out of their way, jerking my phone behind my back. When they finished wrapping the artifact up, they signaled above, and the men pulled it to the surface. I waited for them to be helped out first, giving me time to slide the phone back into my boot.

I would analyze the footage later.

Pain raced along my finger, and I looked down at the angry red welt that had formed.

Just what the hell had we found?

After Malik helped me out of the crawl space, I dusted off my jeans and followed him out of the tomb. Everyone else had already left. I'd been misled: that much was evident.

My research on Jacob Hamilton told me that he believed others were beneath him. He used people to get what he wanted. I had foolishly assumed he wanted a priceless relic to show off to his rich friends. He had told me my role was to authenticate the relic in question. Yet when I inspected the tomb, Avner hadn't asked me to do that. Instead, he insisted I enter the chamber first and confirm it was there. Why?

My assumptions kept me from looking beyond the obvious to ask the most important question. Why would a pharmaceutical company want The Ark of the Covenant? Or, more importantly, the Ark I touched in the tomb? Something about it seemed familiar. Maybe I'd read its description somewhere before. But without more details, it would be hard for me to figure it out. Especially since a headache had started to form at the base of my head. I was positive it was a result of something I had been exposed to in the tomb.

I stepped out into the cool night air and sucked in a cleansing breath. The chilly wind ran over my throat. A raw sensation had settled on the soft tissue, and I swallowed, trying to work some moisture into the area.

Avner was giving instructions to the men placing the Ark in a shipping crate.

I cleared my throat and he looked up. After giving the men one final instruction, he signaled for me. I joined him and he returned my phone to me. 'Your payment should have been deposited by now if you care to check.'

I inclined my head, entered my security code, and pulled up my banking information. He was right. The agreed upon amount had been deposited. I swallowed, my throat now on fire.

'You all right, Shauna?' Malik asked, staring at me.

I squeezed my throat, turning my head to the side to ease some of the discomfort. 'Yeah. Just need some water.' Avner was watching me like a hawk. 'I believe I have been lied to about what we found down there.'

'Oh,' he said.

'Yes. Everyone,' I stepped closer, my heart now ramming in my chest. *'Everyone* knows what The Ark of the Covenant looks like.' I pointed to the crate, Hamilton Pharmaceuticals stamped on its front, that the men were loading in the jeep nearby. 'While that may be *an* Ark, it isn't the Ark in question. So, what is it?'

He instructed the men to get going, then turned back to me. 'Like I said, Dr. Landry. You have been paid. This is no longer your concern.' He climbed in the jeep and his driver got in and started the engine. 'I trust our time here will remain between us.' He pulled out his phone and showed me the display. 'I always find it beneficial to take pictures of my time in foreign places.' He smiled. 'Don't you?'

I looked at the picture of me inside the tomb and screamed inside my head. Well, that answered the question on what they had planned to use against me to ensure my silence and cooperation. But I would get the last laugh when I snatched their discovery from them.

He gave me a condescending smile. 'Be sure to drive safely.' They drove off.

The scent of gasoline and oil punched the air as the other vehicles swerved around us, kicking up sand and dirt while their headlights danced in the darkness. Grit and sweat coated my skin and I suppressed a feverish chill running all over me.

Climbing into our Jeep, I sighed and rested my head on the back of the seat. 'Something's not right,' I said, reaching for Malik's water bottle resting in the cup holder. After draining the contents, I continued, 'What we found is…concerning.' I described the walls and the Ark I'd found. He drove on, following the fading red lights from the other vehicles.

I shone the light on my finger. An angry red rash snaked out from the tip, trailing down to the center of my palm and bursting into a star pattern with tiny white splotches. I'd touched the frigid lettering with my finger. Could it be frostbite? What about the other symptoms? Could it be the substance that had rushed out when I opened the Ark?

With enough distance between us and the tomb, we pulled onto the gravel. Malik pulled a pen light from his pocket and flashed it into the night three times.

I showed Malik my finger.

'I don't like the look of that.'

'I don't like the feel of it. I'm worried I might have contracted something. My throat is on fire.'

An eerie laugh pierced the darkness. Adrenaline rushed through my body. The beast's familiar cackle had me searching for the bright orange eyes of its owner. Hyenas weren't native to this region, but there was no denying the sound of its wicked howl.

'Did you hear that?' I asked Malik.

'What?' he said, searching the darkness. But there was nothing there.

The giggles morphed into whoops as the sound drew nearer, seeming to echo all around me. 'I hear a hyena,' I said in a rush, my heart ramming in my chest.

Malik pulled a gun from under his seat and jumped out of the jeep, his gaze taking in the entire area, his body rigid and alert.

When I stepped out of the jeep, the sound suddenly stopped, leaving a void behind. Like I'd suddenly entered a tightly sealed room. I looked at Malik. 'Maybe...' I shook my head. 'I'm hearing things.' He came over and put his arm around me.

'You sure?'

I nodded. 'Yeah. Just my nerves.' At least, that's what I hoped it was.

A short while later, two jeeps pulled up. My brother Raymond's six foot two inch frame emerged from the passenger side and he made his way toward us. When we were younger, most people believed we were twins. We had the same fair skin, sharp green eyes, and long curly hair. Now we barely resembled one another. Life had dealt him some serious blows. His skin, darkened from being in the sun all the time, sported scars along his muscled arms. His eyes, once kind, now held an edge of hardness. His hair had been shorn to the scalp.

He pulled me to him, and I let myself relax in his embrace.

'Everything go okay?' he asked after a while.

'Yeah. Just...' I looked back the way we had come. 'That wasn't The Ark of the Covenant.'

'What do you mean?'

I started to speak, but stopped when a cough overtook me. 'Malik,' I croaked.

Malik took him through the events, thankfully not mentioning my brief hallucination.

Raymond's lips thinned. He ran a hand over his head in agitation. 'My contact at the dock in Alexandria says they should be departing tomorrow evening, so we stick to the plan'

'Maybe we should take it now.' I swallowed, trying to ease the pain and assuage the thirst. It had to be the air down in the hidden cave. Or, more likely, what was inside that Ark. I really needed to get the inscriptions translated soon. For all I knew, it had been constructed to house a plague.

'Shauna believes something down there infected her,' Malik said, staring at me. 'Show him your hand.'

As I did, I said, 'I can have someone look at it later.'

'Tonight,' my brother said and turned to Malik. 'Have Noelle look her over.' He pulled a device from his pocket. 'This will let you track the Ark's movements. We will follow at a distance.' He glanced back at me. 'Did he take your phone?'

I smiled. 'Yeah, the decoy.' I handed it to him.

'Give them what they're looking for and they will look no further.' My brother used to say when we'd stage our small apartment to appear as if our parents still lived there. We had kept that ruse up for five years.

He examined the phone. 'He put a tracker on it.' He handed the phone to one of his men. 'We'll drive it to one of the hotels and leave it.'

'Why would he want to track my movements?'

'Don't know, sis. But keep your eyes open. Something is not right about all this.'

'I agree. And until we know…' I pulled in a cleansing breath, lungs burning. 'Make sure you protect yourself. Don't open the Ark.' I glanced at my finger. 'Or touch it with your bare hands.'

He kissed the top of my head then turned to Malik. 'Take care of her,' he said and returned to his jeep. 'Remember, stay in touch. '

We watched as they drove away.

'It is odd for them to want to keep tabs on you,' Malik said.

I nodded. We'd learn soon enough what they were up to. But first…I needed to find out just what we had discovered.

I came to in a malaise of madness. Cracking open my eyes, I took in the whir of motion. It was as if Malik's bedroom had joined the other planets in a journey around the sun. The bright morning light drove spikes into my grit-filled eyes while a sea of voices sang a mournful song of death inside my head – their somber melody accompanied by a piercing whistle.

I went to move and found myself plastered to the bed, laying in a pool of sweat. My hand came up slowly, fighting through muscle aches.

'Malik,' I croaked.

The bed moved and Malik appeared. His worried gaze roamed over me. 'I should call Noelle again.' He moved the strands of hair plastered to the side of my face. 'You are on fire, Shauna.'

I swallowed, once again wincing at the pain radiating down my throat. 'I just need…water…shower…medicine.'

He nodded, focusing on my face. 'Noelle left some pain medicine and antibiotics. But…' He moved in close. 'If they don't help, I am calling her again. No arguments.'

I forced my mouth into a smile. 'No arguments.'

After Malik gave me some more pills, he helped me up. I attempted to walk but gave up when my legs started trembling. Malik had to carry me to the shower.

The cold spray bit into my skin, relieving some of the heat. Malik stood behind me, steadying me while the water cascaded down my body. A bone deep ache raced down my spine, and I turned, allowing the mist to buffet my back.

Malik cupped my face and gave me a gentle kiss on the lips. I breathed in his amber and musk scent, letting the familiarity ground me. 'Are you sure you should be doing that?' I asked, resting my face on his chest. 'I could be contagious.'

'Noelle didn't think so, given my contact with you and me displaying no symptoms.' He eased me back, staring down at me out of his dark brown eyes. 'And besides. After last night, if you are contagious, concern over me being exposed should be a moot point.' He smiled. 'You got your germs all over me.'

I shook my head and turned around, grabbing the soap from the rack. 'I just wish I could remember what happened.'

He nuzzled my ear. 'If you're up to it, I can give you a few reminders.'

'Maybe later,' I said, running the jasmine scented bar over my skin and suddenly remembering the way I had jumped him after Noelle left. What the hell had come over me? 'Yeah. I think we should revisit last night.' I turned and looked up at him. 'Real soon.'

He captured my mouth in a bruising kiss. After resting his forehead against mine, nostrils flaring, he held me close. 'You just say the word, my heart.'

Once we had showered, I pulled on a T-shirt and stepped out onto the balcony while Malik made breakfast. While the fever had subsided and the pain in my throat had eased, I still fought against the bone-deep ache thrumming inside of me. I needed some air.

A cacophony of voices filled the narrow avenues as people navigated down the tight passageways exchanging early morning greetings. I sipped my ice-cold water, the frozen cubes clinking against the glass, while my gaze traveled up the neutral yellow walls of the high-rise apartments. Malik and I spent a great deal of time out on this balcony when I stayed with him. I enjoyed watching the people below, cast in shadow, hiding from the heat of the sun. But today the confined space gave way to a gnawing sense of the walls closing in on me.

Something below caught my eye. In the sea of colors, a lone figure wearing a long black robe stood against the wall. I leaned forward, breath catching in my throat as I took in the long wooden stick in its hand. The sun reflected off the polished silver scythe, pulling my gaze to its deadly sharpness. The sickly sweet scent of dead roses filled my nose. The sound of my rapid heartbeat pounded in my ears. Sweat broke out along my brow and my breaths grew shallow. I blinked a few times trying to will the sight away but the figure remained, its dark hood now angled up – staring at me. No one seemed to notice its presence. Like the world moved around him while he stood frozen in place.

Malik stepped out, startling me. He wrapped his strong arms around me, resting his chin on the top of my head. I shivered in his arms.

'What's wrong?' he asked, turning me to him. I looked back, but the figure was gone.

'Shauna?'

'I'm okay. You just startled me.' I turned away.

He touched my forehead. 'You still have a fever. Maybe...'

'It's the heat. I'm fine,' I said, cutting him off. There was no way I was going to tell Malik that I'd seen Death. Hell, I wasn't sure myself. Like the hyena laughter last night, it was only a hallucination. One that could be attributed to the sickness raging inside of me. I would have to deal with it on my own.

He searched my face. I turned away and rested my head on his chest. 'Are you ready to eat?' he finally asked.

I took another sip of my water. 'We have to stop them,' I said. Warning them would have been the right thing to do. The worry I had over why a pharmaceutical company would want to procure The Ark of the Covenant had been answered.

They weren't looking for the holy relic. They were looking for something much more deadly. Something I had obviously been exposed to. A plague? Was that their game plan? To release an ancient plague on the world? Did they have a cure for the sickness? Either way, it didn't matter. We just had to stop them. And I couldn't let anyone I cared about get exposed too. Malik, thankfully, was showing no signs of what I had. So it stood to reason that whatever it was, one would have to come in direct contact with it to catch this fever.

The ceiling fan droned overhead, depositing cool air on my feverish skin while I sat at Malik's desk in my underwear, searching online for past restoration dates for Nefertari's tomb.

I checked the tracking device my brother had given us last night and confirmed the Ark hadn't left the area yet. We could procure it while it was still in Luxor, though that could be too risky. Odd it hadn't been moved yet. What were they waiting for?

The phone rang and I answered.

'Shauna.' My brother's deep voice filled the line. 'The men from last night have been found inside the tomb. Dead.' I called for Malik and put the phone on speaker.

'What happened?' I asked.

'Story being told is they went in looking for something. A few holes have been dug around the tomb and covered up.'

I had to give Avner credit. The ruse was a good one. 'How long do you think it will take to discover the truth?'

'Best guess,' Raymond stated. 'A week at the most. They're going to have to investigate the deaths before anyone can get in and restore the tomb.'

At which point they would find the empty secret chamber in the eastern annex.

'We left the tracker Price put on your phone in the hotel. Still don't understand why he wanted to track you.'

'Maybe he suspected our plan.' I offered.

'Doubtful.' Raymond paused. 'Malik? How's she doing?'

I could have bristled at my brother not asking me but he knew I wouldn't give him the complete truth.

'Still fighting,' Malik said.

'I told you both, if I get worse, we can deal with it. For now, we concentrate on the Ark.'

We went back and forth a few more times before they relented. After hanging up, I tapped my pencil on the desk. Why kill their crew? It didn't make sense. They would have to hire more men to travel with the Ark to Alexandria.

'Does what they're doing make sense to you?' I asked Malik.

'Yeah. Especially given the secrecy of what they're transporting.'

Now that he said it, it made sense. The fewer people who knew about it the better. But it still didn't explain why they wanted to track me. If they were going to kill everyone, why leave me and Malik alive? They could have killed us all once they secured the Ark.

I would have to figure out the puzzle later. I turned my attention to the video I'd captured while in the tomb. An hour later I learned the writing on the wall comprised nine different languages. The phrase, *Do not look upon the goddess... for in her eyes is death,* had been written in Tamil, Sanskrit, Coptic Egyptian, Hebrew, Greek, Basque, Lithuanian, Gaelic and Arabic. The writing on the mysterious Ark gave me some trouble until I realized the word was not in a different language but a combination of the nine on the wall.

Spelled out using a single letter from all the dialects was the word: *Harbinger.*

A portent of death. I went still, remembering the hyena's laughter, and the vision of Death standing in the street. Despite it not being widely accepted, magick existed in this world. Signs and portents were a part of its makeup. Yet I'd never heard of an illness related to magick that could manifest visions. Could that be what they were after?

My skin thrummed as if I had live wire running under it. I shifted in the chair, unable to get comfortable. The medicine had eased the worst of my illness, but its lingering effects still threaded through me. I blinked to clear the hazy film over my eyes and refocused on the task at hand.

For someone to create the space under Queen Nefertari's tomb and place the Ark there, the site had to have been closed for an extended amount of time, when no one had reason to be inside the tomb. I just needed to find that time.

I opened my laptop and pulled up a site dedicated to Queen Nefertari's tomb.

In the fall of 1988, Spanish conservators came to Egypt to help preserve the walls. Workers were in the tomb around the clock, only breaking for lunch and dinner. So, it had to be prior to that or during that time.

In 1934, it had been closed with concerns the visitor's touching and breathing on the paintings were causing them to deteriorate. I couldn't find much activity being reported between those dates so instead, I searched for the phrase and returned only one article. Co-written by Dr. Ayanna Shukuma and Professor Jabari Ebeid, it talked about the concept of death in ancient times and how our perceptions of it should remain obtuse. That to know death would bring about one's early demise. While the entire phrase wasn't in their article, it did have the beginning of it and another one not included on the walls. *Do not look upon the goddess…we all say her name when we take our last breath.*

Sadly, Ayanna Shukuma had died after her last trip to Egypt some years ago. But Professor Jabari was alive and teaching at Cairo University.

Malik set another pill down in front of me. 'Take it, Shauna.'

I took the pill, then got up. 'I need to go to Cairo.'

He opened his mouth to protest, and I gripped his arm. 'No, I need to go. And you need to follow…' I paused, fighting a sudden wave of dizziness. 'Follow Avner and his men when they leave for Alexandria. I can meet you there tonight.' I told him about the professor and the article.

'I don't need to follow them. Ray can track their journey. I should come with you.' He pulled me to him. 'We don't know how this illness will play out. You will need me, my heart.'

I smiled, blowing out a painful breath. 'I'm doing better than before. And there is no guarantee that they won't find the device I planted.'

'No—'

'Listen to me, Malik. Please! We cannot risk this Ark getting into Jacob Hamilton's hands. I have the medicine Noelle gave me, so trust me' – I gripped his face in my hands – 'if I get worse, I will call you. Promise.'

He wanted to protest, but he also knew that I was right. 'Check in as soon as you land. And every hour after that,' he demanded.

I kissed him. 'I will. And you do the same. Do you remember the code?'

Sadness crept in his eyes. 'Yes. If you tell me you love me there is something wrong.'

'You know how I feel. And you know I don't need to say some sappy phrase to prove it.'

He rested his hands on my shoulders, face close to mine. 'Just once I would love to hear the words and know it's because you truly do love me.'

'But you already know that.' I ran my hand over his head. 'Now promise me you will be safe.'

'I promise, Shauna.'

I knew Malik hated my strange rule, left over from a child who heard the words I love you over and over again only for my parents to abandon my brother and me. To me, those last sentiments meant only one thing. The person giving them would never come back.

Once I'd booked a flight to Cairo, Malik took me to the airport. Dread had settled over me as I walked into the terminal. Could I keep the promise to him? To myself? And if I didn't find a cure, my fate would be sealed. I understood that. Accepting it would be hard, but I wouldn't go gently. There would be no hidden rooms or cryptic maps to ever lead another person to its whereabouts. I would destroy that Ark and stop it from spreading a plague across the world if it was the last thing I did.

The cab driver watched me in the rearview mirror while I fought the tremors raging through me. The shivers had started on the plane ride over. The fever suddenly broke, only to be replaced by an all-consuming chill. No matter how many shirts I put on; I couldn't get warm enough. And to avoid the scrutiny from others, I'd put gloves on. The red streaks now covered my entire palm and were snaking up my arm.

The driver pulled up to a large house with a red terracotta roof nestled behind a wrought-iron fence covered in green foliage. He glanced back at me, concern in his eyes. 'Do you need help?'

I reassured him in Arabic that I was okay, and he relaxed. After thanking and paying him, I climbed out and a wave of vertigo overtook me. I stood there trying to orient myself, resting my arm on the open car door.

'Miss,' he called.

'Just need to eat,' I said, turning to smile at him.

He tried to give me a foil-wrapped package. 'Here,' he said.

'Thank you. I can get something inside,' I said, straightening. He nodded, still watching me. I shut the car door and moved away from the cab. After one last concerned look, he drove off.

I'd promised Malik I'd let him know if the sickness got worse but if I did, he'd come here instead of following the Ark. And keeping track of that deadly artifact was way more important.

Once the world stopped spinning, I took out my phone and sent a text to Malik, letting him know I was okay. When he replied the same, I started for the property gate.

Halfway there, a spasm ran down my spine and I stopped abruptly. Wetness stained my cheek. I ran my finger over the moisture, capturing a small drop of the liquid and studied the tiny, pink teardrop. My bag slid down my arm, thumping to the ground, and I followed suit. With frantic movements, I yanked a handkerchief from my bag and scrubbed at my face. A faint pink stain marred the surface of the white cloth.

Not blood, but something.

I stood up, dusted my jeans off, and looked around the quiet neighborhood, eyes landing on a dark figure across the street. Wearing a black, hooded cloak, the figure slowly turned toward me, showing me the vast void where a face should be. I blinked and the hood was replaced by the head of Anubis. The Egyptian God of death. I scrambled back, heartbeat pounding in my chest, and landed against the shrubbery intertwined in the fence. While I continued to stare slack-jawed at it, the Jackal head rippled, morphing into an old man. Black wings burst out his back. Thanatos. Greek God of death.

I screamed, dropping once again to my knees. I covered my eyes, trying to will the image away, but it had imprinted inside my mind and continued to morph into one mythological god after the next, Yama; Mot; Mari; Dagda, until someone placed their warm hand on my shoulder. I jumped at the contact.

A dark-skinned woman wearing a hajib, jeans, and a pale, yellow t-shirt stared down at me. 'Dr. Landry?' she asked, hesitant. 'You are Dr. Landry, correct?' she asked again when I didn't immediately respond. She reached for me, and I pulled back. 'Are you looking for Professor Ebeid?'

'Yes,' I blurted out, eyes shifting across the street. Death was gone. I scrambled to my feet. 'I apologize. I'm not feeling well.' I took a deep calming breath and picked up my bag. 'I am Dr. Landry.'

She nodded and looked across the street. 'Was someone following you?'

I ran my hand over my sweaty forehead. 'No. I just…'.

'You don't look well, Dr. Landry.'

'I know. Can we please just go inside.' Even I could hear the fear in my tone.

After one more look around the area, she reached down and picked up my handkerchief. 'Is this yours?' She extended it to me.

'Yes. I cut myself. I just…' There was no way I could tell her what was happening to me.

She waved off my reply. 'Come. Let me get you some cool tea. The professor is in his study waiting for you.'

I followed her up the walkway and into the chilly house. We were deposited into a foyer filled with antique, dark wood furniture. Rich, brown tile covered the floor with intricate gold, brown, and green rugs scattered throughout.

'I will take you back and bring you and the professor some tea. Would you like anything to eat?'

I shook my head. I didn't have an appetite. I'd thrown up my breakfast and felt that even tea would upset my stomach. 'Do you have any ginger ale?'

She nodded, her eyes dipping to my stomach. 'Of course.' She started down the hallway lined with artwork and family portraits and waved for me to follow.

We stopped at a closed door. She knocked softly on the polished wood. A man called out to enter, and she gave me a hesitant smile before opening the door and signaling for me to go in.

I went into the dimly lit room. Leatherbound books lined the oak shelves. A plush red carpet stretched across the floor leading to the large wooden desk sitting cata-corner on the left side of the room. Behind the desk sat a white-haired old man, brown face heavily wrinkled. He stared at me out of gold rimmed glasses.

'Dr. Landry?' he asked, using the side of the desk to help him stand. He stuck out his hand. 'Thank you for agreeing to come.'

I hurried forward and shook his hand. 'Of course. And thank you for agreeing to speak with me.'

He waved my thanks away and sat down heavily in his chair. 'Please. Have a seat.'

I sat down heavily on the leather covered chair and sighed. A muscle spasm ran down my calf and I reached down and squeezed my leg, biting past the pain. Professor Ebied watched me the entire time.

He glanced over my shoulder. 'Thank you, Irene,' he said and smiled.

Irene set a tray on the desk with a sweating glass of ginger ale and a plate of saltine crackers along with a green and gold tea service. She smiled at me. 'If you need anything else, just ask.'

I nodded my thanks and looked at the plate of crackers. I could correct her assumption about my state but didn't feel it was necessary. Besides, maybe the crackers would help with the nausea. The liquid went down easily, but settled in my gut like a brick. The crackers weren't much better.

'Are you all right?' Professor Ebeid asked, his eyes on the remaining crackers.

'I'm okay. Just…queasy.'

'Ah. I'm sorry to put you out. I've been concerned about the safety of discussing…the Ark over the phone.' He busied himself with fixing his cup of tea. 'I'm not paranoid. I just realized some time ago that we needed a better solution to its existence.' He sipped his tea. The chair squeaked as he leaned back, holding the cup in his hand. 'I knew it would be found eventually.'

'Someone wrote down a cryptic message on where to find it.'

He grimaced. 'I'm afraid that is my doing.' He turned and looked out the window. 'Ayanna believed it would be safe hidden in Nefertari's tomb. She didn't want to return it to Theopetra's Cave.'

'Isn't that in Thessaly, Greece?' I interrupted, my mind racing.

He glanced at me. 'Yes. It was where it had originally been hidden after Pandora had found it. She managed to infect her entire village before succumbing to her illness.' He took another sip of tea. 'At least, that was how the original story was told. Like all history, it morphed into something different altogether. Some even speculated what she'd found was a large storage jar filled with rotting spices.'

Pandora. Pandora's box. A cursed artifact from myth.

I had always believed the story of Pandora was fiction. But her name had been carved into the walls where the Ark had been hidden. Now, thinking of the story of that damned box and how Pandora had opened it to release physical and mental curses on humanity - and given the ancient knowledge of diseases in the past - what I was experiencing now could be seen as a curse. And the mental effects of the sickness consuming me had to have been alarming as well.

I was barely holding it together myself. I could only imagine what the ancients believed had been happening to them.

'Did you write the warnings on the walls?' I wiped my brow. I'd started sweating again.

He nodded, his gaze distant. 'Using the languages inscribed on the Ark. I had hoped it would be enough.' He set his cup down. 'Curiosity is humanity's greatest downfall. The story of Pandora is familiar enough that the warning made sense. I couldn't very well say what it really was. But Ayanna had told her husband with her dying breath.'

'What is it, really?' My mind was drowning in fever. Through the fabric of my gloves I could feel the red welts pulsing on the surface of my skin.

'It is the Ark of Death. It is…Harbinger. One of the three Arks that host the creator gods' powers. It can destroy everything, infecting millions.'

'What?' My eyes rounded and my breath came out in a whoosh. *What?*' I all but screamed. The ramifications of what I had inadvertently let out into the world left me cold and angry. My earlier fears of helping Hamilton Pharmaceuticals acquire some ancient plague they could unleash on the world seemed inadequate now.

A thump sounded outside the room.

'My intentions were noble when I contacted Mr. Price,' Professor Ebeid continued in a rush. 'I had been assured he could deal with the situation discreetly.' He opened his desk drawer and pulled out a bottle of pills. 'Staring down one's own demise does have a way of putting your life into perspective. I could not leave this world knowing that at any moment someone would stumble upon that Ark.' He shook out a pill and took it. 'I had no idea he had involved anyone else.' He studied me; his eyes filled with sadness. 'I was there when Ayanna first got sick. I recognize the signs.'

Adrenaline rushed through me when his words finally penetrated the fog in my mind. I'd been lured here.

The door opened and I turned to the sound. Avner Price walked in with two men trailing behind him. I jumped up and moved toward the wall.

'You set me up,' I accused him. Something else had suddenly registered. The men who had retrieved the Ark had been wearing gloves. Price had to have known touching it would lead to sickness. Yet he hadn't warned me. Why? As soon as I thought about it, I understood. He *wanted* me to get sick. That's why he put the tracking device on my phone.

Price nodded. 'I had to provide a test subject before Mr. Hamilton would agree to my price.'

'What?' Professor Ebeid yelled. 'We agreed you would destroy that damned thing. Not sell it!'

Avner gave him a pitying look before signaling to the man with him. The man pulled a gun from his waistband and shot Professor Ebeid. His body landed on the chair, toppling it over. The thud made my body jerk.

My eyes rounded, going from the now dead Professor to Avner. How could I have miscalculated? I should have brought Malik with me. Should have done a lot of things differently. 'I suppose I'm next.' I needed to figure a way out of here. But the world was once again spinning. Shadows crawled across the walls. A cacophony filled my ears: laughter, crying, screaming, and an eerie church bell ringing while my heartbeat drummed in my ears.

He chuckled, his voice seeming to echo. 'No. Like the Ark, you hold a great deal of value.' He pulled a plastic bag from his pocket. Inside rested the tracker I'd planted in the Ark. 'I found this when I procured samples from the artifact for my own research. I assume you and your companion Malik had intended on tracking us.' He turned the device around in his hand. 'Looks like the one I thought we'd planted on you.' He smiled. 'A decoy phone?' He paused, studying me. 'Tell me, Dr. Landry. Why would you use a decoy phone?'

I didn't answer.

He sighed heavily, irritation evident in the creases on his brow. 'All would have been lost had you not contacted the professor. I have to thank you for that. It took some time to find a suitable host for the disease; one we could study and not worry about others trying to locate them. I had believed you had no one in your life.' He shook his head. 'Sadly, we've had some trouble locating your friend. Malik, right? Was he the one who suggested the subterfuge?'

The anonymity I insisted on with regards to my personal life would be my undoing. I glared at him while the world spun around me. At least they didn't know about Raymond. Despite them removing the tracking device, he would find me.

When my parents first left us, I had promised my brother I would never let them separate us. Only when I wanted to go to college to study, we both knew I needed to explain our existence. So, when they came, I told them my brother had run away and joined a gang.

A few years later, my brother returned home having changed his name from Raphael Landry to Raymond Chase. All traces of his past and previous identity were forever erased.

'Get Dr. Landry's *real* phone.' He instructed one of his men. 'Malik's a loose end we need to eliminate.' He gave me a mock frown. 'I hope you understand.'

He was crazy if he thought I was going to let him just take my phone.

His man started for me, I backed away, eyes darting around for something to use to defend myself. My hand landed on a paperweight. I lifted the heavy object, brandishing it in front of me. My would-be assailant laughed at me, and I brought the paperweight down on his arm. He cried out and moved back. I pushed into his space, pounding at his body. Despite the pain. Despite the futile efforts, I would still fight. For me. For my brother. And for Malik who I hoped one day I could bring myself to say the words he so wanted to hear.

To my very last breath. I. Would. Fight.

The other man rushed forward, knocking me into the bookshelf. Pain raced down my arm and my vision wavered. I swung out, trying to land a blow. He danced back out of reach. I righted myself, chest heaving. Once again, my vision wavered, and a chill sent me into a shaking fit. The paperweight thumped to the floor. My attacker took the opportunity to take me down and roughly search for my phone.

He pulled it from my pocket and handed it to Avner.

'I thought you'd be further along in your illness by now.' He stared down at the display as he searched the contents on my phone. 'But I guess that is a good thing. Mr Hamilton wanted to chart your progression. You really do have very few friends. Ah, here it is.' He crouched in front of me. 'I assume your coming here was to figure out what to do with the Ark once you and your associate stole it from us.'

I didn't respond.

'Rather than chasing him all over the place, why don't we lure him here?' He looked at my phone again. 'Brief seems to be your style. Checking in, I assume.' He smiled. 'This one seems more personal.' He cocked his head to the side. 'More than just a guide, then.' He typed a message on the phone. 'Tell me. How does this sound? *I could really use your help. Meet me at the port in Alexandria in three hours.*'

'Doesn't sound like a message I would send. He won't come,' I said. 'As you said, he is more than just my guide.' I kept my face blank, willing him to put the pieces together on his own. Feed him too much information and he wouldn't believe me.

'Of course. Too impersonal. How about, *Meet me at the port in Alexandria in three hours. I love you.*' He smirked. 'Is it sappy enough?'

'Screw you.'

'I will take that as a yes.' He hit send and I suppressed a sigh of relief. Malik would come but he would also know something was wrong and alert my brother as well.

Avner stood. 'Bring her.' He glanced at the man I had pummeled with the paperweight. The man was still down, barely moving. 'You're useless.' He pulled a gun from his inner pocket and shot the man in the head. 'Dead weight,' he said and winked.

His remaining man hoisted me to my feet. Bile rose in my throat, and I spewed undigested tea and crackers all over the man. I took pleasure in that simple defiant act. He slapped me hard. Blood flew from my mouth, coating the books on the bookshelf.

I spat the remaining blood in his face, hoping it would make him sick.

Before I could relish yet another act of rebellion, someone struck me in the back of the head. I fought hard to keep my eyes open, bit down on the pain radiating down my spine. But darkness crept around the edges of my vision until finally...

The world went black.

I swam up from a sea of confusion and nightmares and slowly became aware of my surroundings. A crushing weight sat on my chest. I opened my eyes to a brightness so absolute it burned my retinas. A horn bleated, echoing in my ears, joining the symphony of voices mumbling in my head – repeating a phrase in several different languages.

'Do not look upon the goddess... for in her eyes is death.'

The beep of a monitor stabbed its way through the chaotic chorus. I turned my head, the only thing I could move, and took in my surroundings: white walls with large bolts running along the seams; medical equipment circling me; a few people wearing dark green scrubs and face masks, their attention on the monitors. In the corner, surrounded by a black mesh harness, was the crate they had packed the Ark in. Hamilton Pharmaceuticals was stamped on the front. Two men dressed in black and armed to the teeth stood in front of it, eyes cast out, unseeing.

I opened my mouth to say something, but no sound came out. All sense of smell and feel had left me in a void. As if I were looking out at a scene I was no longer a part of.

One of the people walked over and peered down at me. 'Good. You're awake.' He signaled behind him and a woman walked over. 'Start blood pressure readings for every two minutes.' He shined a penlight in my eyes. 'The color in her eyes is fading.' He moved in closer. 'Your body is beginning to shut down. We would have preferred to monitor you from the start, but that's not an option now. Can you answer a few questions?'

I glared at him.

'Well. We at least can capture the transition from death to life. That's what we need anyway.' He smiled at me. 'You, Dr. Landry are going to be the key to learning the formula for immortality.'

My eyes rounded. Immortality? How was that even possible?

A door opened and a woman walked in. Late thirties, with light brown skin and hair pulled back in a tight knot, she wore all black like the guards, but she had no visible weapons. After exchanging a brief glance with the guards, her dead, grayish eyes focused on me.

I recognized her from the article online.

Ayanna Shukuma. Professor Ebeid's colleague, back from the dead.

Now it made sense.

'Do you still feel the pain?' the man asked, touching my forehead.

Again, I tried to speak but couldn't. Instead, I screamed inside my head.

'Unfortunately, even if you are in pain we can't do anything about it.' He looked at Ayanna. 'She told us about her own transition. Called this part the calm before the storm.'

The blood pressure cuff tightened on my arm.

'99 over 60, sir.'

He patted my cheek. 'Not long now.' They moved away and Ayanna slowly walked over.

Where am I?' I mouthed to her.

'You're on a ship.' She leaned in, stating the obvious. 'I've been where you are. I even took my own life. But the Hamilton family knew I wasn't truly dead. I'm changed. Renewed. And soon, you will be as well.' She touched my forehead, her eyes filled with sadness. 'But first you must meet her.'

The sickly sweet stench of roses and charred things filled my nose. My chest moved as if being pulled by an invisible string. Spasms shot down my entire body. Yet I remained in place. Secured by the straps holding me on the bed. My gut twisted and bile rose in my throat.

Once again, the blood pressure cuff tightened on my arm. All the while, Ayanna watched me out of those dead eyes. Why was she working with them?

Another spasm overtook me. The woman called out my blood pressure again. '84 over 50.' I roared. At least I thought I did. No sound came out of my mouth.

I remembered what Ayanna had told me. *'Who will I meet?'* I mouthed.

'Harbinger,' she whispered and turned.

I followed her gaze and found a child holding a burned doll in her arms, standing next to the crate. The child's eyes, filled with all colors and none at the same time, swirled with madness and hunger. Her hair, a tangled black web of strands, cascaded down her back. Her bronze skin had familiar gold symbols carved into it, along with the wings of an owl on both cheeks. She wore a blood-coated dress and no shoes.

She extended her hand to me.

My heart slowed.

She smiled. Showing bright, white teeth.

My skin grew cold.
She spoke, the words like the rush of wind.
And the world went black.

THE HAUNTING OF LIFT 3

TANSY RAYNER ROBERTS

Items Recently Found By Me, Sally McNab, In A Haunted Lift:

- A hair comb

- Decades-old letters, sealed and never opened

- A vintage magazine for modern housewives

- Three crackers, neatly stacked

- A lace handkerchief with the initials SG

- A single Christmas ornament

- A porcelain teacup (cracked)

- One of my own baby teeth

Reasons I Believe The Lift is Haunted:

- Strange and sinister items left behind on a regular basis

- A mysterious creaking sound when the lift goes up

- A suspicious complete silence when the lift goes down

- A soft whispering 'woooo-oooh-ooooh' sound if you go down very low and listen

- Cedric the chihuahua always whines and looks terrified when he sees himself in the mirror tiles

- I once saw a headless girl in the reflection of the mirror tiles

- I had regular conversation with an elderly lady who caught the lift at the same time as me at 11am and 2pm every day for a month, who then suddenly vanished in mid-air while discussing the weather

- A hell pit once opened up in the floor of the lift and I almost fell down into this hideous demonspace, but luckily I've been learning some minor spells on the side and was able to close it up without too much drama

- It's lucky Cedric the chihuahua wasn't with me that time; he is not a fan of hell pits

- Or lifts

How To Locate the Haunted Lift:

1. Take the narrow path behind the high school – the one with the blackberries

2. Take a sharp left at the little corner shop that's always closed

3. Walk only on the concrete, not the cracks, along the pavement on the same side as the refurbished cinema that only shows films from the 90s

4. What's the deal with Ethan Hawke, anyway?

5. Go past the cemetery car park to the council building, on East Street

6. Check at reception if you need to be buzzed to an upper floor. Say, for example, because Mrs Engel the deputy mayor always brings her chihuahua to work, and you are paid to come by at 11am and 2pm every day to take him out for walkies

7. There are three lifts in a row, facing a wall of mirrors

8. The haunted one is the third one at the back, right by the big green plant

9. Yes, there's an odd stain on the carpet. Best not to look too closely

Messages I Have Discovered In The Haunted Lift:

- If you peel up the back left corner of the carpet, you will find demonic sigils painted underneath in what I really hope is red nail polish

- Written on the mirror, only visible if you huff on the glass: *Stay Away, Little Girl*

- A piece of very old paper tied up with an actual ribbon, featuring an itemised list of horrible fates suffered by the previous people who took too much interest in Lift 3. Very elegant calligraphy

- On the ceiling one afternoon, painted in something yellow that smelled a lot like mustard: *Get A Real Job, Sally*

- I'm starting to wonder if the ghosts have been talking to my mother

Notable Disappearances Linked To The Haunted Lift:

1. Mr Venn the cashier

2. The police officers who came asking questions about Mr Venn the cashier

3. The very attractive temp who dressed kind of goth and smiled at me sometimes

4. That one lady who was selling fundraising chocolates for her kid's school

5. Her kid

6. Tracy the receptionist

7. Mel the receptionist

8. Amy the receptionist

9. The guest speaker who came in to teach that sexual harassment seminar

10. Me, probably, if I believe anything the inhabitants of the lift have to say about my future

If You Have Found This Diary:

- I'm probably dead

- The ghosts killed me

- Or they opened another hell pit, this time in the wall, and I got sucked through

- Or I'm living in another dimension, on the other side of the lift, where everyone has buttons for eyes (ha, lift buttons) and very dark goatees, but somehow we all pull them off effortlessly

- Or I'm still here but you can't see me, because I have become a ghost

- Maybe I'm writing a message to you on the glass right now. Better breathe on it to fog it up and check

- Maybe I went somewhere else and got a real job

- Like the ghosts (and my mother) kept hinting about

- Or maybe Cedric the chihuahua turned into the three-headed dog of the Underworld and dragged me down there to battle Hades, flirt with Persephone and figure out the proper exchange rate of the Australian dollar with Charon the ferryman

- But I'm probably dead

Items Recently Abandoned in the Haunted Lift:

- A diary belonging to Sally McNab, featuring endless speculations and one very disturbing illustration

- A confused-looking chihuahua called Cedric

- A ham and cheese sandwich in a beeswax wrap

- A mobile phone, locked

If you have any information about the owner of these items, please check with our receptionist at the main desk.

If you cannot locate a receptionist at the main desk, please contact the temp agency and ask them to send us a new one.

Mrs Engel the deputy mayor is looking for a new dog walker, if anyone is available at 11am and 2pm each weekday.

THE LAST RUNT

CLAIRE L. SMITH

THE EDEN FAMILY DAIRY WAS LOCATED MILES AWAY FROM ANY FORM OF city or town pollution, among fields of vibrant green grass that swayed in the fresh, crisp wind. The label on the bottle showed a grinning cow with shining teeth and a speech bubble that read "I'm hand-milked with love and care". On the farm, there were three buildings. The garage, the barn and the living quarters that squeezed in nearly thirty people, ranging from birth to old age. The household had begun as a mix of four families, but after a while, it became hard to determine who was related to whom. They were all Edens now.

Out of all the children that lived there, Alice was the youngest, the smallest. Father used to joke that if she were a cow, they would've roasted her for Sunday dinner the moment she fell from the womb, since she would've been too weak to survive. The entire family would chuckle at that, but the joke tasted sour to Alice. The idea of being shot between the eyes, then stretched out across the table and picked apart made her five-year-old self squirm with unease. As she grew older, the jokes didn't get any funnier, so she assumed she was also born without a sense of humour.

Another joke was that she had to make sure she ate all of her dinner, because after all, if she had been born an ounce smaller, she would've ended up in the patch. The patch was a small, fenced-off piece of paddock at the very back of the farm. It had a low fence but no gate — no one was allowed to touch the land, except for Father and his shovel. At one point, he'd hung a small wooden sign over the fence with the words "the strong shall not suffer the sins of the weak" carved into it. Thankfully, Alice was too young to understand what the message meant.

Alice was always told that she was lucky. She lived a worthy life away from the lazy heathens in the city; she had structure and was able to learn good traits like discipline, perseverance and obedience. She lived in a good home with her family, all graciously given to them by Father.

Father's farm was built on five generations of strong blood, and Alice had lived in the same fields, the same house, with the same people, and the same routine for all fourteen years of her life. Her brain felt pickled in her skull, boredom and fatigue wearing away at her until she felt like an empty shell that only moved to and from her bed and workstation every day. Her relatives were the same. Rooted to the land, the Edens were all that remained from what used to be a vibrant farming town and community. Father spoke little of the time before, only letting details slip through alcohol-lubricated lips. He talked about the Brothers who abandoned the land because they were weak and 'not cut out 'for the noble work'. His speech would begin to slur by the time he got to talking about the drought and the financial hardship, having to herd cows into swallow pits since they were too weak, barely able to afford the bullets. By then, the entire dinner table was captive to his rant, heads bowed as the air grew thick with the intensity. Alice would hold her breath, hoping he would doze off into a drunken sleep.

One night he kept them at the table for hours in a gripping silence as he turned over years of memories in his head before he lifted his gaze towards Alice.

'You would've left me too,' he always said. 'The runts always leave; they leave the strongest to carry on because they know they're not worthy.'

Alice didn't sleep that night, her heart pounding as if Father was still there, filling her head with words that burned her brain. Tears filled her eyes as she struggled to accept that she was truly as worthless as he said. She could still help the family, maybe even become a Mother instead of just a Sister. Yet they always reminded her that she'd never earn the honour of carrying on the Eden legacy. She was destined to disappear and contribute nothing to the family's strength. Surely, she could prove that she wasn't another runt.

The only way to and from the farm was Father's truck, in which he transported the milk to the distribution centre miles away. Not even the manufacturers knew where the farm was — that was part of its appeal. The milk was untainted by milking machines or other technology, the cows untouched by chemicals. Each cow was the result of generations of special breeding and their milk "as pure and strong as it gets". It sold at five times the normal price to really convince the well-off public that they were healthier than those who could only afford the two-dollar supermarket brand milk.

Alice watched Father drive away every afternoon, longing to steal away into the back of the truck and ride down the beige gravel road to see what was over the horizon, beyond the green fields. She'd asked to come with him once, only for him to laugh in her face before driving away. Mother, one of several Mrs Edens living on the farm, told her not to bother Father anymore.

Alice settled for watching the truck disappear into the horizon, imagining the wondrous things that must be on the other side of the paddock fence. It made things easier, to hide in the clouds of her imagination, to dream of an escape rather than face her reality.

Alice didn't notice the shift until a few weeks after it commenced, right after the first spring cow was born. The few conversations she had with her Sisters grew short and impatient. Their eyes avoided her and her requests for help with carrying her quota of milk to Father's truck were ignored.

At first, Alice wondered if it had something to do with the newest addition to the family. Father's new wife, Alice's new Mother. The young woman was quiet, reserved. Her eyes were always wide, and she trembled like a newborn calf finding its feet. Father said her name was Eve, yet the woman's hiking bag said "Louise Jones" on the tag. Alice had noticed it when she was asked to dispose of the woman's things.

She was tempted to ask her about it, yet Father said no one should talk to her until Eve accepted her place.

Things got worse for Alice after that. She wasn't allowed to spend the day outside, picking fruit or vegetables from the garden and pickling them to put in the basement in case of another drought. She was to help milk the cows, and only that.

Mother would also normally put a little bit of sugar in her tea in the mornings, but when Alice took a sip one morning the taste was bitter against her tongue. She assumed Mother had forgotten, but when she asked Mother said, 'Surely you can handle unsweetened tea.'

Alice carried the shame with her until that evening as she helped clean up after dinner, scrubbing the dishes with her hands already sore and worn from a day of milking. She must have done something wrong, and she had to make up for it.

Alice felt suddenly cold to the bone, despite her hands burning from the scalding sink water, as if a chilling wind had blown into the room. She didn't notice Father until he was standing over her, his hands clenched behind his back as he gazed down at her. She stopped, her hands still plunged into the hot sink, frozen in silence before he finally spoke.

'Come,' he said.

Alice wiped her wet hands on her apron and followed Father out into the cold night. The sky was pitch black, blocking out the horizon. It was as if she was trapped in a dark void – the thought caused her to shiver. She wondered how far the sky went, how high she could go, how far she could fly from the farm.

She was hauled back from her swarming mind as Father directed her into the paddock, where her family stood in a wide circle. They surrounded one of the calves that'd been born the morning before. The calf was small, even for a newborn, with knobby, twig-like legs that quivered beneath its weight. Its round, black eyes glistened under the moon as it circled the post it was tied to, its thin neck stretched out as it scanned the dark field. The calf let out a low cry, its voice echoing into the blackness. In response, a deeper groan came from the barn, strained and squealing. The calf's mother calling for her baby.

Alice winced at the sound, the pain in both mother and child's voices causing chills to run up her spine. Father stopped centimeters from the calf and reached for his belt. There was a blunt click before he turned to Alice; a short black pistol was waiting in his open palm. Her stomach dropped.

She glanced over her shoulder to her Mothers and Sisters, searching for an explanation but she was met with only tired, blank stares. They looked like perfect dolls, dead in the eyes, all dressed in similar cream aprons, collared white shirts and ankle-length skirts. The older women's hair, especially the Mothers, had thinned and greyed, their faces worn like aged leather, worked and used yet unable to tear or break. They wore it all like a badge of honour, their faces proof of their years of self-sacrifice and hard work. Alice felt a sense of shame looking at them, her skin still smooth and youthful despite her best efforts. Clearly, she hadn't tried hard enough.

'What's that for?' Alice asked, the gun gleaming in the dim moonlight.

'You're fifteen now. This is your chance to prove yourself worthy of a place here,' Father said before jerking his head towards the calf. 'She's weak. We don't want that weakness in future stock.'

The warmth drained from Alice's face as Father held the gun towards her; the cold breeze passed through her as deeper silence fell upon the crowd. Her eyes drifted towards the calf as it continued to tug on the rope around its neck, edging as close as it could towards the barn. It let out another desperate moan before turning back to her, its black eyes wide with a consuming fear. Alice's mind raced, fumbling over excuses until her words came out in a rambling stutter.

'But sh-she seems healthy, a-and she's standing. And she hasn't been rejected by her mother,' she said, wincing as another strained wail echoed from the barn. 'You could sell her.'

'Oh, you want to give our competition a leg up?' Father barked, impatience tainting his gravelly voice. 'All of these cows are specially bred. They either make the cut or they don't. That's what those rich pricks pay for.'

Alice yelped as Father's large, rough fingers snatched her wrist, forcing the gun into her hand. It felt so heavy in her grasp, although the weight of it was nothing compared to the pressure forced down on her shoulders. Through her fear, a clear thought emerged. *This is wrong.*

'No!' she screamed, voice nasal between her jerking sobs. 'It's not her fault. You haven't even given her a chance!'

Her cry burst from her, passing through the fields like a strong wind, but like the calf's, it fell on cold, deaf ears. Father's face contorted as confusion and rage played across his twitching features.

'Do this or you're out,' he said. 'All by yourself. I won't even give you a ride to that God-forsaken city.'

Alice turned to the rest of the family, most of whom dodged her gaze. Only the Mothers kept their eyes on her, their firm stare devoid of any comfort or support.

'Your Mothers and Sisters have all done this. You've been spoiled,' Father said, 'Are you really that selfish and weak? You won't even help your family?'

Father's words crashed against Alice, her form trembling before she finally turned back towards the calf.

'It's loaded,' Father said, his voice settled but still simmering with rage, 'and don't close your eyes. You'll miss and waste bullets.'

Alice lifted her arm, her sweaty fingers keeping a flimsy grip on the gun. She choked back several sobs as the calf let out a confused groan and took a few steps away from the barrel of the gun. Alice stared into the calf's eyes, allowing the blackness of the pupils to consume her.

She didn't expect a recoil, the gun flying backwards in her grip, smashing against the bridge of her nose. She let out a startled yelp as she clasped her palm over her face, a sharp pain blooming from her nose as she bent forward. She fought back the tears that burned her eyes, her blurry gaze roaming the ground before her.

The calf lay slumped against grass, the tight rope around its neck making its head hover above the ground. Its face was stuck in shock, its jaw slack and eyes wide. Alice stilled, the blood from her nose dripping onto her palm as her eyes locked onto the corpse. Her gag reflex swelled, her eyes watered. She couldn't move. The image of the dead calf burned into her mind.

If anyone noticed that she was hurt, they didn't mention it. Father took the gun from her loose grip before placing it back on his belt. He stared down at the calf.

'As it should be,' he said.

Then the real work began.

The Sisters dragged the calf into the kitchen, slapping her onto the heavy wooden table with a thunderous bang. Alice flinched, a light gasp caught in her throat. Father came back with a set of knives, laying them across the counter. The blades gleamed like diamonds against the large ceiling light.

'Get to work. You have until breakfast tomorrow,' he said to her. 'Mother will help you get started.'

Alice felt no relief as Father left the room. There was still a tight twist in her chest, tears behind her eyes and more sobs lodged in her throat. She stood by the calf's corpse, gazing at its cold form as Mother collected the knives. Outside, the calf's mother was still screaming for its baby, its voice now raw. Every cry felt like another punch to Alice's gut as the stench of death filled her nose.

'Stop feeling so sorry for yourself. I don't know why you had to make it harder on yourself. He asks you to do something, you do it,' Mother snapped at her. 'If we are not strong, and the farm fails, what else will we have? Where would we go? What would we do? We have nothing but this, and nothing else to offer, so you'd better accept that soon or else you'll drag the rest of us down with you.'

Alice didn't reply, leaving room for the mother cow to scream out once again.

'That damn thing better shut up soon if she knows what's good for her,' Mother muttered.

'Sh-she's sad,' Alice said, 'can't you tell?'

Mother paused, her hand resting on the handle of one of the knives. Her entire body stiffened.

'Do you want my help or not?'

All through the night, they worked. First, they stripped off the calf's skin, revealing the layers of muscle, fat and organs. Then, with Mother's guidance, Alice took the calf apart layer by layer, until it was little more than bone. As the night continued, Alice occasionally slipped with the knife. Mother would hand her a band-aid before pushing her to continue. It was finished in time for breakfast, which Alice was meant to cook as an offering to secure her place on the Eden Family Farm.

She wasn't allowed to wash her hands or shower, the stench of blood and flesh seeping into her skin as if branding her. She wasn't to have a bite of what she'd made of the cow's flesh, only the calf's heart, tongue and liver. All raw. The texture was slimy in her mouth and her stomach lurched as she forced it down. Her entire family watched her, their eyes burning holes through her tired, aching body as she swallowed each nauseating bite until her plate was clean. Then she was to commence a day's work as if the previous night had never occurred.

Despite her desperation for it, Alice couldn't find sleep. She'd crawled out of her covers to sit by the window above her bedhead. With her arms crossed over the windowsill and her chin resting on her wrist, she gazed out into the paddocks. She tried to keep her eyes pinned to the horizon, yet her gaze couldn't help but wander down the paddock below to the dark patch that stained the grass. She closed her eyes as her body tensed, trying to push away the image of the calf. The mother's cry still echoed in her head, fusing with the hollow bang of the gun. But there was nothing the cow could do: she was powerless, weak.

Taking in a shaky breath, Alice opened her eyes to find the glare of the sun staring back at her from the horizon. A sudden panic washed over her, horrified that she'd overslept.

Yet, as she squinted she noticed the size of this "sun" – like a giant dome, it smothered the starry night sky. Blinded by the light, she shielded her face with her hand before a small figure in the paddock caught her eye. Her breath stuck in her throat as the calf rose from its final resting place, stumbling slightly under its weight before finally finding its balance. It exited the paddock, following the stretch of the driveway before leaving through the front gate. Alice trembled with a consuming awe. The calf walked towards the sun, and when it reached it, its body burst into flames. The fire ate away at its flesh and bone and yet the calf's form remained, a skip in its step as its blackened feet left the ground and then the calf soared into the orange sky. It flew away until it faded into the vast horizon, free at last.

'Alice, go to sleep.'

Alice flinched at Mother's voice. She was glaring at Alice from a nearby bed. Alice's eyes shot back up towards the window. The black sky had returned and there was no calf on the horizon, nothing but blackness. Confusion swept over her, her mind buzzing, caught between two fading truths. She pushed her scrambled thoughts away as she sunk back into bed, mirroring Mother by laying on her back. She listened to the other girls and women snoring and stirring in the Women's Ward, their beds lined up side by side on either end of the room, similar to the milking barn.

'Why didn't you tell me?' she asked. 'You knew it was going to happen.'

Mother sighed, dragging her hand down her face.

'What's there to say, Alice?' she said, her voice cold and firm. 'Some things you just have to endure for the sake of the family. It is how it is.'

'Do you wish you hadn't killed your calf?'

The only response Alice got was the slight shuffle of Mother rolling onto her side. Mother's silence was answer enough. Alice rubbed her eyes before reaching up to run her fingers into her scalp.

Alice tensed as her fingers suddenly dipped. She held her breath as her fingers frantically circled the dent in her forehead before they dipped into a hole that dug through her skin and into her skull.

Her hands flew over her mouth to smother the pending scream, her eyes bulging from her sockets before she finally gathered the courage to lift one hand back up towards her forehead. Despite finding a smooth, whole surface instead of a deep bullet hole, her heart continued to beat wildly against her chest until morning came.

From that day on, Alice's quota was doubled; she wasn't allowed to leave the barn until she'd finished. Every day, she felt the cows' eyes burn into her, watching her as she milked them, filling bucket after bucket. As if killing one of their young wasn't enough, she was draining them as well. The younger cows seemed to struggle more, groaning and squirming against the restraints while the older ones endured. As Alice struggled to milk them, every croak of discomfort sent a sharp chill down her spine.

Sunlight became a distant stranger as she rose from her stone-cold bed well before dawn and returned to dinner after dark. After a week, she stopped eating, instead opting to crawl into bed for a moment of quiet and rest, dreading to awake the next day. Father took this as a sign of disrespect and forced her to sit at the dinner table until everyone else had finished.

She sat slumped against the chair, staring at her empty plate. She hadn't bothered to fill it with food, since she'd be scolded for having too much or too little. Even if her appetite decided to return, she didn't see the point. She couldn't eat at the same long table where the calf's corpse had lain, where she'd sloppily stripped it to the bone and then swallowed its organs.

She closed her eyes for a brief moment and took in a slow breath in an attempt to refresh herself. Yet, as she opened them, her body locked up in a gripping fear. Her eyes scanned her family as they sat around the table.

The men and boys remained as they were, but the girls and women began to shift. Their skin stretched, discolouring into a blotchy white, their chins extending and their eyes turning black. Alice sat still, her jaw trembling as their faces finally set, their bodies remaining human but their heads now complete with long snouts, large ears, white and black skin and dark, soulless eyes. They sat in silence, eating as if it were a chore. A chore Alice did not have the strength to do. She'd always been the runt, the weakling, the Other amongst the litter of perfectly bred stock. It wasn't until that moment that, for the first time in weeks, she felt the cold slap of clarity. They weren't born perfect – they were *made* perfect.

'Alice? Alice!'

She jolted in her seat and glanced at Mother, who stared at her through her thick lashes, her long bovine ears twitching. Alice swallowed the fist-sized lump in her throat as she met Mother's eyes and flinched as a harsh snort shot from Mother's enlarged nostrils.

'Y-Yes?'

Mother extended her pale finger towards the seat next to Alice.

'Your Sister is talking to you,' she said, before turning back to her meal.

Alice glanced at her older Sister, Emma, beside her. A cold sweat lined her forehead as she forced herself to gaze into Emma's bovine eyes, her own ghostly face mirrored in the endless void of the black globes.

'I said pass the salt, please,' Emma said.

Alice nodded, sucking on her tongue as her trembling hand reached for the salt shaker.

'Here,' she said,.

Despite her cow's head, Emma's features tensed, as if studying Alice's petrified expression.

'Are you sick?' Emma asked, tilting her large head.

Alice's vision began to warp, her jaw drawing open as her eyes fluttered. Her head began to throb, her mind to numb, and all sound faded into silence as the world bled into strips of red. The women's cow heads began to drip with blood from their large snouts, eyes and lips, dribbling into a pool on the table. Generations upon generations of blood, all lapped up by Brothers, Uncles and Fathers as they continued to dig into their blood-stained plates.

Anger rose within Alice. It wasn't just her. They were all unworthy, mindless, weak.

A wave of nausea washed over her before sound found her ears and her watery eyes focused on the scenery around her. The table was clean and the women's heads had returned to normal. Alice's mind continued to buzz, her head still heavy on her shoulders.

'I... don't...I'm fine,' she said, clearing her throat. 'I'll be fine.'

She glanced to her side to find Emma's worn skin restored, the grey bags back under her tired eyes.

'Maybe try and sleep more,' Emma said.

'I have been,' Alice said. 'It's all I do other than work.'

'No, you haven't been sleeping,' Emma replied. 'I've seen you looking out the window all night.'

Alice blinked in confusion. Every night, she fell into a deep slumber the moment her face met her thin pillow. She'd wake up in the same position, as if she'd merely blinked before having to rise again.

'What are you talking about?' she asked.

'You just sit there staring outside the window for ages,' Emma said, her eyes slowly drawing back to her food as she let a brief silence pass. 'You make noises sometimes. It scares me.'

Emma's hesitant words hit Alice like a hard slap. She watched Emma, who returned to eating mechanically with downcast eyes.

Glancing back around the table, she saw Eve, sitting next to Father like a disobedient puppy that wasn't allowed to stray too far from its master. She quickly found that Eve's plate was still full, perhaps even fuller than hers. Eve's intense stare locked onto Alice, sending a shiver down Alice's spine. For a moment, it felt like they were the only ones at the table, like two outcasts separated from the herd.

Father gripped Eve's arm, pulling her towards him. To Alice's surprise, she did not freeze, only jumped slightly as her attention was torn from Alice. Father's jaw was tense as he hissed into Eve's ear. Eve scowled before reaching for her folk and begrudgingly starting to eat the food that Mother had laid out for her. Alice squinted as she noticed a faint bruise forming beneath Eve's eye. She'd apparently tried to get out of bed the previous night, Alice still wasn't sure if the screams she'd heard were real or a part of her hazy dreams.

No one commented on Alice's empty plate, leaving her to sit in silence until she was permitted to leave the table.

The voices started the next evening. At first, the quiet groans echoed in the dark parts of Alice's mind before growing into desperate screams of pain. She rushed into the barn at midnight to check on the cows, thinking they were being slaughtered, only to find them resting in their pens. Yet the sounds continued, growing louder each day, seeping into her dreams until they dominated her every thought. She felt as if every piece of her was being stripped away, leaving only helplessness, weakness. She had nowhere to hide anymore, and everyone knew what she was. Weak.

One night, a sense of clarity broke through the cries. A wild smile spread across her face as a burst of confidence prompted her to slip out of her covers.

Alice snuck down the aisle of beds, descended the stairs and went into the kitchen. Her lungs burned, her sharp breaths scratching at her throat.

She searched the kitchen, climbing onto the counters and rifling through drawers to find what she needed. After gathering her equipment onto the kitchen table, she made her way toward the dining room. Father kept his guns in the cabinet next to the fireplace. It remained unlocked – he was confident no one would dare touch them without permission. Her eyes scanned the many firearms, all neatly polished and presented as if they were trophies.

Finally, she found it. The handgun Father had forced into her hands that night. Standing on her toes, she unlatched it from its holder. It was lighter and less bulky than she remembered, as if her hand had moulded to fit it. She searched for the right bullets, testing a few by sliding them into the barrel to ensure they were the correct ones. She felt a rush of adrenaline as the bullets slid into place, as if solving a puzzle.

She convinced herself that the gun was just a precaution. She had a better plan, after all.

She tucked the loaded gun into her bulky cardigan pocket and returned to her kitchen for the supplies. Her arms full with her loot, Alice stepped out into the night. The heavy wind knocked against her as her hair flowed behind her.

The generations-old barn was already cramped with the hay scattered across the floor and the wood. She broke the lid off the chest-sized bottle of cooking oil and did laps around the barn, trailing a thick line of liquid behind her as she went like a snail.

'Almost there,' she muttered to herself. 'Almost there, I promise. It won't hurt anymore, you'll never worry about being weak again.'

Her first task was completed within minutes. By then, the cows had begun to stir, groaning in confusion at the shadow stalking their barn. Their moaning only added to the choir of screams that filled Alice's head. With a loud cry, she slammed the now empty bottle of oil onto the ground, her veins burning with fury.

'Don't you see?' she screamed at the cows, 'I'm trying to help you!'

They continued to groan at her, caught up in their own growing panic.

Alice tossed the last bottle of oil onto the barn floor. The loud clang reverberated throughout the building. Yet, she heard them still, all their voices crying out in anguish. They were suffering, they were too weak.

She then collected several coils of rope that hung by the barn door. She collected the cows she wanted, the strong ones, the ones that made the most noise, put up the biggest fuss. There were only three out of the small batch of twenty: three strong ones suffering the burdens of the weak, while the weak suffered under guilt. Alice wished she could tell them that she understood, that it wasn't their fault.

The cows still had their nosebands attached, allowing Alice to easily attach a rope to each before leading them out of the barn. She tied them to the fence beside the open gate. They calmed once they were out in the open, soothed by the cool night air.

Alice then returned to the barn and produced a box of matches from her pocket. Her cold fingers pinched a match from the box. She flipped it in her grasp before she struck it against the box. The flame danced on the match like a tightrope walker.

For a moment, the realisation of what she was doing broke through the cows' cries, but it was quickly drowned in the chaos that now reigned in her mind.

The strong must not suffer the sins of the weak. But that didn't mean the weak had to suffer.

Alice relaxed her fingers, letting the match fall from her grip and into the trail of oil. Alice slipped outside, closing and barring the barn doors before stepping onto the grass. She waited, reaching into her pocket for the gun in case any cows broke loose. Her heart pounded against her ribcage. She froze as a loud wail came from the barn, a violent heat beginning to radiate from inside and flames seeping through the doors.

Alice backed up further as the entire barn burst into harrowing flame. A slight smile spread across her face, as the barn glowed a vibrant orange, like the sun with the bright evening stars gleaming behind it. All she had to do was step towards it, and like the calf, she would be free.

Panic rushed through her as the screaming didn't subside. Her head was ringing from the pressure. With a wailing cry, she dug her fingers into her hair, tearing at her scalp as if to claw the voices out.

Her frantic gaze landed back at her chosen cows that stood against the fence, away from the heat of the flames. She gathered her skirt and ran towards them. 'They're not weak anymore, they're happy now. They won't feel bad about dragging us down anymore,' she whispered to them. 'Why are they still screaming?'

Her ears tracked the sounds to the top floor of the house, through the bedroom window to where her sisters slept. The groans suddenly shifted, growing soft, more human. The realisation slapped Alice like a sharp backhand, yet she smiled. They needed help too. They needed her to be strong so they didn't have to be weak anymore.

Alice's euphoric state was interrupted as a flicker of movement snagged her gaze. A shadow creeping from the house through the front door. Alice didn't recognise the figure, but she'd known everyone here for all of her life.

Everyone, except one.

Alice watched as Father's newest wife glanced back into the darkened house behind her before she broke into a run, her footsteps echoing over the crackling of the fire. She was dressed in Father's button-up shirt and slacks, clearly stolen from his wardrobe, instead of her apron and skirt. She also had one of Father's carry bags over her shoulder. Even from a distance, Alice could see the bag was bursting with the spare cans of food from the basement.

Louise ran directly for the truck as if she was sprinting towards a lake in the centre of a desert. Once there, she hunched and fumbled with an object in her hands. Intrigued, Alice climbed over the fence, drawing closer until her shadow covered Louise like a heavy cloak.

Louise gasped as she noticed Alice behind her, her eyes widened like a rabbit cornered by a fox. She trembled and tried to hide behind a fragile mask of bravery. She held Father's heavy ring of mostly unused keys, except for the two that Alice always eyed: the small silver one that unlocked the truck and the slightly larger one that started it.

'What?' Louise snapped, failing to hide her anxiety. 'Get out of here. Leave me alone.'

'Where are you going?' Alice asked.

Louise rolled her eyes.

'I'm getting the hell out of here,' Louise said, trying the keys in the truck door.

Alice turned back towards the cows, their silhouettes black against the flames of the barn.

'We're coming with you,' Alice said.

Louise glanced up from the keys and gazed past Alice towards the paddock which now glowed with the light of the fire. Her gaze flickered between Alice and the barn fearfully before she released an amused scoff.

'Oh sure,' Louise said sarcastically before turning back to the keys. 'Find your own way out.'

Alice parted her lips to reply, but a sudden crash echoed from inside the house, followed by a charge of heavy footsteps.

Alice slipped like a shadow behind the house. There, she leaned against the wall in order to peek around the corner. She watched as Father, a lantern in hand, flung open the doors and nearly stumbled over his loose pyjama pants. He didn't see Alice in her hiding spot; his eyes were trained on Louise, like a hawk zoning in on its prey as it tried to squirm away.

'No!' Louise pressed against the truck door. 'Get the hell away from me!'

'Get back in the house, Eve,' Father barked, unaffected by Louise's terror.

'My name is Louise!'

'And hand it over, you little thief,' he said, holding out his palm. 'Weak cows like you don't deserve to hold it.'

'What are you talking about?' Louise replied, hiding the keys behind her back.

'You don't have the nerve to shoot me,' he replied, 'so hand it over!'

Louise's face flashed with genuine confusion as Father held out an expectant palm. Alice watched with a keen interest as the cogs in Louise's head turned until she figured out what Father thought she had.

'I'd shoot you in a heartbeat, you crazy old bastard!' she screamed. 'So stay back!'

Her voice travelled like a clap of thunder, heavy and booming. Alice wondered if Louise had awoken the others in their beds. But they wouldn't move. No matter what, they must remain in their room.

As her focus shifted back to Louise, Alice felt an aura radiating out of this girl. It was inspiring; intoxicating. Alice had never seen anyone speak to Father that way. She thought it impossible. He was the strong one. Yet, there he stood, bewildered and stunned, his face blank and his eyes filled with panic. He didn't seem to notice the glow of the burning barn.

Louise didn't even need the gun. She'd managed to command Father all on her own.

Father raised his hands, palms facing Louise. He bowed his head slightly in a sign of a thinly veiled empathy.

'Come on now,' he said with a smile, sliding his foot towards Louise. 'You really wanna go back out there? You had nothing – nothing but that bag on your back. You had nowhere to go. I helped you, remember? I can still help you. You don't ever have to worry about anything ever again. All you have to do is stay.'

Even though Alice was not the intended recipient, Father's words sewed a strong doubt into her, like his argument had regripped the puppet strings he had attached to her mind. *Father is strong, Father knows best.*

'Go. To. Hell.'

Alice's eyes widened as she felt the fiery burn of Louisa's voice. With it came a realisation. Father was holding them back on purpose. He wasn't like the cows or the Sisters. He had taught them how to be weak because he was weakest. It was all him. It was his fault.

Rage blinded Alice. It pumped through her veins like the fire she had started. She reached into her cardigan pocket for the gun before stepping from behind the house.

'Father.'

Father turned around. Alice waited until she could see the glimmer in his eyes before she squeezed the trigger.

Louise screamed, but Alice couldn't take her eyes off Father as his body froze and his legs buckled beneath him. He fell on his back, his limbs limp as his chest began to heave, a puddle of red blooming in the centre of his white sleep shirt.

Alice felt a numbing cold at the scene before her. She remembered the calf, its fear now reflected in Father's eyes as he gasped for air.

No. She needed to do this. She needed to help him.

'You were wrong,' she said, a smile flickering across her face, 'but it's okay, you won't be weak anymore. You don't have to suffer anymore, and no one else will suffer ever again.'

Father released a desperate croak before a second bullet shot through the space between his collarbones. Alice watched as he convulsed, trembling and gargling as his lungs filled with blood. Alice felt glad that the calf had died instantly, but she didn't want to waste another bullet on Father. She felt a sickly joy as his chest stilled, his body at her feet, at her mercy for once.

Louise went limp, the keys tumbling from her hands and onto the dirt. Her jaw was slack, her bulging eyes fixated on Father.

'Do you know how to drive?' Alice asked her.

Alice half expected a sarcastic or diminishing comment like the ones Louise had flung at her earlier. Louise just nodded, prompting Alice to pick the keys up and tuck them into her pocket. Louise's face fell as the keys were out of her reach once again.

'Get them inside the truck,' Alice said, pointing to the cows still tied to the fence. 'Did Father show you how to do that?'

'Um yeah but…why?' Louise asked.

'They need to come with us,' Alice replied. 'They're the strong ones.'

Louise took in a long breath

'To sell? Is that what you mean?' she asked, hesitant. 'We'll need cash.'

Alice tilted her head in thought. She'd only ever seen glimpses of money, the tiny pieces of paper and coins she'd sometimes found when folding Father's laundry.

'Maybe,' she said.

Louise's brow creased at Alice's response, yet her eyes lingered back to the loaded gun in Alice's hand. She gave another nod before slowly backing away from Alice as if she was trying to distance herself from an angry lion.

Alice watched as Louise made her way towards the cows, stumbling over her own feet, still caught in a cloud of shock. Alice then turned back towards the house, her eyes seeking the bedroom window once again. She could not deny it, as much as it stung to accept the disappointment. They would have seen the fire, they would've heard Louise and Father's argument, the gunshot. And yet none of them had left their room, or their beds, most likely.

With a heavy sigh, Alice retrieved the final few bottles of oil from the paddock.

'W-what are you doing?' Louise asked as she lead the cows to the truck.

Alice ignored her, fixated on what she had to do. The house was made of wood by Father's Father's Father. It was old, so she knew it wouldn't take much oil, but Alice wanted to be sure that the fire would carry them to a better place, where they wouldn't have to carry the burden of being weak.

Later, with the cows in the truck and the sun beginning its morning climb, Alice sat in the passenger seat, watching the downstairs windows starting to glow as the fire swelled. At last, for Alice, all was quiet. She was the strong one. It was like she was watching the horizon again, all of those nights wishing she could climb out of her window to feel the freeing warmth of the sinking sun, and now she could. And she had given it to all of them as well.

'Um, can we go now?' Louise asked.

It took Alice a moment to register Louise's question. The fire had almost hypnotized her, accepting her in a warmth embrace that she'd never felt before.

Alice felt a rush of intoxicating excitement, her smile widening as she scanned the dash full of buttons and handles. She giggled as Louise turned the key in the ignition and the truck hummed to life around her. Alice clutched the side of her seat as if she was on an amusement park ride as Louise steered them down the driveway.

Alice's stomach turned anxiously as they drew closer to the front gate. She had never seen it so close. She gripped the gun in her lap for comfort.

They pulled out onto the dirt road and turned towards the horizon. Dawn had yet to fully break, but Alice couldn't see the stars through the large clouds of smoke that smothered the sky.

'If you want to take a nap or something, go for it,' Louise said. 'The nearest town will be an hour or so at least.'

'I'm okay, thank you,' Alice replied, too excited to even think about sleep.

Alice didn't register the disappointment on Louise's face or her eyes on the gun in Alice's lap before they returned to the road ahead.

Alice looked over her shoulder at the flickering fires behind her. Perhaps it was her twisted mind, but she swore she could see Mother in the burning window, the flames swallowing her whole as she screamed. Alice raised her hand, waving fondly, content in knowing that Mother would be eased of her burden. To her surprise, she wasn't angry at Mother. She understood. Alice had been weak once too.

Maybe, once they reached the city, Alice could find more weak people and rid them of their burdens. She smiled wider, her mind buzzing with a thousand possibilities as she disappeared into her beloved horizon.

SAPLING

A. J. VRANA

Ioana always said her daughter was born to be a wolf.

Steadfast, unyielding, and fearless, wolves were made to frighten. They were also guardians, protecting family and warding off the malevolence of witches. That is, if one was to believe such tales; yet in the mountains, belief was not a choice, it was survival.

'Name the child Vuk,' the village elder had instructed Ioana and her husband, Nayden. Vuk – *wolf* – was more than an evocation; it was a manifestation of what the child in Ioana's womb was to become. After losing several offspring before they'd drawn their first breath, Ioana knew the culprit was a witch, stealing the souls of the unborn.

The elder's voice had been resolute as the mountain they lived on. 'Make the next one a wolf, and no witch will dare touch what's yours.'

Ioana agreed, and a daughter was born. Vuk was an odd name for a girl, but it was the one bestowed. To make it more palatable for the living, the only surviving daughter of Ioana and Nayden became known as Vuya – a diminutive of the masculine moniker intended for a son. Nayden had been sure that only a boy could've survived the witch's wickedness after the others had succumbed, but Ioana relished their girl's strength.

Vuya heard the story of her naming so many times that she couldn't forget it had she been struck by a bolt of lightning. Of course, she wasn't a real wolf, though her parents had tricked the witch into believing so. Vuya, for her part, was uncertain that there was such power in any name.

But stories held power, and as much as Vuya fought them, they followed her into her eighteenth year, when the unfettered joy of childhood wilted into a wintry gust of hardship, and the solemness of the world bloomed like sorrow at a gravestone.

'Vuya,' came her mother's raspy call, her voice barely penetrating the wooden walls half eaten by water rot.

It'd been a difficult spring, the showers an onslaught rather than gentle nourishment for the trees. Mudslides had buried nearby settlements, and although this one still stood, its bones had grown soft and fetid with decay. Cold and damp seeped into homes, beds, and bodies, making the eldest and youngest sick with fever and cough. Most recovered, but some unexpectedly worsened.

Tugging down the barely dry linens after a merciful reprieve from the rain, Vuya pushed open the craggy door with her shoulder, the world dimming in the shelter of the cabin.

'I'm still here,' she told her mother as she set down the woven basket and began folding.

Ioana lay in the bed, a quilt splayed over her. The gentle slopes of her body shrank under the blanket each day, the porridge in her bowl untouched. She wasn't eating much, each spoonful a struggle.

'Would you make me some *kantarion* tea?' Ioana croaked, her throat scraped raw from the ceaseless coughing that wracked her body throughout the night.

The corners of Vuya's mouth strained to pull wider, to offer something resembling a smile. 'Of course.'

Of course, the tea never helped. *Kantarion* was a common enough flower – as common as rosehip and chamomile. If it truly cured illness, the land would've been stripped of every last petal decades ago. Ordinary herbs were for ordinary illnesses, but whatever gripped Ioana was far from ordinary. She'd been struggling for weeks now, some phantom thing draining the life from her. It was like she'd been poked with a dozen tiny holes, each one leaking vitality until the vessel ran dry.

Vuya poured freshly boiled water over a bed of dried *kantarion* in a pot and kissed her mother atop her head, mumbling her intention to visit Kosta, the village herbalist.

Kosta lived at the very precipice of the settlement – a scant collection of wood and stone structures barely clinging to the mountainside. Aside from a meagre flock of sheep, a few goats and their milk, the village sustained itself on berries, mushrooms, pumpkin, and horseradish. When people became sick in the damp weeks between winter and spring, Kosta was there to provide tinctures. When the green onions and wild carrots wouldn't grow in their usual spots, Kosta never failed to concoct some magical mulch that coaxed the soil into sprouting new life. He was a miracle worker, and without him, the village would've been a far barer place.

Kosta's workshop was something out of the old tales sung by *guslari*: a stone cottage ensconced in flowers, herbs, and shrubs. The thatched roof was as fluffy as a shepherding dog, with reeds and sedge so thick that no storm could penetrate. Framing the path to the front door were four large clay vases the colour of wine, three of which homed small fruit trees unlike any Vuya had seen. There was something *other* in the way their limbs twisted and bent, the bark knotted and lumpy. They were hideous in the winter, but as soon as the ground warmed and the rain descended, dense foliage sprang from the boughs, each tree boasting different coloured leaves. Supple pink buds erupted into cherry-red blooms before the petals withered to make way for summer fruit.

As far as Vuya could tell, Kosta always left them be, refusing to pluck the fruit when it ripened. It seemed a waste, but she wouldn't pretend to understand his reasons. As Vuya passed, her eyes snagged on the dark, moist earth of the fourth urn – always empty. As she turned back towards the house, and before she could raise her fist to knock, the door swung open.

'Child,' Kosta greeted with a friendly smile, the lines around his wise old eyes creasing with mirth. His features were long, even a little gaunt, but his limbs remained robust despite his age. Vuya never saw him eat with the others during festivals. When meat roasted on the summer solstice, and the families gathered for celebration, Kosta was reluctant to partake, always meandering on the fringes of the ruckus and drinking only his own tea. His refusal began after the death of his wife and child many years ago; he was a widower shackled by grief. Vuya reckoned he was simply old-fashioned, his solemness a gesture of loyalty to his departed family.

'Uncle Kosta.' Vuya bowed her head respectfully. 'I was hoping you'd be home.'

The scent of herbs wafted from the interior of Kosta's workshop as he swung the door open and stepped out of the way. 'Please, come in,' he offered, and the young woman obliged.

Despite the modest space, Kosta's little alcove was organised to perfection. Handmade shelves lined every wall. Dried herbs and flowers hung from fish hooks he'd wedged into the wood along the ceiling, filling the cabin with a heady mixture of lavender, mint, and rosemary. His workbench in the back corner was cluttered, the mortar and pestle front and centre. Beside it, Vuya glimpsed a sharp, black stone that glistened like spring water.

'How may I be of assistance?' Kosta leaned forward and placed two knobby hands on the back of his chair, the seat of it concave with use.

Vuya tore her attention from the bits and bobs scattered over every surface. 'My mother is quite ill,' she said. 'I'm afraid her usual teas won't suffice.'

Kosta nodded, humming attentively. 'Tell me about her symptoms.'

'The season has its grip on her. She sleeps all day but won't even blink once the moon is up. Her appetite's so weak that she eats less than a bird; she's nothing but dry skin clinging to bones like leather on a bronze peg. She's always warm but shivering, and the cough has worn her throat raw.'

'That sounds quite serious,' Kosta said gravely, then turned towards his work bench. 'I fear it has little to do with the weather.'

Vuya's heart kicked against her ribs. Her mother was the only family she had. It'd been years since her father died, and she didn't remember him – not what he looked like or what he sounded like. Ioana never spoke of him, saying only that he'd passed after a sudden illness. But Ioana's reticence wasn't enough to keep the rumours tucked under the thick pall of the past. 'How do you mean?'

'Your mother…' Kosta began, then released a heavy sigh. 'She may be under the influence of a malevolent force. Just as Nayden had been before he passed.'

People rarely used her father's name anymore. Villagers whispered that he'd been killed by a witch – Ioana's girlhood rival, and her father's first wife, Iskra. Vuya's mother had tried to keep the rumours under lock and key, but it was like trying to trap water in a basket. In public, most adults kept their fragile veneers of propriety, but behind closed doors, when their children eavesdropped and boredom gnawed at their feet, their mouths loosened. It wasn't long before the gossip reached Vuya through other children: her father had abandoned Iskra while she was with child, and the babe died soon after birth. Consumed by grief and resentment, Iskra turned to the dark arts for retribution, cursing her former husband and his new bride, Ioana. Some said that Iskra had stolen the souls of Vuya's unborn siblings to mend her own loss. Others claimed she'd done it to resurrect her infant. When she failed, again and again, and when Ioana finally gave birth to a child named *wolf*, Iskra lost her threadbare grip on humanity, her hatred ravelling around Nayden like thorny vines and dragging him to his untimely death.

'You don't think it's Iskra, do you?' Vuya asked, a hint of incredulity lacing the question.

The lines of Kosta's face deepened with concern. 'It could be. After all, she failed, did she not? You still live. It makes perfect sense that she'd return to take your mother from you.'

Everyone spoke of Iskra's treachery as though it were an unalloyed fact, but Vuya'd never met Iskra. The woman had been banished, forced to live in the woods well beyond the village. She survived off wild mushrooms and whatever unfortunate creature she happened upon – foxes, squirrels, rabbits. Some say she boiled the blood in their bodies while they still lived, revelling in their anguished throes. The nightmarish image was enough to keep the children from wandering too far from home, and even Vuya hesitated where the trees grew dense and the forest darkened.

'If my mother's illness is something supernatural,' Vuya steadied her voice, 'then there is nothing I can do. Perhaps you have something that can help with both worldly and otherworldly sickness, Uncle Kosta?'

'There are some roots that are beneficial for ailments of various origins.' He scanned his collection of dried wares. 'I can't promise they will exorcise her entirely, but they will do more than chamomile tea, at least.'

He busied himself at his work bench, grinding all manner of sinewy things that Vuya didn't recognise. Kosta was well-regarded for frequently weeding out the root cause of unwanted conditions with little more than a glance, but she noticed that he never used the fruit from the strange trees in his urns out front.

'You have four vases outside,' she observed. 'One is always empty. Is the soil too poor to plant anything?'

'No, child.' He folded a piece of parchment so he could more easily slide his grainy concoction into a small burlap pouch. 'I simply haven't found the sapling yet.'

'*Found?*' Vuya repeated, a curious smile on her lips. 'Is it hiding from you?'

Kosta laughed thinly as he stood. 'No, but it is difficult to excavate. The breed I seek is rare, and I want to ensure that it survives when I finally decide to plant it. You see, these fruit trees are precious to me. I only pluck the fruit for very special occasions.' He handed Vuya the medicinal pouch, then thumped his hand atop the girl's head, her dark hair swallowing his bony fingers. 'If my usual medicines don't work for Ioana, I will give you one piece of fruit from each of my trees. Nothing is more potent.'

Vuya's earth-coloured eyes widened. She never imagined Kosta would proffer something so rare for a peasant woman. 'What would it cost?'

'Do you take me for a peddler, child?'

Vuya's cheeks flushed with embarrassment, and Kosta waved her off, his mirthful laugh lightening the air in the small cabin. 'I am only teasing. A favour will do.'

'Of course,' Vuya agreed enthusiastically. 'I'm not very skilled with medicines, but I'd be happy to learn and help in your shop whenever you need me.'

'Nothing so laborious,' he promised, then smiled widely, his cheekbones bulging through his aging skin. 'You'll help me find my fourth sapling.'

After a week of Kosta's medicine, Ioana began to improve. The first sign was when she asked Vuya for rye bread and hard cheese. Then, her fever broke and her strength improved enough for her to manage a stroll around the periphery of their cabin. The worst of her fears mollified, Vuya happily indulged her mother's every whim, splurging on whatever delicacies she craved. A month passed, and as the soil softened and bourgeoned into new life, so too did Ioana. Long past were the days of grey skies, mud, and bone-thin, frigid hands. Her eyes shone clear as the sun through a crystalline sky, and she plumped like the apricots on the village's fruit trees. Once too sick to stomach a bowl of gruel, she now asked for seconds; once too weak to raise her shaky hands and grasp a needle, she began to sew and tend to her home.

One warm night, Vuya was sleepless, her candle guttering as the last of the wax softened. She'd huddled near the window, enjoying the cool breeze as it wafted through the cracks in the wall. The shutters were mostly closed, the spaces between them black as coal.

Between lazy blinks, she saw the stillness shudder, and her heart stuttered to a stop. Everyone in the village should've been asleep, but the midnight air swelled from the other side of the partition. Shoring up her courage, she leaned forward but kept enough distance lest the night reach for her throat.

Two pallid eyes snaked with pink peered at her through the slits of darkness, wildness brimming from them like a fire licking the confines of a shallow pit.

With a staggering gasp, Vuya reeled back, knocking the candle over and snuffing out the last of her meager light. The shadows roiled. Only the sound of her desperate breaths filtered through the inky shroud. As her eyes adjusted, she scrabbled for the matches she'd placed on the windowsill. Something warm and sticky coated her fingers – hot wax – before she finally felt the four battered edges of her matchbook.

Striking desperately at the rough patch on the back of the matchbook, Vuya fumbled as the flame sparked and died, again and again, until finally, the bud ignited, and a sphere of orange warmed the heavy murk, enveloping her quivering hand.

Wresting control over her fear, Vuya darted to the window. She stared at the outline of each wooden slat but saw no one staring back. Could it have been an animal? A mischievous child out on a prank?

No. Those eyes were old, angry. They harboured a resentment that no child ought to carry.

She didn't dare approach, opting instead to blow out the match and retreat to bed. She could retrieve the remnants of the candle and scrape the cooled wax off the floor come morning.

Rumours of a spectre plunged the village into a haze of suspicion. The shepherd swore to the tanner that he'd seen a shadow skirting the edge of the woods near his sheep pen. The entire flock had been spooked, battering around the fence in a desperate attempt to flee the threat. The old seamstress griped that some creature had absconded with herbs from her garden, and ever since, none had grown back in their place. The soil was as barren as a frost-bitten field, and even the worms shrivelled in their burrows. Whispers and quibbles quickly escalated to accusations and trepidation that Iskra had returned to wreak havoc on those who had expelled her. The butcher bellowed that he'd caught the exiled woman tearing a shank from a recent slaughter, and the following day, the carcass was infested with maggots.

No matter how diligently the villagers went about their daily lives, Iskra never failed to make an appearance. Even Vuya wasn't immune. As dusk dimmed the mountainside, Vuya hurried to pull laundry from the lines at the back of the house. Reaching for a sheet as it fluttered in the wind, a face appeared imprinted in the thin fabric. Emaciated fingers, crooked like broken twigs, reached for Vuya as she scrambled to rip the linen free. Yet nothing lurked behind the mantle.

She searched the perimeter only to glimpse the tail of a robe eddying around the trees. Had she imagined it? Was it a coyote scurrying after a hare? She could never be sure. Again and again, she'd catch the vestiges of a phantom at the threshold of her vision, but there was never anything to grab on to—never anything to perceive beyond the fancies of a troubled mind.

Each sighting robbed Ioana of her recently recovered strength. Illness seized her as fear seized the village, yet no one dared venture into the forest in search of Iskra-the-witch. No one knew where she lived. Some claimed that she bent the woods to her will, leading men in circles in a mirage of wilderness until they collapsed from exhaustion. All were convinced that Iskra was behind Ioana's affliction, and Vuya found herself hard-pressed to believe otherwise. But she had no way to confront her mother's girlhood rival; Iskra was impossible to find.

Ioana deteriorated and the sightings intensified, and Kosta's remedies grew ineffective. At a loss, Vuya returned to the herbalist, ready to exchange her labour for a piece of his ambrosial fruit.

As Vuya trudged towards Kosta's workshop, she saw the three trees in their clay urns. The soil around the boles was littered with cast-off petals, wilted to a dull burgundy. The boughs were lush with a summer's canopy, the fronds firm and supple. Where the petals once sprouted, fruit welled like engorged blisters. The bulbous growths retained the brilliant colour of the tree's sanguine blossoms, the skin a translucent film that shimmered around crimson flesh. Yet their aroma was heavenly – sweet as honey with a floral crispness that reminded her of wild roses. The peculiar plants seemed somehow sentient; what should have been the innocuous flutter of foliage in the breeze appeared as undulating breaths, like the trees were watching the goings-on of the village, absorbing it like nourishment. Vuya suddenly felt welded to the dirt, unable to move past the sentinels as they guarded the path to Kosta's workshop.

How foolish to be paralysed by a trio of potted plants. Sucking in a determined breath, she marched past the trees, her senses buzzing as though a thousand eyes needled her back. Again, before she even reached the door, it swung open, revealing Kosta's tall silhouette.

'Vuya,' he greeted, inclining his head. 'I've been expecting you.'

'You have?'.

'Villagers talk,' he clarified, shutting the door behind her as she stepped into his home. 'Of late, they talk rather fervently.'

'About the witch,' she surmised.

He nodded, dropping onto his rickety old chair by the work bench. 'Do you believe them?'

Kosta wrung his hands together, his gristly skin stained green and brown from whatever he'd been mashing that day. 'I believe the truth is hidden between the words we hear others speak.'

Vuya's face scrunched as she tried to parse his meaning. 'I'm not sure I understand.'

He offered a balmy smile. 'Forgive my riddles. I mean that something sinister may truly be afoot, but paranoia is a marvellous storyteller. The tales people weave when they are frightened lend themselves well to grandiosity, don't they?'

'Are you saying the rumours are fabricated?'

'Some of them, yes, but they may still speak of something real.'

Vuya lowered her gaze as she recalled the outlandish accounts. Then again, had she not seen a face imprinted on a sheet? A figure creeping along the forest's edge? Was she bearing witness to her own fears made manifest?

'You must've gotten word of my mother, then,' she cut her musings short.

'Yes,' said Kosta. 'I hear she is quite ill again.'

Vuya exhaled shakily. 'The tonics and the ointments have stopped working. I need something stronger. I need what you promised me.'

Kosta regarded her with an unreadable expression. He'd always been polite and reserved, uninterested in the theatrics of communal gossip. If he was shocked, he didn't show it, his face a perfect mask of neutrality. 'We did strike a bargain, didn't we?'

'And I will fulfill my end of it. I'll help you find the fourth sapling to join the other three.'

'I would never doubt your integrity or your dedication, Vuya.' Pressing his palms to his knees, he rose from the stool. 'Come, let us pluck fruit from each of my children.'

'Your children?' He referred to them with such affection. 'Do they have names?'

He led her outside and halted before the first tree. Its azure foliage of spring had transformed as the months warmed, brightening to a vibrant teal.

'I'm afraid not. Not all things were meant to be named.'

Vuya had no idea what that meant, but she shrugged it off. Kosta loved his riddles, and she had no intention of making him explain himself to a youth.

Kosta gently cradled the swollen bulb in his palm, its skin sweating tears of pink that stained his fingers. With a small tug, the fruit snapped from the stem. Kosta smiled, a wistful longing in his eyes as he cooed something indiscernible, then handed the fruit to Vuya as though entrusting a newborn to their godparent.

'Here,' he breathed out, his expression brimming with things that

Vuya reckoned were felt only with age. Then, he moved on to the next tree.

Its foliage had deepened to a lovely mauve, the veins weaving through each leaf a light wisteria pink. The fruit was identical; it seemed so soft, so easily bruised. Kosta lovingly plucked a piece from its branches.

Finally, he offered Vuya a fruit from the last tree, its canopy shimmering with an iridescent gold that reminded her of the summer sun.

'There,' said Kosta. 'Now you have everything you need. Take these to your mother.'

'Thank you, Kosta. I won't soon forget this, and neither will my mother. As soon as she is well, I will return and help you find your last sapling.'

'That is all I ask, child.' He gave her shoulder a light squeeze, the sticky ichor from his fingers smearing the white of her blouse.

Ignoring the blemish, Vuya left for home, the herbalist's ambrosia nestled securely in her arms.

Ioana greedily accepted Kosta's gift. Although she'd been unable to smell food for weeks, the aroma of the strange fruit broke through her fugue and awoke her appetite like an animal out of hibernation. Ravenous, she devoured each fruit with her bare hands, refusing to let Vuya slice them into wedges for her. Viscous nectar seeped from the meat and flowed down Ioana's emaciated fingers, its saccharine scent filling their home. She licked away the juice, and before Vuya could wipe her clean with a wet cloth, Ioana sank into the bed, turned over with a moan, and fell into her first peaceful sleep in weeks.

Stunned, Vuya waited several minutes for the fretfulness to take her mother, yet she remained as still as a tarn in winter. She silently thanked Kosta and his odd little trees, then retreated to her spot by the window. Iskra's eyes, peering at her through the darkness, were long forgotten. She plunked down in her stool by the shutters, her heart fluttering with relief. The tension bled from her body, and she succumbed to the pull of exhaustion. Vuya thumped her shoulder against the wall and dozed off, her anxieties finally quelled.

Sometime later, an eerie scratching, like vermin in the walls, scraped against Vuya's awareness.

The moon had risen to its zenith, its silvery light piercing through the gaps in the shutters. Rubbing the dregs of sleep from her eyes, Vuya straightened and searched the darkness. There, in the corner by her mother's bed, was a stooped figure, its face to the floor as its arm swiped under the dresser. Nails raked frantically against the wooden boards, the squeal of friction sending a shudder up Vuya's spine.

Vuya's gaze darted to the bed, and she saw that the sheets lay flat. The bed was empty.

Bolting to her feet, Vuya staggered forward just as the intruder turned to face her. Its chest remained flush with the ground as its head swivelled with an audible click. Something wet and sickly warbled in its throat as thin, cracked lips parted, stretching skin over the hollows of its cheeks.

Under the tangled mess of dark hair that fell over waxen skin, Vuya caught a shred of something recognisable – a pair of deep brown eyes, barely visible in the cavernous pits beneath the creature's heavy brow.

'Mother–'

She choked on the word, the evocation lodging in her throat like a fish bone. The mass of gaunt limbs showed no indication of a response. The thing that should've been Vuya's mother canted its head, then crawled forward, joints bending at odd angles, as though the body had been pieced together all wrong. Another lurch, a wheeze, a sickening snap.

Vuya finally slid a foot back, her heel colliding with the wall. The thing wearing Ioana's skin rasped, lips peeling back as ragged breaths morphed into feral growls.

Something scurried out from under the dresser. Without so much as a glance, the creature dove towards the floor, rooting for its prey. It was a rat, fleeing the peril it'd no doubt sensed. It maneuvered left and right, evading the clumsy assault before it disappeared into a crack in the adjacent wall. Ioana slunk on her hands and knees, back hunched, before her head jerked up and her ravening gaze landed on her daughter. Her mouth was agape, saliva dripping, and two sharp fangs pushed out from her gums.

Vuya's stomach dropped, and her heart revolted, thrashing wildly in its cage. She'd heard the tales, whispered over the mountains, about monsters who rose from the grave and stole what they'd lost from the living. Sinners whose deaths exposed the gravity of their crimes.

Vampires.

No amount of prayer could preserve their damned souls, leaving only the rot.

Ioana had become a vampire.

Vuya's mother – her only family – had died some time during the night, and what remained looked at her with hunger.

Terror like a thousand blunted needles sunk into Vuya from every direction, jolting her from her horrid reverie. She flew towards the door, unconcerned with the state of her dress or the absence of shoes on her feet.

Dread, sorrow, and anguished realisation flooded her with every judder of her heavy footfalls against hardened dirt. Her own mother would consume her blood, and with it, her very soul.

Ioana had been too far gone even for Kosta's fruit to save her. And it was all the witch's fault.

Iskra.

She was the cause of this – the architect of Vuya's misery. She'd stolen her siblings, terrorised her family, killed her father and now her mother too. Rage rippled beneath Vuya's skin as purpose crystalised in her mind.

Iskra would pay for what she'd done.

Bereft of reason, Vuya fled into the woods. She had no concept of where the witch lived, believing instead that her wrath would guide her to the source of her suffering. Despite the darkness, her sight was unaffected, her sense of smell and hearing sharpening like the edge of a blade. It must've been the fear and fury waking her blood. The bounds of her awareness prickled as she glimpsed signs of passage through the thick underbrush. Twigs broken by careless wandering. Trampled grass with prints too large for an animal's paws. The villagers never came this far into the forest; it must have been Iskra.

Moments later, a structure bathed in shadow emerged from between the trees, rising over the slope. It was a stone cottage, mired in dirt and wildlife. Vuya halted after rushing into the glade where the witch's abode lurked like a hunter in waiting. Suddenly aware of the danger, she reconsidered her foolhardy plan to simply confront Iskra.

Before she could gather her wits, the door chirred open, inviting her inside.

Truth beckoned, and Vuya was hard-pressed to refuse.

Carefully traipsing to the blackened hollow, Vuya squinted and found the interior of the cabin nearly empty, save for the silhouette of sagging shoulders and a hearth not unlike the ones found in village homes.

'Come,' a raspy voice called from the murk. 'What you seek is here.'

Swallowing her apprehension like a lump of hot coal, Vuya stepped into the witch's lair. The door remained open behind her – a reassurance that she could leave whenever she pleased. Or perhaps it was only wishful thinking.

'You took everything from me.' The words were out of her mouth before she could stop them, accusations laden with hatred.

The cabin filled with a peal of hoarse laughter. 'How dramatic. Surely you haven't lost everything, and surely not all of it at my hands.'

'You killed my parents.'

'Yes,' the witch confirmed, no hint of emotion in her voice. 'I did.'

Vuya balled her hands into fists so tight, her nails cut crescent moons into her palms. 'Stealing my brothers' and sisters' souls wasn't enough for you?'

Moonlight spilled through the door, grazing the edges of Iskra's skirts. Thickened toenails curled from feet that looked more like worn leather than skin. As if hearing the call of something distant, she stepped forward into the pale glow.

Vuya immediately recognised those pallid eyes, the colour of stone and silver. They'd once stalked her from between the shutters.

The witch's hair was like onyx, with ashen strands that wove throughout. Thin with a hooked spine, she seemed to barely get enough sustenance to keep herself upright as she leaned against a craggy old walking stick fashioned from a thick tree branch.

'I did no such thing, girl.' Her voice sounded like it'd been dragged over pumice, yet in the cracks, Vuya heard her conviction. 'Your parents died so that *you* wouldn't meet your siblings' fate.'

'You lie!' Vuya flung the indictment like mud.

Unfazed by the girl's outburst, the witch hobbled to the hearth and lowered herself to her stool, her body sliced in half by the moonlight. 'Your parents made a pact. They offered up their souls to make you strong so that you wouldn't be taken. And I was the one who sealed that pact. By my hand, their strength was passed to you, *wolf.*'

A pact with a witch was indeed a weighty sin. If what Iskra said was true, then both of her parents would have been damned. Vuya thought back to her mother, crawling on the floor like a starved beast. A vampire.

'Oh, don't look at me like that.' Iskra waved her off, her tone chiding. 'Selling one's soul to save another is not the transgression you village simpletons think. It only made your parents weak, susceptible to illness. They knew they would pass before their time, and it seems your mother's has come. I don't deny my role in their deaths.'

Vuya's mind revolted at the possibility. Could Iskra have been exiled for using the dark arts to *help* Ioana and Nayden? 'Then why did you appear in the village after all these years? Why now?'

She chuckled, the sound like pebbles under a horse's hoof. 'To see if my old rival was dying, of course.' Her nostrils flared. 'I smelled her frailty as soon as the snow melted.'

'You're the witch who took my siblings,' Vuya insisted, dismissing Iskra's denial. 'You attacked my family because you were jealous, because *you* were already damned.'

Iskra's gaze settled on the girl, watery irises boring holes through the marrow of her bones. 'Do you know how many miscarriages your mother had before you were born?'

Vuya's mouth felt like cobwebs, her resolve shaken by this woman's steadfast calm. The question sounded so innocent, and yet… 'She never said. It was too painful to speak of.'

Iskra's lips stretched back, rows of crooked yellow teeth greeting Vuya like a knife at her throat. The witch's eyes were alight with vicious knowing as she replied, 'Three.'

Three. The number echoed in Vuya's mind, ricocheting off the image of her mother devouring not one, or two, but three pieces of fruit mere hours before her death.

Three ripened fruits from three unearthly trees. Three sets of wilting bones buried before they could unfurl with life.

Vuya forced out a stuttering breath, and Iskra soaked in her horror, basking in the upheaval she'd sown with a single word.

Knees buckling as she turned, Vuya stumbled and caught herself on the doorframe, the world listing before her eyes. She pitched forward, determined, even as Iskra's laughter reverberated all around her. The witch may have been wicked, but what use was there in lying when truth cut so deep?

Vuya tore through the woods, her limbs strengthening with every stride. The world seemed brighter than it should have under the midnight canopy, the call of owls and the scurry of rabbits a cacophony that rent her senses. She could smell the loam beneath her feet as she sprinted towards the village, every grain jagged between her toes.

Kosta's workshop appeared like a phantom from the verge of a nightmare. Under the guard of the bone-coloured moon, Vuya saw the three fruit trees glistening with otherworldly light. She'd once thought their strangeness alluring; now they were wholly aberrant. Gripped by a ferocity she'd never known, she dug her hands into the soil, emptying the first vase to unearth whatever thing festered there. When her knuckles scraped against the roots, she yanked at them until they came loose.

An abomination had always lurked beneath the ethereal façade of Kosta's saplings.

The roots were bent together, shaped like a human fetus, limbs knitted in a grotesque display as the bole sprouted from the infant's belly like an umbilical cord. The knots in the wood were as gnarled faces, some of the smaller offshoots reminiscent of fingers and toes.

Dropping the tree back into its container, Vuya retched, bile burning up her throat as her stomach evacuated itself. After heaving for breath, she spat out the acrid taste and wiped her mouth, then shambled towards the other two urns.

Each tree was the same; the lush exterior disguised a sinister seed: roots shaped like an infant just large enough for the womb.

'Did you miss your brothers?'

Vuya whirled towards the voice, the last of the three abominations still in her grasp. Her hands were shaking uncontrollably even as she gripped the base of the bole with all her might. Every hair on her body stood on end, skin prickling with revulsion as she met Kosta's gaze.

She'd never seen him like this. The kind old man with a playful, fox-like smile had metamorphosed right in front of her. Spindly fingers steepled together as he emerged from his workshop, his expression fiendish, his eyes shining with unspent malice.

He needn't say more; Vuya knew she held one of her long-lost siblings, warped by a man she once thought a friend. While she could barely contain her charges against Iskra, she was now speechless.

'You were always meant to be the fourth sapling,' he filled the silence as he moved closer, gliding like an apparition.

Vuya's mouth opened, questions tangling on the tip of her tongue as she stared down at the gnarled thing she still held. *How? Why?* But nothing came out. Her eyes must've spoken for her, pleading for an explanation. A reason.

Kosta stopped by one of the vases, the displaced tree lopsided where Vuya had dumped it. The old man plucked one of the leaves, and it furled in his hand as though recoiling. 'Your mother's sin was that she devoured her own children.'

He was referring to the fruit he'd given her – fruit that had grown and ripened from the desiccated bodies of Ioana's first three children.

'The fruit is what changed her into a vampire,' Vuya realised aloud, her breath hitching. She dropped the third tree, stumbling away from it as though stung.

'As I intended,' said Kosta. 'My intention was for her to sate herself with your blood.'

'You helped my mother recover in spring,' said Vuya.

'The fruit hadn't ripened, and your mother was too ill. I needed her to live long enough to feast when her children were at their sweetest, their most succulent.'

'But why?' Her voice sounded so small. 'Why would you do this?'

'So that two would become one. Mother and daughter – both souls united in a single vessel.' He swept aside his wool coat, brandishing a wooden stake strapped to his belt. 'Hawthorn,' he informed her. 'The only blade that can fell a vampire.'

Heat simmered up Vuya's esophagus, and her joints locked with tension as sweat slicked her neck, suddenly scorching beneath her dark mane. Though the moon was their sole lantern, Vuya could have sworn she felt it like a blazing white flame on her skin. 'You made a vampire purely to kill it?'

Kosta's eyes widened a fraction. 'How wasteful that would be. After you survived the womb thanks to that meddlesome witch, I waited and waited for the next best thing – Ioana, engorged with your essence in a dark union between mother and child. Once staked as a vampire, your souls would emerge together like a butterfly from a cocoon, ripe for picking.'

His stare dragged down to the fourth urn. 'I would have buried it here, wings still fluttering with desperate struggle, and the fourth sapling would've joined its family.'

'Family?' Vuya spat. 'You destroyed my family!'

'And I made my own.' His eyes glistened with twisted reverence. 'This one, I'll never lose.'

'The only family you'll know are the maggots I leave you to,' she seethed.

This appeared to stun the old man as his fingers brushed the top of his stake. 'There's no name that'll keep you safe this time, Vuya.'

Jaw clenched, Vuya forced her words through her teeth, her gums aching as something pointed cut through the meat. 'Keep my name from your vile mouth.'

Colour drained from the world, leaving it as grey as Iskra's eyes. Vuya's shoulders tugged forward against her say so, and the urge to fall to her hands nearly consumed her. She felt too tall, too lumbering. Fingers curled and contracted, knees buckled and inverted, and an anguished cry shattered the still night air as she collapsed, her rage devouring her from the inside out, re-making her in its image. Teeth gnashed until they'd become too sharp, too lethal. She snapped and snarled, tail whipping and ears flattening against her fur-covered skull. Stygian like the night that made her, Vuya beheld the world as though reborn.

She could no longer read Kosta's expression, but she smelled his horror blossom like a carrion flower, the stench of it mingling with a less bitter scent—a resignation and awe at having witnessed something most unexpected.

'My, what big teeth you have,' he breathed out, ensnared by wonder.

Vuya had no taste left for his voice. She lunged at the man who'd stolen her life, locked her maw around his throat, and tore through his flesh, crushing the poisonous source of all his deception. He would never utter another lie again.

Tongue coated in malevolent blood, Vuya watched Kosta's lifeless body crumple to the ground with a weak thud.

Wracked by grief, she lifted her nose to the sky and unleashed a harrowing howl that shook the mountain. When she was finally empty, she turned away from her brothers and faced the approaching scent of decay.

Ioana had followed the carnage. She crouched several feet away, transfixed on something only she could see. Then, the scent of Kosta's fresh blood stirred the devil in her, and her head swivelled towards the wolf. A hiss crackled in her throat as she writhed, her eyes as hollow as Vuya's heart. She prepared to leap, her elongated nails sunk into the dirt, but the wolf was faster. Springing forward, Vuya ate the distance between them and knocked the vampire to the ground, pinning it beneath her paws. The thing that was not her mother thrashed wildly, arms flailing and saliva spattering across her chin. She was starved, yet nothing in this world could slake her hunger.

The wolf's fangs embraced the vampire's neck. Kosta may have concocted the poison, but Vuya had poured it straight into the well. By the daughter's hand had the mother been cursed to walk as a soulless revenant. Now, Vuya would right her wrong. With a quick jerk, bones shattered, tendons unbraided, and skin ripped like wet paper. Ioana came apart like a doll. Her head lolled on the ground. From her unhinged jaw, a large butterfly with violet and silver wings hooked its pin-like legs over her lower lip, then quavered from her gaping mouth.

It wobbled through the air, slaloming past Vuya and towards the wreckage that Kosta had wrought. She yearned to join this frail creature that homed the vestiges of her family – to cradle it before it slipped away. Tiny purple blades beat against the night air as the butterfly circled each vase, then hovered over the one that'd remained undisturbed. The one meant for the wolf.

Delicate as a spring blossom after heavy rain, the vampire's soul descended towards the urn and settled on Vuya's empty grave.

HOUSE, MEET YOUR MATCH

KATYA DE BECERRA

FOR SALE BY OWNER:

Sweetgraven Mansion in the Victorian Countryside

A rare find!

This dramatic Federation Queen Anne mansion is full
of character! Boasting original décor (in near perfect
condition), twin turrets and a stunning wraparound porch
(look at that sunburst detailing!), this charming fixer-
upper cannot wait to find its forever-and-ever family.
With a stunning family salon, four cosy bedrooms, and so
much more, this historical gem will not remain available
for long – not for this low, low asking price.

Need more encouragement?

For the outdoorsy types, a beautiful pond on the property will add a hint of mystique to the atmosphere as you enjoy your romantic picnic, while an adorable hedge maze will keep the little ones entertained with its twists and turns.

And did you know that Sweetgraven Mansion possesses Victoria's first-ever psychomanteum? This quirky mirror-lined room would make a nice vanity space – or use it as intended, to summon spirits from other realms. How fun! You will never walk these halls alone.

Don't miss out on this marvel. (Definitely not haunted).

Contact: Germane A. Nevis-Towns from *History Comes Alive* Real Estate.

I am dreaming of sinking into the earth when the humming of a car awakens me.

I come alive, one loose shingle, one dusty brick at a time.

They're here! They're heeeere.

My excitement dissolves into fractured echoes. I am weak from my slumber, but I will not stay weak for long. Soon I will feed.

I crackle my misshapen joints. When my mullioned eyes fly open, fully for the first time in what feels like an age, the light of the afternoon sun stuns me. I am not a creature of daytime; too many shadows nested in my corners. They snack on light, they gorge on warmth. They are never sated.

The new arrivals exit the car – this Volkswagen has seen better days – and trample the overgrown grass by my porch. They stop at the edge, that dark line where my shadow bifurcates the lawn. They look up at me, and I look at them.

They are: two women (in their thirties?) and two children (about seven, eight?), boy and girl.

Four sets of hopeful eyes on me.

A spark ignites in my empty belly. I love them instantly, this family. But I exist for a reason, and that reason is not love.

It is not too late to warn them with a roar: *I am a house unlike all others! I will tear you apart, I will gorge myself on your fears as your nightmares come alive. I will devour your very souls, like a whale swallows an entire civilization of plankton in one greedy gulp, hungering mouth open wide!*

But I stay silent. I watch and wait.

Memories come forth, of faces, so many faces. Never happy and carefree, the way they were on Day One before they tasted my bitter agony on their tongues. No, in my mind, their features are always twisted in fright, smeared in tears and blood, mouths gaping open, readying for a scream.

My gut rumbles, shrunken with hunger, pipes straining to burst.

I have been starved, deprived of company of the living for far too long. But like lungfish calcified in the drought, I only need a drop of water, of life, to break my torpor.

Oh, how divine they smell, the new arrivals.

Their scent intoxicates, it pulls me in. If only I could move from the spot where my cursed roots have merged with the dark earth. I can sway in the wind, I can shiver, I can tighten my corridors around those who dare inhabit me. But I can never leave.

Through the murky glass of my unwashed windows I watch them haul their meagre belongings out of the car. My new tenants, my company.

My meal.

As I think that, the thing that lives in the hedge maze rears its bloated head, its expectant rictus almost lurid.

'Full of character indeed. Looks like it's about to fall apart,' says one of the women. Her copper-red hair is cut short, her eyes stand out against pale skin. Those eyes are the same shade of mossy green as the pond in the back, its surface overgrown with water lilies, its depths festering with phantoms.

'It's a fixer-upper, Anya. The listing was clear about it,' replies the other woman. Her skin is of rich brown shade, her crow-dark hair falls to her waist in waves, her eyes are dark, reflective. If I look long enough, I can see myself in them. My sunburst detailing looks like a deep-sea kraken, readying to devour. I look away.

'Still can't believe we've bought it without inspecting in person, Nisha. It could be all rot and black mould inside,' Anya says, her sceptical eyes trained on my façade.

Mould! I hold back from baring my teeth at such a vile accusation. How amateurish it would be of me to let mould take over. I do not need to resort to such measures, thank you very much. I produce enough of my own nightmare fuel to make the walls bleed, to make the rooms as suffocating as a tomb.

'I'm sure it's not,' Nisha replies. 'Anyway, this is the only house we could afford on such short notice. And it's even fully furnished!'

'Right. But what about that agent, *Germane*. We've never even met him,' Anya keeps on.

'He's just a shut-in, avoiding contact with people – can you blame him after the pandemic? He was always so quick to answer our emails... This place was a total steal!'

'When something's too good to be true...' Anya says under her breath.

They are repeating an old argument, I suspect, saying their respective lines. But they are not going anywhere. Of that I am certain.

I miss the rest of the conversation as I zero in on them for a closer look. I study the shadows beneath their eyes. I try to read between the lines, see the hidden meanings behind the silences, understand the real story here. The pair are beautiful and full of vibrant energy, but underneath it all, they are exhausted, wary.

Only a special kind of person comes to a place such as me: one without options. It is just my incredible luck that after years of abandonment I have an entire family worth of them about to walk my halls.

Come inside... Come inside... I whisper, impatient for a taste.

My graveyard breath caresses their faces. But they do not flinch.

'I'm starving!' says the boy child, eyeing me sideways. 'Mums, can we order pizza?'

'I don't think pizza delivers here, Jai,' says the girl child. She smirks mischievously. 'This place looks... haunted.' Covertly, she reaches for the back of her brother's neck.

'Mums!' Jai shrieks as he twists out of his sister's grip. 'Freya is trying to scare me!'

'You're being a scaredy cat!' Freya shrieks back, giggling in her twisted joy. I think of the four of them, she might be my favourite.

'Stop it, both of you, you're going to annoy the neighbours!' Nisha is looking around.

But there are no neighbours to speak of – places like me repel people. Those who can leave, leave.

The children cease their bickering all the same.

'You can help me make sandwiches. What do you think? Turkey and cheese sound good?' Anya asks the children, but her attention is on me. She studies how the wind moves against my walls. Does she see me shiver even when the wind stills?

'Sure, Mum,' the children say in near unison.

The family heads inside, and I brace for that sweet moment when they step over the threshold, the moment they seal their fate.

Jai and Freya are the first to step into my domain. The porch is still vibrating from their steps but they are already rushing upstairs. They are fearless, unburned by life, still innocent. They do not walk, they run. My windows vibrate with their high voices.

I track them as they explore the upper-floor rooms, as they pull at the doors and pout if they meet resistance. Not all of my doors are meant to be opened; not yet. I will show myself eventually, but I reveal my presence by affecting little things first. A random item out of place, a cold spot, a draft that has no reason to be there, a voice whispering close to your ear.

Children are usually the first to notice something is off, way before their parents catch on. The little ones see shapes in the shadows, they notice words written on the steamed-up glass in the bathroom before those vanish without a trace.

But children are never believed until it is too late.

Holding hands, the women follow their offspring inside. Their skin ripples as they pass through a freezing spot right by the door. Nisha shivers. Anya soothes her, a gentle hand gliding effortlessly against skin.

Concerned, Anya looks around my reception space. 'I really don't know about this... There has to be a reason why this place is so cheap. I mean, besides the silly ghost stories. And why on earth is it called Sweet Grave?'

'It's Sweet*graven*, I think,' Nisha replies. 'But yeah, it does sound weird. And maybe it *is* infested with ghosts, but does it really matter? We're out of options. This *has* to work.'

Anya gives her a look, still not fully convinced but thawing.

'If it helps, we can rename it. What's the opposite of "grave"?' Nisha goes on, determined.

'I dunno. Cheerful?' Anya shrugs. 'Or maybe an elevation of some kind, like a hill? No, wait. A cradle!'

'That's it, we can call it Sweet Cradle. *Sweetcradle*?'

I chortle at that. The sound is like wooden shutters hitting the window frame. Only there are no shutters on my windows.

'What the hell was that?' Anya asks, her voice rising in alarm.

'Wood settling in?' Nisha says. 'Old houses are noisy.'

Whether she herself believes it or not, I do not know. Her mind is closed off to me at the moment, but soon I can have a look. When they sleep, I will go for a wander, I will explore the neural spaces nestling between their thoughts.

'Dibs on the biggest bedroom!' Jai yells somewhere upstairs.

'That's where Mums will sleep!' Freya rebuffs.

'Then dibs on the second biggest bedroom!' Jai does not give up.

'You'll share the same room, for now!' Nisha shouts, but I doubt they hear her. The pounding of their steps rattles me to the core.

My doors are swinging, slamming as the children and their mothers explore. I creak and I moan. But instead of frowning in unease, this family exhales in relief. Even Anya has mostly relaxed.

Home, home at last! That is what I read from the women's content faces, from the secret little smiles they exchange as they roll up their sleeves and prepare dinner, as they call their children down to the salon, where the four of them devour their meal in quiet solidarity.

Are they so eager for four walls and a roof that they do not notice the boneyard air from my lungs, the unnatural echo from the deep of my gullet?

It begins.

Anya and Nisha sink into bed in exhaustion. I watch them. I hold my breath. I listen to their night-time whispers, to the rustling sounds their bodies make against clean sheets.

I can sense it, their past. Its dark gravity invisible but formidable all the same, lurking underneath the surface. Both women have been through a lot – a thin cloud of sadness clings to them, a shimmering patina over their eyes. But there is also joy, so much joy. They hold each other close. Instead of 'I love you', they say, 'thank you for existing'.

And they thank me for existing too.

'I'm grateful, for this house, and for you,' Anya whispers. 'I'm sorry I was giving you a hard time earlier. I take it all back.'

'I just can't believe our luck.' Nisha replies, also a whisper. 'We finally have a home. Together.'

They kiss, a light touch of lips that does not last long but its effect lingers like a bewitching scent of a rare flower. I cannot look away.

I wait for them to fall asleep, for consciousness to loosen its grip. Snippets of memories repackaged as dreams spill out from slumbering minds like gossamer strings, a nocturnal spiderweb.

I slip into their heads with ease – I imagine it is like sinking into a warm bath. But this bath will not stay warm for long. This is the way my poison works: it leaks into the dreamscape, enhancing minor fears into catastrophes, stretching insignificant uncertainties into gargantuan monsters.

Dreams are where I excel, are where I am most powerful. I can reshape any dream into a nightmare. I know nightmares the way a studious child knows their ABCs. The one in which you think you are alone in a dark room but something is breathing quietly behind you? I practically invented it, perfected it on countless test subjects.

The one in which you are pursued by a horrifying presence, a figure rushing at you, all claws and teeth?

The one in which you think you can fly but fall to your death instead?

The one in which you think you are awake but you are not, far from it?

Me, mine.

I do not throw all of it at once at these two women. I start small. As I move through the terrain of their minds, I add a couple of my personal touches – a little darkening here, a strange figure there.

I slowly pull the blanket off their still forms.

I exhale, and the air in the room grows gradually colder. The human body will eventually wake itself in alarm as the temperature plunges. But these two barely even stir. They wrap their limbs around each other, creating a cocoon of warmth. Neither wakes up with a start, a scream on her lips.

How puzzling.

I thicken the darkness at the foot of their bed so that it resembles a tall figure, too tall, its limbs burdened with too many joints. I stare at them, glare at them, but if they sense my presence at all, they do not show it. I exhale noisily, my icy breath touching their faces. Still they do not move. I watch their chests go up and down, inhaling, exhaling, so damn calm.

Are they too exhausted from their trip to pay attention?

I repeat familiar acts, these sequences I have mastered into a form of art, until the arms of the clock inch toward five in the morning, dawn closing in. Anya is gently snoring. Nisha is talking in her sleep, deep whispers in a foreign language I do not understand.

My last chance to frighten them. I take a closer look at their dreams, searching for opportunities to twist the familiar into the uncanny, to replace the divine with the grotesque. But I find that their dreams are scary already. My additions blend in, lost amid the frightening memories.

Anya dreams of escaping. Of leaving behind her country, the only home she has ever known, a home that has turned into a prison for her. First they said people like her didn't exist; then they said: it's okay, as long as you're quiet and don't parade yourself on the streets – what if a child sees you, their mind instantly corrupted! But then they said: you cannot be tolerated, your existence contradicts the ideals of the state, somehow threatens its identity. *They must think I'm very powerful*, Anya sarcastically reflects.

When she is arrested for the second time, slapped around and threatened with worse, she knows it's time to go. She's lucky, her passport is still valid and she has friends waiting for her across the border. It took months to plan the escape, but she has been preparing for years. She ran to survive, to live. Sometimes, when she is alone, she cries for a life that could have been. But she is happy now, with Nisha, with the children.

Nisha has also escaped, I learn, but the dangers she faced were of a different kind. Before Anya, before this family they have made together, her life was a suburban paradise. She was a "domestic goddess". That was what he called her, anyway. At first. But then the blissful fog wore off and Nisha could see things as they were…

I learn so much about them while walking their dreams like a shadow. I experience their fears, relive their terrors, relish in their joys, taste the sweetness of their hope. It is difficult to tear myself away.

Eventually, I retreat from the bed, watching them tangled in each other's arms. I am still hungry, having not succeeded in terrifying them into delicious terror, but I fall into a peaceful slumber all the same. And as I sleep, my own dreams materialise and roam the corridors as apparitions. They glide and glide, translucent phantoms, while the thing that lives in the hedge maze stirs more awake.

Over the course of our first few days together, I learn more about my new tenants' lives before they came to invade my halls. One anxious brush stroke at a time, a full picture forms from snippets of disturbing dreams and hushed discussions and moments of reminiscence.

I learn more about Nisha's marriage, how it ended with her fleeing into the night.

Her husband started to show his true colours. Everything seemed to set him off – a dish out of place, a patch of dust, a streak on an otherwise immaculate window. Nisha was a "goddess" no more, and the suburbia was no Eden. Perhaps it never was. Nisha knew how to be a good wife, in theory, but nothing she did was good enough. He never touched her in a way that would expose the rot of their marriage to their neighbours at once, but she feared that kind of terror was yet to come. She could already imagine attempts to hide the evidence of his increasingly aggressive "corrections": a side fringe, a double-layer of concealer, a dab of foundation. *Dark Peach. Espresso. Spicy.* So many shades that compared beauty to delectable cuisines of faraway countries but none of them quite right, none a perfect fit.

Nisha did not know she was pregnant when she left, the twins already learning the taste of freedom inside her. When she found out, it felt right to take care of new life, to see this new beginning, especially so when Anya came into her world.

They met at a café. So clichéd. I can read the irony from their minds: Who even meets people in "real life" anymore? After settling into her new reality, having erased her trail with help from friends, Nisha landed an admin role at a law firm. It was one of the few employment options in the small town she came to call home. Her office was right next to the police station. Nisha was wary of the latter. She's heard of police, unwittingly or otherwise, letting estranged husbands know where to find their runaway wives. But work was work. With the twins in the crèche, she needed the money.

Anya was a life-saver, a beacon of light and a source of laughter in Nisha's life.

Having reinvented herself in this foreign land as a small-town barista, Anya worked at a café that Nisha frequented.

Anya must have spotted a fellow runaway in Nisha. It started with a "newbie in town" discount that seemed to exist for Nisha alone, and then Anya asked her out. Their first date was at a local drive-in cinema. A *Little Shop of Horrors* singalong.

One morning I overhear them singing in the kitchen, a soulful duet, something about Seymour. The children are there too, rolling their eyes in response to the musical display. But I sense their delight too, joy concealed by sarcasm. This is the song their mothers sang on their first date. After that, their falling in love was effortless, akin to a movie montage but less cheesy. Though reality did bite eventually.

In the pandemic, Nisha lost her job when the law firm's operations shrank, while Anya's cafe barely made any profit at all, with the customers drying up. To add to their growing list of troubles, both women were facing the end of their respective leases. It was time for a change. They needed to find work and a new place to live – together. Nisha's children took to calling both of them "Mum". My heart melts at this, but I must remain stoic, must guard my darkness from their light.

I learn it was Nisha who saw the ad in some newspaper (the framed clipping is now displayed on the wall, next to a casual photograph of the family together). Despite my humble location in the countryside, my ill fame had spread far and wide. I was even featured on *Most Haunted*, having allegedly expelled – often bloodily – anyone who dared to inhabit me. As a result, my new residents acquired me for a record low sum. It cost them their combined savings, all of it, leaving them with no safety net. But what other choices did they have? And how could they resist anyway – a whole house for barely the price of a studio apartment?

And so here they are. Home, sweet home. By next month, the twins would be enrolled in the local school. The family would set its roots. The longer they stay, the harder it will be to leave. But something tells me leaving is the last thing on their minds.

I learn that my new tenants didn't even leave a forwarding address with their previous residences. My dark heart does a strange flip at the revelation, causing glasses and plates to rattle in the cupboards. This family, they are mine. I think of Nisha then, of her fear-drenched nightmares. Her husband a hulking figure in the dark. And a new shudder goes through my heart, this time because of worry. I fantasise for a moment what I'd do to him if he ever finds his way here. My stomach growls.

One morning, I catch Jai standing in the living room, studying the framed newspaper ad, his face scrunched up in concentration. If his sister is more adventurous and outgoing, Jai's nature is inward. He loves crosswords and puzzles. I look over his shoulder, holding in my cold breath, as Jai moves the words around on a piece of paper, trying different combinations for "Germane. A. Nevis-Towns", the agent listed as my representative. Will he ever figure out this riddle?

They get to work, cleaning, painting, spinning my cobwebs into ghostly fairy floss that ends up in the trash. No corner is safe, no shadow undisturbed.

Every night after watching them labour all day, I work just as hard, undoing their efforts. The paint peels off, the wallpaper falls away, accumulating in discarded folds on the floor.

'It's too damp!' They say. Or: 'The glue needs to be stronger!' Or: 'We need to buy more paint!'

They do not give up, determined to transform me.

But what is worse, so much worse, is that nothing I do seems to scare them.

'Real estate this cheap is so hard to come by,' they repeat like a mantra, while bringing in more paint and starting to work on my walls all over again.

'A home with such beautiful, strong bones,' they say, as they spray Windex all over my murky windows.

As if all I need is a deep carpet clean to change my nature. As if.

Fear me! I scream as I lengthen my corridors and make my windows shake against the onslaught of invisible wind. I hate to admit it but I am growing desperate.

I roar: *I have driven families stronger than yours to madness! I have made them believe in monsters!*

But even Anya barely reacts to my tricks as days go on. As for the rest of the family – they just giggle in response.

'Our home is wild!'

'Our home has character!'

Oh, just you wait, I howl.

Wait till you meet what dwells in the hedge maze. Wait till that thing drains colour from your hair and life from your eyes. Wait till it sinks its clawed hands into your heart.

But the idea of them encountering the worst of my emanations, the one that haunts the hedge, also makes me... wary, unsure. I feel almost... protective of them? This is wrong. So wrong. I am a house unlike all others. I am not a home.

I cannot look away from Anya's face, so innocent and relaxed in sleep, with that frown between her eyebrows smoothed over. I cannot help but smile at Nisha as she whispers in that language of hers, what I guess is her mother tongue. I may not understand it but I know the meaning all the same – love and gratefulness, and safety in her woman's arms, with Anya sleeping peacefully next to her.

It takes a special kind of woman to stay in a haunted house and not only survive, exist, persevere, but to thrive. Desperate. Stubborn. Determined.

I know this now.

One night, I wake the children.

Their mothers have proven immune to everything I have to offer, but perhaps the little ones will give in.

I let Freya glimpse me first as I stand in the corridor, a menacing shape just outside the room she shares with her brother. My dark outline resembles that of a woman, tall and still. Years of projecting societal fears and grievances onto women has shaped this archetype of a vengeful female ghost, and it has proven most effective with previous tenants.

'Hello?' Freya says as she sits up in her bed and waves at me. 'Who are you?'

'Wow! Who is that?' Jai asks, stirring from sleep.

Is that a tremble of fear I hear in his voice?

I float toward him. I expect him to freeze in terror, to curl up into a shape of the unborn, and for cold sweat to coat his skin. But instead he stands up and comes closer, comes to me. His sister joins him.

'Are you the ghost that lives in this house? What is your name?' The children ask.

What is wrong with them? Why are they not frightened? Have they learned no fear from their mothers? Have they never waited in fright for their closet door to slide open and unleash misshapen monsters upon them?

I entice the children to follow me into the night, Pied Piper that I am. As if bewitched, Freya and Jai spill out from their room, all giggles and hushed murmurs. To me, this is not a game, but to them it is. Awake and alert, they watch me, they see me, and their fascination eats away at my shadow flesh. It does something else to me too.

I want them to know me, to understand what I am.

And so, instead of outside, where the foetid pond awaits and where the hedge maze shimmers in the night, I lead the children to the circular room full of mirrors where my heart rests, dormant. In this room, their reflections multiplied, Freya and Jai swirl and spin. When they notice me staring at them through the glass, they laugh in joy. 'What else do you have to show us?' they ask. 'What other secrets are there for us to discover?'

I let them play, let their enchanting laughter warm my insides. I am still hungry but not as ravenous as I was on the day of their arrival. Maybe I have grown mellow in my old age.

Later, as I sleep, instead of restlessly roaming the corridors, my phantom visions move about as ballet dancers do, on light feet. They do not scuttle, they waltz.

Our first weekend together.

Anya packs a picnic basket, while Nisha dresses the children in gumboots and Windbreakers. The summer has turned unusually cold. For now the clouds are like whipped cream against the restless blue, but today's forecast promises afternoon rain.

Nothing, not even the promise of a deluge, will dissuade this family from consuming their feast outside, together.

They sit by the pond, seemingly undeterred by the rotting smell of its water. Their backs are to the hedge maze – the thing that lives there studies them from a short distance. Ever so patient.

'We really need to hire a gardener,' says Anya. 'I think our renovation skills don't cover… whatever that is.' She points absently over her shoulder, at the maze.

'It looks creepy!' Jai offers his opinion after a long look. 'Like everything else here… but I like it, I think.'

'Let's go play?' Freya stands up, tucks her sturdy pants into her knee-high gumboots and ushers her brother toward the maze.

Nisha says, 'I don't want you going in too deep, not before we had a closer look at what's in there.'

'Don't worry, Mum!' Says Freya. 'The house won't let anything hurt us.'

The idea of them wandering into the maze, right into the hands of a monster, is perfection. Or it should be.

Freya's assertion, her voice so sure, catches me off guard. I thought children had short memories. I imagined our communion in the mirror room last night would already be fading from their minds, retreating to the realm of dreams and fantasies. And yet, they remember enough to speak of me as if I matter, as if I am real to them, a force, an entity that exists to guard, not to frighten.

As Freya and Jai near the hedge maze, something tickles at my sense of presence, a warning originating deep in my gut.

I realise that I have been so obsessed with observing this family that I have barely fed on them, and yet I am not starved. Each time Freya or Jai laugh or simply acknowledge my presence, I am a little bit more sated. Every time Nisha and Anya exchange a comfortable smile, I smile too. This family, this assemblage connected by the silken strings of love and yearning for a home has…softened me. My desire to frighten and to feed on their fears and screams gave way to something else. Something I am not familiar with.

Whatever this is, it drives me into the hedge maze after the children. The thing that lives there is part of me but it is not under my control, not fully. If I am the ego, then the hedge entity is id, all hunger and aggression. I must hurry.

Inside the maze, the sweet stench of decay hits me first, disorients me for several seconds. As I regain my focus, the children vanish behind the next turn.

Listen to your mothers! Do not go in too deep! I scream but the maze swallows my warning.

The thing that lives in the maze comes alive, it sniffs at the children, following them and beckoning them to go in deeper at the same time. It is a stalker and a lure. While it is a part of me, it is also a separate entity, having evolved in accordance with its own rules. I catch a glimpse of it and I tremble – it is tall enough to match the height of the hedge, its shadow stretches both ways, ignoring the sun's position. This thing is sleek like the pond's rotten water, its skin falls off its body in filthy strips, trailing behind it. This thing, this embodied *creature*, is an accumulation of my history of terror, the side effect of my feeding on fear, a monster born out of a monster.

The need to protect rises in me as the creature tricks the children into a dead-ended corridor. To follow them, I stretch as far as I can, as far as the bounds of my earthly roots allow. I wedge myself between the children and the monster of the hedge.

Freya is the first to see the creature in all its gory glory. She is trying to scream, but the sound is trapped in her mouth, lodged in her throat. The monster grabs Jai and pulls him closer. The creature's maw is wide open.

'Nooooo!' I roar as I lunge, sharpening my shadow and using it to pierce the monster. I tear and hack at its nightmarish matter, ethereal chunks flying left and right, until it lets go of Jai.

Jai is shouting for his sister to run, but she refuses to leave without him. She helps him up and they scramble out of the maze together, just as the rain begins to fall.

What the hell is wrong with you? The thing that haunts the hedge maze hisses at me. It tries to break free of my hold. Its instinct is to chase, to terrify, to feed on fear.

They are mine, I hiss back. *Not for you.*

I do not let the monster go until Freya and Jai are out of the maze.

I repeat, *This family is mine.*

It is mine to protect.

The idea surprises me but it feels right to nurture this new beginning.

In time, I even let them paint my walls.

My cobwebs dissipate, and instead of death, I come to smell of detergent, roast, cake. I become this thing that can foster feelings other than fear: inhabitable, liveable.

My story used to begin anew with each arrival, but it would always end the same: with the family fleeing into the night. This time, instead of me reshaping them into a barbed-wire ball of fright, they have changed me. After a century of living my lonely dark dream alone, I am now a home.

I have finally met my match.

(I am so happy they have answered my "for sale" ad. Eventually, Jai even solved the anagram for Germane. A. Nevis-Towns.)

Sweetgraven Mansion.

The twins turn eight.

An age has passed since this family claimed me as theirs. Since then, Nisha and Anya have made friends, and so have Freya and Jai.

The hedge maze has been trimmed in half, its mystery dimmed. The scary thing that calls it home is still there but I hold it back, having muzzled its urges. Evil cannot always be eliminated but it can be trained to behave itself.

This birthday party serves as proof that change is the only constant. Even the most vile of haunted houses can be reformed, if its tenants are persistent enough.

Sometimes in my sleep I revert to my old ways and my walls seep red, but by morning I come to my senses and clean myself up. My cold spots warm up, my shadows dissipate.

I observe now as the children play in the back yard, their eyes sparkling with wonder, bellies full of cake. Nisha and Anya, content and calm, stand to the side with the other parents, sipping on sweet bubbly.

A girl, a neighbour's child, wanders off. She is new to these parts – once my family tamed me, some of the other houses nearby attracted new tenants, promising renewal and cheap real estate. This girl stands by the edge of the pond. A safety fence surrounds it now, a precaution to keep the little ones safe.

The little girl spots something in the pond, a set of fingers emerging from the brackish water, their tips stained black. Is it some kind of fish, she wonders as she leans over the fence, bringing herself for a closer look. The fingers stretch further out and it is now a hand. It waves at the girl. The girl's mouth shapes into a terrified O and she runs away screaming. Her fear tastes acidic on my tongue.

I retreat, the ghoulish hand submerges back into the primordial soup of the pond.

One last thing to say before I fully commit myself to this newfound bliss, this love a house shares with its people.

It happens sometime after the twins' eighth birthday though my memory grows foggy. A man comes skulking at night, peering through my windows. I catch him muttering about 'that bitch' as he glares at my porch like a hungry ghoul. He says 'Nisha', a name like a swear on his drunken breath.

It is him then, the one Nisha escaped. Things click into place. I watch him for a short while, as he walks my perimeter, looking for a way in. My heart shudders in my wooden chest. I can't let him anywhere close to my family.

I pull air into my lungs and I exhale with all my might. This impulse that I direct at the man goes against his will, against the reason he came here in the dead of night. But he obeys, for such is my power.

He walks, his steps uncertain, mesmerised. He's like a marionette in my grip, but also not quite. He is awake, he is aware, and yet something (me) is pulling him closer and closer to where my darkest ego dwells. Into the hedge maze.

They never find him, Nisha's husband, never even think to come here to look for him. When the thing that dwells in the maze is done with him, there isn't much left to find.

His bones sink to the bottom of the pond, where a lovely family of fish makes a home in his ribcage.

Old habits die hard.

TWISTED ELEGANCE OF THE DEEP GREEN SEA

ANNIE McCANN

'To breaking news now, the body of Australian diplomat Terry Herman has been recovered from Pelabuhan Ratu, West Java, Indonesia. Pelabuhan Ratu, translated from Sundanese as Harbour of the Queen, is a popular tourist destination for many Australians. The locals are shaken by this tragedy. A local fisherman told us he found Herman's body washed up on the harbourside in the early hours of this morning. Here's Sam Jackson, live from Pelabuhan Ratu…'

In my sleep deprived state, I jump out of bed and run to the TV. Not even the bite of the cold Western Sydney morning is enough to keep me under two doonas. The cameraman zooms in on the scenery. A picturesque stretch of beach with white sand and tropical forest against the deep blue ocean. Breathtaking mountain view and hillside villages. You would not think tragedy was capable of striking here.

The screen pops up with a caption "Hadi, local resident" centring on a thirty-something year old man wearing a brown and black batik shirt and white T-shirt, standing next to the reporter.

'Many Australian come here,' Hadi says, staring at the camera without blinking. 'Like swimming, holiday, we sad this happening in our country, we feeling sorry for Australian peoples, when Akbar finding this man, we all shock you know, he wearing gree–'

The TV screen ripples like water, swallowing all sound. When it returns, the reporter is wrapping up the segment. 'Oh, it would appear there is a technical difficulty there…to other news now…'

I stare wide-eyed at the TV as the sun is slowly rising, light splitting through the drapes but not bringing any warmth.

'No…' I exhale before my iPhone goes off with the alarm I set the night before.

I switch it off, then head to the kitchen. I put the kettle on, then start the electrical fireplace in the living room. Within minutes, the house is warm, yet a chill goes down my spine. The door next to me creaks open, startling me, but it's just my brother Raffi emerging from a deep slumber.

'*Kenapa* Dek?' Raffi yawns. 'You look like you've seen a ghost.'

Ghosts…

I don't know what it is exactly, but something is wrong.

Today my brother and his mate, Iwan, embark on their trip to Indonesia. West Java, to be precise. They have been planning this trip for months, including a visit to the famous Pelabuhan Ratu. The very place that has suddenly hit international headlines.

'And we return to our developing story: the body of Australian diplomat Terry Herman has been recovered from the harbour of Pelabuhan Ratu…' I can hear the returning news segment from the kitchen; it makes me flinch.

'Dek, where's the new *teh melati*? You said you bought some yesterday,' my brother asks for jasmine tea but I ignore him.

'Dek?'

I am unable to move, standing still from the kitchen as I study the sparkling beach behind the reporter on TV, looking for…what?

'INDAH!' Raffi shouts my full name at me.

'Kang Raffi, listen to this!' I grab the remote control and turn up the TV volume.

As the reporter repeats the information, an enlarged photo flashes up on the TV. A middle-aged man, wearing a green tropical shirt and shorts. The image is captioned: last photo of Terry Herman.

Astaga…oh no…

I turn to my brother but his look of bewilderment shows he's not getting the news.

'OK, so an Aussie has been found dead in Indo; not new, Dek,' he huffs.

'No, you don't understand, Kang. They found his body washed up in Pelabuhan Ratu – and in the photo they showed on screen…he was wearing green!'

'So?'

Honestly, Mr No Freaking Idea dot org. I call him Kang out of respect as he is my older brother yet it's like I'm the older one here.

'So? You can't remember the golden rule Mah told us as kids?' My frustration is coming through. How can he be so calm?

'Dek, I'm pretty sure that diplomat got himself in trouble after a few too many. Besides, you remember how superstitious Mah used to be… Anyway, I gotta hit the shower. Iwan is going to be here soon.'

Just like that, my brother dismisses me and hurries off to the bathroom. I am left standing in the middle of the living room looking at our last family photo taken. It hangs on the wall, next to the clock chiming the next hour above the sound of the TV.

I'm lost in my thoughts, the memory of Mah telling us about Pelabuhan Ratu while travelling in her sister's van through villages we refer to as kampung. Pelabuhan Ratu, a great tourist destination for families with only one rule: never wear green, especially for men, otherwise–

The front doorbell rings through the house, shaking me back to the present.

'*Selamat Pagi.*' My brother's fiancé, Bunga, dressed in a purple fur hoodie and knee-high boots, greets us in a singsong voice.

'My brother won't be long, Kak, he's just in the bathroom, silahkan, masuk.' I hug Bunga as I welcome her into the house.

'Uber will be here in half an hour, where's your brother?' Iwan barges in after Bunga.

'Hello to you too.' I roll my eyes.

Raffi finds Bunga in the kitchen, where Iwan helps himself to my fridge…again. He's the human Dyson that sucks my fridge clean. It is difficult to tolerate my brother's irritating mate first thing in the morning. I avert my eyes as Raffi and Bunga exchange their version of pleasantries. They have been together for as long as I can remember, but only recently got engaged. Their wedding is set for the end of next year, giving Raffi time to level up at his job as planned, before getting married. The warmth in my heart returns seeing how happy they are together. If only our parents could see this but the warmth is now overshadowed by an ice-cold feeling returning, chilling my veins. The news comes back on TV, headlining their developing story again. My stomach is very tight and not from lack of breakfast.

'Kang Raffi, wait!' I take him by the arm, leading him to my room.'You really shouldn't go. But, if you have to… Just… Please be careful, OK?' I whisper.

'Dek, what are you so worried about? You've been tense all morning.'

Tears well up. I try to hold them back. I want to tell my brother – the only family I have left since our parents' Malaysian airlines flight disappeared in 2014 – that since I woke this morning, something doesn't feel right. The news from West Java, the heaviness of my heart. I take in my brother's face and how much he looks like Abah. I never had closure with the loss of our parents, their bodies never recovered. We couldn't even give them a proper burial. I can't bear the thought of losing my brother. I wish he would reconsider this trip with Iwan. But words are failing me this morning.

I can't explain my fear, why I don't want him to go – how the news story is something he really should listen to, but he insists on going to this place with Iwan. It's imperative to their research, he says. Last time my brother and Iwan went to Jakarta, they came back saying they had no choice but to return. It was strange. Before that, Kang Raffi couldn't wait to get home to see Bunga.

My brother insists the reason for going back is simply to tick a bucket list item off, but I was not convinced. I once demanded he tell me what he was *really* doing there. He told me he was scoping the area for a potential restaurant location.

I couldn't ignore the gnawing in my stomach at Kang Raffi's cagey behaviour then. I can't ignore it now. Iwan is not above dodgy dealings and I'm worried "research" is code for a secret drug thing. But with the news today, dread overtakes me and I can do nothing more than give Kang Raffi a tighter squeeze as though this is the last time I will see him.

'*Kenapa* Dek!?' My brother pulls me in with a hug, like when we were little and I was afraid of thunder and lightning.

'*Hati Hati*, ya Kang.' I sniff, pleading with my brother to be careful.

'*Tenang, calm down*...I'll be back in a couple weeks. Bunga will check in from time to time. We'll keep in touch.'

A horn in the driveway signals the arrival of the Uber driver. Raffi heads out to the living room with Bunga and Iwan, taking his suitcase and getting his passport off the coffee table. I watch from the window as the three walk out into the driveway. The driver helps them load their luggage, then waves them into his car.

My brother gives me one last wave when panic strikes me.

I rush out of the house barefoot. Forgetting my robe and sandals, I run to the end of the driveway, but I am too late. The Uber has driven off.

I am standing alone on the freezing pavement. Tears spill from my eyes, now there is no turning back.

Why didn't I see it before?

Feeling nauseous, that knot returns to my stomach as dreadful realisation hits me.

My brother, my only family, is heading straight to Pelabuhan Ratu in a green hoodie.

Trudging through dense, endless jungle and there is no way out.

Humidity intensifies, seeping into my skin. Damp, rank air, a violation of the senses. I am desperately looking for a coastline or a main road. There are very few highways in kampung. Only small roads link the southern portion of the province to the central part.

I am startled by a green figure in the corner of my eye.

Long ebony hair goes past her waist, a heart-shaped face with daunting dark, almond eyes, so strong they pierce through the soul upon just one look. The most beautiful woman I have ever seen in my life floats before me.

Floats?

Floating in the air like a mermaid out of water, sporting a green strapless top: a traditional kemben tucked into batik sarung, her emerald-green salendang draping around her body, billowing in the wind below. Her beautiful eyes staring at me, holding me captive, traditional gamelan sounding in the background. Soothing sounds of the West Javanese gong and suling, so soothing I am caught in a spell. Suddenly, scales appear across her face, emerging rapidly from her left eye down to her chin. Half of her face turns into a sea serpent, teeth morphing into sharp, lethal fangs.

An evil cackle escapes her lips with enough force to throw me across the jungle, and I hit a nearby tree. This beautiful floating mermaid is now a monster advancing upon me, inching closer and closer, the stench of death encroaching. My heart is beating fast. I can no longer feel my feet, my hands, numbness consumes my body but my legs flop about, scrambling. I am trying to scream for help, but I cannot conjure even the slightest sound. The floating mermaid is zeroing in on me, like a snake about to devour its prey, but she stops still.

Suddenly, translucent hands penetrate out of the snake's chest, reaching for me. Frozen in fear, I squeeze my eyes shut, bracing for the hold of these ghostly hands.

'What do you want?!' I try to scream, but my mouth is sealed shut.

'What is rightfully mine,' she answers, reading my thoughts.

The gong and suling grow louder, drawing me in. I close my eyes, sinking into the ground.

I wake with a sudden jolt, drenched from head to toe.

My clothes stick to my legs, chest and back. I'm in bed, not the dense tropical rainforest from my nightmare. My fingers cramp up after holding my doona so tightly. The music of the gong and suling, freakishly close, is only my phone ringing on my bedside table. My cousin's name, Fera, glows from the screen.

I answer the phone, sounding more irritated than intended. 'Fera... it's 2am,'

'Oh ya? It's only 11pm here.'

My cousin clearly has no concept of the time zone difference.

'*Ada apa*, Fera? What's going on?'

'Have you spoken with your brother recently?' She asks. Her tone sends me bolt upright, all drowsiness gone in an instant.

'Why?' I ask. He's been gone for over a week and I haven't even received a text but I just assumed his phone was out of range.

'He came to visit us,' Fera answers slowly, then pauses. There's static on the line that sounds like the distant roar of ocean waves.

'*Terus...* go on...'

'With his new wife.'

I drop the phone into my lap and I stare wide-eyed at my bedroom door.

My brother's new wife? But Bunga stayed behind. I was with her earlier in the day. Fera must be mistaken. I scramble to pick up the phone again from between my sheets.

'When did this happen?' I demand.

Before Fera can answer, I have a new call coming through.

Bunga.

Oh no.

Without saying goodbye, I hung up and answer Bunga, who is sobbing on the phone.

'Please let me in. I'm right outside.'

A cold blast intrudes as I open the door just in time to see Bunga, pure rage on her face. I don't know what to say other than to welcome her in. Bunga remains silent as I switch the electrical fireplace on before bringing her a glass of water. My phone is ringing again – Fera is trying to call back, but I ignore her.

'Kak, tell me what happened? Why are you here at this hour?' I whisper.

'I trusted you,' is all she can manage.

What is she talking about? Before I can ask, Bunga holds up her phone. She's showing me an Instagram account – not hers. It is my brother's. There's a photo of Raffi, with his hands wrapped around a beautiful woman. The caption "Just Married" stares at me from the screen.

Bunga fury is the same as the fury in my heart. Anger, betrayal, disgust. How could my own brother do this? How can he hurt the best thing that has ever happened to him?

BASTARD!

'Ya ampun Kak Bunga, How? When? Why?' I'm lost for words.

'I was hoping you could tell me.' Bunga's serious tone catches me off guard.

'What do you mean, *Kak*?'

'You really had no idea your brother was planning to marry another woman all this time? All that bullshit about Raffi and Iwan having to go there for research? It was just talk, wasn't it. You're his sister! How could you not know?'

Her accusation cuts deep but she's right – how could I not know? If this was really Raffi's plan all along, then he betrayed us both. But he seemed so in love with Bunga, none of this is making any sense.

'*Kak…sumpah…*I had no idea Kang Raffi was going to do this. I know my brother can be stupid, but I didn't think he was such a complete dumbass to do something like this.'

Did my brother fall for one of those online dating sites not realising he copped a scam bride who's only looking for a ticket to Australia?

'I knew the day I saw the news something wasn't right. I didn't want him to go,' I say, thinking aloud. This is what my premonition was all about – not about something bad happening to my brother, but about him doing something so stupid, so irreparable.

'What are you talking about? What news?'

I tell her about the Australian diplomat washing up on the shore of Pelabuhan Ratu. Bunga's expression changes from cold fury to spooked. I don't blame her. The more I tell her, the more questions are raised. We decide the only way we can get any answers is by calling Raffi, but despite several attempts through Whatsapp, he's still offline. Surely he can't be out of range for this long especially since Fera mentioned him turning up with a new wife just a few days ago.

'Think Indah… Think!'

Iwan…

I call Iwan through Whatsapp but he is offline, too. He was also last seen on the app two days ago. My heart is beating fast. Something is definitely not right. These boys live in the virtual world – how can they be offline? Especially in a tourist attraction with strong wifi like Pelabuhan Ratu. I check other social media platforms and Iwan hasn't posted anything since their arrival almost a week ago.

Another dead end.

I go to Raffi's account. No stories in his feed, but I see the posting Bunga showed me earlier. At first glance, it appears to be my brother and his new wife. They look happy. The pinned location is Pelabuhan Ratu. Zooming in for a closer look, I study the picture, desperate for clues. It's taken on the shoreline, sun beginning to set on the Southern Sea behind the newlyweds. I squint for a better look of their faces and notice something odd about this woman. The longer I look at her, the more I see her skin rippling as though covered in scales.

I blink and the image goes back to normal – perhaps it's pixelated.

But that's not it. I look closer and a memory comes surging at me like a punishing wave. I know this woman; I have seen her before. In my subconscious! I jolt upright, knocking the magazines off the coffee table where my feet were resting.

I startle Bunga. 'Are you OK? Indah? Kenapa?'

I can't find my voice. Shock is taking me over. Bunga stands next to me, tugging at my arm. Sudden tears fall from my eyes; I can barely face her.

'My brother is in trouble.'

Cheap emergency flights to Jakarta are easy to find when you're willing to forego the pleasures of in-flight meals and entertainment. Bunga fell asleep as soon as we boarded but I'm wide awake. Taking advantage of in-flight wifi, I bootup my laptop and wait for my Aunty's Skype status to glow green.

@Ana_Suheni8: Assalamualaikum Sayang.

@Indah_House10: Waalaikumsalam Uwa... kumaha damang?

@Ana_Suheni8: Saeh, Allhamdulilah. Let me practise my English, Neng...I got your text, I am so glad you contacted me about Raffi. I knew something was not right when Fera told me he visited with a new wife who was not Bunga! Astaga...Neng...what do you know of Nyai Roro Kidul?

Nyai Roro Kidul.

It takes me a moment to remember the story Mah used to tell me when I was growing up: about a young, beautiful princess who was heiress to the throne somewhere in West Java. Upon the death of her mother, her father remarried. However, he didn't know his new bride was a witch, jealous of his daughter's beauty. So jealous, she cast a spell on her, which drove her out of the palace to Pelabuhan Ratu, the Southern Sea. There, the princess was able to wash the spell off in the water, only to have it reignite when back on land. She had to make the sea her home.

I type it into the Skype messenger.

That is one story, my aunt confirms. *But there are many others – many legends formed in West Java about the mysterious Nyai Roro Kidul, but none truly reflect the truth.*

My Aunty stops typing for a while, leaving me in suspense. I can see she starts and stops typing several times before finally finishing the sentence.

Neng – Nyai Roro Kidul is real.

Now it's my turn to stop typing.

I knew Aunty could be superstitious just like Mah, but I never thought she would fall into the trap of believing a myth to be real. The archipelago of Indonesia is made up of over 17,000 islands, and while Nyai Roro Kidul is connected to Pelabuhan Ratu, each island has its own legend, which more often than not gravitates towards a horrific end for those tempting fate. To this day, Fera is convinced she once crossed paths with a tuyul when she lost her phone. Sure, like an undead infant known to steal gold from houses would be interested in my cousin's Android.

Uwa, but what would Nyai Roro Kidul have to do with my brother? I finally have the courage to type but the captain signals it's time to land. Before I can get an answer, my connection is lost.

Uwa Ana meets Bunga and me at Soekarno Hatta Airport and drives us straight to Pelabuhan Ratu. Jakarta's humid air seeps into my skin and down my back – there is no respite, not even with the aircon blasting in the car. I have no time to think, settle or plan. All I know is my brother's life is on the line if we don't get to Pelabuhan Ratu now. We drive a thousand miles an hour, the smell of diesel wafting through the car, cars beeping.

It's too much; I fall into an anxious sleep and dream of her… *Nyai Roro Kidul,* the pinnacle of West Javanese legend, now a recurring nightmare. My feet are sinking into the sand as I gaze upon the waters in front of me. Ocean breeze a welcoming respite from humidity and the smell of saltwater. And here she is, a beautiful monstrosity, floating in the Southern Sea, head above water, trying to wash her cursed skin only to have the scales grow back when she steps on land, and now she's walking towards me.

'What do you want!?' I scream at her but only a cackle escapes her lips as she retreats back into the Southern Sea, vanishing before my eyes.

I bump my head against the window, the slamming of brakes jolting me awake. Darkness surrounds the lands with the exception of faint light glowing up ahead. We have reached Pelabuhan Ratu. I welcome the ocean breeze and salt air after three hours of humidity in a nauseating car ride. I unfasten my seatbelt. Both Bunga and I jump out of the car.

'Where to?' I ask Uwa Ana.

My Aunt gives us directions to the town centre where she tells us to locate Cafe Gaul. According to her friends who frequent Pelabuhan Ratu, Cafe Gaul is the go-to place for local information. They've heard of a man by the name of Hadi, said to be a well known tour guide, and he's always in this cafe. If anyone can help us, it's him. At the sound of his name, a chill goes down my spine but I don't know why.

Hadi.

Why is this familiar?

No time to dwell on this now as Uwa urges us to move. Bunga and I run ahead, using our phones as torchlight, navigating the dark dirt road descending down a winding path toward the shore. A man of small build wearing a white polo shirt and knee length shorts greets us like he was waiting for us the whole time. How did he even know we were coming? This stranger looks alarmingly familiar but I can't place him. Before I can think any more on this, he introduces himself in Bahasa Indonesian, with the creepiest grin I have ever seen in my life.

'Nama saya, Hadi.'

I don't know why, but I feel compelled to tell him why we are here, replying in Bahasa Indonesian. His smile turns serious when I show him my brother's latest Instagram post. Hadi nods and indicates for us to follow him. Leading us down a trail through a small village off the beaten track. Darkness sets in, not even our iPhone torches are sufficient to light the way.

Before long, we reach a small hut. Hadi opens the door, inviting us inside. Suspicion uncoils immediately. I have heard too much about what happens to young girls stepping into strange rooms. Before I can talk myself out of it, Bunga enters, so I follow.

The room is green like the sea from floor to ceiling, yet there is no breeze to comfort me in this humidity. Sweat beads on my forehead and runs down my back, the sickening heat making me dizzy in this strange place.

A picture hangs from the far wall, drawing me in. As I take a closer look, the distinct smell of paint or turpentine wafts from the portrait of a beautiful woman, ebony hair falling to her waist, much like the woman in my dream. Well, my nightmare. Floating above water in a green strapless top: a traditional kemben tucked into batik sarung, her emerald-green salendang draped around her body, billowing in the wind below.

No...

I whip my head around and see Hadi, only moments ago standing by the door, now an inch behind us. But he's not the Hadi we met on arrival. Half of his body has changed into a black serpent's tail, scales all over where his legs should have been. His face is half skin, half scales. Sharp fangs now protrude through his top gums, and he's boasting a smile as though he is a predator about to devour his prey. Bunga pulls me back to the wall, whispering to keep calm. I am trying to keep control of my bladder when I find we are trapped between this monstrosity that people only ever see in movies and the shrine of Nyai Roro Kidul behind me. The door behind Snake Hadi is our only way out. I take a shaking step forward and he hisses.

'What the hell are you!?' Bunga shouts at him, clearly holding it together better than me.

'WHERE IS MY BROTHER!' I demand, trying to swallow my fear.

I don't even know if this is real or a nightmare from which there is no awakening. Right now, I just want to find Kang Raffi. Instead of answers, I am met with laughter, but Hadi's lips are not moving. His voice invades my mind, like a whispering djinn, all too happy to tell me the Goddess of the Southern Sea will claim any soul she pleases, especially souls of ignorant fools who dare encroach on her land in the forbidden colour, and that, as her most loyal servant, he will lead them to her. The last man was no match for her, yet he brought too much attention to the harbour. This time, she knows better.

The last man?

The last man washed up in Pelabuhan Ratu was headline news the day my brother left for this forsaken place. Then it hits me. The morning the news broke, a reporter interviewed a local who claimed to have found the body of the Australian diplomat. That local is the Hadi who has now transformed before me.

Hadi is behind all of this!

He must have enticed my brother with the prospect of a business deal, only to lead him to his demise simply because he was wearing the forbidden green. Yet the reason why it's forbidden is unclear; only that green somehow draws the Goddess of the Southern Sea to the forefront. But those stories always tell of unusual activity, like fishing boats disappearing mysteriously or a tsunami devastating the beach and local residential areas. Nothing so personal, where an enchanting woman rises from the ocean, infiltrating the land and seducing and claiming the souls of unsuspecting men in green.

Hadi's whisperings in my mind become louder and more intense, creating a migraine I am trying to ignore. I can barely keep my eyes open. I clench my fists, nails digging into my palms, drawing strength to remain alert. Bunga and I came here to find my brother and we are not leaving without him.

Adrenalin suppressing my migraine, I find the strength to hit Hadi right in the middle of his chest with an open palm, forcing him to stumble backwards. Without a moment's hesitation, I stomp forward, attempting to hit Hadi in the face but I trip over my own two feet and fall to my knees. I try to get back up but Hadi takes this moment to strike, tackling me to the ground. I cannot escape his strong grip that's pinning me down. I struggle to breathe, gasping for air but I am slowly losing oxygen while he finds this amusing as a grin stretches across his face, boasting two fangs like a cobra about to devour its prey.

This is the end, I just know it. I came all this way to save my brother and it was all in vain. Mah hasn't just lost a son, she will now lose a daughter. I am starting to lose consciousness, dots forming in my eyes when suddenly Hadi collapses on top of me. The stench of sewerage and beach water radiating off him assaults my senses. Just when I thought I would be stuck under Hadi forever, a pair of strong hands drags me out from under him.

Bunga - ya ampun, I forgot she was here! She hugs me while

repeatedly telling me I'm OK as she helps me back on my feet. I see the metal fold up chair she used to knock Hadi out a moment ago but our moment of victory is short-lived as Hadi slowly regains consciousness and rises from the floor. Both Bunga and I are frozen in fear as Hadi starts to advance upon both of us.

'Foolish... so foolish... only death awaits you both now,' Hadi says, fangs protruding through his gums once more. Anger replaces my fear. I've had enough. I am exhausted, I am dirty, I am pushed over the edge and no longer in the mood for a half-man half-snake monster. With a closed fist, I punch Hadi right in the mouth, knocking out one of his fangs as he lands on the ground with a thud. He's very still but it's not enough for me. I run up to him and kick him repeatedly in the stomach and his snake half.

Incoherent shouts of rage are forced out of my mouth. Not even I know what I am saying, besides my brother's name. I don't realise I move outside of the hut as I am kicking the daylights out of Hadi. Out of nowhere, arms wrap around my waist from behind, pulling me away from Hadi's limp form that is now leaning against a tree. I turn to hit this new assailant but it's Iwan, looking bruised and battered.

'What the hell happened to you!?' I push away from him.

'Iwan!?' Bunga gasps, as she runs out from the hut.

'Indah... your brother is in trouble,' Iwan says.

'No shit!'

'I'm serious. Neng...We got separated two nights ago and I've been looking for him all this time. I'm sorry we couldn't tell you or Bunga why we were really coming here.'

I channel my rage from Hadi to Iwan and punch him square in the mouth. Shock is written all over Iwan's face. I cannot believe him. They lied to us, their stupidity put us in danger. I am too enraged to speak. Too numb to feel the pain that must be radiating from my hands as I see the cuts and bruises all over them. A rustling nearby steals my attention. Hadi is propping himself up on his elbows from the dirt ground. The snake part of his body fades from black scales to bruised legs and feet. He's crawling away through the shrubs.

Iwan stares at Hadi's retreating figure in awe. 'The guy whose ass you just kicked? He's a loyal servant to Nyai Roro Kidul.'

'I am really starting to get sick of hearing that name.' I sigh.

'He'll lead us to her! Let's go!' Iwan beckons us to follow Hadi's retreating figure.

The three of us break into a run, trying to keep quiet, to not to tip off Hadi that he's being followed.

'Dek...listen to me,' Iwan says as we track the servant of Nyai Roro Kidul. 'Raffi and I have been following the story of men going missing right here in Pelabuhan, we are a part of a secret society run by the West Javanese community back home who are on a mission to figure out why men seem to go missing around these parts never to return. And not just that, strange things have been happening on the island for a while. Parts of the shoreline are dangerous for swimmers and for good reason. Fierce waves coming in from the Indian Ocean — water coming in with the power of a nuclear-blast shock wave — we think that's all her!'

'All this because men wear green on the shoreline?' Bunga asks, keeping up with us.

'It draws her out,' Iwan confirms. 'But things have gotten so much worse! Nyai Roro Kidul is real, Dek. She has the power to move a sleepy fishing town with more ease than a wave over sand. She can reduce homes to rubble forcing locals to move to higher ground. It's not natural what's been happening here. '

'Then what?' Bunga asks. 'What happens to the men she seduces?'

Her question hangs unanswered.

Ahead, Hadi disappears up the hillside, into a building that looks like a hotel designed to resemble an ancient West Javanese building overlooking the Southern Sea. What a view! But...before getting on the plane to Jakarta, Bunga and I studied the maps, and I don't recall seeing this hotel. This part of the beach should be empty.

My hands are tingling, something isn't right. The building gives me a dark premonition but before I can articulate my fears, Bunga rushes up the hill, heading straight for the building. This is so unlike her. Bunga - the very person refusing to go skydiving with me on my birthday now leads the way to what could very well be a trap. I look to Iwan for other suggestions but he just grabs me by the wrist and runs after Bunga.

We run up the stairs two at a time and on the second level, Iwan signals us to duck and keep quiet. Glass breaks somewhere in the rooms above us, followed by the sounds of a struggle and my brother's voice crying out for help.

I take the lead this time, running up the stairs to the highest level of the building, which only has one room – Room 13… *of course.*

Ya ampun…

My brother's scream breaks the silence of Pelabuhan Ratu's night.

Without another thought, I push the door open.

This room, like Hadi's hideout, is green from floor to ceiling. No windows, no balcony to enjoy the view of the sea. Just a green box of a room, with a small closet to one side and a white bed in the middle. Raffi is cowering naked in the corner of the room, while the bed is claimed by the creature from my nightmare. She, too, is naked, her skin a discoloured green. Her long ebony hair is matted and stretched out across the bed.

And then my eyes are drawn to the lower part of her exposed body.

With her legs open, a black snake as large as a python exits her and slithers down the bed and toward my brother. Horrified, Bunga collapses at the door, Iwan catching her just in time. I look for anything I can use as a weapon.

The snake is inching closer and closer to my brother. I am running out of time. Panicked, while the monster is focused on Raffi, I run to the closet and open it, looking for anything useful that can help us out of this. The closet is full of regal costuming, batik materials and gold jewels. Someone of royal stature definitely lived here once upon a time. I wonder whether this monster killed them when taking it over and creating a lair. The hissing is getting louder and my brother screams, sound so chilling, it is bound to stay with me for the rest of my life.

A shiny silver catches my eye. I lean closer and see it is a keris, a traditional, double-edged dagger with a wavy blade. I remember hearing about these weapons being more lethal to spiritual beings than any other weapon. How did the creature miss this? Testing the theory, I grab the keris. Struggling to keep my sweaty palms firmly wrapped around its handle, I leap forward, taking stabs at the snake but missing as it shifts from side to side. Its hissing grows louder as it advances on Kang Raffi.

A stench suddenly violates the air, as if the strong odour of durian encountered my brother's dirty socks. It is coming from the snake. As it hisses, the stench becomes so overpowering, my eyes are watering. I am losing focus, trying to hold my breath and breathe at the same time. I am stumbling, trying to stab the snake, but missing over and over again.

Exhaustion, fear and frustration cripple me. I slash with the keris but trip over my own two feet and land with a thud.

A blood-curdling scream jolts me and I see the keris has stabbed into Nyai Roro Kidul's leg. She turns to me, piercing eyes looking deep into my soul. In a panic I wrench the keris out of her leg and stab the snake right in the centre.

The snake, wounded, freezes, as does Nyal Roro Kidul.

Her eyes turn to glass as the snake breaks free from her body and turns to sand on the floor. Bleeding, Nyai Roro Kidul faces me but she does not attack. Instead, she turns translucent – just like the ghostly hands I once saw in my nightmare – and vanishes through the green wall.

As she disappears, all signs of a struggle – blood, sand, and the dead snake – vanish too, as though she has never been here.

My brother is still cowering naked in the corner. I ran with a sarung to cover him. He is shaking feverishly. I become aware that Iwan and Bunga have entered the room. Iwan falls in next to me, but Bunga stands back, clearly having mixed feelings about the whole situation. Raffi covers himself, tears streaming down his face.

'Dek… Neng… Indah…' my brother gasps.

'Maafin Kang Raffi ya Dek,' Raffi apologises in a shaky voice. All I can do is hold my brother while his body trembles. Shushing him, telling him it'll be OK. As my brother finally regains some control, the trembling slows down and he manages to tell us of the fateful day down the beach when an enchanting woman approached him and caught him under a spell. He tried to get away, but her hooks were buried so deep there was no escape.

'The moment our eyes connected, that was it. My surroundings became a blur, all I could see was her. Her frightening beauty, so captivating, one step out of line was a death sentence.'

Raffi only seems to remember meeting that creature in human form on the beach. He can't remember any wedding or visiting Fera with this woman or even the photos that are still on social media. My brother suddenly breaks down in tears, repeating Bunga's name over and over, the pain coming through his cries as he realises Bunga may be lost to him forever. Their relationship, their plans, their love. Bunga suddenly pushes through and embraces Raffi. Iwan and I are left to watch them sobbing in each other's arms.

'Ayo bangun Dek,' Raffi calls.

The winter morning is keeping me under my doona, yet the scent of nasi goreng and fried egg is enticing. I rise, put on my robe and slippers, and head to the kitchen, where Bunga and Iwan are already digging into chef Raffi's special breakfast.

It is so good to be home in Australia. Raffi promised he was done with the Sunda Society – after we left West Java, there has been no word of men going missing on that island again.

'To breaking news now – the autopsy report of deceased Australian diplomat Terry Herman has now been released...' The TV drones.

I take my breakfast to the living room to listen in.

'Authorities are still unclear on the actual cause of death but an unusual finding of a large snake bite on the diplomat's lower abdomen may be the possible cause. Though locals have not confirmed any snake sightings, Herman's death still remains a mystery. Here is Sam Jackson with more...'

The view on the screen switches to Pelabuhan Ratu, at the very shoreline where my brother was ensnared by the beautiful yet deadly Nyai Roro Kidul. Is not Sam Jackson on camera but a familiar face, captioned as "Hadi: local resident". Just seeing him on TV causes my stomach to knot. Hadi puts on a great act, pretending he is upset about the death of the Australian diplomat and with the influx of tourists now coming to Pelabuhan Ratu, he is hoping there won't be another death, especially if tourists stay safe and don't go near the water after dark.

I am sure my brother can hear my eyes roll from all the way in the kitchen.

A shiver takes over me as my attention is now caught by what is behind Hadi. From the Southern Sea a translucent figure slowly emerges from the water, like a floating mermaid. Ripples around her become waves, crashing on the shoreline. The sky turning from blue to grey, a storm is brewing as the camera zooms out from Hadi and focuses on the news reporter, Sam Jackson who is standing on the shoreline holding a microphone and wearing a teal green shirt.

NO TIME FOR MAYDAY

SARAH GLENN MARSH

SKYLAR HAS BEEN STARING AT HER PHONE FOR SO LONG THAT WORDS ON the screen have begun to blur together. She ignores the babble of unfamiliar voices around her, the glare off the ship's fresh white sides reflecting the persistent heat, and even the muted sun-drunk blue of the harbour that normally wouldn't have to compete for her attention.

I don't want this anymore. I don't know that I ever did. Maybe I should have told you sooner. But you're still, like, my best friend, Sky. I hope we can keep that.

Friends. They had been, briefly, so long ago now she can hardly remember. But she said it as if all their time offscreen, the in-jokes, the love songs that stacked their shared playlist over the past two years had ever been just–

'Put that away. You'll make yourself seasick before we even take off,' Margot tells her briskly, swiping a summer-bronzed hand toward Skylar's phone.

Skylar lets Margot grab her cell without protest and watches silently as it disappears, screen still glowing, into Margot's oversized designer beach tote; she knows Margot is only doing this because she cares. She's a good friend under the glitz and gloss, loyal, even if her whirlwind Insta-fame following a fling with a popular *Bachelorette* castoff has gone to her head lately.

'*Take off*, huh?' Skylar teases halfheartedly as she makes her way to the deck rail, seeking more distance from the crowd. She gives the generous expanse of Florida beachscape a cursory, unimpressed glance. 'What, Marg, are we on a plane? I think you mean *set sail*.'

Margot rolls her eyes. 'I've never been on one of these things before. I'm not even a good swimmer. Sorry if I'm not up to date on my maritime—'

The behemoth of a cruise ship beneath them gives a great shudder as if protesting something slithering against its great white underbelly. Margot grabs Skylar's arm, the sound of her gasp drowned by a blast from the ship's horn that announces their departure. After a few seconds of ringing silence, a Calypso band begins to drum an upbeat tune, drawing a handful of dancers already splashed out on the free drinks that have been circulating on deck for the past hour.

Just like that, *Seas the Day* begins its maiden voyage, a five-day, round-trip sailing to beautiful, humid, rum-soaked Barbados filled with influencers like Skylar and Margot who were invited along to party while promoting this new cruise line.

Recovering, Margot decides, 'Let's get a few shots with the beach behind us while we can. I need something to post tonight.' She grabs two drinks from a tray as it sails past, offering one of the stormy blue concoctions (complete with little paper umbrella) to Skylar.

She takes it, but doesn't taste it, instead watching as Margot plucks the umbrella from her glass and tucks it behind her ear, its yellow paper bright against her dark hair.

'Not your flavour?' Margot sighs when Skylar sets her drink precariously on the rail. 'Look, this is my vacation, too, and your misery is contagious. This could be great. Think about it: Free concert, free booze, free…views.' She stops, thinking she's lost Skylar again. Her friend stares moodily toward the sea as her long, dirty blond hair lifts in the warm breeze. Margot hasn't seen Skylar this down since the two first met at a streaming con a few years back, when Sky lost a beauty blogging award to someone who *didn't* tell creepy stories while teaching viewers how to blend foundation.

'I wouldn't even be here if it wasn't free,' Skylar says eventually, distantly; she was at least half listening. 'This whole thing is going to suck; only old people go on cruises for fun.'

'What old people?' Margot asks, arching her brows above her sunglasses. 'The oldest person I saw today was the woman running the temperature screening when we checked in, and she couldn't have been fifty.' She takes a sip of her drink and makes a face; it's stronger than she expected for a freebie. 'Either the old people are hiding in their cabins, or everyone else is here for the same reason we are – they had nothing better to do with their summer. Seriously, look around. See anyone you recognise?'

Skylar takes a slow sweep of the deck packed with twenty-somethings. 'She's on a few apps,' she says, nodding subtly to a Black girl surrounded by admirers at the bar. 'Some kind of singer. And the girl in the yellow bikini – she runs a fitness blog. And that guy in the Speedo makes the worst cringe content with his frat buddies…' Eyes narrowing, she asks, 'Think these guys could be more obvious about their thirst for promo?'

Margot shrugs, growing impatient. 'Screw it, we're already here, so let's make some content and get some new sponsors out of it. Money's money – we win if they do.'

She lifts her phone – a brand-new, waterproof model, the same as Skylar's, gifted to them by the cruise company when they accepted the trip invite – and motions for Skylar to lean in. Behind her tall, narrow frame and Margot's petite, curvier one, palm trees and high-rise hotels grow imperceptibly smaller as the ship glides sluggishly, almost reluctantly, toward open water, the horizon a confusion of deep blues bleeding dizzyingly into one another.

Skylar doesn't see the ocean or her reflection, her focus turned back to a night in early spring, huddled together in the dark with Ava to watch her favourite scary movie. Eventually, ghosts had been forgotten in favour of lips and hands and words, a combination Skylar would have sworn at the time was love – but now, those words about what Ava never wanted are burned into her brain, so small but somehow strong enough to reshape her entire reality. Maybe the love had only ever been in her head. Maybe she had just wanted it enough to make it real for a time, rather than seeing what was true, what was in front of her all along.

'Try looking less like you're in the middle of a root canal, Sky,' Margot commands, dredging her out of the drowning pool of memory with an arm wrapped around her shoulders like a life preserver.

Skylar dutifully pastes on a smile – sponsored by a tooth whitening company and a new lip stain – and tries to concentrate on something she knows to be real, hoping to anchor herself to the moment. There's the overpowering scent of Curaçao from the drinks, Margot's coconut sunscreen, the tang of salt in the wind, and the heartbeat of the ship itself, a deep thrumming beneath their feet that churns in time with the waves the further they stray from shore.

'Good enough,' Margot declares after flicking through a few shots. She pockets the phone and offers Skylar her hand. 'Come on.'

'You want to leave the party already?' Skylar feigns surprise. 'And we were having so much fun mingling with our peers.'

Margot grins at her – a real grin, Skylar thinks, not the one she uses to sell weight loss tea and protein powders. But can she be sure? What does she know about real, anyway?

'The fun is coming. Let's check out our room. No, our *cabin*,' she amends, pleased with herself for using the correct term. 'We're going to get cleaned up, made up, and drunk on free booze. And then we're going to find a cute girl so you can get laid and forget all about what's-her-name.'

'Cruise ships have crazy high rates of sexual assault among–'

'Passengers, yeah, I heard you the first twenty times on the flight here,' Margot interrupts as the automatic doors yawn open wide to admit them. 'And these ships wreck the environment. I *know*. But unless you want to make us both miserable all week, I suggest you worry more about what you're going to wear tonight.'

Skylar follows her friend into the ship's immaculate interior, her sandals sinking into plush carpet. As she breathes in the oppressive chill of the new and powerful air-con system, she continues to sense the deep and restless churning beneath them, the heart of the ship, her anchor to this reality.

Slipping quietly past a couple tucked away on a bench who seem to have no idea about the party they're missing, she wonders if she's capable of forgetting Ava. If anyone can forget something they might have just imagined in the first place.

Late that night, Skylar lays in bed beside Margot with her eyes shut tight, unable to fall asleep, listening to the waves slap against the hull interspersed with her friend's snoring.

Their plan of hopping between the ship's bars was cut short when Margot got sick; Skylar suspects it's the vague sensation of rocking that never ceases, but Margot insisted the drinks were too strong, just like at the sail-away party. Skylar wouldn't know; she hadn't been in the mood to try one before Margot crashed out.

Hoping to lull herself to sleep by recalling the details of something familiar, Skylar thinks about the time her family went on a cruise to Mexico when she was a kid. She's remembering the way the ship lurched beneath them as they sailed through a summer storm, how they huddled together in their cabin and longed for solid ground, when a noise rises above the familiar din of the boat's creaks and groans – a thud, scattered between the breaths of the waves.

It sounds like someone just knocked something heavy off a table. And it's close – closer than the hallway.

Skylar's eyes snap open, quickly making sense of the shadowy shapes around them: the curtains that open onto the balcony, the vanity packed with make-up bags, the TV above the mini fridge, the small uncomfortable couch pushed up against the opposite wall, and there – where there shouldn't be – a man, crouched by the closet, rummaging through their shoes and bags and dresses.

He's tall and broad-shouldered, built. Probably one of the fitness junkies who was dancing by the pool earlier, half out of his mind from partying too hard. Yet his movements are too strong, too deliberate to suggest intoxication.

Drunk or not, he shouldn't be here. And there's no way in hell she's letting him steal their shit.

Skylar loves horror movies; she loves seeing what someone can endure when pushed to the edge, what they can survive. But she's never wanted to be in one. She's never thought of herself as a final girl, the one who makes it to the end somehow; she's not the fastest runner, she's not particularly strong, and while she was a decent student, she wouldn't call herself clever. All the same, she reaches silently toward the nightstand for the glass of water she poured for Margot earlier.

Once she's taken aim, she demands, 'What the hell do you think you're doing?'

The man turns quickly – definitely too fast to be anything but sober. She can't make out his face, even in the scant light seeping from under the bathroom door; there's only a collection of fuzzy shadows gathered together to vaguely suggest the outline of a nose, the sharp curve of a hollowed-out cheek. He snarls, low and guttural, almost like he's choking on his own tongue.

Skylar's heart roars in her ears as she nudges Margot, trying to wake her. But her friend snores on as the man launches himself toward the bed, a hand outstretched.

Skylar hurls the glass, but rather than connecting with flesh, it shatters against the mirrored doors of the closet – closed doors, though the man had left them open – raining glittering crumbs all over the carpet. The hulking shadow is gone, vanished mid-rush.

'What the hell?' Margot demands, plenty awake after the crash. She fumbles for the light switch on the wall.

In the far corner of the room, just before it fills with a soft yellow glow from the lamps above the bed, a pinprick of red light blinks out like some reptilian creature closing its eye to avoid notice. But when the lights come on, that corner is empty save for the faint lines of what might be, with their luck, the beginnings of a brownish water stain.

Maybe Skylar just imagined that brief red glow, like she imagined their visitor; like she imagined a girl as smart and funny as Ava could ever love her.

'There was a man,' she explains dully to Margot's ashen face as her friend takes in the aftermath. 'Or I thought there was.' She swallows over a dry tongue and adds, 'Sometimes these keycards work on more than one room – I'll check with the help desk tomorrow. He was looking through our closet, and then he ran at me, but...'

But what? But the glass went right through him? But he disappeared? Skylar isn't in a horror movie. She knows this. She's on a big, busy, brand-new boat where no one has ever died. She's having some trouble with reality right now, and no one needs a reminder of that.

'Bad dream,' Margot says firmly, faithfully, because even if she drinks too much and her plans aren't always the best, she's a really good friend.

'Right,' Skylar agrees, because she doesn't know what else to do; she doesn't mention the gurgling sound the man made, or the little red light in the corner of the room.

'Go back to bed,' Margot urges, drawing up the covers tight around her neck. 'Ugh, it's freezing in here. They think this is comfortable? Because I'm mentioning it in my review.'

Skylar glances at the goosebumps covering her own arms; the cold is the last thing on her mind. 'I can adjust the thermostat. I should clean up that glass any—'

'Housekeeping will get it in the morning,' Margot interrupts, burrowing into her pillow and yawning pointedly.

Skylar still hears the disappearing man's wet, ragged breathing too well to be tired; even if he wasn't real, the adrenaline hasn't worn off yet. If she didn't know better, if the evidence wasn't right in front of her to show that there was never a looming figure of a man in their room, she would swear he's still here, just out of sight – tucked into the closet, peering out from a crack in the doors, waiting until her guard is down.

What concerns her more than their phantom watcher, however, is her mind slipping further from reality as they sail into deeper waters. She leaves the lamps on even as her eyelids grow heavy, wondering why the new lights seem to smell faintly of ash and yet hoping they're strong enough to appease her wild imagination into keeping any more shadows at bay.

Margot's mood sours further when, after a night of broken sleep, she finds the day has dawned grey and overcast with a bite of chill in the wind that feels like late fall instead of August. This drowns her plans of sunbathing by the pool all day to make up for their still-frigid room – which, despite what the thermostat insists, is not the comfortable 75F they set it on. Turning it up only made the room smell like something burning.

Margot's not the only one grumbling over her morning coffee at this turn in the weather, however; the ship's staff mill around the dining room, smiles plastered to their faces, trying to sign up twitchy, restless social media moguls for free tours of the ship, pitching it as a rare chance to go behind the scenes.

'Told you cruises suck,' Skylar whispers to Margot as they're led down a sweeping staircase and into the ship's kitchens for an *exclusive* look at some large vats of soup and a glittering array of sugar-dusted desserts.

Margot scowls — Skylar knows she shouldn't be giving her friend such a hard time, not after how nice Margot has tried to be — and lifts her phone, the camera at the ready as usual. '*Exclusive content* doesn't suck,' Margot counters tightly, snapping a few shots of herself with a strawberry held to her glossy lips.

Skylar's phone is still in Margot's bag, she realises; she doesn't have the heart to look at it anyway, followers and sponsors be damned. If she has to read a text from Ava calling her *bestie*, there's no telling how many shadow men she'll unintentionally conjure in their room tonight.

Their perky tour guide soon ushers them out of the kitchen — nimbly and wisely stepping into the door of the large wine cellar to prevent anyone from swiping a bottle or two as they pass on their way out — and leads them to the ship's photography studio, where she tries to sell them on a variety of discounted photo packages.

Skylar feels sorry for her; she's got the wrong audience, a bunch of influencers who already know the best filters and lighting and would never pay someone else to try to make them look their best when it's all at their fingertips already.

The guide must sense this, too, as her speech grows more halting and awkward with each passing moment. Unable to bear the awkward any longer, Skylar wanders away from the group, looking at the framed art hung proudly on the walls as the ship rumbles steadily beneath her. There are a couple shots of the ship's interior: the lit-up casino, the multi-tiered chandelier dripping crystals above the central foyer with its marble floor and baby grand piano, the (per the caption) state-of-the-art fitness centre. There are images of ocean swells as captured off the ship's balconies, tropical seascapes, and even sample photos of shiny happy people dressed in their finest formal wear. And then there's a smaller photo that catches Skylar's attention purely for how unremarkable it is; one in an ordinary wooden frame.

The image itself is old, a black-and-white still of another ship. The HMS *Orpheus*, she can just make out from the faded text on the boat's side. A man in a crisp dark suit and white cap stands on the dock in front of the ship — his ship? —his expression as heavy as his beard, arms stiffly crossed.

She leans closer, trying to make out details despite the photograph's decaying state and not sure why she cares, just that it's better than listening to their tour guide. The picture – or more likely the frame – gives off the faint odour of cigarettes, of smouldering ash.

Margot puts a heavy hand on her shoulder, pulling her back from studying the old picture a little harder than necessary.

'Ouch, Marg, what's your deal?' she demands, turning to glare at her friend.

But Margot is across the room, under a glossy canvas showing a white sand beach complete with a hammock strung between palm trees, talking to a younger girl who runs an up-and-coming YouTube cooking channel.

There's no one behind her at all. Just several yards of plush new carpet separating Skylar from the rest of the group.

She inhales deeply, trying to clear her head, but the smell of ash lingers in her nose. For a second, she thinks of heading outside for fresh air, but a glance out the nearest window at the steely sky sends her toward their cabin instead.

It's still freezing inside; with a huff of irritation, she dials the temperature all the way up to 80F. That has to do something, she reasons. As she flops down on the couch, she notices housekeeping did indeed sweep up the glass, and makes a mental note to leave them a huge tip at the end of their stay.

Margot's oversized beach bag sits beside her, still packed for the pool day that's not going to happen. Skylar plunges her hand into the depths to retrieve her new phone that's somehow still got a charge; this, at least, has been a better gift than the cruise itself, actually holding up to its lofty promises of waterproofing and a longer battery life. There's nothing from Ava. Not even when she connects to the ship's free wifi. But that's not what she's looking for, anyway.

She heads to Google to search for the HMS *Orpheus*, curious why a ship from a hundred years ago would matter enough to this big new one to earn a spot on the wall.

It's not a happy story. The *Orpheus* was a cargo ship sailing from England to the U.S., doomed from the start, though its crew had no idea. The hazardous materials they were carrying hadn't been packed well back at the dock, so when they hit rough seas on their crossing, chemicals leaked from crates in the hold, poisoning everyone on board with noxious gas and ultimately causing a fire in the engine room as they lay dying, gasping their last breaths.

Why would anyone on a cruise to paradise want to be reminded of an old, doomed ship? Maybe, she wonders, it's somehow a sister ship to this one. *Seas the Day*'s parent company could be registered in England, for all she knows; she didn't read much of the fine print beyond "free cruise," being freshly broken up with and just agreeing without a second thought when Margot decided it sounded fun.

Skylar tosses her phone aside and draws her knees up to her chest; it should be boiling in their room by now, but it isn't. Growing even more irritated, she crosses the room to adjust the thermostat again, only to yelp and jerk her hand back as the touchscreen burns the tender pad of her index finger.

At least one thing in the room is getting hot.

Margot reappears not long after, realising Skylar ditched the tour; Skylar doesn't even think to tell her what she's been reading. There's no need to make her friend worry about her even more, especially after last night. Instead, they huddle down in blankets and watch a movie they've both already seen, one of a generous six free options, until they agree it's time for lunch.

Up in the cafeteria, rather than jumping right into the winding buffet lines, they choose a table set against the long glass wall so they can at least pretend they're enjoying the ocean. Neither of them mentions that the horizon they're sailing towards looks even darker than the heavy clouds that hang overhead, and it's not yet two in the afternoon.

Eventually, Skylar grabs a tray and fills it with whatever she can quickly grab – some waxy-looking fruit, yoghurt, and French fries that look like they came from a freezer bag. Margot, having a little more patience, returns some long minutes later with a fresh plate of shrimp alfredo.

'If the sun doesn't come out by tomorrow, I'm going to start thinking you're right about cruises,' Margot confides, twisting long noodles around her fork with a flourish. 'Not sure what the point of coming here was if there's not even anything decent to record for–'

Her lips shape a few more words, but Skylar can't hear them over the sound of violent retching from two tables over.

One of the fitness gurus, red-faced, is getting sick over his plate of grilled shrimp. It's a mess. Cruise staff seem to crawl out of every crevice, appearing in a blink to try to contain the splatter zone. Skylar's pulse quickens as the noises intensify, hoping someone with some real medical training will rush to the man's aid – it sounds almost as if he's gasping for air, strangled by his own vomit – but she dimly realises it's far too much to expect that any passenger on this boat will be able to help while they wait for the ship's doctor to arrive.

With the space around their table getting more crowded, Skylar and Margot are on the verge of leaving their seats when the retching stops as suddenly as it began – colour drains from the man's face, but his regular breathing resumes, his eyes glassy and, Skylar thinks, unseeing. The strong hands that had clutched at his throat now hang limp at his sides.

'Tyler, are you okay, man?' one of the guy's friends asks as the cruise staff seep back into the walls, or wherever it is they came from.

'Quite all right, thank you,' the man answers calmly, almost formally, as though he hadn't just been fighting for air.

Skylar's seen a few of his videos; she doesn't remember him talking like that.

Before she can think on it more, Margot swipes the apple off her tray and stands. 'Let's go eat in our room – this whole place smells like puke.' As Skylar stands to follow her, taking a banana and her still-sealed yoghurt, Margot adds, 'I only ate the one shrimp, so hopefully I don't get food poisoning, too.'

'You'll be fine. He's just possessed,' Skylar murmurs, quickening her pace to exit.

'What the hell, Sky?' Margot calls, staring after her.

She hurries to catch up, and they're just passing through the café doors when another red light in the corner catches Skylar's eye; this time, she grabs Margot's elbow and motions subtly toward it. 'Do you see that?'

'What, the security camera? You–'

'There's one in our room, then. I saw that same light last night, after the man – or whatever it was – was looking through our closet,' Skylar says, her voice low (low enough, she hopes, to avoid being picked up by the camera's audio) and urgent.

Margot raises an eyebrow. 'Pretty sure that's illegal. And you're avoiding the issue. Listen, Sky, maybe this whole thing was just too much right now.' She pauses, pulling her friend to the side of the doors so they won't block the flow of people coming and going. 'If you need to go home, I'll understand. We can fly back once we dock in Barbados tomorrow. Spend the rest of the week at my place, if you want. At least there's sun so we can actually use the pool.'

She doesn't hate the idea. 'Yeah. Okay. That might be good.'

As they trudge back to the room with their less-than-satisfying lunch, Skylar thinks about how she must sound. Paranoid, for one, about the cameras; and even if she had seen one in their bedroom that vanished somehow, so what? They invited a bunch of influencers on this free trip. For all she knows, the right to film them at all times was in the fine print she didn't read. And calling that man possessed; Margot probably thinks she's delusional now, too. Maybe she is. Maybe Ava's messed her mind up so thoroughly that she doesn't understand what's real anymore. After all, cruises are a breeding ground for norovirus, and why would this boat be haunted, anyway? It's brand new.

Still.

While Margot settles in with another of their free movie choices, Skylar curls up on the opposite end of the couch under a blanket to ward off the chill and announces lightly, 'I just need to take my mind off *her*, that's all. I'm going to work on my profile on a couple of dating apps, I think, at least see what's out there.'

Margot gives her a long, appraising look, but finally smiles – the one Skylar thinks is genuine. 'Good. Use your main pic from Insta. It's hot.'

Skylar opens her phone, but she doesn't search for any apps. Instead, she hunts for anything else she can find about the HMS *Orpheus*, city of origin: Liverpool.

The captain, Gordon Turner, was much-loved by his crew – he'd sailed with many of them before their ill-fated trip, had gotten them through the roughest weather and earned their loyalty in return. His body was found among the dead when the ship was eventually discovered rocking lifeless on the waves, and no one was more distraught than his teenage son. He was presented with his father's captain's hat and some of his other possessions by a friend at the burial.

As she reads more about the Turner family and the boat pushes deeper into churning waters, the unmistakable smell of spoiled milk creeps under her nose. Margot, half scrolling through her own phone and half watching TV, doesn't say a word about it, if she notices at all. So Skylar tries to ignore it, choosing to think about her ex instead;

at least those delusions, the ones where they were in love, are more pleasant to inhabit.

That night, when the ship's usual groans and the hiss of seawater glancing off the hull are interrupted by distressed shouting from Margot, Skylar thinks longingly of their flight home tomorrow afternoon as she turns in the chilled sheets to check on her friend.

'Whatsit?' she slurs, her tongue still thick with sleep.

But Margot doesn't answer. Her breathing is still deep and regular, her body limp.

As Skylar starts to roll back over, her friend says a few more words, this time louder and more clearly: 'You don't give a damn about the people on this ship.'

The room is already cold, it's never stopped being cold, but now she's frozen in place.

'Wh-what was that?' she somehow finds the nerve to ask. No answer. She takes a deep breath, and – shoving down the part of her that feels like a complete idiot – asks, 'Captain Turner? Gordon?'

Her only answer this time is a thud, as though something has fallen from the narrow space above the closet – but Skylar knows they didn't put anything up there, for one thing.

For another, the sound is too heavy, like all the weight of an overstuffed suitcase or even a grown person dropping to the ground, but by the light spilling from under the bathroom door – her makeshift night light after what happened the evening before – she sees there's nothing on the floor but two pairs of castoff sandals.

Margot's rhythmic breathing has already resumed. The longer Skylar listens, unable to fathom trying to sleep again, the more it seems as though her friend is breathing in sync with the rush of the wind-tossed sea, waves lashing hard against their side of the ship with every long exhale.

The next voice to wake Skylar isn't Margot's but the tinny garbled speech of the cruise director over the hallway speaker system. It's still dark – what time is it? Her phone says 9am, but the charcoal-washed sky outside disagrees. Groaning as she untangles herself from the blankets, Skylar staggers closer to the cabin door so she can hear better. The handle is warm in her hand, almost uncomfortably hot, as she pulls to open it just a crack; but it's a fleeting heat, ultimately unsatisfying and – she suspects yet again – only wishful thinking.

She tunes into the words from the loudspeaker as the ship rolls beneath her, She grips the door to keep herself upright.

'Ladies and gentlemen, again, we apologise for the inconvenience, but due to Hurricane Ava shifting course, we won't be arriving in Barbados today as scheduled. We'll circle port until it's safe to dock, and in the meantime, head to the bar of your choice for free drinks and entertainment. You're in good hands.'

Hurricane Ava?

Skylar's head feels fuzzy, like she didn't drink enough water the day before – which she probably didn't, she realises. She clings to the door a little harder than necessary in case the ship takes another hard dive to either side and sends her reeling as she listens to the message repeat.

'Ladies and gentlemen, again, we apologise for the inconvenience, but due to Hurricane Isla shifting course...'

Shaking her head at herself, Skylar shuts the door, resigned to repeating the message to Margot – she's going to be disappointed, too – and spending another frigid, gloomy day on a ship that had promised nothing but fun and sun in emails.

She steps into the narrow bathroom first to splash water on her face. Whatever comes out of the taps first isn't water – it's darker, shades of reddish brown like rust cascading between her fingers and smelling faintly of metal and char. She closes her eyes, then opens them again to clear water and a sink that now smells only of Margot's citrus face wash. She soaks her cheeks liberally until she's chased away what little colour remained there.

When a man's voice says in a gravelly rasp against her ear, 'You look lovely, my dear,' Skylar doesn't whirl to face the mirror, doesn't succumb to the urge to swat at the unseen mouth whose breath tickles her hair. Instead, she answers tartly, 'Thanks,' before slamming the bathroom door shut in an attempt to wake Margot.

Her friend takes the news about as well as Skylar expects. 'You're right. Cruises suck. We're never doing this again,' Margot declares as she pulls on a pair of joggers and a fuzzy pink crop top. 'Let's go up to one of the bars?'

'You can't seriously be thinking about drinking right now,' Skylar groans, about to point out what time it is – not yet ten AM – when the ship lists hard to the right and sends her stumbling.

Margot catches her, her fingers digging into Skylar's shoulders harder than necessary as a tremor runs through her hands. 'I'm not,' she says, not yet letting go. 'I just think…it might be nice to be around other people.' For a moment, Skylar thinks she sees a glimpse of some other Margot peeking out, a stranger who's uneasy and craving the security of others. But then she adds, 'You know, instead of freezing our asses off down here,' sounding entirely herself again, and Skylar isn't sure what she saw after all.

There aren't many people in the hallways or on the staircases leading up to the bars, though walking is currently the only means of getting around; due to rough seas, the elevators are off-limits, access walled off by bright lines of yellow tape.

Several of the people they do see are currently in the midst of being seasick, from a popular food blogger hugging her knees at the base of the stairs to a travel guru retching into a potted palm tree.

'Guess everyone ate the shrimp yesterday,' Margot tries to joke, but it sounds hollow, her words swallowed up by the wave of silence filling a space usually bustling with activity.

In the bar Margot chose – Gordon's Club, Skylar notices, the name gleaming in gold letters above the dimly-lit entryway – there are a couple other brave souls who have ventured out of their rooms. One guy alone at the end of the bar is talking without pause at the man mixing drinks, who only seems to be half listening.

'…so I'm trying to leave the bathroom, right? And I could twist the handle, but like, every time I pushed, nothing happened. And of course it didn't lock from the outside. It was like somebody was standing out there, somebody heavy, holding the door shut. But I'm the only one in my room, you know? I'm travelling solo,' a pause here, as if this is the part where usually he would brag about getting more hookups this way. 'Anyway, eventually whoever it was got bored, I guess. It just stopped.'

Skylar and Margot leave a few stools between them and the storyteller for good measure.

As Margot asks for two ice waters and the bartender gives her a Look, someone at one of the tables behind them starts gagging and retching.

'Does anyone else smell that? Smells like smoke,' the storyteller observes, perplexed, glancing over at Margot and Skylar as the bartender rushes from his station with rags in hand to attend the spill.

Skylar shrugs. When the bartender returns, three vomit-soaked rags later and not looking remotely green – a veteran of his trade, it seems – Skylar surprises Margot by ordering one of the blue drinks with the umbrella in it.

'Seriously – is something burning?' the storyteller asks, a touch more heat in his voice.

Skylar doesn't attempt to answer this time.

She clinks her swirling blue glass against Margot's water as her friend stares, wide-eyed, and says flatly, 'Cheers to another day in paradise.'

None of this is even real, she reminds herself as she drains the glass in a few befuddling gulps. Besides, if it were, what could she really do about it?

To Skylar's utter lack of surprise, two of those blue drinks are enough to encourage her to take a nap on one of the low couches at the back of the bar, her head in Margot's lap while her friend scrolls aimlessly through her phone, out of content to post.

They should be taking a taxi to the airport right now to arrange a flight, but instead the ship circles the island like a shark cornering its prey. Skylar dozes off and on, listening to the chorus of people getting sick and the occasional heavy thud from somewhere as though one of the lifeboats has come unmoored, banging against the ship in the high wind.

Margot is in the nearest bathroom when a much closer, much more tangible thud startles Skylar off the couch and out of her alcohol-induced torpor. A woman, probably in her mid-thirties, the bar's only other occupant at the moment, has just collapsed in her seat and – no doubt aided by the violent rocking of the ship – crumpled to the floor, spilling the contents of her bag everywhere.

As the bartender checks her pulse, Skylar sits near her (her legs too shaky to be trusted with much else), trying to help by scooping her things back into the bag. There's an assortment of papers, a few hair ties, and a name badge – the logo for a media company stamped boldly onto the front beneath the woman's title, *Associate Producer*.

Producer of what?

Skylar wishes her sluggish brain would catch on and let her fingers move faster as she rifles through some of the woman's papers. What is *Dark Waters: Haunted Reality TV Like You've Never Seen?* It's stamped across the top of every page.

This is completely out of control, someone – presumably the woman – has scrawled on a memo affixed to the topmost page. *We have to call it off before the storm and*

It stops there, no punctuation, as if the writer had been about to say more when – what? She'd gotten sick?

'What are you doing with that?' the bartender snaps suddenly, yanking the papers and bag from Skylar's stunned grasp.

She dimly notices the long papercut slashed across her hand, evidence of her nosiness, and the way the bartender so casually leaves the woman on the floor in favour of using the phone on the wall to call someone – hopefully medics.

Skylar stares at the woman's pale, sprawled form and realises she needs to do something more. Or rather, she should, if any of this were really happening. But for all she knows, it's an act. Something the little red lights in the corners of every room on this damned ship will be eager to capture for the next segment of *Dark Waters.*

She glances toward the bathroom, willing Margot to hurry up in there so she can tell her friend how right she was.

They're being filmed. Internet stars offered a free vacation in exchange for unwittingly being on reality TV. *Haunted* reality TV, apparently. But how could they get a ghost onto a brand-new boat? Maybe, Skylar reasons as she fights the rolling floor to get back to the couch without slipping, the haunting is as manufactured as the rest of this experience, like the overpowering drinks that are clearly being served on purpose to make everyone sick or paranoid or something that's good for ratings.

Five minutes later, with no medics and no Margot in sight, Skylar staggers past the woman still prone on the floor (the bartender now notably absent, along with the woman's bag) to the tune of smooth jazz music playing on an endless loop, heading to the bathroom where her friend was supposed to be quickly fixing her hair.

'Marg?' Skylar asks as she pokes her head in.

Sure enough, her friend is there, though she doesn't answer, and she's apparently forgotten she wanted to throw her hair into a messy bun; Margot stands with her back to the door, busy doing something near the hand dryers.

It takes Skylar's brain a moment to catch up with what she's seeing: Margot's nails, ripped down to bloody stubs from scratching so deep into the wall. Flakes of plaster like snow in Margot's dark hair. And where the layers of wallpaper and insulation hang like skin on either side of an open wound, exposing the bones of the ship, a rusted sheet of metal and a few letters: MS OR.

She doesn't have to guess at the name; Margot's busy writing it over and over among the mirrors and above the dryers with the blood from her own torn fingernails.

HMS *ORPHEUS*.

A piece of the old ship, embedded in the new. Perhaps one of many.

So that's how they did it, Skylar realises dully, the alcohol still strong enough to suppress her fleeting urges to panic. They didn't fake a haunted ship for their show; they built one on purpose, using scraps from that doomed cargo liner. And they lured people onboard, having no idea how dangerous it would be. Just for entertainment.

'Margot!' Skylar shouts, her heart lodging in her throat. 'Stop!'

Her friend keeps on scrawling the name with her own blood.

It isn't until Skylar grabs her by the shoulder and turns her that Margot's glassy stare breaks; she blinks, and after a moment of breathing hard, vomits all over Skylar's feet.

Moving quickly to help her friend, Skylar catches a man's face in the mirror out of the corner of her eye, his skin mottled purple, frothy pink spit oozing from his mouth. He watches her sadly as she grabs a handful of toilet paper and uses it to dry Margot's damp face.

It's as unreal and yet vivid as her memories of Ava, and for some reason, that helps her feel a little more distant, as though she's watching it all happen on-screen to somebody else. A little red light above the mirrors stares steadily at her as she finishes cleaning up her friend.

'I don't feel good – let's go back to the cabin,' Margot says, sounding weak but more or less like herself.

Skylar, relieved to hear her friend's voice even through her numbness, puts an arm around Margot's shoulders to guide them down the stairs. Neither of them mentions their missed flight home. After all Skylar has just learned, she can't be sure if she's imagining the wet, raspy breathing that follows them back to the cold refuge of their room.

'Do you smell smoke?' Margot asks upon re-entering the cabin.

But Skylar doesn't; she only smells the almost sickly-sweet odour of the strawberries on the cheese plate that someone dropped off while they were gone, "with compliments and apologies for the delay in beginning your tropical escape."

With the boat rocking so violently, there's little to do but wait out the storm. They settle in on the couch with blankets, and although Skylar grabs the remote, their small TV remains silent as she finally tells Margot everything – about the HMS *Orpheus*, about *Dark Waters*, and how she fears many passengers are possessed by the spirits of the former crew.

She leaves Margot's incident in the bathroom out of it.

When she finishes, she expects her friend to tear into whoever thought building a haunted ship on purpose was a good idea; to grab her phone and start documenting the utter bullshit for her followers, if nothing else.

But Margot, her eyes having grown glassy once again throughout the telling, merely leans over and vomits, nothing left in her stomach now but bile.

Resigned, Skylar grabs the room's small trash can and hands it to her friend to use as a bucket. They're staying in the cabin, she decides, until they're finally in port, and then they're out of here without a backwards glance to get some help for Margot.

All there is to do in the meantime is listen to the lifeboats slam into the side of the ship each time it lists too hard to one side.

Or perhaps, Skylar thinks, as a much closer thud rings out from the hallway, it's not the lifeboats she's hearing after all. Maybe it's echoes of the old crew hitting the ground in their final moments.

It makes as much sense as the acrid stench of smoke now pouring under the cabin door. It can't really be on fire, Skylar reasons, though she still gets up to check, leaving Margot blankly hugging the trash can and gazing around the room as though she's never seen it before. It's part of the haunting, or part of the illusion. If there were a real fire, there would be–

Sirens.

The first blast from the fire alarm sends a jolt up Skylar's back. She can hardly feel the ship beneath her anymore, hard as it's fighting against the waves, but the blare of that alarm brings her sharply into the moment.

She hurries to lead Margot to their muster station like they practised in the lifeboat drill on the first day; they'll be going home soon after all.

As she grabs her friend's arm and tries to tug her to her feet, she remembers how the HMS *Orpheus* was found: a burned-out husk with charred bodies on board thanks to the fire that started in the engine room.

'We need to go *now!*' Skylar pleads, trying to snap Margot out of it. She picks up her friend's untouched phone lying on the cushions – the one thing Margot could never do without – and shoves it in her jeans pocket, then pulls her friend roughly toward the door.

In the halls, a handful of other people are making the same wild dash to the lifeboats across a rapidly tilting floor. Yet many seem to be absent, or else are wandering aimlessly, staring into corners or at the walls as if they see something Skylar can't.

Keeping a tight grip on Margot's forearm, Skylar drags her toward the automatic doors that will admit them to the lifeboat station, get them out of this frigid air into the warm, high wind. There's no time for mayday, and even if there were, Skylar doubts anyone on board would have sent out a distress call. Someone wanted all this to happen.

They've just stepped onto the rain-lashed deck when a dull roar hits Skylar's ears and the ship tilts too far, tilts in a way it wasn't built for.

It only takes an instant, though it feels much slower than that, the way she wheels through the air and plummets like a stone into the dark water far below. The sting of it is like the assault of so many knives at once on her exposed skin, and then she's hurtling into deeper darkness. Yet she kicks upward, struggling against the urge to sink without really understanding what she's fighting for. What there is to return to. She surfaces, gasps for air, and begins to tread water. Around her are other bodies, some – like her – fighting against the current, and others merely bobbing there as though they're content to let the ocean carry them away.

By the ruddy glow of the burning ship, Skylar tries to pick out Margot. Margot, who can't swim. She calls her friend's name, but she can't even hear herself over the high keening of the wind.

Dimly, through a haze of rain and smoke, she realises at least one lifeboat is already on the water. And it's actively picking up passengers. She swims toward it, pushed back by the waves but determined to get closer. Those onboard can help her look for Margot before it's too late. It can't be too late yet.

As she gets closer, she catches a few words as a slightly older woman she recognises as the producer from the bar lifts someone partway from the water. 'This one, Mr. Turner?'

'Yes, yes – look at his eyes. He's one of them.'

Turner, Skylar tries to think over the wind screaming in her ears and a mouthful of air choked with ash – the captain of the *Orpheus*? No, she realises as she squints against the rain, not the man from the photograph – that wouldn't have made sense, anyway. But he had a son. She remembers that from her searches. His family line could have carried on.

And now this man she's never seen before, the captain's descendant, is – what? Pulling the possessed passengers from the water, giving his ancestor's beloved crew a second chance at life?

She's startled from her frantic thoughts as a dark-haired girl swims past her with surprising strength and grace, close enough to touch.

Margot.

Skylar breaks her tread and tries to grab her friend's arm once again, but Margot slithers out of her grasp without a backwards glance and continues toward the nearly-full lifeboat.

She's gone. Lost to her, like Ava, like this vacation, like the world she thought she knew.

Skylar reaches toward a piece of deck railing that got blown off in the explosion from the fire. It's too flimsy to be much help, so she slows her careful tread, knowing she'll have to keep this up at least until the storm passes.

Something hard pokes her in the leg each time she moves; Margot's phone. It's a miracle the thing still works, but it does, the water-proof promise fulfilled. The familiar blue glow of the screen provides some comfort as Skylar shivers in the waves.

Somehow, there are two signal bars. The ship's wifi hasn't gone offline yet despite the boat taking on water.

She unlocks it – she knows the passcode – and opens the camera, zooming in on the lifeboat that is content to ignore the bodies still bobbing in the water, one or two face down, a few others treading water like her.

The rain lessens its assault, the storm beginning to clear already.

Maybe, she supposes, she's a final girl after all. The only one who took a closer, longer look at their trip to paradise. Or maybe she's not so special. Maybe she's possessed by a dead sailor, too, and the lifeboat will be circling back for her soon – how could she know?

For now, all that's left to do is the thing she's best at, the thing that got her here in the first place, the thing that could alter everyone's reality if she can upload enough proof of what happened here: she starts filming.

IGNORE THE DEAD BODIES, PLEASE

GILLIAN POLACK

Belanglo Forest in the springtime is very pretty, as long as one ignores the bodies of dead backpackers. It's surprisingly easy to ignore those bodies, if you make your way lightly through the undergrowth in the early morning and celebrate being alone. I have tested this and am very skilled at it. The trick is to watch for branches and snakes and tricky bits of slope, but to avoid anything that looks potentially human. Don't look. Don't see. Be happy.

Watch the sun rising. Contemplate the kookaburra's shout and the magpie's warble. Look down and across selectively. You'll be fine.

Two university students were doing this precise thing, one sunny morning.

I met the group of students this pair belonged to. Their bus stopped at my favourite pub. 'The oldest continually licensed pub on this whole continent,' a girl declared. I looked at her and wondered if glasses would help her distance vision. I'd just come from the pub she thought she was at. I used to see a murderer of backpackers at that same pub. I did not talk with him. Why would I? Nor could I tell the police what I knew. I come from those parts of the forest that are not well-logged and certainly not much-visited. They are on no map. I joke that they're a wood, because entering them is going into the woods, which is a dangerous pastime. Admitting who I was and where I lived and how I knew about the dead tourists would destroy my pleasant lifestyle.

I may be getting tired of dead bodies in Belanglo. I breathed the dark air that day and decided that, despite the number of times I'd issued dire statements, despite how tired I am of humans and all their stupidities, just this last time, a warning would be kind. It was the same warning I had given each of the backpackers.

'Leave Belanglo while it's still safe. If you must venture here, do not take the dirt road that is on no map. If you reach the town hidden in the forest, leave straight away. Above all, do not go to the hotel in that town.'

Everyone ignored me. I wonder why I bother. I've never saved a single life with my warnings.

It was an odd group. It perturbed me. People who should not know each other, acting as if they were friends. I decided to keep an eye on it, just in case these young people came my way. If they did, I would disappear before they saw me. I do this with the murderers and their evil friends. It would hurt no-one if I watched these stupid young people. That's the value of keeping an eye out.

My nickname (never my proper name) is Lisa Yaga. I do not live in a hut on chicken's legs, but my grandchildren call me Baba Yaga and pretend that I do. I put a bowl of chicken legs on the table and they scream in pretend horror. One day I might move closer to them. Leave Belanglo.

That is all you need to know right now. Possibly all you need to know about me, ever. You know as much about me as anyone ought to, and the fact that I'm telling you this story is enough. I can be a good friend. I can be something quite different. Pretend horror is not the only kind of horror. What Australians think they know about liars and shapeshifters from their European pasts has been corroded by time. Lies can be tiny and subtle. Shapeshifting doesn't have to be dramatic. I don't have to fit your vision of me. I'm not an enemy and I'm not a friend and when humans intrigue me, I will play along with them.

I saw the students leave the pub. Their minibus was full of joking and laughing and young things behaving as if they had forever and a day.

I watched the white bus turn onto the road into the forest and wondered what would become of this group.

The cabin in the woods was a bit more sophisticated than the Sydney students had expected. There were four rooms with bunks and there were showers and toilets and the kitchen had electricity and running water.

'Not really camping at all,' said Tones, who, Allie suspected, thought himself a superior being. He walked like a superior being and he never waited to see what anyone else would do before acting on his decisions. He also looked past Allie, in that way she knew too well. The way that meant he didn't accept her existence.

'We're in a log cabin,' said Pete who had already demonstrated his penchant for the obvious to the point where even Allie wished his comments would vanish into oblivion. Allie overheard Jessica whisper "Captain Obvious" to Barbara, every time. She wished the whispers would also vanish. This was not shaping up to be a comfortable weekend.

'Bags I not cook dinner,' said Stephanie, who Allie had known since primary school. Stephanie took one of the bunk rooms with Barbara and Jessica. There were three empty beds but, 'You can have a room to yourself,' Steph told Allie.

Allie decided to pretend they were being kind in giving her a private room. She knew they weren't. She had been in class with Steph two years now (adding to their childhood together) and she knew the crowd Steph belonged to. Steph's life centred upon herself and she only ever saw others in relation to her own needs. While Allie had thought this was mostly harmless when she agreed to camp, she hadn't expected that Steph would be part of a group of three. When it was too late to stay home, Allie discovered that this weekend was only even borderline on the harmless side.

She wasn't entirely unprepared. Allie had put her magen david in a drawer at home the moment she knew Steph was coming. Steph was always easier to handle when she forgot Allie was Jewish. If Barbara and Jessica were Stephanie's friends, then Allie was better off keeping to herself. Maybe they *were* actually being kind in giving her the room?

She could hear everything they said to each other through the spaces between the planks that divided the rooms. At least she was safe from being provoked into talking. Passing might not be that difficult this time. Allie had helped unload the food from the van and she could eat every single item without indicating her background. Her grandmother would be unhappy about some of it, but honestly, it could have been worse. There was no pork, and there was no seafood.

These were the words that she kept in her head when, having unpacked, she returned to the common room. *It could have been worse.*

Seven students and one staff member. Dr Peveril had brought what he called "games".

Why had she agreed to come? Because the whole weekend would have been cancelled unless they had a full minibus. Dr Peveril had talked about the brilliance of the forest for stargazing and Allie had drifted into agreement.

It was cloudy outside and stargazing was postponed. Instead, Dr Peveril brought out a tatty handmade book.

'If we can't have science, we'll have magic,' he declared in that strangely pompous way that is almost comical when said by a middle-aged man without quite enough hair. Everyone was a bit dubious, even Boris.

On the drive up, Allie thought that Boris was the most enthusiastic person she'd ever met. Tones was the most cynical and also the one who she most distrusted. Pete was the bridge that brought cynicism and enthusiasm together. They'd all known each other for years, if the jokes were anything to go by. And they each had an interest in one of the girls. When one of the jokes uttered on the bus scared her, it was too late to back out, since they were already kilometres from anywhere. Yet another fine reason to have a room of her own, Allie thought. She felt very alone.

When Dr Peveril had read out a few choice excerpts from the book, Allie felt even more alone. Everyone else laughed at each and every choice morsel their teacher read. Allie pretended to laugh, because her best way of getting through the weekend was to copy everyone's behaviour, but she felt as if she'd walked into the beginning of a bad horror movie.

For his game, Dr Peveril, had given them the choice between a deal with Satan, summoning a demon, and seeking eternal life. Tones chose the deal with Satan. Dr Peveril himself was going to incant eternal life, and everyone else was supposed to summon a demon.

Tones went first, his Latin sonorous and rather bossy. His pronunciation was, Allie suspected, all kinds of wrong. In his harsh low tones, the words sounded more like a Scandinavian language than anything else.

Nothing happened. Of course nothing happened. Satan did not come because Christianity was not the way the universe operated. Allie clung grimly to the safety of her own belief. She ignored the smugness of Tones' expression when he finished. It was as if he saw something or knew something or–

They all sat on cushions in front of the stove and the book had to travel from one person to the next. 'Just read it out. Your chant is in Aramaic, but has been transliterated,' Dr Peveril encouraged, 'Don't worry about pronunciation. Read then pass it on.'

'No sacrificial blood?' asked Tones.

'No evil monks?' Boris added.

'Just the words,' said Dr Peveril.

'It says here to read with sincerity,' Barbara noted, for the book was in her hands.

'Get a move on then,' said Tones. 'I've got cards we can play when this is done.'

Each of them read, in turn. Even Allie. She changed one word, however. The demon they were supposed to be summoning was named "Azazel". Her Yiddish professor had told her that the Jewish equivalent of "Go to hell" was "Go to Azazel". She didn't care how fictional demons were, she wasn't going to call on Azazel. "Ashmodai" she said instead at the appropriate point. No-one noticed. Allie finished her reading and handed the book on and wondered when she would grow up and stop giving in to this kind of puerile pressure.

'If you don't mind,' she said, when the book was closed, 'I'm going to bed.'

'Let the professor call on eternal life first,' instructed Tones. 'And supper. You can't go to bed until after supper.'

Allie was doomed. She stayed.

Dr Peveril read his section slowly and with much careful and joyous enunciation. The boys cheered him on. It was a long set of words, just as obscure as the rest. Bits were familiar and were supposed to be in Hebrew, but Allie didn't understand it. Maybe she'd confused the word "Azazel" with something else and it wasn't a demon's name after all. Too bad. She'd rather the whole thing was nonsense.

When Dr Peveril finished, there was a silence.

'How do we know if you've got eternal life?' Barbara asked.

'Wait fifty years,' joked Pete. 'Who wants a drink?'

'None of you are old enough,' said Dr Peveril.

'When did you come to Australia?' Steph liked to know things, apparently.

'Last summer,' he answered.

'I know what you did last summer!' crowed Boris.

'The drinking age here is eighteen.' Allie felt a bit forward, saying anything, but it was an awkward situation. She felt more awkward an instant later, when three reproving sets of eyes glared at her.

The situation was defused perfectly naturally when Barbara screamed. She pointed to Dr Peveril's right hand. 'Look!' she said. The edges of the hand were visible, but the hand itself was transparent.

No-one drank. No-one ate. No-one said a word. Not even Dr Peveril. They made a closed circle around him and stood there, fascinated, still, silent, and watched him fade. His clothes kept their shape until the very end. When the man was entirely gone, the clothes fell into a heap. Rain started drip-dripping on the roof. After a few seconds, its heaviness filled the silence. The teens drifted out of the circle.

'What do we do now?' asked Steph.

'Wait until morning,' Tones said. 'He'll be back. This is just a stunt. I'll put his things in his room and wait for him there. Give him a shock when he turns up.'

'How did he do it, though?' asked Pete querulously. 'I couldn't see any tricks. It looked...'

Disturbing was the missing word. Allie wasn't going to say it.

'He'll tell us tomorrow,' said Tones, firmly. He was more confident than anyone else in the room. Again. Maybe that confidence was what they needed at that moment. Or maybe he really thought he knew what was happening. Either way, Allie wanted to get into the van and get back to Sydney immediately.

So did Barbara, who said, her voice fragile, 'Our phones don't work here. We need to go.'

'We can't drive in the dark,' said Pete. 'Not on unsealed roads, in the rain. We'll be fine tomorrow. We'll drive back to Bowral and find a phone and get help.'

Whether anyone slept that night was a moot point.

Allie didn't. She was alone in her room. She kept the light on and pretended to read a book. Every noise spooked her. Allie nearly moved in with the other girls, but she heard them talking far too loudly and what they said discomfited her even more.

'It's part of the Jewish conspiracy,' were the overheard words that stuck in her mind and turned over and over and over. The small red flags that had nagged at her on the way up were real. She should never have come on this excursion. The rain pelted down on the roof and her mind flooded with fear and her brain would not rest.

At one point, she thought she saw a tall black man standing over her. A very tall black man, dark enough to be part of the night. Allie thought of the professor and shuddered.

'I'm Ash,' the man said, conversationally in a comfortably deep voice. 'I can't come now, but I'll be with you tomorrow.' Then he was gone as if he'd never been.

Allie pretended that she had not read that transcript of an old incantation and that Dr Peveril had not softly and silently vanished away. She was scared of the night, but even more scared of the day.

The next morning I decided to find out what had become of the group. I walked to near the hut and stood at the back of it for a while. Once I had absorbed the events of the night before, I watched the sun rise, insofar as the trees permitted.

The moment dawn glinted on the lower branches; a young man left the hut. A few minutes later, a young woman left in the same direction. The path they followed was on no map. The air was brisk and the sun held a soft warmth and at that moment, at that time, it would have been possible to look at the two walking a mere forty metres apart and think, 'These two young people are similar.'

Let Barbara and Tones walk in this quiet, quiet morning before consequences meet them. There were unexpected beginnings here last night. Enjoy the sunshine while you can.

When this walk is over, I'll leave you. I may return with more gloom and foreboding, or I may not. I don't know what will happen next. There are...variants. The past is far safer than the present.

I will only return if I am forced to. If this is a happy summer camp, then the story will stop suddenly, in the middle of things, without me and without peril.

Enjoy the sunshine. If you can.

The day started bright with wisps of sunlight creeping through the clouds. Allie washed and dressed and went out for a walk before everyone woke up. The driest grass route took her past the pond. As she walked into the forest, she turned to look back at the cabin and noticed two of the others were going the opposite direction to her. Soon one was out of sight and a few minutes later the other was gone. It was a much safer disappearance than Dr Peveril's.

'I will only walk for a few more minutes,' she told herself. 'I just need to walk off last night. It was horrid, from beginning to end, and I do not need it stuffed into my brain. At breakfast Dr Peveril will appear and tell us about the joke.' Her walk didn't last more than three minutes. She was watching for wildlife and her eyes caught on what looked like an arm, randomly resting at the base of a grevillea. Allie decided that her eyes were playing tricks and that breakfast would be better than fresh air. She returned to the cabin and helped get breakfast together.

Dr Peveril wasn't there. Nor were his possessions. 'Tones is taking care of them,' said Boris.

Tones returned just in time to finish the coffee. He was barely in time to miss the rain.

'We need to go,' said Stephanie. 'Where's Barbara?' Everyone looked around. She was missing. Allie wondered if Barbara was the person she had seen walking behind Tones. She wasn't even certain it was Tones she had seen, however, and her mind was unreliable anyhow, given she thought she had seen an arm in the undergrowth. Not to mention strangers who blinked in and out of existence at the drop of a hat. *Allie is not a reliable witness*, she told herself, and remained silent.

'We can't go,' Pete pronounced. 'Look at that rain.' It was pelting down again.

'Remember the road?' Jessica reminded him. 'It dips down big time about a kilometre from here. If there's too much rain, we won't be able to get through. I'll go look. Does anyone want to go with me? I don't mind the rain, but I'm a bit creeped out right now. I'd rather not be by myself.'

'I'll join you,' said Tones.

'Me too,' said Allie. She, too, felt as if she was the murderable victim in a horror movie and Tones had made the deal with the devil (even if no-one had even seen the devil) and should not be left alone with any single other person.

The three of them plodded, splashed and waded through the drowning forest and found that the road was already impassable.

'Let's tell the others,' said Tones. 'We can wait it out in an electric bunker, or we can do what the old lady told us not to do and take the other road.'

'It's dirt. Won't it be washed out too?'

'It'll be messy, but it goes uphill. Should be fine.'

It was almost fine. They had driven a long way from the hut, however, before the minibus became stuck. Everyone piled out to look.

They looked at each other, wondering what to do.

'We need to get sticks,' Allie said.

'Good idea.' Steph grabbed Jessica's hand as if she were her last, best hope and the two of them went in one direction.

'This way,' announced Tones and grabbed Allie by the arm and dragged her off, back the way they had come. 'I know this bit of the forest,' he said. 'We should be at the right place in just a moment.'

Allie wanted to ask what "the right place" was and why she was the one Tones had grabbed when he had talked past her and ignored her earlier, but she remembered how he had come back alone that morning, after walking in this direction for over an hour and that Barbara had gone separately but had not come back at all and no-one had even asked about her and maybe she didn't want to know, at all.

She must've made a noise, however, for Tones looked down at her until he caught her eyes. 'I'm not going to rape you or anything,' he said, almost seriously. 'You're too ugly for me. We're nearly there. Stop worrying.' The prosaicness of his insult made her catch her breath. It made his behaviour much more real.

Pete caught up with them. Allie took advantage of the distraction and pulled away. Ran. She hid behind a tree. Tones simply grabbed Pete's arm and took *him* into the forest.

Allie froze behind her tree. The drips of water splattering on her did not melt the fear. She should have gone with them when Pete went with Tones. She should have. She could not. Dead bodies, missing teachers, missing students, the way Tones had not looked directly at her... No-one peered back to see if she was coming.

'What did the old lady say?' Allie said it out loud. 'If you reach the town hidden in the forest, leave straight away. Above all, do not go to the hotel in that town.'

'That's a good idea,' said a deep voice behind her. Allie jumped. 'It's me. Ash.'

'What are you doing here?'

'You asked for me. *They* asked for my cousin.'

'Who are you and who is your cousin?'

'Ashmodai, Demon King,' and Ash bowed. 'That's me. Azazel is a being you don't want to meet.'

'Does he also have an Australian accent?'

'Pfft,' said Ash. 'I speak this way because my girlfriend gives me trouble otherwise.' He said this with such a soft smile that Allie relaxed a bit.

'Tones didn't call on Azazel,' she said. 'He made a deal with the devil. That was what the game was, anyhow.'

'Stupid place to play games like that. This forest is unsafe.'

'It's for logging. I mean, it's built specifically. Not natural.'

'That's the point, perhaps? The unnatural forest hides another place that is differently unnatural.' Ash smiled, a different smile, a grim one. 'We'd better go. If I take your bag can you walk for twenty minutes?'

'Through the town?'

'Back the way we came.'

'The road out is flooded,' Allie felt all kinds of helpless.

'I can handle floods. We have coffee, anyhow.'

'Coffee?'

'Judith's with the car. She brought a lot of coffee. She said she had no idea if you'd need it, but she most certainly did. I hope you don't mind Sydney.'

'I live there,' said Allie, still helpless.

'Newtown?' asked Ash, hopefully.

Allie shook her head. 'Canada Bay.'

'We can find it.' Ash took her bag and they turned back the way they had come.

Allie had no idea what she was walking into, with this very tall guy who claimed he was the Demon King. It said a lot about her last twenty four hours that she felt safer walking back with him than into a town with Tones. She wanted to say, 'I'm worried about the others,' but, to be honest, she was worried about herself and didn't know if they needed saving or if she did. They would each have to take their chances.

Gradually, the remaining students clustered around the car, carrying wet sticks and drab damp branches. Steph returned first with Jessica, then Boris, and finally Tones.

'Where's Pete?' Boris asked Tones. 'Didn't he leave with you?'

'He and I argued.' Tones shrugged. 'I said I was coming back here. He said he'd make his own way.'

'I don't think we're going to get the van out of this,' Jessica said. The mud was deeper than before and the van was perfectly mired. Everyone stood there, in the wet, looking down. The circle they made was no longer perfect.

'There's a town up the dirt track,' said Tones.

'The one we were warned about,' said Boris.

Steph said, impatiently, 'This isn't a horror story. Let's just go. We need help.'

So they went. The track was on higher ground than the road. Jess and Steph exchanged a relieved grin and everyone walked more lightly. No-one asked about Allie.

They walked and they walked and they walked. Finally, the group encountered a perfectly ordinary brick house. It could have come from Sydney, or Melbourne, or Bendigo, or even Wagga Wagga.

'We should knock on a door,' said Tones, casually.

'No need,' said Steph. 'Look.' After the house, the path became a road and down the road more houses were visible. 'It's a town. In the middle of nowhere.'

'Let's find a police station,' suggested Jessica.

'Or a pub.' Boris always suggested a pub. He was the one who found the pub in Berrima for everyone, before Belanglo was more than a place on the map. The same map that missed this town and the hill it stood on.

I'll go into the next house and ask,' said Tones. He knocked on the first door on the left. Steph, Jessica and Boris waited outside when Tones was let in.

Yes, it's Lisa. I'm not back. I never left. I was watching quietly, because they are such stupid young things. I'm sympathetic, but I don't have any reason to interfere. Old agreements hold, even when stupid young things get hurt. I still don't know if I should do anything, or remain a neutral observer. I'm tired of it all. All the humans and their hate and their frailty and…

I'm going silent again. It's easier that way.

Inside the house, Tones was almost brusque. He half-mockingly saluted a portrait on the wall. It was encased in mourning ribbon. 'Hi, Uncle Adolf,' he said towards it, casually, then, to a man seated in a dark red armchair, 'Hi, Dad. I have something to add to the chart. I've got to be quick. They think I'm asking for help.'

'Don't mock the portrait. Doing good work doesn't excuse you from proper respect. I'll phone the hotel and let them know you're coming.'

'No, Dad. Yes, Dad. That'd be great, Dad.'

His father frowned at him.

Tones went to a map of the forest and town which hung in the very comfortable living room. The map was on the wall, just beyond the wine-dark Chesterfield. Next to the map was a desk with seven drawers. From one drawer he took out a pink triangle and from the next, a blue – one representing Barbara, the other, Pete. His father walked over, 'No-one Jewish?' he asked.

'One of the girls said her friend was Jewish. Allie. She doesn't trust me – she ran away into the forest. I'm hoping she'll end up here. There aren't many places to go, now that you've closed the road.'

These people did not have permission to close my road.

'That took a lot of doing.'

'If we can put Allie on the map, it'll be worth it. Her family escaped us, decades ago. We can mop up a little.' Tones' voice was smug, but his face was serious. He pinned the pink triangle very close to the log cabin in Belanglo, and the blue a little further away, just off the dirt track the group had entered the town by.

'How many are there?' His father sounded like an accountant.

'Three outside, and Allie to come.'

'It's about time. He'll be happy.'

'I used the papers you gave me, last night. Peveril fell for it, hook, line and sinker. He wanted to live what he taught us in class,

I suspect. So much occult history that he doesn't recognise the real thing. I remade the oath, and the others all consigned themselves to Azazel.'

'And Peveril?'

'He found his own fate. He asked for eternal life. It'll be a hundred years before he can even blow a breeze into a room. All he can do is watch.'

'As long as the old woman isn't watching, too. She's not as friendly as she once was.'

Too right I'm not.

'She gave us a warning on the way here but she buggered off. She won't do a thing. This little town is too precious to her.'

'She'll do anything to keep it alive. Go do what you must do,' said Tones' father. 'Take this.' He pulled a gun out of the same drawer the triangles were in, checked it for bullets, then gave it to his son.

Another rule of mine, broken.

'One more thing. Tones, wipe that smug look off your face. It gives you away, every time.'

Ash walked as if he were half a metre taller than he actually was. He walked for five minutes. Allie jogged. Given Ash was well over two metres tall this meant... Allie's brain refused to process who he was or how tall he was. She couldn't help noticing that sometimes his eyes were blood-red. She knew that he was masking his real height and his real eyes, but whenever she tried to think about what this meant, she was prevented by the mass of cotton wool that filled her mind. These last few hours had overwhelmed her.

When the car did not appear and the wet mud of the road became a lake, Ash tried to call his girlfriend.

'We have to go back,' he said to Allie a minute later. 'The forest is playing tricks on us. Phone's cut off. Road has gone. This is not natural.' He had a look on his face that said *How dare anyone play tricks*, but then he smiled. 'We're going to the town that doesn't exist. This could be fun.'

'An old lady–' Allie began.

'Warnings, I know. We can't get out this way and you have a murderer somewhere around here. We really don't have a choice.'

'Then why will it be fun?'

Ash looked down from his great height, deeply reproving. 'I am the Demon King, remember?'

'I'm glad I'm not Christian,' Allie said, almost fervently.

'What's your Hebrew name?' This was unexpected.

'Oh,' said Allie, 'Yehudith bat David.'

'Another Judith, then. Good. If I use any part of your Hebrew name in any way, be ready to run.'

'OK,' said Allie. She didn't feel all trusting.

'Why did you walk out on your friends?'

'They aren't my friends,' Allie was honest. 'But if I'd known there was help, I would've asked for them, too.'

'When did your family come to Australia? My girlfriend's came here with the Gold Rush.'

'Jews migrated here that early?' Allie was surprised. 'My parents came with the big wave. They were in Teresin together. They never talk about it, except to say that it was there they met.'

'The rest of your family?'

'Mostly lost in the bog of horror that is Auschwitz. I want to go back to Europe and explore all the places my family came from but it means facing death in every single one of those places.'

'Is that why you're hiding your background?' He sounded inquisitive rather than condemning.

'Hiding? Oh, you mean that I'm not wearing a magen david. I normally wear one, or maybe a chai, but there are things about the people at the log cabin... Steph and her friends make me uncomfortable. I left everything at home.'

'Hiding from them. And yet you'd help them. Why?' The last word was an interrogation folded into a single syllable.

'Why help or why hide?' All the while they talked, they walked back to the log cabin Allie was so heartily sick of, and then followed the other path, the one that was better not to take. Ashmodai walked more slowly this time, as if he, too, were reluctant. They wanted to leave, but not to find the others. *We'll catch up with the others, even if I'm not pretending to be the Red Queen and hurrying nowhere*, Allie thought.

'I was hiding. When we were briefed on what to take, one of the group made an ashtray joke. I dated an Israeli who made ashtray jokes. I learned then that those jokes trigger me but might just show appalling taste in humour and no understanding of the Shoah. But I thought it was a good idea to be careful. Especially as Steph is ambivalent about all things Jewish.'

'Why did you come here at all?' Ash's voice was piercing, as if he'd found a stupidity and wanted to jump on it.

'Because without me everything would have been cancelled.'

'Simple guilt, then.'

'Simple guilt, Allie agreed.

'Who made the ashtray joke?'

'Jessica. Which is funny, retrospectively, because Tones is the one who creeps me out. You know, the sort of person you never want to be alone in a room with?'

Ashmodai said, drily, 'I've never experienced that feeling.' Allie looked up and up and up towards his face, and she laughed.

Ash smiled a small smile, then looked ahead. 'I can see three of the others.'

'Small mercies,' said Allie. 'I can stop feeling guilty.'

'I will visit the owner of the town,' said Ash, seriously. 'Stay safe with the rest of your group. Don't go wandering off alone.'

'I don't want to be with them, though.'

'There's safety in numbers.'

Ash faded before Allie's eyes. She wanted to believe that he was fictional. Allie also wanted to believe that the last twenty-four hours were all a dream. If wishes were horses...

While Tones was inside the house, Allie joined the others outside.

'Tones has gone inside to get help,' Steph said.

No "Where were you?" or "Are you OK?" No explanations of the missing party members. Allie wished Ash were still around. 'I never thought I'd want the Demon King to be hanging out with me', she added to her mind's conversation. The others were too quiet. There were silences to fill. Allie knew she wasn't welcome, but Ash was right – she was still safer with others than alone.

'This town's not on my map,' offered Boris, after a while, waving the tourist map.

'There shouldn't be any town in the forest at all. These woods are only a few kilometres across in any direction and you've got to go to the highway to reach all the towns,' Jess suddenly looked apologetic. 'Sorry,

I looked it up to see how we could see stars in a wildly populated region. That's how. This town doesn't exist.'

'Do you remember the path to the town?' asked Steph, looking at the forest behind them. 'I can't remember which way we came.'

Jessica nodded. 'We took Belanglo Road to get to the hut, so it should continue after that,' she said.

'But it didn't,' said Steph.

'That's right, it didn't. There's a path going north that leads to a camping ground and another that leads out of the forest. I didn't see those other paths.'

Allie wanted to say 'They were probably washed out by the rain' but she didn't feel comfortable talking when she wasn't welcome. She waited out the silence.

It was Boris who spoke. 'This must be the camping ground,' he said. 'More like a B&B. I hope Tones found help.'

At that moment a door snapped shut, politely. Everyone looked towards the sound. Tones emerged from the house, looking serious.

'We can get help at the hotel down the road,' he said. 'Allie, I'm glad you found us.' He led them down the road, still solemn.

The hotel was an old-fashioned Australian pub, with advertisements for $10 steaks on Tuesdays painted on the side of the building in bold red letters.

'Let's all go in,' said Jess. 'It's the safest thing to do. Safety in numbers...'

Allie refused. Every single one of the campers threw down reasons and arguments and berated her. Allie simply stood there and said 'No,' as many times as she needed until everyone else fell silent.

'I'll wait with Allie,' said Tones, finally.

'Me, too,' said Boris.

'Jess and I will go in first, then,' Steph said, firmly. This time, no-one argued.

Fifteen minutes later, they had not come out. 'I'll pry them from their drinks,' said Boris, 'And find out if anyone can help us.' He went in.

Fifteen minutes later then he too had not come out.

Every minute that passed worried Allie more. She looked up and down the street, but saw nothing. Not Ash. Not anyone. She cast surreptitious looks at Tones.

Tones looked as if he were trying very hard to not smile. It was the scariest not-smile Allie had ever seen. At that moment she wondered if he really had made a deal with the devil. She was about to speak when Tones said, 'Now they're all being stupid. We should join them.'

'In being stupid?' Allie asked, tentatively. For the first time since they met on campus the previous day, Tones looked directly at her and saw her. His eyes were a surprising warm brown.

'I am never stupid,' he said.

Allie didn't want to enter the hotel with Tones. Her whole body resisted it. Tones obviously saw the resistance, for he took her by the wrist and began to drag her towards the side door of the hotel.

'This is not turning into a stupid horror movie,' Allie said, forcibly.

Tones laughed and said 'Too late.' He pushed her forcibly through the swinging door.

The size and colours of the red and black room intimidated her. When she stood and looked, it was worse. The walls were painted a dark rust-infused black and the swastikas were all red as fresh blood. From the high vaulted ceiling and the dark tile floor, the swastikas lined up in serried ranks, creating paths for the eyes to follow. The paths converged at an altar. On the wall behind the altar a horned goat's skull poised, as if ready to attack. The black altar was crowded with bowls of dark fluid. The smell of blood filled the room. Next to each bowl rested a head.

Allie recognised each and every head: Barbara and Pete; Steph, Jessica and Boris. The eyes in each head were wide with horror. The blood in three of the bowls still steamed.

'Satan,' Allie said aloud, everything becoming clear. She turned to leave. Tones blocked her way out.

'The others were snacks,' he said, his tone even and pleasant, as if this were a normal conversation, not one drowned by blood and red and black. 'You're the main course.' Out of the darkness stepped a man so tall that his head was close to the high ceiling, so pale that his skin looked translucent. 'Azazel – here is the last of your people.'

'She is none of mine,' said Azazel, his accent thick with age and languages.

'She called you,' said Tones. 'In the forest.'

'She did not,' said Azazel. 'I will take her anyway. I will enjoy tormenting her. You may have the head and the blood. I want only the soul.'

'The soul is not yours,' said a far deeper voice. 'The head and the blood are her own.' Out of the black emerged a man so dark that Allie had to squint to see him, so tall, that his head, too, brushed the high ceiling. His eyes burned red.

'My master and Azazel will deal with you.' Tones was confident. Allie's fear froze her into stillness.

'Is that so, Azazel? Will you deal with me?' The deep voice was playful and Allie finally recognised it. *Ash.*

'I do not want your crown,' said Azazel.

'Then go. Now.'

Azazel, the demon that toyed with human souls and then ate them, bowed low, then stood straight and stepped back into the wall until he was gone.

Tones called out 'Help!' It was as if a crowd had waited at every door, for the room was filled with angry people. 'He dismissed Azazel,' said Tones, pointing to Ashmodai.

'We still have our lord Satan, and our weapons,' said an older man, who looked very like Tones.

Allie looked at Tones again and saw what was in his right hand. They were carrying guns. The goat's skull began to glow with cold blue light. The light floated to the couch and a body started to form.

Time for me to step back into the story.

'That's enough of that,' said a woman's voice. The cold blue light faded and all that remained on the wall was the skull of a dead animal. 'Remember me? I gave you permission to rest here, when you escaped Europe. I said that as long as you didn't bring any other beings into my land, I would let you worship your non-existent lord in your obscene way and all I would do was warn people, because you are alone in the world, as I was when scientists invaded my home two hundred and fifty years ago and argued that I was an invention and a liar and that the universe was not shaped in a way that supported me. I said that and I held my promise. Now you have guns and demons and I will not stand for it.'

'Shoot her, uncle,' Tones urged the older man.

Lisa Yaga stood her ground.

'You would destroy her town and her forest? You're a murderous child. A nasty child.' Ash said. Nevertheless, he did nothing. He looked to me, and waited.

'This is not your place, Demon King,' said Tones' uncle. He smirked. 'There's little you can do.' He raised his gun and pointed it at the old lady.

That would be me. I wasn't happy, but I was caught out by Ashmodai. I never expected to see him in Australia. I shook my head at him. As I did this, I heard a shot.

Lisa collapsed.

Something hurt. I found myself on the ground, watching. I always watch. But this time, everything changed. My world spun out of control.

Ash raised his right hand slightly.

The red and black room flooded with light. The light became the sun shining through wet leaves. They were all in the forest. The bowls of blood and the heads spilled over the wet green undergrowth, and those heads were looking at the old woman, on the ground with them. She glowered back, but couldn't move. Standing in their midst was a goat. It grumbled at them and wandered off, eating as it went. It did not touch the blood. As it left, the heads faded.

They were killed in my wood and did not belong in a tree farm.

I tried to pull myself upright. I hurt, but I'd live.

Ash wasn't as interested in me as I was in him. He was talking.

'Your god was in an ordinary goat?' Ash puzzled, and, as he spoke, his size diminished until he was merely an extraordinarily tall man. His skin remained as dark as ever, and his eyes still glowed red. 'You're very stupid.' He made a sweeping gesture and then Tones, his uncle, everyone – was gone, except himself, Allie, and Lisa, bleeding on the ground. 'Let me see,' and he knelt by Lisa.

'He thought he was clever,' Lisa said. 'It's my leg. I can't stand.'

'We should get you to hospital,' said Allie.

'First ring the police,' said Lisa fiercely. 'I gave these people a safe place after their war and they abused it. I want them in jail.'

'What can the police charge them with?' asked Allie. 'There are no bodies.'

'There are many bodies, hidden in these woods,' said Ash. 'It may take the police some time to find them all.'

'What did you do with those...people?' asked Lisa, with as much spite in her voice as she could bring. 'And why is the King of Demons in my forest, anyway?'

'My friend called me,' said Ash, looking at Allie. 'Let's find my girlfriend and get out of this place.' His red eyes faded to a slate grey. The sky lifted and the rain stopped and the sounds of the forest started up again as if nothing had ever stopped them.

'But what did you do with them?' Lisa asked again.

They lifted me and started carrying me out of my domain.

'I sent them to Azazel, of course.' said Ashmodai. 'Allie, I'll give you a way of calling me if you encounter them again.'

'Why didn't you kill them?' demanded Lisa.

'Why did you give them refuge in your forest?' asked Ash.

'I'd like to know the answer to both questions,' Allie said timidly. 'Also, why did you want my Hebrew name if we weren't going to use it?'

'This isn't a fairy story,' said Ash. 'Not all plans magically become outcomes.' He looked down on the woman he carried, 'You allowed this family to call a dark spirit, given power by their lust for murder. All the deaths are on you.'

'Are you judging me?' asked Lisa.

'No,' said Ash. 'I'm instructing you. You may not go back into your safe little world until you have done enough good to balance the evil you supported here.'

'Do you have the right to make her do this?' asked Allie. 'I mean, you're the Demon King, but is she a demon?'

'It's complicated,' said Lisa.

'Then why was Satan a goat? I mean, isn't he the Devil?'

'Christian beliefs are also complicated,' said the Demon King. 'And none of our business.'

'I was going to be sacrificed to him.'

'To a goat,' said Lisa. 'That was on me.'

I thought these people knew what they were doing.

'And Dr Peveril?' Allie's voice sang with tension. She wanted answers and was being given none.

'It will be a long while before he has even the semblance of a body,' said Ash, gentle again. 'We will say that he disappeared with the rest of the party.'

'So I'm the only survivor?'

'You and Tones,' said Ash.

'When Tones escapes Azazel, he will face me. The police can wait.'

The small old lady looked, in that moment, more dangerous than the Demon King.

THE DEVIL'S BARGAIN

L. J. M. OWEN

CHEWING HER BOTTOM LIP, KAT CONTEMPLATED A WALL OF SCUDDING GREY clouds approaching from the south. The winter sun sat low in the west, skulking toward the forest on the horizon.

Splashes of petrol soaked through her pant leg, the sharp benzene scent snapping her back to reality. She shoved the bowser pump into its holster and shook her boot. Standing in a service station on the edge of Tasmania's Livingston National Park, struggling to concentrate, she weighed up which road to take from here.

She'd booked a suite at a remote resort on the other side of the park, part of a month's leave from work. The resort was so deep in the ancient wilderness that there was no mobile phone signal. She yearned for that isolation; it would give her a chance to settle on a course of action to deal with Dave.

Trouble was, the route from her current location to the lodge was either a four-hour circumnavigation of the densely wooded park or less than two hours straight across on a mix of logging roads and unmapped dirt tracks. Her B&B host that morning had warned her against a direct crossing. He'd urged her to instead take the sealed road that skirted the vast reserve.

Kat headed through the petrol station's glass and metal sliding doors to pay. As she hopped back in the vehicle, her jeans squeaking on the rented 4WD's polished pleather seats, a smatter of raindrops smacked against the windscreen.

She needed to decide. If she took the safe route, she would arrive well after nightfall and might miss the resort bar's opening hours. However, if she went straight through the park she'd arrive around dusk and could warm herself with a whisky by the resort's enormous stone fireplace.

Kat assumed the B&B host had underestimated her ability to handle a vehicle. She'd spent her childhood living with remote communities in one mountain range or another. Life with her anthropologist mother meant she was more than capable of looking after herself.

And she wanted an evening of whisky to silence the ghosts of memory.

After an hour of sleet and twisting roads, inching along one of the rutted tracks that ran between the plantation logging roads and fighting to keep her vehicle from sliding into the trees, Kat had to admit the B&B host might have been right. It looked like she wouldn't arrive at the resort until long after dark.

She reached the end of a dismal trail of sucking clay and mud and turned left onto a proper dirt road. *Demon Days* began playing through the speakers. As much as she liked Gorillaz, and the distraction they provided during long nights in the office processing government tenders, she wanted to listen to something else. Mari had loved Gorillaz too, and right now, Kat needed a break from reminders of her sister. She groped for her phone on the seat beside her to choose a different album.

A flash of something small, brown and shadowed flung itself across the road in front of her. She slewed to a halt.

The deafening squeal of jammed brakes heralded a truck coming too fast in the opposite direction.

Her heart jumped in her chest.

Kat locked eyes with the horrified driver of a logging rig as he skidded around the bend. Screeching tonnes of shiny metal drifted in slow motion toward her.

She swore, prayed that she would survive, remembered that she didn't believe in anything, wondered if she should reconsider that, wondered how she could be having all these thoughts in what must have been a split secon–

Kat regained consciousness with a jolt.

Bony forearms cut into the flesh behind her legs and shoulders, bruising the tendons at the back of her knees. Someone was carrying her as though she were a small child.

She forced her eyes to open. Through narrow cracks, she glimpsed the rainforest canopy far above, and a nest of brown and grey beard closer by. Hairy nostrils washed a wild, rotting scent across her face, mingling with murky mint notes from the surrounding undergrowth.

Was it the driver of the truck that hit her? Each step he took caused a nauseating crunch in her right shin. Fantastic. A broken leg meant hospital, x-rays, a cast, the opposite of her planned timeout.

'The woman's awake,' said a deep voice to Kat's left.

Her spine stiffened. Where was her phone? Kat hadn't let her mother know she was going on an interstate trip. Not that she'd necessarily notice Kat's absence…

Someone else groaned, as if waking up. The truck driver must also be alive.

'Should we knock him out again?' said a voice from behind her in ringing, confident tones.

She pushed fear's grip aside and strained to capture every sound.

'No,' said her carrier, his disturbing breath washing across her face again.

She could make out at least three sets of footfalls. Two of the walkers were breathing heavily, including the person carrying her.

'May as well slit his throat now then,' said the disdainful voice behind them. 'He'll bleed out by the time we get home.'

Kat's heart pounded against her ribcage. Who were these people? Where were they taking her? What were they going to do with her?

'Don't be ridiculous,' said the man carrying her.

'Kyle's not here,' the toffeed voice took on a petulant edge. 'This guy's not going to pass the test, so why not get it over with?'

'We can't know that,' warned the man carrying Kat.

'You just want to eat him,' said the deep voice to her left.

It was everything Kat could do to not punch the nose of the man holding her and attempt to scramble away from these people. But what would that achieve?

'Don't be like that,' said the petulant one.

She was obviously injured, outnumbered and alone. She needed to stay calm to give herself the best chance of survival.

'You carry him then.' The deep voice again.

Nothing made any sense. Was she in a hospital already, sedated after the crash, hallucinating? She'd never done well on opiates.

The person carrying Kat shifted her body in his arms. 'Enough.'

Nope. The pain in her leg shrieked that this was real.

'What do we do with *her*?'

'I know what to do,' said Petulant.

Kat's stomach lurched again. The teasing tone in his voice reminded her of Dave at work; how she imagined he must sound when he cornered young women in the office. Young women like poor Raelene. Young women who reminded Kat of her own sweet, dead sister. Mari.

'Don't be a perv,' said Deep Voice.

'It's just a joke,' Petulant whined.

'Your jokes are shit.'

The man carrying Kat slipped and swore, smacking her leg onto the ground and causing a blinding white pain that ripped a scream from her throat.

Someone was patting her cheek. She must have blacked out. She tried moving her mouth.

'She's okay.'

'That leg looks bad.'

It was time to take control. 'I need an ambulance,' she mumbled, forcing her eyelids to open again.

One of three hazy shapes snorted. 'Ambulance.'

Petulant. His amusement made her skin crawl.

Her transport, Bad Breath, picked her up. At some point on the trudge uphill, Kat lost consciousness again.

The light was different now. Less bright. Was it night? Was she inside?

She squinted. The ceiling was close to her face. A tent of some kind?

A flap lifted to reveal three men silhouetted against a dim sky as they crowded in to stand over her, bearing lanterns that filled the space with blue-tinged light. Kat saw her own jeans folded over a stool next to her,

'Are you awake?'

Bad Breath. Kat recognised his voice, calm sense of control, and the beard. She grunted.

A much older man with a crusted red cravat around his wrinkled neck said, 'See, she's fine.'

His voice, even in those three words, told Kat this was the petulant man with the posh voice and disturbing jokes. He wasn't what she'd pictured at all. That meant that the third in the trio, a solid young man who looked to be related to the other two, was Deep Voice.

'Will,' Bad Breath pointed to himself, 'Scott,' the youngest man, 'and John.' That was old Petulant.

'Kat. Where am I? Who took my jeans off?' she grimaced as a wave of pain shot through her leg. 'I need to go to hospital, is there a chopper on the way?'

Bad Breath Will avoided her eyes. She glanced at the others; Scott looked worried, John smirked.

An agonised groan ripped through the air outside.

Kat winced. 'Is that the truck driver?'

Will ignored her question. 'No-one was going to find you on that road, not for a while. We've brought you home because you would have died out there. *I* took your jeans off to get a better look at your leg.'

Why did it seem like he was apologising? How could she feel both safe and in danger at the same time? It was jarring. 'Where's my phone?'

'I'm sorry about this,' Will said, ignoring this question too, 'not sure if it's a true break or you've only cracked the bone, but we're going to have to bind that leg to keep any swelling down.'

Kat knew what that meant. Her childhood was spent in remote places like this; broken bones had been set by local healers in mud huts, never people in white coats and sterile offices. 'Give me something to bite down on, and alcohol if you have it. Let's get this over with.'

All three men seemed surprised.

She wasn't what they expected. Good.

Kat took several slugs of cheap vodka, barely registering the awful taste as she willed the muzzy haze of alcohol to embrace her. A cloth was wedged between her teeth. Then, searing pain. A scream began in Kat's throat but ebbed behind her lips as she drifted out of awareness...

Scott brought her to consciousness again, and supported her head while she sipped water. Pressure from her bladder signalled urgency. She asked where the toilet was.

Without speaking, he draped a blanket around her shoulders then wrapped an arm under her back then said, 'Okay?', and lifted her.

The slap of icy outside air on her cheek brought her fully to her senses.

'How long have I been here?' The horrified eyes of the truck driver as he careened towards her car swam across her mind. 'And how's the truckie?'

Scott wouldn't answer.

When she signalled she was done, he helped her from the bench of a foetid pit toilet. Part way across a muddy clearing of campfires, huts and tents he eased her onto a rough-hewn wooden seat next to an equally rustic table and began ferrying more water and a plate of scrambled eggs to her.

Kat looked around between bites of food. There were ragged polytunnels, patchwork netted gardens and the *bok-bok* of chickens nearby clucking soft assurances to each other. Watching Scott's back as he cooked another batch of eggs, she secreted a small, sharp knife up her sleeve.

A shout from a hut on the other side of the settlement told her where the truckie was. His protests made it clear he was restrained. Why?

When she asked the question of both Scott and Will, who she now realised were father and son, they both looked away, scowling.

Their gentle care for her, but grim disdain for the trucker, made her deeply uncomfortable. If this was a hostage situation, why was she unrestrained? Because of her injury? Because she was a woman?

Big mistake. Fifteen years of corporate hell meant she was well versed in planning complex operations under duress; the pain of a broken leg wouldn't stop her.

She began devising her exit strategy the instant Scott returned her to her tent.

The next few days passed in an almost monotonous, domestic routine.

Life at a survivalist camp, or whatever this place was, involved a lot of shovelling. The three men spent hours each day in the drizzle moving soil between areas of their haphazard garden and the floor of the chicken run. The scent of stir-fried egg and vegetable rice wafting from the campfire grill hung in the air each day.

Kat rested her makeshift crutches against one of the tables outside and sat to watch them work. She stared at the wet, yellow, knee-high grass surrounding the camp, then, with her eyes, traced the narrow paths beaten into the stubble by pademelon wallabies. They hop-thumped through in single file every night.

Her mind bounced, too, between planning her escape to civilisation and gnawing indecision about what to do if she got there. As far from ideal as her current predicament was, with a broken leg and apparent imprisonment, it didn't feel much worse than the distress that threatened to engulf her whenever she thought of home.

She had no proof of Dave's attacks on Raelene. The girl's own tearful plea for help before dying by suicide had revealed her colleague's monstrous behaviour. The flicker of guilt on his face when Kat had confronted him over Rae's death was as good as a confession.

A seasoned liar and spin-doctor, however, forty-five year old Dave had instantly flipped the narrative and turned himself into a figure of pity, reinventing his crimes into a doomed secret love affair with a seventeen year old intern that had ended in the tragic loss of his soulmate.

Kat was furious when their colleagues believed his lies.

If…no, *when* she returned to her normal life, she'd have to deal with him.

She hadn't been able to make things safe or right for Raelene. Just as she hadn't understood what had gone wrong for her adored sister.

Only after they lost Mari to suicide did Kat and her mother understand. The sixteen year old had been suffering the aftermath of being raped by another student at school. Kat, haunted most days by Mari's memory, had wanted so desperately to help the distraught Raelene, but had failed her too.

Kat still wasn't certain what she should do. Should she go to the police and tell them of Raelene's accusations? She had no proof, and any investigation would surely lead to her becoming a pariah at work, with nothing to show for it.

Alternatively, should she swallow her revulsion, pretend to believe and befriend Dave, and see if she could find anything in his phone or personal effects to back up Raelene's claims?

Angry screams from the truckie shattered her thoughts.

Holy shit. What were they doing to him?

And what might they do to her?

Between dealing with three criminals here or one at home, she'd go for the one in the office. But she needed to get out of here first.

Deep breath in…

She faced a choice of paths once more.

She knew they were currently uphill from the location of her car accident, though how far into the opaque forest she wasn't sure. That meant if she could make it downhill without being discovered she should be able to follow the road back to town. It would be slow, predictable, and incredibly painful.

Or, she could try going in an unexpected direction, up the hill behind them to see if there was a road on the other side. It would also be slow and incredibly painful, but at least it would be unpredictable. But, for all she knew, there may not be a road in that direction. It could be all wilderness between here and the west coast of Tasmania.

Choosing the riskier option was what put her in this situation in the first place. The safer, more predictable route downhill it was. And in a few days' time, a full moon might allow her to see where she was going.

During the days that followed, she gathered small items to aid her escape. An abandoned shopping bag could serve as a backpack. Scratched, empty bottles became water bladders. And she pretended to a larger appetite than she had, secreting any non-perishable food in the shopping bag.

At night, to the squeal of possums, thunder of wallabies bounding by and terrifying grunts of Tasmanian devils, she whittled by torchlight in her tent until the ends of her crutches were sharp points. She hoped they would grip the slippery, leaf-strewn forest floor.

It seemed the men had no concerns over her possible escape. They didn't question her increased appetite for crackers, nor seem to notice the improvements to her crutches.

The night before her intended breakout, Kat registered something on the edge of hearing. Snatches of what sounded like someone on the phone. Someone speaking in a slow, definite voice followed by long, silent pauses.

If they had a phone and were talking to someone on the outside, it might explain the periodic conversations she'd overheard. It sounded, some nights, as though the men were discussing blue chip stock trading. She thought she must have that wrong, though. Why would a survivalist cult, or whatever they were, living deep in pristine old growth forest, argue over stock market investments?

Perhaps they were more connected to modern life than she'd assumed. If they had a phone, could she find it and call for help?

When Scott brought her food to the table outside the following morning, she asked again if he would help her get to a town, even if he dumped her there and left.

He shook his head. 'Sorry.'

The thing was, he looked genuinely apologetic.

'But you could. I need you to call someone to come and get me.'

'No contact with the outside world.'

Kat held up a chipped vodka bottle that now held water. 'Really?' There were many bottles of the same brand in reuse around the camp. 'I call bullshit.'

'I can't help you, okay?'

'Then what are you planning to do to me?' She waved a hand at the makeshift hut holding the trucker. 'To him? Why not just let us go?'

Her voice rose as she gesticulated, drawing Will and Petulant John from behind the chook enclosure.

'I want to take care of him now,' John said.

Will's face darkened. 'No.'

'We have to wait...' Scott began.

'Pointless,' Petulant snorted. 'He'll fail the test.'

'What test?' Kat asked.

Will ignored her. 'Can't do the test before Kyle's back.'

'She doesn't have to be here.'

Kyle was a she? The unseen fourth member of this bunch of nutters being a woman explained the plush armchair Kat had glimpsed in the camp's main hut, a single point of stained pink and gold in the otherwise black, brown and muted green palette of the camp.

'No!' Scott said. 'It has to be all four of us.'

Kat nudged Scott. 'What test?'

John smirked. 'You'll know soon enough.'

Scott looked sad; Will looked thoughtful.

Kat felt the skin on the back of her neck prickle, the hairs rising.

None of them would speak to her again that day, though she heard urgent whisper-arguments from inside Will's hut. She went to bed that night with trepidation for a bedfellow.

Shouting ripped her from sleep.

'Calm down,' Kat heard Will say.

Shadows moved across the canvas of her tent, cast by torches. She could hear one or two of the men running.

'I know now, I know. I'll expose you all! The world should know!'

Then came the sounds of a scuffle, someone falling heavily to the ground, then fist-thumps.

'Told you he'd fail.'

The last voice was John. Whatever the test was, the trucker had not passed.

A terrified scream cut through the night.

It didn't sound like a Tassie devil.

Kat emerged from her tent the next morning determined that this would be her last day here. She paused to wipe sand from her eyes and painful dreams of Mari along with it, then hobbled to Scott's side by the edge of the deep green forest.

'Where is he?'

He knew which "he" she meant. His eyes flicked to the dense trees below them. 'He was…no good.'

That sounded final. 'What have you done with him?'

'What we had to.'

His voice was slow, deeper than usual. It conveyed the weight of the world on his shoulders.

'You said something about needing Kyle here to test him. Who's she?'

Scott's eyes lit up. 'My mum. Her full name's Kylie.'

'So John is?'

'My uncle, her brother.'

These people were all the one family. 'What's the test?'

'Sometimes we have to…stop people coming into parts of the reserve, okay?'

'Why? Are you growing something?'

He glanced over his shoulder toward the two older men and shrugged.

'What did you do with the body?'

Scott's head pulled up and back, clearly unnerved by her stoic tone. With villainous Dave, Kat was already dealing with something that felt as heavy as murder; it made the killing of the trucker seem somehow less shocking.

Scott dragged his foot in the blackened soil beneath their feet. 'All you have to do is disturb the dirt a little and they'll come at night and investigate.'

He was looking into the rainforest again.

Kat was lost. 'Who?'

'The Tassie devils. They're scavengers, and they eat everything. Never a trace left. They even eat the bones.'

As Kat hobbled back toward her tent to digest this new and somewhat horrifying piece of trivia, the aroma of barbecued meat invaded her nostrils. She spied Petulant John sitting outside one of the ramshackle huts ripping cooked flesh from blackened ribs and licking juices from his chin with a long, unhealthy looking tongue.

Large, curved ribs. The wrong size and shape for beef. Or pork. Or even venison, if there were feral deer in the park.

John grinned at her. 'Want some?'

Drops of blood fell to form dark patches on the stained cravat encasing his unshaven, wrinkled neck.

Her stomach lurched. Not all of the logger's bones had gone to the devils; not yet.

Kat forced herself to stare into old John's eyes, sniff with disdain and limp away.

'She's got balls, I'll give her that,' he said to no-one in particular.

Once hidden in her tent, Kat allowed her body to convulse with dry heaving and silent sobs.

It was clear that no-one from her regular life was looking for her. No choppers, no sounds of vehicles anywhere within earshot. When she hadn't turned up to the resort they'd probably charged her a cancellation fee and moved on. Her hire car wasn't due back for another week, and she was on leave from work for another week beyond that. Her mother was good at leaving her be for weeks at a time, so no help there.

As the night closed in, Kat could see that the time was right to attempt her escape. The air was almost still, the moon shone brightly in a cloudless sky, and the men were hitting the vodka hard. Their raucous laughter echoed across the camp, reflected back by the chamber of towering trunks surrounding them.

She needed to go. Sharpened crutches, check. Boot-like cast made from rags tied around her leg, check. A bag containing what food and water she'd been able to sequester. Check. It was now or never.

Bwark!

As she snuck past the chicken house, one of the silly things stirred on its perch and cried.

Thump! Thump!

The squawk had startled a mob of nearby pademelons, who now thundered away from the edge of the compound, small yet hefty bodies crashing through the underbrush, smashing feet and tails into the ground as they tore through.

Kat held her breath, listening for any movement among the men. Nothing, but...

As she breathed out, she detected a faint bark. It was a strange hoarse noise, like a dog with laryngitis. Where was it coming from?

Behind the chickens.

Kat crutched toward the sound. Was it captive devils? The adults of that ferocious scavenger species sounded like several hells' worth of daemons, especially when mating. Perhaps the pups made this soft coughing sound?

The barks were coming from inside one of the larger sheds. She planted her crutches carefully and lowered the shopping bag to the ground in front of her.

She bent forward to peer through a gap between double doors. And gasped.

Her eyes traced moonlit stripes along a canine-like back. The rarest mother on Earth raised her head to look straight at Kat while one of her pups nuzzled into her pouch.

Kat stood completely still, aware of every movement of her chest as it rose and fell with her breathing. She didn't want to startle the little family; didn't want this wondrous moment to end.

The Tasmanian tiger's eyes, inky black in the dim light, were filled with the calm of a mother suckling her young in safety.

Joy filled Kat's chest, warm and tingling. *They had survived.* Somehow, despite a determined campaign by English invaders to drive them to extinction, and a near-universal belief that they were no more, this mother and the four pups tumbling around the dirt beneath her feet meant that the tigers had survived.

'What are you doing here?'

Scott startled her. The sudden shift in weight jarred her broken leg. 'Ow!'

The tiger growled a warning to her cubs; they scrambled to hide behind her.

Kat held her breath. She glanced down to check that her bag of supplies was lying in a shadow, then turned to confront him as he crossed the campground clearing. 'What are you...? Why are you...? How?'

He closed the distance between them with two final strides, and glanced inside the pen. 'It's okay,' he crooned to the tigers, then sighed as he looked at her. 'Now that you know, what are you going to do?'

Kat narrowed her eyes. 'What do you mean, "do"?'

'There's plenty of people who'd pay good money to get their hands on Tina here.' He gestured at the once-again content mother.

She cocked her head to the side. 'That makes no sense. You're obviously protecting them, why would you ask if I would tell the world abou— oh.'

She stared at him.

He stared right back.

'This is the test, isn't it?'

He said nothing.

Kat realised that, in this moment, her life hung in the balance. She glanced at the little family again. It was the easiest decision she'd ever made. 'I'll never put them in danger. I can't explain it, but I need to help you protect them.'

He gave a deep chuckle. 'Dad said you're our type of person.'

She thought for a moment. 'Does this mean you'll finally help me get back to town?' She tapped her leg. 'To a doctor?'

The smile fell from his face. He shook his head, his long fringe of mousy brown hair swaying. 'I'm sorry; it's not possible for you to leave.'

'I see,' Kat said, swinging a furious crutch at his shins, 'I can't leave, but at least you won't kill me and eat me.'

He jumped out of her way and blanched, but said nothing.

Kat's face burned bright red with fury, frustration and the urge to cut Scott to pieces.

They stood, side by side, motionless as she decided on her next move. She had no idea what was going through Scott's mind, but at least her captor couldn't know what was on hers, either. She hoped.

Kat pushed her jaw toward the Tasmanian tigers. 'I want to be alone with them.'

Scott grunted and began to wander away. She was certain he was moving to his hut to watch her through a window but waited ten minutes or more, making a show of observing the tigers then slowly trundled toward the toilet, leaving her precious bag of provisions by their shed. Without overacting, she played on her reduced mobility, never taking more than a few steps without wincing in pain.

Even if they thought she'd run – well, hobble – they'd expect her to take the easy way downhill. They wouldn't expect her to go up and over the mountain behind them and down over the other side, to freedom, hospital and painkillers.

She hadn't lied, though. If she got away, she would never tell anyone about the tigers. She hadn't been able to save Mari or Raelene, but she *could* help protect the miraculous Tina and her children from the predations of men.

She waited for her second attempt at escape until she heard Scott and Will sink back into their drinking session and John snoring his bandsaw snore.

Thankfully, this time she didn't disturb the chickens. She took one more peek at the legendary inhabitants of the shed, retrieved her bag, and left the mud-drenched compound for a long slow climb uphill with crutches.

After what seemed like several night's worth of pounding bruising to her armpits, she topped a slight ridge and looked into the next valley.

Yes! Even from this distance she could see a bright snake of dirt wending its way through the pitch black swathe of trees below, and a road equalled cars and people and freedom…

She began the steep descent.

One crutch must have hit a rock because suddenly she was on the ground, sliding on her back. Somehow, she hadn't reinjured her leg, but how was she going to get up?

Lying on her back, she felt rather than heard the footsteps at first. Her attempt at escape had failed already.

The steps grew firmer, then audible, as they grew closer. How had the men discovered her missing and found her so soon?

A woman, tall and rangy, came into view and smiled at her. 'Kat, I presume?'

Kat's surprise meant her mouth curled into a tight 'O'. She realised how ridiculous she must look, sprawled on the ground in the middle of the night, wrapped in her boot of rags and damaged clothing.

Even in the pale light of the moon, she saw that the approaching woman had the same aquiline nose and high cheekbones as Scott and John. Her plummy tones confirmed her identity… Kylie.

'But how do you know who I am?' Kat blurted.

Scott's mum gave a throaty chuckle as she offered a hand. 'We have a two-way radio between home and my Landrover,' she pointed toward the road, 'parked down there. Scott let me know you'd wandered off into the forest.'

So that's why it sometimes sounded like one of the men was on the phone. They were.

'Are you hurt?'

Kat gestured toward her broken leg, stone-faced. 'No more than I already was.'

'You're a stoic one, aren't you? Will mentioned it more than once.'

Kat slumped. 'You're going to make me go back.'

'Scott said you'd seen Tina and her cubs…'

The awe of that revelation washed over Kat again.

'…and I was headed back to interview you in the morning.'

'To decide if you'd let your brother eat me?'

Kylie gave her a lop-sided grin. 'Will told me you were direct.'

'You don't deny it?'

'That we're working to protect the tigers? Or the thing John does?'

Kat's stomach lurched again.

Kylie shrugged. 'That's just his thing, I'm afraid. It has nothing to do with our purpose; he's a damaged old man with appalling proclivities, but we need his support to protect the tigers.'

'He's a bit more than "difficult".' Kat's leg was throbbing. 'Can we sit?'

'Sure.' Kylie continued talking as they found two chair-height fallen logs to rest against. 'John lived all over the world before choosing to be here with us. We couldn't have protected the tigers for as long as we have without him, without his money.'

Kylie sure was chummy for someone who was deciding Kat's fate.

'We used to live in Sydney. Parents sent us to private school, university, called in favours to get us jobs at the right firms.'

'Sounds like hell.'

Against the bright midnight sky, Kylie nodded. 'It actually was. John cracked first. He's much older than me. It was a world of full wallets and empty souls, he said, and left.'

How could a young man of principle have turned into the old man at the camp?

'I kept working,' Kylie continued, 'met Will, had Scott. We were on a hiking trip down here when we happened upon one of Tina's great, maybe great-great grandmothers, and that was it for us because we knew we had to dedicate ourselves to their survival or we'd always regret it.'

Having looked into Tina's dark eyes, Kat understood completely.

'I don't know what happened to make John like he is,' Kylie continued. 'He'd been gone for years and suddenly turned up, medivacced home from Siberia, barely clinging to life. He'd been in a bus accident in the middle of nowhere, stranded for weeks. He'd never talk about it, but whatever happened, well, ten people went out but only two came back.'

'So you capture men and bring them here for him to eat?'

The woman shook her head. 'Only when people come onto our land, looking for something that doesn't belong to them. If they see the tigers then yes, we capture them and test them. If they expose what we're doing, everything is lost. So yes, we can't risk letting them go, so we kill them.' Kylie searched Kat's face for her reaction. 'It's shocking, I know. But John only eats those ones. He's a scavenger, like the devils.'

'How many have you killed?'

'Six, over twenty years.'

'But why us? Me and the truckie? We weren't looking for anything.'

'One of Tina's older cubs had escaped. The boys were trying to get him back when he ran across the road and caused your accident. They couldn't be sure what you had seen, and we take no chances...'

Kat's morbid curiosity nudged her to keep prodding. 'But how do you do it?' Her cheeks reddened. 'Get away with it, I mean?'

Kylie shrugged. 'Tourists get lost in the forest all the time. And men sometimes run away from their families. We make sure their cars aren't found. When I leave here, I'll take this latest one's phone up north, turn it on briefly, then mail it to Melbourne and get someone to switch it on there and put it in the garbage. It'll look like he's absconded from his life and stowed away on a ferry to the mainland.'

Kat swallowed hard. 'And *my* phone?'

Moonlight cast shadows into deep puckers on Kylie's forehead. 'That's up to you.'

'I'd never do anything to hurt the tigers. I mean, after all these years, they're still here.'

'Yes, and no.'

Kat cocked her head.

'I call them Schrodinger's Tigers, because they can only survive if a handful of people like us know they're alive, but...'

Kat finished for her. 'Everyone else must believe they're dead.'

Kylie nodded. 'My family knows, so we created a sanctuary for them. We invest the money John and I inherited, use it to keep our camp going and slowly buy up as much land around us as we can.'

That explained the overheard stock market discussions.

'But, they're supposed to be extinct,' Kylie continued. 'Conventional wisdom says they didn't even live in this part of Tasmania, yet here they are.'

'But *I* know.'

'It comes down to this,' Kylie said, her voice almost as deep as her son's. 'Can you convince me you won't reveal our secret?'

Kat went to answer several times, then stopped.

They fell into silence, staring up at the stars.

She faced a life-altering choice.

She *had* to help protect Tina and her kind from facing a second extinction and she *had* to honour the memories of Raelene and Mari, return home and try to protect other girls from the brutish Dave because men like that didn't stop at one terrified teenager...

But which one was more important? Who should she work to protect?

For fifteen minutes, perhaps more, the women sat quietly, their breath condensing as clouds of mist around them, the cold seeping into Kat's throbbing leg.

She gasped when a resolution finally swam to the surface of her mind. Perhaps she didn't have to choose at all.

She reached out to pat Kylie's hand, then explained her epiphany.

The woman listened solemnly until Kat ran out of words, then tugged at her backpack. 'I have milk powder, chocolate and rum. They're usually just for me.'

'Like the special chair?'

'Like my chair.' Kylie smiled. 'It's a long time since I shared a boozy hot chocolate with another woman.'

Kat sighed dramatically. 'I'm partial to whisky, but under the circumstances I *suppose* I could make an exception.'

Kylie chuckled.

'But tomorrow, you'll help me get to a hospital?' Kat held her breath.

'Yes.'

Kat's answering grin was so wide her cheeks ached.

Her bruised armpits protested as she stood for the journey back to camp. 'I need to go slowly.'

'That's okay,' said Kylie. 'We have a lot to talk about.'

On Kat's advice, Kylie and her family invested in an IT company days before it rocketed in value, the result of landing a large government tender. Now, six months later, the family was negotiating the purchase of an adjoining 2000 acres to the south of the compound. Every acre would augment the buffer between the tigers and the outside world.

Visiting the compound, as she now did on a monthly basis, Kat leaned over a pen containing one of Tina's daughters and nudged a yipping cub toward a morsel of meat that she'd placed on the ground. The tumbling, striped bundles were at the in-and-out of the pouch stage and mum looked to be thoroughly over it.

Kylie patted her arm. 'It's done.'

Kat's bargain with herself to protect both the tigers of this forest and some young women in an urban jungle had worked. She wished with all her heart that her sister Mari could see this day and maybe, just maybe, forgive Kat for not saving her.

Excitement and trepidation swirled in her veins as she moved toward the camp's main dining table, then stood between Will and Scott. They watched John, a metre or two away, savouring a joint of meat.

Kat felt lightheaded, nauseated and victorious all at once.

In front of them, John grinned, and dabbed with a paper serviette at juices from the roasted thigh that smeared on his chin. 'City boys are more tender,' he smirked.

Part of Kat's breakfast threatened to launch itself into her throat. She swallowed.

In the end, it had been an easy trap to bait. Dave had lapped up Kat's apparent new sympathy for him over Raelene, and bought into Kat's insistence that he needed a break from the stress of his life. Why not go with her on an all-expenses paid trip to her new holiday home in Tasmania?

'But don't tell anyone we're going together,' she'd added. 'They might get the wrong idea.'

He'd winked at her. 'Of course.'

John sank his teeth into Dave's thigh and chewed industriously.

The Tasmanian devils would dispose of his bones later.

ABOUT THE AUTHORS

CHUCK MCKENZIE was born in 1970, and still spends much of his time there. He is not dead yet. He writes things, and sometimes people publish those things, which is very nice.

CLAIRE LOW is a Chinese-Thai Australian writer and visual artist, living on Cammeraygal land. A former newspaper journalist and magazine editor, she is twice shortlisted and highly commended for the Marjorie Graber-McInnis Short Story Prize. A firm believer in ghosts and all types of monsters, she used to force her colleagues to take part in a scary gift exchange, has a gothic doll collection, and likes to celebrate Halloween all year.

RAYMOND GATES is an Aboriginal Australian writer currently residing in Wisconsin, USA, whose childhood crush on reading everything dark and disturbing evolved into an adult love affair with horror and dark fiction. He has published many short stories including several for Clan Destine Press, and is working on his first collection of short stories and first novel. Learn more at: http://www.raymondgates.com

SARAH ROBINSON-HATCH is a writer and book lover who lives in Melbourne, Australia. Since graduating from RMIT University with a Bachelor of Communications and an Advanced Diploma of Professional Screenwriting, Sarah has worked in both the literary and film and TV industries. When not writing, Sarah can be found hiking, playing the cello, or binge-watching the latest TV shows.

ELLE BEAUMONT loves creating vivid and fantastical worlds. She lives in Southeastern, Massachusetts with her husband and two children. When not writing, she enjoys candle-making, crocheting, and taking care of her menagerie of animals. More than once, she has proclaimed that coffee is the lifeblood, and it is how she refrains from becoming a zombie.

JASON FRANKS is a novelist and comics writer. He's best known for the novels *Bloody Waters* and *Faerie Apocalypse* and the Sixsmiths graphic novels. He works at the intersection of science fiction, fantasy, horror and comedy, but he'll stalk a story into any genre – especially if the destination looks like a dark alley. Franks' work has variously been short-listed for Aurealis, Ditmar and Ledger awards. He lives in Melbourne, Australia, with his wife, his child, and a brace of sorely neglected guitars. Find him online at jasonfranks.com.

CANDACE ROBINSON spends her days consumed by words and hoping to one day find her own DeLorean time machine. Her life consists of avoiding migraines, admiring Bonsai trees, watching classic movies, and living with her husband and daughter in Texas – where it can be forty degrees one day and eighty the next.

NARRELLE M. HARRIS writes crime, horror, fantasy and romance. Her 40+ works include vampire novels, erotic spy adventures, het and queer romance, and Holmes/Watson romance mysteries *The Adventure of the Colonial Boy* (2016) and *A Dream to Build a Kiss On* (2018). In 2017, her ghost/crime story *Jane* won the 'Body in the Library' prize at the Scarlet Stiletto Awards. Her recent works include *Grounded, Scar Tissue and Other Stories* (nominated for the 2019 Aurealis Awards for Best Collection), and *Kitty and Cadaver*. Narrelle was also commissioning editor for *The Only One in the World: A Sherlock Holmes Anthology* (2021) and *Clamour and Mischief* (2022). In 2023, she is co-editing *This Fresh Hell* with Katya de Becerra and *Sherlock is a Girl's Name* with Atlin Merrick, along with writing more fiction. www.narrellemharris.com.

GREG HERREN is the award winning author of over forty novels and over fifty short stories. He is also an award winning anthology editor, and his most recent anthology was *Land of 10000 Thrills: The 2022 Bouchercon Anthology*. His most recent young adult novel, *#shedeservedit*, is nominated for the 2023 Agatha Award for Bes Children's/Young Adult, and his most recent mystery (as T. G. Herren) *A Streetcar Named Murder* is a finalist for the Lefty Award for Best Humorous Mystery. His ninth Scotty Bradley adventure, *Mississippi River Mischief,* will be released in September 2023. He lives quietly in New Orleans with his partner of 27 years.

EUGEN BACON is an African Australian author of several novels and fiction collections. She's a finalist in the 2022 World Fantasy Award. Eugen was announced in the honor list of the 2022 Otherwise Fellowships for 'doing exciting work in gender and speculative fiction'. Her short story collection *Danged Black Thing* made the 2021 Otherwise Honor List. Eugen has won, been longlisted or commended in international awards, including the Aurealis Award, Foreword Indies, Bridport Prize, Copyright Agency Prize, Horror Writers Association Diversity Grant, Otherwise, Rhysling, Elgin, Australian Shadows, Ditmar Awards and Nommo Awards for Speculative Fiction by Africans. Visit her website at eugenbacon.com and Twitter feed @ EugenBacon

CLARE RHODEN lives on Bunurong land in Melbourne, Australia, with her husband and an overly-smart poodle cross called Aeryn. Clare started writing stories early and hasn't worked out how to stop. Her dystopian trilogy The Chronicles of the Pale features genetically-enhanced wolf-dogs and was inspired by the worldwide refugee crisis. She is currently writing a companion to her Great War novel The Stars in the Night, and her middle grade fantasy How to Survive Your Magical Family was published in September 2022. Clare's short stories appear in several anthologies. She has a sizeable list of academic publications and her PhD thesis was published in 2015 by UWAP Academic as The Purpose of Futility: writing World War One, Australian style. When not writing, Clare usually has her head in a book. She might be reviewing for Aurealis magazine, or she'll be editing the next project of many in the pipeline. There are always many in the pipeline. Find her at www.clarerhoden.com.

C. VONZALE LEWIS is the best-selling author of the Blood and Sacrifice Chronicles and various short fiction. She resides in Hesperia, CA where she spends her days plotting the demise of her enemies. All her stories tend to be dark with a little mystery thrown in and some love to round out the mix. When not writing, she enjoys reading, spending time with her husband, and binge-watching British crime fiction.

TANSY RAYNER ROBERTS is an eclectic author, podcaster and abandoner of craft projects. Her recent books include the Teacup Magic series, *Gate Sinister*, and *Gorgons Deserve Nice Things*. She also writes crime as Livia Day. Find her at tansyrr.com

CLAIRE L. SMITH (she/her) is an Australian author and visual artist. She is the author of the gothic horror novella 'Helena' and the coming-of-age horror novella 'When We Entered That House'. Her artwork has been featured in various anthologies by Tenebrous Press and The Ghastling, as well as on the covers of publications from Off Limits Press and Ghost Orchid Press. Her website is www.clairelsmith.com

A. J. VRANA is a Serbian-Canadian academic and writer from Toronto, Canada. She lives with her two rescue cats, Moonstone and Peanut Butter, who nest in her window-side bookshelf and cast judgmental stares at nearby pigeons. Her doctoral research examines the supernatural in modern Japanese and former-Yugoslavian literature and its relationship to violence. When not toiling away at caffeine-fueled, scholarly pursuits, she enjoys jewelry-making, cupcakes, and concocting dark tales to unleash upon the world. Her published works include *The Chaos Cycle Duology: The Hollow Gods* (2020) and *The Echoed Realm* (2021) from The Parliament House Press and Tantor Audio, and a short supernatural horror story, "These Silent Walls" (2020), printed in *Three Crows Magazine*. Her latest folk horror story, "Sapling," will appear in Clan Destine Press' anthology, *This Fresh Hell*. She has been featured on *Business Insider* and *Psychology Today*.

KATYA DE BECERRA writes atmospheric horror featuring determined characters, complicated families and enigmatic places. Critics called her debut *What The Woods Keep* "a thoughtful and compelling horror fantasy" (The Bulletin) and "a narrative that will keep readers enthralled" (Booklist), while her second novel *Oasis* earned a starred review from Booklist. Katya regularly publishes short fiction in anthologies and literary magazines. She is also co-editor of the anthology *This Fresh Hell*, which reimagines and subverts horror tropes in new and unexpected ways. As a child, Katya wanted to be an Egyptologist, but instead she earned a PhD in Cultural Anthropology and now works at a university, where she teaches and researches as well as supervises graduate students in Anthropology, Creative Writing and Education. Katya is a short version of her real name, which is very long and gets mispronounced a lot. Her third novel, *When Ghosts Call Us Home*, is forthcoming in 2023. Her website is www.katyadebecerra.com

ANNIE MCCANN is an Indonesian-Australian Muslim, born and raised in the western suburbs of Sydney, NSW. An avid reader, book blogger and emerging writer, she created a network of readers called Read3r'z Re-Vu in 2009, co-founded a network of Muslim writers called The Right Pen Collective in 2019 and is one of the Australia Reads Ambassadors endorsing reading for all ages. You will also find Annie emceeing celebrity and literary panels every year at conventions such as Supanova, Comic Con, Book Fair Australia and many more. Passionate about diversity, inclusivity and representation, Annie works tirelessly to lead by example in 'bridging the gap' through her networks, showcasing diversity in content, breaking down misconceptions and shining positivity to connect the wider community. When she's not reading, writing or emceeing, you will find Annie either jamming to the King of Pop: Michael Jackson, old school hip-hop and R&B or watching her team: Parramatta Eels play in the NRL.

SARAH GLENN MARSH is an author of several young adult fantasy-horror novels including the Reign of the Fallen series. She is also the author of almost a dozen award-winning picture books including *The Mystery of the Love List* and the Junior Library Guild selection *Dragon Bones: The Fantastic Fossil Discoveries of Mary Anning*. She lives with her husband, daughter, and menagerie of pets in Richmond, Virginia. Find her at www.sarahglennmarsh.com.

DR GILLIAN POLACK is an award-winning Jewish Australian speculative fiction writer based in Canberra. The first ever Australian Jewish fantasy novel (*The Wizardry of Jewish Women*) is set in the same world as her story here, and has just one character in common. This story itself is the result of a promise Gillian made her father on his deathbed, and she owes several of the names used to the residents of Café Moose. Her most recent novel is *The Green Children Help Out* (French superheroes), and her best known novel is *The Year of the Fruit Cake* (what happens when an alien takes the body of a perimenopausal woman). She was the 2020 recipient of the A. Bertram Chandler (lifetime achievement in science fiction) award. She is also an ethnohistorian with a special interest in how story transmits culture, both Medieval and modern. She is an Ambassador for Australia Reads.

DR L. J. M. OWEN is a multi-award winning writer, festival director and reading advocate. L.J.'s novels include *Olmec Obituary* (2015), *Mayan Mendacity* (2016), *Egyptian Enigma* (2018) and the standalone *The Great Divide* (2019), the latter long-listed for the 2020 Ngaio Marsh Awards. At the 2020 Scarlet Stiletto Awards she won the Scriptworks Award for a Great Film Idea, the Liz Navratil Award for Best Story with a Disabled Protagonist, and the International Association of Forensic Linguists Award for Best Forensic Linguistics Story.

In 2019, L.J. founded Australia's southernmost literary festival, the Terror Australis Readers and Writers Festival (TARWF). She is also the Convenor of the annual TARWF Children's Short Story Competition, Convenor of the Tasmanian branch of Sisters in Crime Australia, and a Tasmania Reads advocate.

A passionate supporter of emerging, disabled and regional writers, L.J.'s guiding principles are kindness, inclusivity and the love of books. Along with her environmentalist partner, L.J. is the caretaker of an extensive menagerie on a bush block of Tasmanian devils.

Clan Destine Press Anthologies

The Only One in the World

Since his first appearance in 1887, Sherlock Holmes has been the quintessential English sleuth, alongside his loyal companion and biographer, Doctor Watson.

But what if they had come from some other place in the world, or another time? How would they differ from Conan Doyle's creations? How similar might they remain?

Holmes and Watson are herein re-imagined in new cultural contexts, different genders and sexualities, and in stories rich in foreign detail that still reflect their origins.

Thirteen writers from around the world, with cultural or historic expertise, explore the possibilities with stories set in Germany, C17th England, Ireland, Australia, Russia, South Africa, India, Poland, USA, Ancient Egypt, Viking Iceland, and even the entire world.

You'll discover Holmes and Watson are not only unique in original canon, but the Great Detective remains singular in every world!

Stories by: Kerry Greenwood & David Greagg, Greg Herren, Atlin Merrick, Jack Fennell, Lucy Sussex, Jason Franks, Natalie Conyer, Lisa Fessler, Katya de Becerra, Jayantika Ganguly, LJM Owen, Raymond Gates and JM Redmann.

ISBNs: 978-0-6489586-2-8 (hc)
978-0-6488487-8-3 (pb)
978-0-6489586-3-5 (eB)

Who Sleuthed It?

Fingers and feelers and paws and wings
Solving thrillers and chillers and secretive things.

An anthology in which animals help their animal friends, or human sidekicks, solve diabolical crimes and whimsical mysteries in 19 stories by Australian, American and Irish authors.

Kerry Greenwood, Elizabeth Ann Scarborough
Meg Keneally, Narrelle M. Harris
Livia Day, David Greagg, Atlin Merrick
Fin J. Ross, Vikki Petraitis, Tor Roxburgh
Lindy Cameron, CJ McGumbleberry
Chuck McKenzie, Jack Fennell, Craig Hilton
L.J.M. Owen, GV Pearce, Kat Clay
and Louisa Bennet

ISBNs: 9780645002126 (hb)
9780648848769 (pb)
9780648848776 (eB)

aurealis
awards
FINALIST

Clan Destine Press Anthologies

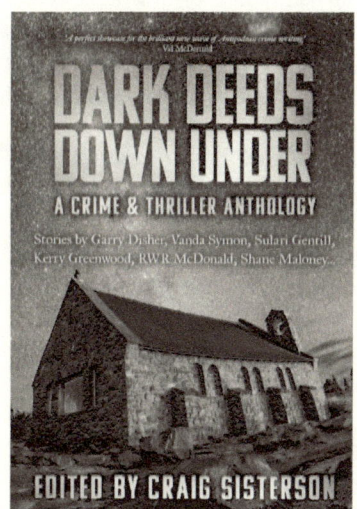

ISBNs: 978-0-6453167-9-7 (hc)
        978-0-6453167-8-0 (pb)
        978-0-6453168-0-3 (eB)

Edited by Narrelle M. Harris

ISBNs: 978-1-922904-16-4 (HC)
       978-1-922904-17-4 (PB)
       978-1-922904-18-8 (EB)

aurealis
awards
FINALIST

A Vibrant Southern Constellation of Crime Writers

Dark Deeds Down Under features the very best of
modern Australian and New Zealand
crime and mystery writing.

Spend time with some of your favourite Aussie and
Kiwi cops and sleuths – Hirsch, Corinna Chapman,
Sam Shephard, Rowly Sinclair, Murray Whelan – and
the edgy stars of some cracking standalone tales.

Travel the criminal trails of two countries
from the dusty Outback to South Island glaciers,
from ocean-carved coastlines and craggy mountains
to sultry rainforests or Middle Earth valleys,
and via sleepy towns to the seething underbellies
of our cosmopolitan cities.

The 19 dark deeds herein are perpetrated by:
Alan Carter, Nikki Crutchley, Aoife Clifford,
Garry Disher, Helen Vivienne Fletcher, Lisa Fuller,
Sulari Gentill, Kerry Greenwood, Narrelle M. Harris,
Katherine Kovacic, Shane Maloney, Renée,
R.W.R. McDonald, Dinuka McKenzie, Vanda Symon,
Dan Rabarts & Lee Murray, Stephen Ross,
Fiona Sussman, David Whish-Wilson

**A clamour of rooks. A mischief of magpies.
A storytelling of crows.**

All the corvids – rooks and ravens, jays and jackdaws,
crows and magpies – have the best collective nouns:
from tidings and titerings, bands and trains,
to a parliament, a party, and an unkindness.

Clamour and Mischief is a veritable storytelling
of adventures featuring corvidae, the bird family
known for its intelligence, cunning and connection
with folklore and urban legends.

Our storytellers come from around the world
and include award-winners, and fledgling authors
in their professional debut.

Herein are 16 striking stories imbued with the
humour, darkness, wisdom and magic
of the birds which inspired them.

Stories by: Raymond Gates, GV Pearce, Eugen Bacon,
Geneve Flynn, Alex Marchant, Jack Fennell, RJK Lee,
Lee Murray, Dannye Chase, Narrelle M. Harris,
R.D. White, Jason Franks, Katya de Becerra,
George Ivanoff, Tamara M Bailey, Gabiann Marin.

Clan Destine Press Anthologies

The rising dread of damn good mysteries.
A horde of criminally good horror writers were
invited to take a walk down the mean streets of crime.
Their task: to make your blood run cold, to scare
you witless and to make your skin crawl.
And most of all to make you think.
The rising dread of a good mystery doesn't really
need anything supernatural to keep you on the edge
of your seat. But put the two together — crime fiction
and horror — and all sorts of nasty business comes
out of the woodwork. Sometimes literally.
The stories herein include urban monsters,
Victorian-era mathematicians, contemporary lawyers,
near future police, and outback ghosts.

Edited by Alan Baxter — award-winning author of
horror, supernatural thrillers
and dark fantasy, liberally mixed with noir and
mystery — our Damnation Games are played by 19
Aussie, Kiwi and international authors:
Gemma Amor, Joanne Anderton, J. Ashley-Smith,
Alan Baxter, Aaron Dries, Gemma Files, Geneve Flynn
Philip Fracassi, Robert Hood, Gabino Iglesias
Rick Kennett, Maria Lewis, Chris Mason,
Lee Murray, Cina Pelayo, Dan Rabarts,
John F.D. Taff, Kyla Lee Ward, Kaaron Warren.

ISBNs: 9780645316841 (hb)
9780645316858 (pb)
978-0-6453168-6-5(eb)

www.ingramcontent.com/pod-product-compliance
Lightning Source LLC
Chambersburg PA
CBHW020839020726
47497CB00005B/1164